# The Hytharo Redux

## Book One Of The First Hytharo

### Jonathan Weiss

HELIXIC
BOOKS

HELIXIC BOOKS

# DEDICATION

For my brother, Daniel, who was the first person to read
of Spiric's original steps into the Droughtlands and was so
intrigued by what he'd read that while driving to pick up some
takeaway pizzas and talking about it with me, he drove straight
past the place and on for another ten minutes before he realised
what had happened.

Never before or since have I seen anything else get in the way of
that man and his pizza, which inspired me to keep going.

And for my wife, Kayla, and anyone else who has put up with
my chaotic aspirations.

# CONTENTS

1. From Dust                        1

2. Last Memories                   17

3. Trial By Ruin                   31

4. To The Depths                   45

5. The Last Hytharo                63

6. The Boundary                    75

7. It Had A Name                   91

8. Kurkress                       101

9. The First Rune                 115

10. The Scythes Strike            131

11. Past Lives                    143

12. Respark                       155

| 13. | Doubt Underfoot | 163 |
| 14. | Through Red Mountains | 173 |
| 15. | The Hunter Descends | 185 |
| 16. | Fragmentation | 201 |
| 17. | Viceroy | 209 |
| 18. | By Invitation Only | 223 |
| 19. | An Honoured Guest | 235 |
| 20. | Excited Delirium | 245 |
| 21. | Long Shadows | 257 |
| 22. | Understanding Intention | 271 |
| 23. | A Forgotten Translation | 283 |
| 24. | A Veiled Threat | 299 |
| 25. | Storm, Sand And Fire | 315 |
| 26. | Buried Memories | 327 |
| 27. | Nothing Beside Remains | 339 |
| 28. | Boundless And Bare | 353 |
| 29. | Lone And Level Sands | 363 |
| 30. | A Place Where Time Stands Still | 371 |
| 31. | Echoes Of Those-Of-Glass | 387 |
| 32. | Erase Traces | 399 |
| 33. | The Depths Of Memory | 415 |

34. The Forest                          429

35. To Dust                             443

Pronunciation Guide & Glossary          458

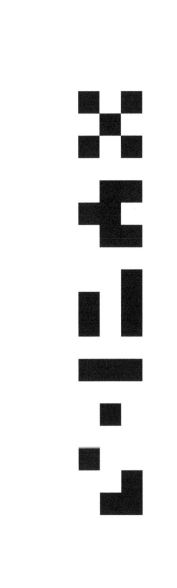

## CHAPTER ONE

# FROM DUST

T HE OLD MAN DRIFTED through the desert ruins. These days his boots were more hole than leather, but that didn't matter, for his feet never dipped less than ten feet from the ground below. Around him, massive pillars of glass and iron stretched higher than anything another living soul had ever seen, but he knew that they ran so much deeper.

His shadow darkened his path, cast long and far over the red dunes by the sun beating down on his back. Despite the overwhelming warmth, he pulled his duster tighter around his shoulders. A blast of sand broke over him a moment later. Once he felt it settle, he continued, eyes darting to every shadow cast by the ruins as he passed. Something he searched for would be lurking there. Something he saw thirty years ago.

The pillars spanned for miles and stars appeared in the sky by the time he neared the centre. His camp was close, near one of the larger structures, but he didn't head straight for it. A gut feeling pointed him further south. It was as if something wasn't meant to be there, though he wasn't quite sure what. The ruins certainly hadn't moved.

He stopped, comparing the map he pulled from his coat to his surroundings. He had sketched it himself over the course of the last dozen or more years —he'd long lost count— yet massive chunks of detail were missing and what remained had been long smudged into illegibility. He gave up and stuffed it back into his cloak before moving on.

In uncharted territory, he pushed the blocky blue runes on his arm to burn harder. They'd been going all day and his focus was yet to break. Their essence drove him higher into the air, the winds beneath flapping through his cloak. A gentle ripple in the loose sand below now marked his path and the old man's brow matched the pattern. It wasn't as much of a disturbance as a true footprint, but it was still a worry. The forms of a dozen little iron-balled creatures rustled free of their burial in his wake, an early start to their nightly patrols.

The old man had taken to calling them "skuttlers," a deceptively innocent name for the strange machines he'd witnessed produce many mangled corpses when an overly curious beast strayed too close. At this altitude, they paid him no mind, instead sprouting several pairs of spindly little legs and wandering aimlessly back along the rippling path he'd created. At an intersection, more skuttlers appeared, far too many to be just to greet him, their routes a good deal more arbitrary than he'd previously observed.

Scanning the streets, the old man spotted what the skuttlers must be after. Nestled in the dunes, a single thin hand poked out, its fingers twitching. Should he help? No, it had to be a trap. A trick of the ruins to lure him in. The old man had once called them fractures, a word now almost forgotten for lack of use. He chuckled at the thought. Most words were like that nowadays.

He began to drift away, thinking more about the makeshift cot in his camp than what that hand could possibly belong to. It wasn't even the strangest thing the old man had seen that day. Before it was gone from his sight, he risked one look back at the hand, now far in the distance.

He froze.

The hand was no longer alone and abandoned. A dark figure crouched over it. A shadow which light could not pass through.

For the old man, thirty years was up.

But the spectre wasn't here for him.

# ✕ ◀ ıl ▼ ⸗

From the moment he woke, panic was the only thing Spiric knew. Pressure all around, seeping into his clothes, ears, and mouth. He clamped his jaw shut, the crunch that familiar one of sand. It was pressing, crushing, all-consuming, and completely immobilising. He tried to kick with his legs. There was a little give, but not enough. He didn't even know which way was up. He couldn't twist, his hands—

*Hands!*

One was free! Free to flap about uselessly in the air. His fingers clawed at the surface, pulling and pulling in vain. All common sense vanished, and he forced his jaw open to desperately inhale, but only sand flowed in.

Then something fleshy was grasped around his free hand. He grabbed back and it yanked at him like a rabid animal about to tear his shoulder clean from his socket. The sand loosened in small gives around him, chunks dislodging from his clothes, releasing him from its deathly grip.

Then he was free.

Gasping.

Choking.

Coughing.

But free.

On hands and shaking knees, he caught his breath. It clogged in his throat, thick and unfamiliar.

*Why would air be unfamiliar?*

The question left Spiric with a frown as he moved gingerly to his feet. Each sway of his body and tilt of his head seemed to have him moving through water.

*Water.*

Voids below, he was thirsty. The thought struck him as he took another wheezing breath and the thirst was suddenly quenched. He blinked in confusion, the air stinging against his eyes. It was like something was wrong with it. It was thicker and unnaturally so, like it had been changed by a magic far beyond his understanding. The sky above him was cloudless, a perfect gradient of pink and blue.

The sunlight was blinding. He didn't know how long he'd been trapped under the sand. It might as well have been eons. Using both hands to shield his eyes, Spiric looked for his saviour, but there wasn't another soul in sight.

All he could see were rows and rows of pillars, their walls of splintering glass giving way to hyper-machined metal. They were giant and arranged in a perfect grid, the space between them a flowing wash of dunes that lapped up their sides. Iron rocks were buried among the red waves, a fraction of their shining, bulbous shape visible in the freshly disturbed sand.

'Skyscrapers,' Spiric whispered under his breath, not sure where the word had come from.

But the squirming in his gut as he stared into the dark voids told him he'd been here before, and it wasn't good. The way they jaggedly thrust into the sky was foreboding enough, yet the gloom held within was an added terror. He tore his eyes away from them and looked down the rows between.

He'd felt a hand, a real human hand, but there was nobody around. Just a flicker of a shadow in the darkness of the ruins. He swore quietly under his breath, picked a direction, and started walking, the late afternoon sun beating down on his back. As he went, he wracked his brain for the reason he'd ended up here, trying until his head was pounding, but he could not yield a single useful recollection.

His name was Spiric. He could remember his mother telling him it meant *from dust*, but he couldn't remember her face. He was fourteen —no, fifteen years of age— though he couldn't be sure which it was. But if he was alone in this haunting wasteland, what help would such a number be to him?

The lightly mottled traveling cloak hanging from his shoulders threatened to tear as he tried to hitch its collar over his exposed neck. It was composed of layers of once fine and now fraying fabrics of greys and yellows which would've blended into any sands other than the scorched orange that now surrounded him. When he sniffed at it, it smelt faintly of smoke, but Spiric couldn't be sure if it was that of a campfire or something far more deadly.

The tunic underneath also carried the same odour. It was a

stiffened leather of bruised brown, its sheen having long been creased and crumpled from its original form, its texture far too coarse against his soft flesh. The only garment that didn't irritate him was his trousers, but they were ragged enough to be seen as robes by this point.

At least his boots, besides the minor scuffing at the toe, bore some signs of good workmanship. The pale red leather reached halfway up his shin and was adorned with all manner of trailing straps and silver buckles that clanked softly as he walked.

Spiric sighed as he ran his hands across the various pockets and pouches that spotted the front of his tunic.

*Empty.*

No food, no water, no maps, no weapons, and no ink. The latter meant no magic, either. He checked his wrists and sighed again, this time in relief. Running up the underside of his right forearm was a series of deep crimson runes. There were five in total, each a blocky arrangement of squares that lay in an invisible three-by-three grid.

With these, he could send up a flare, or even send out a pulse to detect the person that had saved him from his shallow grave. Yet once again, the words came to his mind without definition or origin. He looked back to the runes with a stern frown. They weren't a permanent mark. He could feel the slightly raised notes of dried ink as he ran his fingers over their surface.

He imagined painting them on, subtlety miming the action with his left hand, though his instinct was to do it with his right.

So how had these runes ended up on his right arm, just under his wrist?

*Are these even runes for me?*

He stopped in front of one of the glass-walled buildings, staring at his reflection. His dark hair, usually glossy and tousled, was flattened with the same grit that coated his face. His features were soft and boyish, as to be expected with his roughly estimated age, but he also felt a yearning instinct that they should be sharper, more aggressive.

He tried to let a flash of anger cross his face and chuckled shily as the reflection only returned a bewildered and panicked look. It was apt for the situation. Even his eyes, glinting the same blood red as the runes on his wrist, struggled to muster the beginnings of fury.

The thought disappeared from Spiric's mind as he caught a glimmer of movement behind his reflection. His eyes fixed on what looked like a small metal tube that hurtled through the air. He started after it, stumbling down the dune and breaking into an ungainly run. It wasn't long before his legs were vehemently protesting from the misuse, and they gave in after only a few dozen metres. The rest of his body followed, tumbling into the sand and landing him next to one of the strange, grey metal-shelled boulders.

Spiric pounded the dust with a clenched fist. A puff of sand rose in reply to his frustration and flew straight into his eyes, blinding him. When he'd cleared his vision, the flying canister had already disappeared over the horizon, falling from view as it landed. He chided himself as he stood.

It was all pointless. He'd been stupid to chase after it and all he'd gotten for it was a boot full of sand.

Spiric gazed open-mouthed at the buildings around him as he caught his breath, not recognising any of them. He turned back to his path, but the wind had already swept up his footsteps. In their place, one of the boulders had emerged from the ground, revealing a multitude of stubby, clanking legs that were only supported by a joint at the base of the body.

It looked a bit like a tiny munbrak. Those were unpredictable creatures at the best of times, their scaly brown hides storing juicy meats and an explosive temper. This metal rock with legs didn't seem to have either, so Spiric wasn't sure why his memory had decided to connect it with the animal.

But as he looked closer, he realised this creature didn't have scales. It scuttered around to face him, extending a thin black tube with a glowing glass tip from its top and pointing it in his direction. The glass flashed with a blue light as it inched closer, looking almost inquisitive.

Spiric crouched to be level with it and was about to lean closer to inspect it when a man's gruff bark cut the air.

'Boy! Don't move.'

He turned, rising slowly as he found the source of the noise. An old man stood at the top of a dune, around thirty metres away. Spiric stared open-mouthed, all thought of the machine lost as it shuffled a few paces closer to his turned back.

The old man was nothing but frantic. The endless layers of his draped rags fluttered in any direction the wind tugged them, his shock of wispy grey hair going with it, spare for the matted chunks that blended into his unkempt beard.

His brow was severe, jutting out so far it almost obscured his watery blue eyes. In the back of Spiric's mind, he could recall the colour of the eyes meant something, but this too escaped him.

'Were you the one that saved me?' he asked as he took a step up the dune.

'I said not to move,' the man snapped, his voice hoarse. He began rustling through his many pockets and pouches, buried within what he seemed to call robes. 'That thing behind you—'

Spiric twisted to look at it. Now the shell wasn't so smooth. Cracks had formed, a dull orange light leaking from within.

'—has got an eye on you. Another step and we both die.'

Spiric's face turned to a confused frown. 'What do you mean? I don't even know what that thing is!'

'You don't need to know what something is for it to kill you!' The old man paused abruptly to squint at him. 'How did you get this far without knowing what a skuttler is?' He grunted something to himself and went back to his pockets.

Spiric glanced back at the skuttler again. Now that it had stopped moving, the little machine seemed confused. Its strange eyepiece swayed low to the sand in a methodical search, the shards of what had once been its shell now pointing outwards like needles, revealing the swirling machinery that frothed at its core.

'What... what's it going to do?' Spiric asked, not taking his eyes off it.

'That doesn't matter!' the old man barked. 'But what I'm about to do is waste the last of my ink to save your sorry hide!' From a pocket at the small of his back, he withdrew a frayed brush and a narrow glass vial. The latter swished with a sky-blue liquid that matched his eyes and seemed to steam from the moment he unstoppered it. The old man began hastily dabbing the ink on to his exposed forearm in the rough shape of runes.

'You're worried about water? When did it last rain?' Spiric asked as the man stashed the near-empty vial.

'Last rain!?' the old man guffawed. 'It hasn't rained since the time of the Hytharo! Eons! They've been dead for far too long!' Pausing again, the man peered at him. 'How did you end up here, boy? Thinking about rain as well?'

'I don't know!' Spiric yelled, finally giving into his exasperation. 'I don't know where this is, how I got here, or even who the hell I'm meant to be! All I've got is empty pockets and these runes that someone *must* have put on me!' He thrust his arm forward, presenting the five blood red runes to the old man. From this far away, he wouldn't have a chance of making out the pattern, but they seemed to shock him, nonetheless.

Silence lingered between them. The only sound Spiric could hear was the faint ticking that grew behind him. Lapping waves of warmth came with it, each one making his skin prickle more than the sun ever could. The old man watched him, hesitating before speaking.

'What's your name, boy?'

'Spiric. What's that sound?'

'I'm Grethard,' the old man said calmly. 'I need you to stay very still. The skuttler's started its count. I think we've only got one more move before it blows.'

Spiric took a deep breath. 'What will happen when it does?'

'I'll be picking up the pieces of you until dawn,' Grethard said quietly. 'When I come at you, I need you to grab my hand. You can do that?'

Spiric only risked the slightest nod.

Grethard reached his hand forward, revealing the three blue runes on his wrist.

'This is going to be fast,' he muttered.

One by one, the runes slid into his palm, each stacking on top of its predecessor and burning white. The winds picked up around him, disturbing the dunes enough that they began to swirl. The old man crouched, the rippling gusts calming as he did, yet the air surrounding him was warping into a dancing shimmer. He sprang forward without warning, a fury of sand and wind carrying at his heels as he careened towards Spiric with an outstretched hand.

Spiric snatched at it, and suddenly he was yanked into the air, the sheer force of Grethard's grip almost enough to yank his shoulder from its socket. The sky and ground blurred into a single twirling mess as he soared before it was suddenly replaced by a flash of fiery yellow light and the deafening boom that followed.

The old man's grip disappeared and Spiric crashed bodily into the sand, only having enough sense left in his dazed and ringing head to curl into a ball as a mixture of thrown sand and shrapnel rained down upon him. The orange haze hadn't even cleared when a set of strong hands was hauling him to his feet. Spiric swayed as Grethard began to dust him off in a rough and vigorous manner. Grethard's mouth was moving, but the ringing pitch that stabbed at Spiric's eardrums turned every word into a distant horn blast.

Twenty feet away, sand settled into a charred crater. The explosion had burrowed as deep into the dune as Spiric was tall, and the only sign of the skuttler that'd caused it was the shrapnel that dotted the surrounding sand. Some of it had hit the glass walls of the nearby skyscrapers, but not a single pane was more broken than it had already been.

Instead, the strange metal spines hung suspended halfway through their face, almost like the glass had been created with them embedded there. Skuttlers from the surrounding avenues of glass had deployed their own legs and were shuffling over to investigate, their spindly metal necks craned as the blue light at the tip flashed rapidly.

Before Spiric could see more, Grethard took his hand and

dragged him back, pulling him around the corner of a nearby skyscraper where the opaque glass of its walls blocked his view. Spiric wanted to ask why the skuttler had tried to kill him or why it had been so enthusiastic in giving its own life to do so, but the old man shushed him.

'Now, let's have a closer look at you.' Grethard paused for a moment, holding him by the shoulders and struggling to remember his name. 'Spiric... right?'

He nodded, his dazed eyes focusing on the old man's apprehensive face. Grethard's stare was almost off-putting, he was staring at Spiric like he was a ghost.

'Red eyes... I've never seen red eyes before...'

Spiric shrugged out of Grethard's grip, checking his reflection in the ruin's glass wall. They were still red, just as he'd seen before. But what was strange about that? While there was precious little he actually could remember, he'd always had red eyes, even if he couldn't now recall why. He turned back to Grethard, his uncertain expression making Spiric doubt if they were his eyes in the first place.

'It's something to do with magic, isn't it?' Spiric said, tugging at a memory. What if Grethard could help him remember? He held out his wrist, presenting the strange red markings again. 'Do you know what these runes are? Why I'm here?'

Grethard glanced down at Spiric's arm, still hesitant.

'Could you help me find out?' Spiric added, trying hard to hide the desperation in his voice. From the corner of his eye, he could see the sun going down, painting the sky deep orange.

Grethard looked away without answering. He scanned their surroundings, maybe looking for more skuttlers, or something worse. The coast was clear, but this only made the old man's frown deepen. He looked back to Spiric and nodded for him to follow.

'Stay close, and don't stare at the shadows.'

The warning was cryptic, but Spiric obeyed, keeping his eyes fixed on the horizon as they stalked through the ruins. The path Grethard took them on was erratic. Sometimes they'd take a detour to avoid a herd of skuttlers or a pathway filled with twisted metal from a fallen structure. Other times they stood at the mouths of empty alleyways, where Grethard would produce a map, tracing his finger along their path before landing on a hastily scrawled cross.

The skyscrapers grew taller as they walked, looming overhead until they closed in from above. They all but blocked the setting sun, casting them in the shadows the old man had forbidden Spiric from looking at, yet these didn't seem to scare Grethard the most. Every now and again he'd throw a furtive, side-long glance at Spiric, his pace always seeming to keep him a few steps further from him than necessary.

'What are these ruins?' Spiric eventually asked.

Grethard remained silent.

'Who built them?' Spiric added, as if the train of thought seemed innocent enough.

Still nothing.

'Did you... did you build this place?'

This got a chuckle from Grethard.

'No, I can't let you believe that,' he said to himself. He stopped, finally letting Spiric draw closer. 'I didn't build these. Nor anyone I could have ever known. There were a people a long time ago. Advanced. More than anything we can reckon or imagine. But they're gone now. I've heard them called "those-of-glass." This, things like the skuttlers and other more mysterious things, is all they left behind. Most of it buried under the sand.'

'What do you mean by "other things"?'

'Things that are best forgotten. I went looking for them and saw things that drove men mad. Magics unbound by runes. Paralicts —objects cursed with that magic— that defied all sense and behaved exactly the opposite of how you'd expect. Phantoms that... Look, Spiric, these are the things that many believe were the downfall of the people who built this place and they're scared of it. Scared of people who've had anything to do with it.'

'But you're not scared?' Spiric asked. 'Are you?'

'Of course I am. That's why I'm out here, Spiric. I'm an exile. By the looks of it, so are you.'

## CHAPTER TWO

# LAST MEMORIES

THE SUN WAS NEARLY gone when Grethard's pace slowed out the front of yet another skyscraper. Spiric watched him as he eyed its length up and down several times before mustering the courage to approach a rent in the glass where the ruin's outer wall met the dunes. He waved for Spiric not to follow before disappearing into the darkness. The tense moments of isolation made his heart race as each second dragged on, but Grethard returned quickly enough, handing Spiric a small metal rod.

It was hefty, its body as thick as his wrist and maybe a foot in length, one of its ends capped with glass. With a confused expression, Spiric looked between the inert metal and Grethard, who made a quick shaking gesture with his arm, a kind smile forced upon his face. He mimicked the motion, causing something inside the rod to rattle with a sound Spiric was sure would attract more skuttlers. But before Spiric had even stopped, the glass end of the rod began to glow green.

The light was gentle at first, no match for the brilliant rays of the setting sun, but as Spiric shook the rod more vigorously, it grew in strength. Soon it was enough to illuminate the guts of the gloomy skyscraper.

'It's an old torch. Surprised it still works, but you can use it for now. I know the place well enough. It's more so you don't trip over.'

Inside the ruin was a long room of low ceilings, barely divided up by the toppled remains of decayed walls. Spiric swept the torch across the breadth of the massive room, his breath catching in his throat as the green light seemed to linger in a haze at certain spots. Grethard paid the phenomena no mind as he began leading Spiric deeper.

His path twisted around concrete pillars, past piles of thin metal desks and skirted collapsed sections of the floor that yawned with bottomless pits. With each step, the carpet released a puff of dust, and the knot in Spiric's stomach grew. It felt like a trap, but there was nothing Spiric could point to that was a danger. When he was sure Grethard wasn't looking, Spiric shone the torch into one, yet the darkness was truly impenetrable.

The old man stopped again at the foot of a spiralling set of stairs. A single silver pole supported each wafer-thin step that sprouted outwards like the feathers of a bird. They'd reached the centre of the skyscraper. Night had fallen outside, or perhaps light simply didn't reach this far into the ruin. Grethard crouched slightly, his face appearing ghostly in the light of the torch. He looked calm, yet his voice was restrained to an unpractised whisper.

'These stairs go up and they also go down. It's important that you never go down. Got it?'

'But what's down there?' Spiric couldn't help asking.

'Boy, do you think what you see around you is *all* of the ruins? Most of it is underground, along with the danger. We'll be safe as long as we stay above the sand.'

They started up the stairs. Spiric's boots clacked on each step, the sound sending a jolt of terror up his spine. He attempted to step softly, or only on his toes, but the sound still came. Ahead, Grethard climbed in perfect silence, indifferent to the racket being made behind him. Spiric used this to calm himself. He didn't even know what he was trying to hide the noise from.

A dozen floors later and open sky was suddenly above them. Spiric found himself momentarily awestruck by the busy field of stars that stretched out across the dark blue of the night. The acute ache in his legs eventually distracted him from the view and he hastened to follow Grethard across the skyscraper's roof.

Despite the arduous climb, the old man had a spring in his step, like that of one who'd just arrived home after a long day.

*Maybe this was home for him.*

The skyscraper's roof was a barren expanse of unnaturally smooth grey stone, spare for Grethard's little settlement. Shelves, tables and chairs, looted from below, no doubt, were arranged in busy rows that converged at one corner of the rooftop where a dormant brazier sat.

As Grethard fiddled with it, Spiric quietly made his way up and down the little alleys of curios, holding his fading touch close to each object in the hopes that one would stir up a memory.

There were vials upon vials of different oils and powders, stacks of identically misshapen ingots of purple metal, complicated-looking instruments that had entire shelfs dedicated to them, and dozens glass jars. They took all shapes and sizes, some filled with strange leaves of marbled colours, others with crushed shards of blue rock, and even some containing rather ordinary-looking sand.

*Why bother with sand? There was plenty of that around.*

Spiric dismissed the thought. He'd rather believe Grethard had a reason for it, otherwise he'd have to face the reality he'd been taken in by a madman.

He kept moving, now among what looked to be Grethard's personal library. Books in all shapes and sizes lined the shelves, bound in either cloth or ragged leather. By Spiric's estimate there had to be more than two hundred. The collection seemed so mismatched that it could only be the result of a combined inheritance that stemmed from the last dozen hermits that'd preceded the kook.

Spiric leaned around the shelves to look at Grethard. The brazier now bore a gently dancing flame, spitting up from the hot coals at its base and giving off a pungent, oily aroma. The old man threw in a few more lumps of coal, dusted off his hands, and beckoned Spiric closer, handing him a patched blanket when he approached.

'Gets cold up here. At night, I mean.'

Spiric traded the torch for the blanket, draping it over his back as he sat on a stool near the fire. He watched as Grethard busied himself, first finding his own blanket to wear, then rummaging through the pack he'd shrugged from his shoulders.

From it, he pulled a couple of fat-looking lizards and began to gut them over the fire with a blunt knife. The gizzards spat and hissed jovially in the coals, but he wasn't distracted by the spectacle as Spiric was. Grethard was focused on carefully skewering the remains with thin iron rods, each one just long enough to be haphazardly perched across the rim of the brazier. The oily smell was soon replaced with that of burning scales, which was just as pungent.

The old man continued around the rooftop with his pack, stowing the day's findings one by one into their proper places. With his eyes glazed over from the firelight, Spiric couldn't make out what each thing was, but he still watched curiously. Each item required Grethard to lean both elbows heavily on the shelf to steady himself, forcing a low grunt as his gnarled fingers scrabbled at the worn lids of jars or scratched-up cases.

There was no haste in this process, so it was a long while before Grethard finally kicked his scuffed boots off and sat down at a table next to the brazier, only just close enough for him to stretch out and warm his blackened toes.

The old man still didn't say anything. The peace was nice. Spiric hadn't realised how on edge these ruins had made him. Walking across the sands had been like being the prey in a hunting ground, a feeling that was all too familiar. But Grethard didn't seem bothered by it. Maybe he was used to it. The old man was more than content just to sit and scribble away at his map, taking great care not to punch through the already fraying cloth.

'What am I?' Spiric eventually asked.

'Hmm?' Grethard looked up from his map, twirling a pencil between his stubby fingers.

'I don't remember where I came from, how I got here or where I am. This doesn't happen often, does it?'

Grethard leaned back in his chair, and Spiric counted five different pops from his bones as he stretched.

'No, no it doesn't,' he answered. 'Never, really. That's why I'm so perplexed by you, to tell you the truth. I thought I'd seen most everything that the ruins could throw at me, but you, Spiric... You're a puzzle. That little bit out of place. An anomaly.'

Grethard stared pensively, leaning on his desk with his head propped up on his fist.

'If it were any other boy I'd found in these wastes I'd be confused enough, but red eyes?'

'They mean something.' Spiric couldn't keep Grethard's gaze for long. Instead he opted to watch the coals as they started to glow red. 'Something magic, right?'

Grethard took a deep breath and recited his next words almost as a poem. 'Yellow are Curiktic, beacons of the sun. Green are Kretatic, magnates of machine. And blue are Reythurist, weavers of the wind. And... no, you have to be one of these.'

'Yellow seems closest to red,' Spiric said dolefully. 'It just... it seems like... like there's something else.'

'We can find out tomorrow,' Grethard said. He moved closer to the fire, turning a skewered lizard to reveal the curling scales on its roasted underside. 'Nearly done,' he muttered to himself. He checked the others with bare hands, paying no mind to the searing heat carried by the metal skewers, before lumbering back to his desk, his interest once again firmly fixed on his map.

'What about you then?' Spiric asked. 'Who are you?'

'I'm Grethard,' he answered without looking up.

'You're an exile,' Spiric shot back.

The old man put down his pencil. 'I suppose I do owe you

more than that. I was a scholar for the Academy of Breggesa. You know of it?'

'Breggesa... The town... small upstart kind of place, isn't it?'

Grethard bellowed with laughter, and it echoed back at them from across the ruins. 'You've got a sense of humour, boy! Place like Breggesa being an upstart? Ha!'

Spiric frowned. Now that he tried to picture the town, he couldn't so much as conjure a memory of having visited, let alone a reason why he'd call it "upstart."

'If only it were an upstart. Too big for its own good, really. Last I was there, the Academy ruled the damn place. It was always about runes and axioms, finding new meanings of them, new ways to make ink. Little, incremental improvements, you see? All of it to do with the way we currently knew magic. It was the only thing the Academy was interested in.'

Grethard paused for a moment, looking out over the edge of the rooftop and over the silhouettes of the ruined skyscrapers. It was as if he were inviting Spiric to say something. He took the bait.

'But there's more, isn't there?'

A grin spread across the old man's face as he returned his gaze.

'I was one of the scholars who thought so. Maybe there always has been more. Things that we could learn from these places, left behind by those-of-glass. The magic of these ruins isn't bound by runes and axioms like ours is. Not sure what it's bound by, if anything at all. That's why the Academy forbade the topic entirely. Why I wanted to find out. I got a good ten years of research in, right under their noses, before they caught me. Kicked me out. Said I was tainted by those-of-glass.'

'Were you?'

There was a tense pause as Grethard stared into the fire. Spiric almost regretted the question.

'I saw a shadow,' Grethard said slowly. 'I couldn't explain it to them, so they believed I'd seen something far worse.'

'Like what?' Spiric didn't even think to hold his tongue.

'A shadow dancer. That's what they called them. It's what they're most scared of. I barely know how to describe it. They're all myths and hearsay. I think they were alive once, like you and me. But something happened to them. Died to their own magic. Now they lurk ruins like these. Watching. No idea what for, but they haven't shown interest in me. Not yet.'

'But what's so dangerous about them if they just watch?'

'Why would they watch us?' Grethard shrugged. 'Why take an interest? That's just the problem, Spiric. No one knows. It's the tyranny of questioning that even their name invokes that drives people to insanity, even their own death. It's said that, once seen, they stalk you, whisper dark things to you and drive you down a path of self-destruction until you're just like them. That's not even counting what people say their magic can do.'

'You mustn't have seen one then,' Spiric said. 'You're still alive.'

'I am alive, yes,' the old man said as he checked on the

lizards. 'Still, is this the life I wanted to lead? Tucked away from civilisation in a place where no one can follow me?' He picked up a skewer with a blanket-wrapped hand, ripped the skin off the sizzling lizard with his teeth and took a bite, pausing before chewing to blow hot vapour from his mouth. 'Still, there are things to enjoy.'

He motioned for Spiric to take a skewer. Wrapping his hand with his own blanket, he took the one that looked the thinnest. He was already grateful for the charity Grethard was showing him and didn't want to be greedy.

'You said there's no rain,' Spiric said before digging in. Up close, the sight of the curled scales set his hair on end, as did the thought of trying to eat it, but without a better option, he pushed through, instantly getting a dozen scales stuck painfully between his teeth.

'Not for eons. Legend has it there was another people alongside the Curiktics, Reythurists and Kretatics, called Hytharo. They made it rain. Made it storm. But they died out, no one knows why. The last one must have done something to save us, though. Locked the water in the air itself. We breathe it to live, but most people take it for granted. What they don't take for granted is getting actual liquid water. No water—'

'Means no ink. No ink means no runes. No runes means no magic,' Spiric recited. 'But I have these runes. Do you think I could be a Hytharo?'

Grethard shook his head slowly. 'Eons, boy. A thousand

years.'

Spiric dejectedly looked down at his forearm. He willed the runes to move, to stack up in his palm as Grethard's had done, to burn white and do... something.

'You sure you don't remember anything, Spiric?' Grethard asked gently. 'About how you got here or before? I've seen people get knocked on the head hard enough to forget things. You don't seem nearly cross-eyed enough for that.'

It was a question he'd been asking himself. He took another faltering bite of the lizard. He got fewer scales this time, and aside from how salty it was, it wasn't too bad. He swallowed the mouthful before it burnt off the rest of his tastebuds and wondered if that was the source of the improvement as he took a third bite.

'I was running. I don't know why. And I knew these buildings... we called them skyscrapers.'

'Skyscrapers?' Grethard muttered to himself. 'Only the Academy call them that.'

'I was alone,' Spiric continued, staring into the fire. 'I was alone and afraid.'

'I'm sorry.'

They ate in silence for a while longer.

'Thank you for pulling me out of the sand,' Spiric eventually said. 'It was you, wasn't it?'

Grethard slowly shook his head.

'I felt a hand,' Spiric asserted, panic starting to rise in his

27

chest.

'And I saw a shadow.'

Spiric felt his mouth go dry. The skewered lizard was now even less appealing. 'Do you think it was a shadow dancer?'

'I saw a shadow,' Grethard repeated. 'That's all I know. I saw your hand. A shadow bent over it and then you burst forth. I followed you from a distance because I didn't know what you were. You could have been a trap. A fracture to draw me in. Another anomaly of the ruins themselves. But we still don't know what got you here or what you were before. We can find out tomorrow. For now, eat and rest.'

Grethard was right. There were too many mysteries to solve for one night. He finished the lizard, then choked down the other one the old man offered to him. Once they'd both finished, Grethard handed Spiric a spare bedroll and motioned towards one of the low-hanging canvas shade cloths.

Spiric went over to one nestled between the low wall at the rooftop's edge and the last of the cluttered shelves, leaving the old man to his map work. The canvas was frayed enough to allow a few stray glimmers of starlight through, but their light was no match for the still-cooking brazier. It washed across Spiric with a warm orange glow. With his cloak bunched up as a pillow, it even made the thin bedroll seem comfortable.

Spiric reluctantly closed his eyes. The only sounds were the crackles of the hot coals, the scratching of Grethard's pencil, and the wind crossing through the ruins. It was a low whine, like that of a distant, dying animal.

What if there was something other than him and Grethard out there? A shadow dancer? If what Grethard had seen was true, then it could've been the shadow dancer that'd pulled him from the sand. But could it have also been the one to land him there in the first place? What if it was still following him?

All these questions whirled through his head as sleep gently blanketed him, but his final thought dismissed it all. If Grethard could survive however many years he'd spent alone, Spiric could survive the night.

## CHAPTER THREE

# TRIAL BY RUIN

THE NEXT MORNING, SPIRIC woke with a start, fighting against whatever was holding him down. Only once he'd opened his eyes did he realise it was just the blanket. For a moment, he'd thought he was buried in the sand again, trapped with no way out. It had only happened once, as far as he knew, but the sensation was far more familiar than it should be.

He sat up, the top of his head grazing the low canvas. The sky was purple from the predawn light, yet it was still dark on the rooftop, spare for the faint glow of last night's coals. Spiric stood, throwing his tattered cloak around his shoulders, and walked to the edge. The ruins now stood silent. The eerie wind was gone. But other things lurked between the walls.

Strange, spindly-legged creatures that stood ten feet tall with bodies only as big as a man's head. They seemed to float more than they walked, keeping in tight packs of four or five, some even slowly climbing the walls into the ruins themselves.

There were more skuttlers about, but they stood dormant, tucked away at the corners of the ruins and blanketed by the drift of sand that had moved in overnight. Maybe that was how Spiric had ended up buried. He'd just gone to sleep in the dunes and hadn't noticed himself getting crushed and suffocated. He snorted at the idea. If only it were that simple.

He eventually found Grethard next to the brazier, snoring merrily despite being face down in his bedroll. Toying with the idea of waking him, Spiric decided against it. At this very moment, the old man's collection of books intrigued him far more than any tales their owner could tell. Books didn't have a tendency to tell half-truths and obscured facts in order to hide things.

The previous night he'd thought them dull and uniform, but in the morning light the leather spines shone in all different colours. Sky blue, deep green, and a particularly large yellow one caught his eye at first, but eventually he focused on a neatly tucked-away red one. Spiric pulled it out, running his thumb down the line of runes embossed on the spine before flipping it open.

Each page was dense with hastily scrawled paragraphs of

faded black ink, some sections only as legible as the physical scratches the quill had left in the paper itself. The words flowed in whichever direction they pleased, yet no matter how much Spiric skimmed and flicked between the pages, they all revolved back to a convoluted and rambling history of Hytharo politics and the necessity of sacrifice. Whatever that meant.

Spiric forced himself to slow on the next semi-legible page he encountered, hoping for some hint of how this all might connect to him, how it might tell him what Grethard was hiding from him, but quickly found himself frustrated by the writer's manner, blundering along with phrases that should've ended long ago as they began to repeat themselves.

'You can read that?'

Spiric spun with a start, almost dropping the book as he caught sight of Grethard rubbing his bleary eyes.

'Well, yes, but this isn't anything special, is it?'

Grethard paused for a moment before shaking his head. 'It's not often boys your age know how to read. Either from a rich family or you taught yourself like I did. Never mind the book, though. We've got work to do. Eat this.'

He tossed Spiric a small hessian pouch, which he dropped the book to catch. Inside were a few strips of dried, blackened meat. Somehow it was even saltier than last night's lizard.

He followed Grethard around as the old man prepared for the day, stuffing vials and supplies into his pack as Spiric attempted to gnaw heroically at what the old man had implied was a meal.

'There's one thing I saw yesterday that I still don't understand. There was this metal canister flying through the sky. I followed it, but it was gone so fast.'

'A canister?' Grethard thought for a moment, then lit up. 'You must mean mortar mail!'

He dashed across the rooftop and Spiric followed, both coming to a stop before a long, upright metal tube with a strangely funnelled end. The night before, Spiric had figured it was either a chimney or a telescope. Grethard unlatched a cover at its base, flinging it open to reveal a heavily scratched metal cylinder. He whipped it out with the kind of glee that his wrinkled face hadn't been contorted into for decades and unscrewed it.

'Nothing!'

'But I saw—'

'Must've been a misfire,' Grethard muttered, reattaching the lid.

Spiric's eyes went wide. 'Was it meant for someone else?'

Grethard let out a low chuckle. 'I'm the only exile out here, Spiric. There've been a few of us with a talent for stepping on Academy toes. I'm the only one that made it this far.'

'But you could take me to them? The Academy, I mean. They could tell me who—'

The old man silenced Spiric's jabbering with a wave.

'Not until we find out more. I shudder to think what would have happened to you if you'd run into someone not as...

embracing of the ruins as I.'

'Fine,' Spiric mumbled.

A small grin cracked across the old man's face. 'Let's get on with it, then.'

Back down at the dune level, Grethard unfurled his map. Spiric watched as his stubby finger traced a path across it, following a new line he must have drawn the previous night. A line that passed through several of the scribbled crosses.

'Where are we going?' Spiric asked, still eyeing the map.

Grethard roughly folded it away as he realised Spiric was looking. 'We're going to find out if you're really a Hytharo.'

A flash of excitement rose in Spiric's chest. 'Do you think I am?'

But the old man shook his head. 'During my time in these ruins, I've learnt that certainty is nothing but a death omen. It leads hopeful men on dangerous paths that have unpredictable ends. I want to think you a Hytharo, Spiric, if only to bring you back to Breggesa in the hopes that your discovery can convince them to accept my return, but I need it to be proven. Red eyes and red runes aren't enough.'

'Then how?' Spiric asked.

'I need to see you use them,' he said. 'I need you to bring me water.'

The old man's task weighed heavy in his mind as they set off, trekking a winding path as prescribed by his tattered map. There was less stopping and starting compared to last night,

35

and the skuttlers they passed didn't even seem bothered by their presence. Most of them were still dormant, likely waiting until sunset to re-emerge.

Nevertheless, Spiric still kept his distance from them, holding back his questions of who had created them and why they still guarded the ruins with their mechanical lives.

Soon they were passing a small pack of the gangly creatures Spiric had spied from the rooftop earlier that morning. From down here, their thin legs wavered in the heat haze, and when he and Grethard drew closer, the creatures staggered away in fright, disappearing down alleyways or climbing the walls themselves.

'They're called yherdras and they're deadly,' Grethard said, watching as the last one disappeared from view. 'They weigh almost nothing, which is why they don't set off the skuttlers, but if one of them gets a feeler around you, the poison will have you dead in minutes. Credit to them, though, I've seen them go down the ruins and come back up again.'

'But you said it was dangerous down there,' Spiric said.

'Not to them. They seem to sense their way through things we can't see. Though when they come back, if I'm lucky, they're full of water.'

'So that's how you get water? Why don't we just hunt one then? If water's what you—'

Grethard shook his head. 'It's not that easy, Spiric. They're wily game and I'm not worried about your skills as a hunter. Come on.'

They walked alone for miles, their only company being their warped reflections that crossed the glass walls around them. Spiric kept glancing over his shoulder, waiting for something to jump out from the corners of buildings, the dark gaps framed by shattered glass in the walls, or even from above, whenever they passed under the wire-supported bridges that hung loose between some of the buildings.

The wind began to pick up, only truly felt when they passed through intersections where it would hurl grains of sand at a rate that stung his skin. Even when they were sheltered from it, the continuous low howl still carried through, echoing from all around. It was occasionally punctuated by the distance creaking shift of metal, but that did nothing to put him at ease.

It was impossible to tell how far they'd travelled. Looking back the way they'd came, Spiric only saw dune after sweeping dune, a sea of red punctuated by the pillars of glass that refracted the sky's blue light.

Grethard's silent lead had only given the questions whirling through Spiric's head time to mutate. When the old man had first mentioned it, the idea of being a Hytharo had excited him, even if it was just the prospect of having an inkling of his identity back. If that were true, then it meant he was the only one of his kind. How had they all died out, how had he escaped, and how had he even ended up here?

But if he wasn't a Hytharo, what was he? When he finally found the courage to voice the question, Grethard had only replied with a shrug, and his imagination raced to fill the void with terrifying answers.

Eventually the old man brought them to a stop next to yet another skyscraper. Spiric leaned heavily on the glass wall. It was unnaturally cool under his palm, but welcome. He turned and leaned his back against it, feeling the midday heat draining from his skin.

'Don't lean on that,' Grethard snapped.

Spiric savoured it for a few more seconds before he complied.

'There's a light-bend around this corner. Strange places. Best not to go in together. No telling what you'll see. I'll meet you on the other side. Wait a bit for me to go through and then it'll be your turn.'

Grethard set off for the corner of the ruin and Spiric could again feel the panic twisting in his gut.

'Wait!' he cried out. 'What's a light-bend? What am I even supposed to do?'

It was too late. Grethard was gone from sight, his footprints already fading in the sand. Spiric dashed after him but staggered to a stop as soon as he rounded the corner of twisted iron.

The path before him shimmered, a solid border of refracting light. It drew a perfectly straight line across the sand before him, disjointing the dunes and making them look like they had cliffs and drops that were physically impossible. The skyscrapers that walled both sides didn't make sense, either.

Tightly packed, they wavered like long reeds, curling inwards and out, only holding still as Spiric forced his eyes to focus on one particular point of them. Even this was dizzying, as it made the surrounding view swirl faster.

Spiric swore to himself, his breathing speeding up to keep in tune with his pounding heart. He wanted to run or just lie down in the sand and give up. He was a fool for even thinking of following Grethard, but what option did he have left? He was alone. Alone and afraid.

He sucked in a deep breath, taking another step closer to the border of the shimmering air. It rippled at his presence, the movement of it giving him goosebumps. He just had to make it through and find Grethard on the other side. The old man had made it sound easy. Perhaps it was.

Spiric clenched his eyes shut and took a lurching stride forward. In an instant, it felt like the whole sky was pressing down on his shoulders. His knees fought to keep him upright, and when he opened his eyes, he almost toppled.

A dull red haze had engulfed him, so thick he could only see ten feet around him. The sand blended perfectly with it, so it looked as though there was no border between it and the air. The only thing that remained constant was the skyscrapers above.

Spiric stared, wide eyed and open-mouthed, as they seemed to stretch taller and taller into the sky until they united over him. Shaking his head, he looked back down at his arm, hoping at least that would look normal. The runes were still there, still red, no, now black! They flashed between the two colours, but no matter how hard he focused, he couldn't pick the point at which the runes changed.

'Do something!' he hissed at his arm.

But the runes began to fade off, fragment by fragment until his flesh was bare. Spiric swore again and spun around. The border was gone. The only way out was forward. He turned again. In the mist, there was a figure ahead, their back to him. Could it be Grethard? Spiric squinted. No, too short. They were his height.

Spiric gritted his teeth and staggered forward.

The figure did as well.

Spiric stopped.

So did the figure.

Was it a reflection? No, it should be facing him! Spiric eyed it, waiting for it to make a move, but it was still. He took another step, the figure doing so at the exact moment. Was it copying him? The thought made Spiric freeze.

He had to check. Slowly, he turned his head, watching out of the corner of his eye as the figure's head also turned, then shifted his gaze to what was behind him. Another figure! But it was closer now, and Spiric could make out his own clothes, his own cloak, his—

Spiric snapped his eyes forward. The figure in front was gone. Spiric started walking, his shuddering breath barely registering in his ears. The red haze grew thicker, closing in to trap him until he couldn't even see his feet.

The only sight that remained was the enormous skyscraper that stood in the distance, yet this was not made of glass like the others. Its obsidian faces stretched upwards as Spiric followed its length, towering so high that he had to crane his neck to glimpse its peak. Eventually its base broke from the ground and it hovered into the sky, instilling a terrifying familiarity in Spiric as he fought to tear his eyes away.

He looked back down, and this time he definitely wasn't alone. Human-shaped silhouettes moved lazily through the fog, some walking across his path, some by his side, but one stood in his way. Watching him. Waiting for him.

Spiric couldn't stop for it. He felt like he'd lost control of his own legs. As he drew closer, the edges of the figure grew sharper, features starting to cut into the blackness of where a face should be. Spiric watched in horror as black eyes formed on the creature. It was unnatural, Spiric could remember that much! Nothing had black eyes like that, nothing! Except...

'Shadow dancer.'

The words slipped out of Spiric's mouth by accident, but he was sure they were true. It was now face to face with him, curiosity almost seeping through its featureless expression. Spiric's eyes stung as if he hadn't blinked for days, and his throat had closed up a long time ago from the fear.

'Please,' Spiric choked. 'Help me.'

The figure cocked their head and a hand came rushing out of

the centre of its chest, trailing flecks of shadow like smoke. Spiric couldn't even scream as it grabbed his collar and wrenched him forward.

He thrashed as he hit the ground, spraying dust in every direction until his flailing fist caught something bony. There was a yelp of pain and then a thud in the sand next to him. It was just Grethard, grasping his knee with pain painted across his face and a glare of frustration fixed on Spiric. Next to them, the barrier of light shimmered harmlessly and the haze was gone.

'What the hell are you playing at, boy?' he bellowed.

'What am I— what... what were they!?' Spiric said, pointing a shaking finger at the light wall as he scrambled away from it.

'They?' Grethard groaned as he got to his feet. 'That's just another fracture. It does nothing but distort light. There is no "they" to it!'

Spiric shook his head quickly as he scrambled away from the light-bend.

'But there was more than that! There was a haze, and it was like I was following myself, or being followed by myself, and then there were these shadows... dozens... one of them... one of them had black eyes like I've never seen before.'

Grethard stared at him, long and hard, in a way that made Spiric feel guilty for jabbering. Had he actually seen any of it? How long had he even been in the light-bend? Doubts began to pop up in his mind, crossing out everything he thought he'd seen.

'Maybe it was just the light-bend,' Spiric added sheepishly.

'Maybe,' Grethard said, his tone short. 'We should move away from this place. It does funny things to your head. Like making you punch old men to the ground.'

## CHAPTER FOUR

# TO THE DEPTHS

G RETHARD HAD ALREADY TURNED his back and started walking, his last muttered sentence biting deep into Spiric. He hadn't asked to go through all that. As he stomped after the old man, more mutinous thoughts marshalled themselves in his head. What if he didn't need Grethard? He could just strike out on his own. Maybe there actually was someone else in these ruins who would be kinder. What if he could just overpower the old man, take the pack and run? If Spiric could knock him off his feet by accident, who knew what kind of damage he could do if he intended it.

Spiric's fists clenched for a moment, but then released. The anger didn't sit right in his gut, the mood instantly replaced by a wash of hopelessness. He wouldn't have made it nearly this far if it wasn't for Grethard. Trusting the old kook was the best he could do. He just needed to find water and force Grethard to admit what he really was.

*A Hytharo.*

They walked for a long while, their path weaving still more strangely. It was like the old man was taking him into the very heart of the ruins. Grethard made keenly sure to point out the fractures they passed, their occurrences growing more commonplace.

More howling tunnels of sand and wind, more light-bends blocking their path and even things Spiric hadn't seen before. Streets that turned to bottomless pits that he couldn't see the depths of. Sections of buildings that floated disjointed and free from their lower floors, only tethered there by narrow beams of white light. Then there were the shadows that flickered in the wrong direction, rebelling against the sunlight.

Nearer to the centre, Spiric was sure the skyscrapers would grow larger and more clustered, but the exact opposite happened. The few that survived to poke over the dunes were twisted wrecks at best. Soon they were gone entirely, the sand under them steepening into a massive basin. Spiric felt a strange calm trickle through him as it all just turned to an empty desert of flowing sand.

Over near the horizon, Spiric could pick out the distant

skyscrapers that formed a rim surrounding the sandy depression. It was as if they held back the dune, but how could that be possible? How had this space not been filled over and over in the thousand lifetimes that had passed it by?

'What are we searching for?' he eventually asked Grethard. The question came out in a crackling voice, stiff from the past hour of disuse.

'Another fracture. Look.'

One of Grethard's crooked fingers pointed to a spot somewhere to the left of the centre of the basin, but Spiric followed the spirit of the gesture instead.

A bulbous dome sat at the very bottom of the basin, its height only barely reaching the same altitude from which Spiric peered at it. Golden tiles shaped like hexagons and as tall as he was scaled its surface, each one only separated from its neighbour by a border of dull black.

The sun bounced off it with dances of prismatic light. Spiric was mesmerised by the way it painted the dunes washing against the dome's sides with faint and fleeting rainbows.

Tilted halos of shrapnel and scrap metal hung fifty feet above it in tranquil orbits, effectively at eye-level for Spiric. Rust-coloured particles snaked off either side, forming a pair of ethereal tendrils that reached to the sky, where they entwined like helixes.

Spiric didn't find the dome itself imposing, nestled so deep in the pit, but he didn't trust it. Why was it out here, all alone?

What happened to all the other buildings? And why did the display of suspended metal above it seem so familiar?

'This one I understand the least,' Grethard said, breaking the silence. 'The composition of the metal, the flow of the shrapnel's orbit, the force which twists it into that shape... I've spent decades charting it, testing it, observing it, yet I've discovered nothing I can be sure of. I sometimes wonder if I'd need a thousand lifetimes in this place to see it repeat, but I'm an old man. I don't have that kind of time.'

'Then why bring me here?' Spiric asked hesitantly. 'What could I find that you haven't already?'

Grethard threw him a sidelong grimace, looking as though he was already regretting his next words.

'Water,' he whispered. 'Within that dome is a way down to the city that lies below the sands. The domain left by those-of-glass. A place where everything is a fracture, where normalcy is an anomaly. As a Reythurist, I can search through the air to sense what lies there without venturing down myself and I felt pure liquid water.'

The last three words were spoken with an awestruck reverence. He turned to Spiric and took his right hand, brushing his coarse fingertips over the runes on his wrist.

'If you are a Hytharo, then you will be able to stand inside that dome and summon the water without having to venture into its depth. Together, these five runes must form an axiom, a sentence of meaning for you to cast into the world. I only hope that the opportunity of their use will help you find a piece of your memory.'

'Will you come with me?' Spiric asked, gently taking his arm back.

Grethard slowly shook his head. 'As much as I would like to witness the first Hytharo axiom to be used in a lifetime, I worry it will influence the chance that you recall something. You said you remembered being alone, yes?'

Spiric nodded. 'Alone and afraid.'

'Then the inside of that dome is one of the most terrifying places I have set foot.'

'But what if I'm not?' Spiric blurted.

'Not what?'

'A Hytharo.'

Grethard let out a derisive snort. 'For the sake of the gods, boy, I'm already having a hard time accepting that you are! Don't tell me you are, as well.'

'But what if—'

He was interrupted as Grethard took a loud, sighing breath to still his temper. When he opened his eyes to look at Spiric, it was with a twinkle of reassurance. 'I know I warned you of the dangers of certainty in a place like this, but that doesn't extend to what you hold in your heart.' Grethard shrugged his pack from his shoulders, produced the canister that had been delivered by the mortar mail and placed it gently in Spiric's hands. 'Go. Prove yourself a Hytharo. Not for my eyes, but for your own mind.'

With Grethard's reassurances swelling in his chest, Spiric went marching into the basin, the canister rattling in his hands. For once he believed the old kook. He just had to use the runes, the axiom they made up, and then Grethard would have no choice in accepting him as a Hytharo, because Spiric would know beyond the shadow of a doubt that he was.

Even the word Hytharo was starting to feel familiar on his tongue. Each time Spiric whispered it to himself, the sense only grew, to the point that he wondered why he was still doing this if he was so damn sure.

But his certainty crumbled as he crossed the shadows cast by the rings of suspended metal. Their orbits wobbled at Spiric's presence, tilting from their odd angles as he neared the dome until they were parallel to the earth, the pace of their revolutions almost completely halted.

As Spiric drew closer to the golden dome, it began to shimmer in the heat haze. A low hum had slipped into the air as well, a sound Spiric sensed more in his throat than his ears. At the very base of it, where gold met sand, a few of the strangely shaped tiles lay scattered and half-buried in front of a dark breach.

Spiric stared into the dark entrance of the dome. The borders were charred, as was the sand around it, but it couldn't have been recent. This thing was ancient, dormant, Spiric could just sense it. Judging by the tiles on the ground out here, whatever had forced the breach had been trying to get out, not in. He shuddered. What was down there that needed to escape?

He crouched beside one of the sunken tiles. It was easily large enough for him to lie on. Despite the blanket of dust, the gold itself still glistened. Spiric set the canister aside for a moment and ran his hands over it, wiping the grit away and feeling the finely etched patterns underneath. But he didn't get a chance to see it. The grit had flowed around his hand like liquid, returning to its original position.

'Spiric! Behind you!'

He spun at Grethard's call, his hand racing to a non-existent scabbard at his hip. A pack of yherdras, half a dozen strong, had appeared behind him. The beasts must've been stalking them the whole time and Spiric kicked himself for not once looking over his shoulder to catch them.

But there was no need for panic. They were moving towards him with a serene gait and Spiric slowly stepped to the side, watching them warily as they passed through the breach and into the dome. He was not their prey. At least, not yet.

Up close, the creatures were even stranger. Their bodies were coated with sharp grey-blue hairs that rippled with each step and their eyes could only just be seen through heavily lidded slits. None of them even looked at Spiric as they passed. He glanced back to Grethard, who was still standing at the rim of the basin, but he was barely a speck in the distance.

Steeling his resolve, Spiric followed the yherdras and was

immediately enveloped by darkness. He kept walking, his ears twitching at the sound of thick sand crunching underfoot. Only three steps in and he'd lost the benefit of the midday sun. Not wanting to risk getting wrapped up in the leg of one of those beasts, he forced himself to stop.

Something had been rattling in the canister. With a bit of fiddling, he popped the clasp on the lid and reached in, pulling out a short metal rod. The glass end of it glinted green in the gloom. It was the torch!

Spiric didn't even pause to consider why Grethard had hidden it in the canister. He started shaking it, the rattle echoing around the dome as the green light grew stronger and stronger. Soon it was so bright Spiric could barely stand to look at it. The furthest reaches of the inside of the high dome were illuminated, revealing a network of strange inward-pointing spines.

The yherdras were contently climbing across them, using each spike like the rungs of a ladder. Below them, another basin had formed, steeper than the one outside and centred around a pitch-black pit.

A slow drift of sand constantly drained down it, but Spiric couldn't tell where it went. He didn't want to guess, either. He scanned the dome one more time before he swore quietly to himself. None of it looked familiar. Wedging the canister under his left arm, he held the torch to the runes at his right wrist, but they still sat dormant.

Spiric stretched out his hand towards the pit in the vain hope that he'd sense the water Grethard had told him of, but the only thing he felt was that he was about to fall over. He let his hand drop, kicking himself for thinking it would be that easy. Or that it would even work. What did Grethard know about being a Hytharo? In hindsight, the old man's musings had been nothing but guesswork, and Spiric had been stupid for believing it.

But what other choice did he have? To dejectedly trudge back up the sandy basin and tell Grethard he wasn't a Hytharo? The prospect of it filled him with a wave of indignant fury and he pushed the thought from his mind. No, he was going to find water, even if he had to find his way into the city below the sands to get it.

He shone the torch over the pit and his newfound determination melted.

*Was it safe?*

But before the idea of fleeing could return, a movement caught his eye. Above, a yherdra had started to descend from the ceiling like it was suspended by wires. Spiric held the green torch high but saw no such connection. It floated on its own, its thin legs spreading wide as it drifted towards the pit before tucking quickly as it disappeared. One by one, the rest of the pack followed until Spiric was alone.

He could remember something Grethard had said about the strange creatures, that they survived these ruins by not only being deadly to the touch, but also having an innate sense of where the danger lay. If they could go down there, then surely, so could he.

Carefully, Spiric inched closer to the hole, each sliding stride of his feet giving him the feeling he was on frozen ice. Soon he was overlooking the void. It was wide, easily wide enough for the yherdras to spread their legs on their descent, so why hadn't they? The walls of the shaft were clad with a strange white padding, long stained red by the constant trickle of sand running down them like droplets of water. Peculiar metal instruments jutted out every now and again down its length, mounted of flexible arms that had long ago rusted in place. Right in front of Spiric was a ladder, the first rung a little bit too inviting.

Grethard had said the deep was dangerous. Impossible for someone to survive with their sanity intact. But if that was where Spiric was to find water, if that was the way to prove himself a Hytharo...

Stubborn courage formed in Spiric as he mounted the rungs and began his own descent. This was an act of spiteful and self-inflicted rebellion, hatched because he couldn't even bring himself to believe he was a Hytharo without completing the old man's task.

The rebellion quickly turned to drudgery as the ladder's descent went from a blood rush to a chore. Coordinating the canister in one hand and the torch in the other was difficult enough, but some of the ladder's rungs were completely absent, as if it had been made to be climbed in the opposite direction. Even the strange gadgets that sprouted from the walls were too far away to aid him.

Spiric hadn't even remembered to look down. A moment later, he regretted having the thought. Below was still inky blackness, yawning wide and somehow pulling at his precariously placed feet. The yherdras were long gone from sight, and Spiric could only hope they were waiting for him at the bottom as his guide.

His ears popped uncomfortably and his fingers grew achingly numb, but his exhaustion was all but forgotten when his boots hit the floor with a splash.

Spiric glanced down. He was up to his ankles in…

'Water.'

It came out as a gasp. The entire room was flooded to be a foot deep with perfectly clear water. The ripples emanating from his boots subsided as he stared in frozen awe, the metal grating underfoot barely distorted by the pool's refraction.

Spiric held the still glowing torch close to the surface, tinging his reflection with a dazzling green. He turned, looking to a gap in the wall bordered by breached steel. Beyond it were more buildings than he could ever fathom. The enormous bases of the skyscrapers he'd seen above the dunes were clustered with crowds of smaller towers, all of them linked by intricate bridges of glass and golden cabling.

Unlike above, it was all perfectly preserved, hidden from the world by a cavernous ceiling that the skyscrapers pierced like spears. Spiric took a few more steps out into the undercity, the ground beneath the water line turning from metal to impossibly smooth stone, and his footsteps silent, spare for the water lapping against his shins.

Pillars of steel surrounded the base of the metal shaft he'd just descended, supporting a canopy of glass that undulated like a piece of fabric frozen in time. In the light of his torch, it looked like the underside of a green ocean caught in a storm. Spiric chuckled to himself. If only Grethard could see him now. The old man wouldn't know what an ocean was. Or a storm. But Spiric did.

*Because I'm a Hytharo.*

He looked down at the water, forcing his mind back to the job at hand. Standing in it, feeling the hem of his trousers sway about his ankles in the gentle current, felt right. It was that affinity Grethard had blathered on about.

He crouched low, unsealing the canister and filling it to the brim. Once the lid was back on, he tipped it this way and that, but it seemed watertight enough. If Grethard was telling the truth, then this could be the most water the old man would see in his life.

It made sense for Spiric to stand up and leave, but something compelled him to stay low to the water. It wasn't nearly as dangerous as Grethard had warned. Even the yherdras had left to go about their business. He could enjoy it a few minutes longer.

Wedging the torch in his front pocket, Spiric knelt, the water now around his waist, his palms hovering just above the surface. Droplets leapt up to his fingertips the moment he touched it, a handshake from an old friend and, unable to restrain himself, Spiric plunged his forearms in.

His breath rushed from his body as cool relief replaced it. It was a welcome change from the desert heat. He swirled his arms, watching the currents catch and fade. Even in the green light, the runes on his wrist still showed up crimson.

If only he knew what they did. What they said. Grethard had told him it was something to do with water. He pulled the marked arm up and eyed the axiom closely. If he willed it enough, the runes would even twitch! He touched his palm to the surface again, closing his eyes and willing the individual runes to move, but when he looked again, they hadn't. At least the ink itself hadn't washed off.

The sound of sudden, rapid splashing in the distance distracted him and he looked up. There was movement out there! Spiric leapt to his feet, grunting as the weight of the full canister tugged at his belt where he'd tied it. The sloshing noise was drawing closer and a ripple was starting to reach Spiric's feet.

The yherdras burst back into sight a few seconds later, all six of them galloping for their lives across the water towards him.

Spiric made to run, but the water clamped his boots in place, sending him toppling over with a splash. Suddenly he was fully submerged, his arms flailing until he punched solid ground, pushing himself out of the water and coughing violently. Water sprayed over him as he tried to clear his eyes, only vaguely aware of the gust of bodies flying past. Once Spiric had found his feet, he could only watch the last yherdra scarper up the shaft towards the surface.

He coughed up water as he got wearily to his feet. Completely sodden, his traveling cloak weighed heavily on his shoulders. The torch in his front pocket only bore a dull light and no matter how much Spiric shook it, it would only give enough to see about ten metres out. Maybe it was time to go. If there was something the yherdras had been so desperately running from, it likely wouldn't be something he wanted to find himself chased by, either.

He began backing towards the ladder, not taking his eyes off the alley from which the yherdras had barrelled forth. The spot was too far to be illuminated by the ailing torch, but he swore he could see a small spark of blue energy sporadically dancing there.

Spiric squinted harder, for all the good it would do. If his mind wasn't playing tricks on him, it seemed to be drawing closer. He waited, rooted to the spot as a certain pitch began to fill the air. It was a low hum, a sound that rang in his skull rather than his ears, growing heavier in tone until it caused the water at his feet to start quivering.

Spiric wanted to scream, to run, but fear kept him still. His eyes burned as he stared into the darkness, his mouth agape and his throat closing up. Spiric glanced down at his arm. If those runes were going to do something, this might be the last chance they had.

When he looked back up, a shadow stood at the edge of the torchlight, just like the one he'd come face to face with in the light-bend. It took another deliberate step closer, its darkness not wavering despite the dull green glow.

'What are you?' Spiric breathed.

The silhouette cocked its head and the shadows faded away. A man's thin, pale face was revealed, an almost hungry grin splayed wide across it. His nose was sharp, cheekbones sharper and worst of all, his eyes were familiar. Black irises stared back at Spiric, drilling into his soul. A magnificent black greatcoat hung from his shoulders, the fabrics rippling in the non-existent breeze as thousands of ornately adorned silver runes flashed across it.

'Shadow dancer,' Spiric whispered.

The figure nodded, spreading his arms slightly as he did so. He took a single step forward, the motion causing his clothes to shimmer in and out of sight. His boots were little more than leather wraps, but even they weren't necessary. He walked upon the water itself, his steps not even causing a ripple.

Spiric tried to lurch away, but the water caught at his feet once more and he stumbled, only just catching his balance as he became aware of the tingling sensation on his right arm. He looked to the runes and almost yelped in surprise.

The first one had reached his palm and he winced as it burned white hot, now branded into his skin as the next followed it. But the shadow dancer was suddenly before him, the phantom's very presence freezing Spiric from fear as his pale grey hands reached towards him. The thin fingers traced either side of Spiric's jaw before snapping into a vice-like grip and tilting his head upwards.

A gasp escaped Spiric and he couldn't breathe in to replace it. The third rune burned as the shadow dancer inspected him, tipping his head to get a good look at his eyes, but Spiric couldn't focus enough to stare back for more than a second. The phantom's face was a fearsome blur that sent his skin numb. Another rune burned, cutting through the sensation, searing into his palm with enough pain to force Spiric to utter his last words.

'What do you want?'

The shadow dancer frowned, relaxing their grip just enough for Spiric to hack and cough between desperate gulps of air. As he recovered, the shadow dancer spoke. The words were not fierce. They were not a threat. They were a request.

'I want you to remember me.'

Spiric barely heard it. His palm stung as the final rune burned and, following what little instincts he had left, he shoved it to the water at his feet. A crackling web of lightning arced from his fingers, enveloping both him and the shadow dancer as the entire undercity was lit bright blue, all its shadows suddenly erased.

The jagged ropes of energy surged across the water, licking off the buildings and coiling onto the wires that connected them. It crashed into the distant cavern walls and thunderous rumble replied, then the water returned as a roaring wave, tall enough to batter the stone ceiling and tear through the once-sturdy skyscrapers.

The shadow dancer's face warped into an expression of jubilant wonder as the colossal wave bore down on them. He turned back to Spiric, fixing him with those deep black eyes as he roared a single word with maniacal delight.

'Hytharo!'

## CHAPTER FIVE

# THE LAST HYTHARO

T HE WAVE HIT WITH bone-shattering force. Spiric spun
like a rag doll, his breath escaping through clenched teeth
as he was battered by what seemed to be every solid surface in the
undercity. If Spiric had passed out, he wouldn't have known.
There was only insurmountable pressure, just like being buried
in the sand again. He wanted to scream and thrash, but his
muscles were wound tight, keeping him curled in a ball.

Blackness engulfed him.

Black as the darkness from under which he'd been pulled
from.

Black as the eyes that begged him to remember.

But they'd said one thing. They'd told him exactly who he was.

*Hytharo.*

# ✕ ◀ ıı ▀ ▚

Sand crunched beneath him as waves lapped upon the shoreline. The water was an indecisive blanket, only ever tempted by the notion of completely covering him. Spiric didn't open his eyes. He barely even registered he still had them. His skin was still prickling back into existence, each heartbeat giving him a few more inches of feeling. His mind was a puddle that only summoned useless thoughts. Someone was calling his name, but he couldn't be sure who. Or why. Or if he was bothered to find out.

It took all his effort, but eventually he rolled, sinking further into the wet sand. Spiric cracked an eye and soon recognised the set of robes that was rushing towards him.

'Spiric!' The call was a mix of panic and amazement. 'Spiric, what have you done?'

A pair of hands clamped on his shoulders and lifted him out of the mud, shaking him to his senses. Before he could say anything, he was coughing up water. It didn't even hit the ground. In mid-air, it flashed into vapour and disappeared into the sky.

Grethard was blabbering, all usual calm lost. 'I can't believe it! It's impossible! I don't even know if there's a word for—'

'It's a lake,' he croaked. Spiric's mind had snapped into sharp focus, but he still couldn't believe what he was seeing.

The sandy basin was empty no more. Frothing water spanned its surface for nearly a mile across, the top of the golden dome at the very centre, shining brighter than ever now and washed clean of eons of grit. Where Spiric had ended up, now the shore, was at the edge of the ancient border where the skyscrapers ceased to poke through the sand around the basin.

His thoughts flitted wildly across his mind as he took it all in. What if the basin was empty of skyscrapers because it had been flooded like this before? What if he *wasn't* the only Hytharo here? Or what if he was, and this was all set up for him?

'Spiric, I need you to tell me how this is possible.' Grethard was still speaking as if he hadn't drawn breath. 'Because water like this hasn't been seen for eons, since the—'

'Hytharo,' Spiric finished for him. 'I am Hytharo.'

'Impossible,' Grethard snapped, this time on a reflex. 'We still can't be sure.'

Something in Spiric's head snapped. How could Grethard still have even the shadow of a doubt? After sending Spiric down there into the unknown? Even when water swelled before him in this desert basin?

'You're wrong!' Spiric bellowed with everything he could muster. 'Surely I've now proved I'm nothing else. I've done as you said. All I need you to do now is just listen to me! I saw a whole city down there! Flooded with water! And a shadow dancer! A shadow dancer walked out of the darkness and told me I was a Hytharo.'

Grethard was backpedalling, his mouth agape, so Spiric pressed on.

'He recognised me. He asked me to remember him. But that was all.' Spiric held out his now bare forearm. 'The runes are gone because they helped me escape. Carried me up in a wave the size of a skyscraper.'

He looked back out over the lake. Tendrils of white vapour were peeling off the water's surface. They reached for the orbits of rusted metal, interlacing with them as they snaked up the twin spirals above. Eventually it collected as a white mist in the sky, battling vainly to remain there.

To Spiric, it was almost familiar, but then he remembered everything Grethard had been telling him for the past two days.

'You've never seen a cloud?' Spiric asked.

'Never,' Grethard said, still staring at the sky. 'They're myths, like everything else you just said. All of it together at once can't be a sign of anything good. If you saw a shadow dancer—'

'You believe me?'

Grethard nodded slowly. 'I'm praying that you're lying. At least about the shadow dancer. But as a Hytharo, you could change this world, Spiric. You could bring water back! It wouldn't have to all be desert, it could be like this!' He waved out over the lake, which was already half drained. 'Whatever that last Hytharo did, you could undo it.'

'Whatever that last Hytharo did, they did it for a reason,' Spiric said firmly. 'I need to remember why. I need my memories back.'

Spiric wasn't sure if he'd seen it right, but it almost looked as if Grethard had deflated slightly.

'We'll find your memories, then,' the old man conceded. 'But right now, that shadow dancer is my concern. They tend to linger in the ruins, so if we leave, we can only hope it doesn't follow.'

Deep down, Spiric knew it was a false hope at best. His memories and the shadow dancer were linked. He had called Spiric out as a Hytharo. Even Grethard had said he'd seen a shadow pull him from the sand. Could that have been the mysterious spectre, too? The shadow dancer would follow him, that was for sure, but Spiric wasn't about to tell Grethard this. Not now that the old man had stopped being so damn stubborn.

Grethard glanced down at the canister still tied to Spiric's waist. 'It's full?'

Spiric gave it a shake, letting it slosh happily against his hip.

A small smile broke out on the old man's face. 'We'll be set for the rest of our lives. However long that ends up being...'

Grethard led the way, picking a cautious path through the ruins back to his rooftop camp. Each step was preceded with hesitation, each turn a double take. Grethard forbade them from sharing a word, lest it attract more peril than they were already in. Whenever they passed a distant light-bend, Spiric saw the shadow dancer lurking there. Even in the glass of smashed-out windows, dark flickers set his nerves on edge.

Spiric waited outside the tower where Grethard's camp was. The old man didn't even question it. The sun was going down, the cold coming to replace it, but that wasn't why Spiric was shivering. In his mind, those black eyes were still watching him. Waiting for him to remember. He didn't have to dwell on it for too long, for Grethard had returned quickly, muttering something about packing light.

'Where are we going now?' Spiric asked.

'To find friends.'

Grethard had already started walking, hobbling under the weight of the bag slung over his shoulders. But Spiric didn't follow. The old man stopped, looking back with confusion.

'Are you coming or not?'

'I need to know more than that. You owe me as much.'

He looked at his boots for a moment, then nodded. 'I suppose I do. I'm sorry. Been a long while since I've needed something as obtuse as "manners." There's a commune, all academy exiles, like me. They think they guard the gateway to these ruins, but... Well, they're our first step to getting to Breggesa.'

'Thank you.'

Together the pair set off through the dunes, following the last rays of the setting sun in the west. Spiric kept his eyes to the ground. The less he looked at the skyscrapers around them, the less his mind wandered to the shadow dancer.

Soon all he could think of was how tired he was. How his body ached. After those desperate moments of fear and panic, Spiric wasn't sure if he'd feel like normal again. The exhaustion had beaten him down to nothing and he was ready to collapse in the sand.

It was something he'd felt before.

The memories came back one by one, faint flashes across his eyes in a dark haze when suddenly he was walking along the same path as he was before, only now he was heading into the mass of skyscrapers.

A limp had taken him. He'd been running for days and his breath was ragged. A sandstorm clouded the ruins, but over his shoulder, he could see the men hunting him. There weren't as many as before. Four or five at most, their figures little more than ebbing shapes in the clouds of thrown dust. The sandstorm rushed towards him, clouding him in darkness.

When his vision returned, he was huddled in a dark corner, deep inside a skyscraper, trembling as frantic footsteps came down the stairs. He was wild-eyed and ragged, just as the rest had been, desperate to find the last Hytharo. The last one who could make it rain.

He looked from the man to his own shaking wrist. There

were seven runes there. Runes he'd been given. Runes he'd been saving.

He blinked and suddenly he was with others. They'd fled as refugees into the desert without direction, tinted goggles covering their crimson eyes lest they give themselves away. Red chalky mountains surrounded them, narrow valleys bearing them passage. There were five of them, but there was a mournfulness on their faces. They knew they were the last and so did their pursuers. It only made the hunt more fervent.

The rocks began to crumble underfoot, ground down by a deafening wind until they were nothing but sand by the time his vision returned.

He was knelt in the dunes among the ruins. His chest was heaving, his eyes watering from fear, exhaustion, or something else. The others were gone. Gone and he was the last. He fell forward, driving his fists into the ground as a scream escaped him. Frustration, despair or rage, he didn't know what caused the sound. They could find him for all he cared. They'd taken everything from him in their panic and now all they'd wring from his tired body were the last few drops of rain.

A figure stood before him, only more than a shadow wrapped in a black cloak. They crouched, offering a hand. But he didn't take it. The pale face, the black eyes... they frightened him more than anything he'd seen in the weeks of chaos leading to this point. But the smile, wide and curious, almost seemed familiar...

'I know you!' Spiric cried out.

He was walking again, Grethard beside him. He'd startled the old man.

'After only a day or two?' Grethard said with a weak chuckle.

Spiric ignored the joke. He doubled over, his palms pressed into his closed eyes like he was trying to remember a dream he'd just woken from. He couldn't let the memories escape, but blinding starlight was the only thing to bloom in his vision.

'I know why... why I was alone and afraid,' Spiric said slowly. 'I was with other people. Hytharo, just like me. We were the last, but we were still being chased to make rain. We had to keep running, just to stay alive, but...'

One final flash of memory came to him. Once more, he was deep in the skyscraper, this time free of his hiding place. His pursuer was motionless on the floor, the smell of smoking skin in the air. On his right arm, only five runes remained.

'But who did you know, Spiric?' Grethard's voice was gentle and coaxing. He went to put a hand on his shoulder, but Spiric stumbled away.

'I remember the shadow dancer. I remember his face. He was the one who buried me. He saved me.'

'And then he dug you back up yesterday. But why would he wait so long?'

Spiric opened his eyes. He'd been pressing on them so hard they felt swollen in his skull. The visions were slipping through his fingers like they were sand. But now he had a path. A direction.

'I don't know why he'd wait,' Spiric eventually said. 'He knows something, and I must know something about him, too. Grethard, I need to know who that shadow dancer is.'

Grethard was silent for a long time, considering Spiric very carefully. There was a fear in his eyes, but he didn't look like he was about to let it take hold.

'Let's keep moving. Dark's coming.'

The skyscrapers didn't seem as threatening in the dim starlight. They were just mountains of glass, idle and quiet. Spiric watched instead for the small critters that skittered across the dunes. Most common were the six-legged lizards dived into the sand like it was water at their approach. In the distance, skuttlers clanked and tumbled out of the skyscrapers before beginning their night of aimless patrols. Birds with long, narrow bodies circled above, their wings still as stone as they rose and fell in the eddies of the breeze.

The skyscrapers grew less frequent, each one shorter and further flung than the previous. It was only when they reached what looked to be the last one that Grethard pulled them to a stop. There was nothing but barren dunes beyond it. Their usual beige-red tones were dyed a dark blue in the sun's absence. Spiric didn't want to think about how they were going to cross it the next morning.

Only the highest level of the skyscraper was above the sand. Its rooftop was featureless, spare for some kind of concrete hut they couldn't crack the door on, but between that and the waist-high lip of the roof's edge, there was just enough shelter to hide from the chilly winds. Grethard threw down two bedrolls from his pack, and they didn't waste any time making use of them.

To Spiric, it was as useful as a blanket covering stone, but before he could consider complaining, the sound of Grethard's snores was drowning out the wind. Anything was better than the low howl it made as it caressed the endless dunes.

Spiric wished he could've drifted off as quickly as the old man had, but the flashes he'd just remembered of his past life kept running through his mind.

The feeling of being stalked.

The journey through red mountains.

The heavy footfalls chasing him.

The smell of burnt flesh.

The shadow dancer's smile.

## CHAPTER SIX

# THE BOUNDARY

T HE DUNES SMOOTHENED INTO a single arduous and uphill slog, large enough to make Spiric wonder if the ruins themselves were in one giant basin. The high horizons eventually grew jagged, which could only mean mountains were ahead. When they finally came into view, Grethard gestured vaguely towards them.

'We should find the village up there. But I don't know how much to expect from them.'

'How long since you were last there?'

Grethard shrugged. 'A decade or two, give or take.'

The old man's pace soon slowed and Spiric could see why. A

long line of steel posts stretched out in either direction towards the horizon. They were perfectly uniform in height, completely round and untouched by rust, holding their position even as sweeping dunes engulfed them. Whatever had placed them there had done so with perfect attention paid to their intervals, and the passing eons seemed to have had no say in the matter. Spiric felt his pace quicken under him and he had to restrain himself just to stay at Grethard's side.

'What are these for?' Spiric asked.

'Keep something in, keep something out...' Grethard gave one of the pylons a kick, producing a dull metal groan. 'Whatever they were, I don't think they do anything anymore. You'll find a lot of things on these lands that are like that, but sometimes you'll get caught by surprise and find something that does the opposite.'

'Like a fracture?'

'Yes, and other relics you might find. Things you can take with you.' Grethard smirked slightly. 'Things like yourself.' He gestured forward. 'After you.'

Spiric leapt over the boundary and was almost disappointed by the complete lack of sensation. He'd been expecting a shiver, at the very least. Spiric occasionally glanced back at the posts as they faded into the distance. There was an odd foreboding about them now that he was on the other side. One he couldn't quite put his finger on.

A flash of shadow appeared between the pylons, and Spiric

looked away quickly, silent dread setting in.

As the day wore on, the barren sand underfoot slowly turned to red rock, the occasional patches of dead scrub being the only interruption as the mountains loomed before them. The path grew steeper, and Spiric had to use his hands to stop himself falling off the larger of the boulders. Grethard followed behind him, his arms folded behind his back as he tested each step with a light kick before planting his foot.

This high up, Spiric laid eyes on the ruins again. The glass shimmered in the afternoon sun. The air joined it, a single wobble of heat haze large enough to blanket the entire area.

He felt a sudden urge to turn back, as if his memories were still trapped beneath the skyscrapers' sands. He fought against mentioning it to Grethard. The old man would probably call him stupid.

As they continued on, the mountains rose up to block Spiric's view of the ruins and quell his regretful curiosity. The cliffs captured them in a high-walled valley, nature's poor imitation of the unsettling structures they'd left behind. Smouldering grey clouds lingered overhead, growing thicker and more acrid as they neared the valley's exit.

Smooth plains of rock stretched out before them for miles. Fissures and jagged cracks lined the surface as it inclined downhill, drawing a path to a very different set of ruins. A smattered circle of tumbled sandstone and salvaged plate metal surrounded a toppled watchtower, its iron skin covered in a rash of rust. Unbroken, it would've only stood a dozen metres high, but now it lay in three distinct sections, ashes gently wafting from the breached metal. The rest of the shacks were even smaller, though Spiric could only guess the original size from the amount of debris.

'This can't be the village, is it?' Spiric asked Grethard.

A forlorn droop in the old man's face answered him.

'There's smoke,' Spiric said, pointing at the tower. 'This would've happened not long ago.'

'I'd hope not,' Grethard murmured.

'There might be survivors,' he offered back.

'Along with what did this, whatever "this" is.'

Grethard started his way down the rocky slope towards the wreckage, but Spiric lingered for a moment.

What if this had something to do with him? Had his reappearance or even his escape from the shadow dancer caused this? A small voice in the back of his head snapped at him to stop being so self-centred and he set off after Grethard, skipping across small boulders to catch up.

Stepping through the small, ruined village was just as unnerving as being in the undercity. Despite the afternoon sun blazing down on them, the small shadows cast into the wrecks were pitch black. Spiric peered at each one as he passed, praying not to see a sign of movement. He set out on a wide, arcing path around the village under the guise of looking for clues as Grethard picked through the burnt-out shacks. The old man had barely grunted at his excuse, kicking over a pebble just to hear it clatter against the silent sky.

Alone for the first time, it began to play on Spiric's mind that he was yet to see a sign of another soul having ever been here. No survivors, no bodies, and as he glanced at the smoke wafting from the fallen tower, no smell of burnt flesh, either. He shivered at the thought, brushing away the faint memory of it. There had to be something left, a clue as to why everyone had disappeared.

*Hopefully the Hytharo left something, too.*

He was halfway around the village and over the way, the mouth of the next valley had come into view. It was a narrow split in the cliff face, and Spiric thought he could make out a figure standing there, but quickly dismissed it as rocks. It was a shaky assumption, but the thought of investigating it and being proven wrong made him shudder.

When he returned to Grethard, the old man was standing before one of the small ruined huts, slowly paging his way through a book Spiric hadn't seen before with a nostalgic smile on his face.

'There's no one here,' Spiric said.

Grethard mumbled something back at him, still engrossed in the book. As Spiric lingered closer, he could see a diagram of a skyscraper on one of its pages, the author having neglected to sketch the middle of it.

'What are you reading?'

The old man snapped the book shut and looked to Spiric, the same grin still creasing his face. 'A book I wrote many years ago.'

'Before you were exiled?'

'Yes. From when I was wrong.' He threw it back into the rubble, where a stray cinder happily took to the meal. 'You'd do best not to read it.'

Spiric resisted the urge to dash in and stomp out the stubborn ember, but his curiosity for the old man's past was flaring hot enough to match the rapidly igniting volume. 'Is there anyone here?'

'Not that I can see, though I haven't checked that fallen tower. I've got a funny feeling about it.'

Something flipped in Spiric's guts as he looked to the tower. The wreckage was no more than a speck of dust compared to what he'd just been through, but there was something about this particular ruin being so... so fresh. He felt Grethard's elbow nudge at his shoulder.

'Can you check it?'

He couldn't think of a reason to refuse before his legs were marching under him like he was a soldier acting upon royal orders. The metal shell seemed to grow larger as he approached, like the shed skin of a gigantic iron snake. Its surface was covered in rivets and rust, the edges of portholes and hatches chipped and bitten. Pungent smoke filled Spiric's lungs as he stood before one of the breaches, but there was something else there, too. Something far more rotten.

He braced himself and squeezed through the gap.

*Burnt flesh.*

*That* was what that smell was. It hit him the second he was inside, and he was already all too familiar with it. He fought the urge to choke on it, his eyes straining as they adjusted to the gloom. Bodies, at least a dozen of them, came into sight, scorched and half-rotten. Spiric doubled over to retch. How the smell hadn't leaked out was beyond him.

'Stay where you are.'

Spiric's foot slipped as he flinched at the voice, his impulse to twist to find it instead sending him tumbling into the wall. The impact produced a ringing drone of hollow iron and he lost his bearings, forcing him to dart his eyes between the dozen dark hiding spots the voice could have come from. It had been a woman's voice, a low, hoarse whisper that was far too cool for the fact they were surrounded by the dead.

'I'm not here to hurt you,' Spiric called to one of the shadowy corners.

'Sure you're not,' the voice snapped back from another. 'You're one of the Academy Scythes, aren't you?'

'A Scythe?' Spiric stammered. He held a breath in his throat, hoping they'd say something back to reveal themselves, but the silence, spare for his throbbing pulse, proved them smarter than that. 'No, no academy here. Well, the old man outside is an exile, but otherwise—'

'You're lying,' she hissed. 'Who are you, really?'

'I'm a Hytharo,' Spiric blurted. 'A storm caller.'

Silence lingered again and Spiric heard the girl's breathing quicken.

'There's no such thing,' she spat. 'They're a story, nothing more!'

In the dark, he shook his head. 'My eyes are red. Just come into the light, it's proof enough.'

A blinding flash of fire burst out of the gloom. It snaked from a bare hand and billowed to the metal above, the image of a yellow rune seared into Spiric's vision as he lurched blindly away from the flame. He keeled over backwards, landing with a crunch on the edge of the tower's breached wall and tumbling through it.

Outside, he hit the ground jaw first, sliding into a heap as dust blanketed him and the taste of metal filled his mouth. Blood spat from his lips as he desperately cried the old man's name.

'Gretha—!'

A hard kick to the guts cut Spiric off and flipped him over. Before he could squirm away, a foot came down on his chest, knocking the air from his lungs and pinning him to the ground. The jagged pieces of shrapnel affixed to the woman's boot bit painfully into his flesh, threatening to pierce it if Spiric so much as whimpered.

His attacker was perfectly silhouetted by the harsh midday sun. The only thing he could make out was the thin metal tube pointed directly at his heart. It was connected to a device that glinted menacingly in the bright light that the woman wielded like a curved dagger.

'What are you!?' she roared at him. 'Some kind of trick?'

'Steady with that now,' Grethard said in a calm voice.

Spiric risked turning his head, catching sight of the old man cautiously edging towards the scuffle.

'Or what?' the girl spat. 'This mad idiot says he's a Hytharo! You're nothing but scavengers and fakes!'

'But I'm real!' Spiric snapped.

'Then quit squinting so I can see your eyes,' she barked back.

She leaned in closer, and Spiric could make out a young and battered face, maybe as old as he was, but it looked to have felt a few more years go by. Her skin was tanned like leather and dappled with freckles, complemented by wild flowing hair like fire and a pair of scowling yellow eyes that went wide the moment she got a good look at his.

'No way...' she breathed, her voice low.

Spiric gasped as the metal tube was jabbed into his chest and the girl was suddenly roaring at Grethard.

'Where the hell did you find him!?'

Spiric looked up to see Grethard silently pointing in the direction of the ruins. His other hand was open and outstretched, motioning desperately in an attempt to placate the wild girl. For a second, Spiric could've sworn he saw a trace of blue in his palm.

'*Those* ruins!? No one's been able to get in there for decades!

83

That place ain't right! Are you—'

An almighty slap of wind blasted over them, sending both him and the girl tumbling. There was a loud bang and another flash of light as they went. When Spiric came to his senses, he was face down on the rock again, still half-blinded and now deafened by the high-pitched ringing in his ears.

Spiric wobbled as Grethard rushed over and hastily pulled him to his feet, not even checking the boy for wounds before leaving him swaying in the wind and diving to tackle the wild girl.

The scuffle was hidden behind Spiric's blurred vision, only coming into focus as the old man wrenched the strange weapon from her hands and shoved her away as roughly as he could. The girl staggered valiantly, but her efforts only sent her dropping backwards into the fallen tower, where she landed with a sharp cry of pain.

'She could have damn near killed you!' Grethard muttered as he came back to Spiric, the calm gone from his voice.

'How?' Spiric slurred. He eyed the void into which she'd fallen, worry growing with each second she didn't emerge.

Grethard waved the object he'd confiscated in front of Spiric's face, causing half a dozen brass cylinders, each about the size of his finger, to fall out of it. He recognised the thin metal tube, now smoking, that was connected to a series of crudely welded steel mechanisms with a hand grip of bent strip metal wrapped in leather.

'What is that thing?'

Grethard slapped his free palm to his head. 'That's right, you're from the past! This is a hand cannon, made to loose metal pellets into people so fast it'll punch a hole clean through them. We're *all* lucky you're still alive!'

The last part was shouted in the direction of Spiric's attacker, who forcefully made a rude gesture at the old man as she clambered out of the wreckage. Despite the nasty looking-gash on her left leg, she put her fists up and assumed a fighting stance, shifting her weight gingerly from foot to foot. For some reason, Spiric now felt sorry for her.

'I'm not here to fight, and I don't think you're in any state to, either,' he said. 'What's your name?'

'I ain't telling you squat!'

He faltered for a moment before continuing. 'My name is Spiric. I woke up buried in those ruins only a few days ago and I've been trying to figure out who I am since then. Either you can help or you can stop trying to kill me.'

'And why the hell should I help you?'

'Because he could make it rain again, and he doesn't know when to keep his damn mouth shut,' Grethard said flatly. 'Besides, we've got your hand cannon and you've got nowhere to run, so you might as well come with us, at least to the nearest town.'

She glanced between them, her eyes narrow, and Spiric prayed she made the right choice. With a very pronounced limp, she staggered over and shook Spiric's hand hard enough to make his knuckles crunch. When she moved to do the same for Grethard, she made a snatch for her hand cannon, but the old man pulled out of reach in the nick of time.

'You'll get this back when you've proved you're not still trying to kill the boy,' Grethard scolded. 'Now, what's your name?'

'Byreth, but you'd better forget it when the time comes, got it?'

Spiric nodded quickly, not sure what "the time" meant to her. 'I'll try to, I guess... What were you doing here, anyway? You didn't...?'

Byreth glanced back at the tower and shook her head. 'Dead and burned by the time I got here. Hid once I saw you two coming. Thought you were the Academy back to finish the job.'

'No, this isn't how the Academy operates,' Grethard said quickly. 'When I was with them this was unheard of. This is scorched earth.'

Byreth looked up at him. 'Really think this is still your old the Academy, old man? How long's it been since you last seen 'em?'

'His name is Grethard,' Spiric interjected, trying to be helpful.

The old man leaned forward, an odd leer crossing his face. 'Much longer than you've been alive, young girl.'

'Whatever,' she sneered back. 'They've been rolling through every town and camp near a ruin for the past month, incinerating everything. I dunno what's got into them but by the state of the poor saps in there,' she jabbed a thumb at the fallen tower, 'they only hit it in the last days.'

'So then what were you doing here?' Spiric asked.

'Scavenging,' she said, indifferent to the accusations she'd made. 'See if the Academy left anything good behind, but they did a pretty clean sweep.'

Grethard shook his head slowly, staring off into the distance. 'This isn't normal at all. It's like they know something's coming.'

Spiric met Grethard's gaze, a pit growing in his stomach.

'Do you think it's me?' he said softly.

The old man shushed him, then looked to Byreth. 'There's a town still nearby, right?'

'Tah, there is,' Byreth grunted. 'It's where I came from, bit over a day's walk. Path was crawling with Scythes on the way here so we'll have to take it slow.'

'Scythes?' Spiric said in disbelief. 'What's a—'

'Academy flyboys,' Byreth explained. 'You'll know 'em when you see 'em, just pray they don't see you.'

She made to start walking but gasped in agony as soon as she took a step with her injured left leg. Spiric felt his stomach curdle as a fresh wave of blood pulsed from the wound.

'This is both your faults,' she spat as she lurched over to a collapsed wall and sat on it. 'One of you owe me some ink for this!' She checked her wrist and swore under her breath. 'Just about using my last runes, too.'

She hoisted up the leg of her haphazardly patchwork trousers, suppressing a wince as the wound was exposed. It was a long gash that ran the length of her shin, deep enough that blood pooled in it, but Byreth didn't seem concerned by it. Holding her open right hand near it, she pushed the last three yellow runes from her wrist and into her palm, letting them burn white for only a second before thin jets of bright orange flame appeared at her fingertips. Grethard had already turned away, murmuring an excuse about checking the perimeter, but Spiric watched on, transfixed.

It was like she was sewing her own flesh as if it were cloth, pinching and searing in rapid jabs, moving from one end of the wound to the other and back in quick sequence. Soon the whole thing was nothing but a long ugly line of swollen and tender scar tissue.

'Is it always that bad?' Spiric couldn't help asking.

Byreth shook her head. 'I'm just no good at it. Besides, how would I practice without constantly cutting myself open?'

Before Spiric had to muster an answer, Grethard had returned.

'We're all clear,' he muttered.

Byreth sneered at him. 'Sure we are!' Without waiting for another response, she turned and began marching towards the gap in the mountains, carrying a quick pace that Spiric found himself almost jogging to keep up with. Grethard followed up at the rear, casting furtive glances at the scorched town as they left it behind.

Spiric wanted to ask the old man what he'd hoped to find in the village, had they still been alive to see them. A warm welcome, perhaps? With the way Grethard hinted at his past, who would be looking to give him one? The addition of this wild and rugged girl certainly felt like it did little to increase the odds of a good reception. But without them, Spiric would be travelling alone, fleeing from the shadow dancer just as he'd fled from those desperate hunters in his past.

He dreaded remembering it again.

## CHAPTER SEVEN

# IT HAD A NAME

D ARKNESS FELL RAPIDLY AMONG the rocky crags of the mountains. They'd marched across precarious paths, climbing higher and higher until the stone and dirt under their feet turned from red to chalky grey. Cold accompanied the night with fangs sharper than at the desert floor that gnashed through Spiric's cloak and into his bruised and beaten skin.

As he followed Byreth across a ridge and out into another gale, he envied her for not even shivering. She wore her travelling cloak as more of a grand cape, leaving her muscled arms exposed to the elements outside her sleeveless tunic. The garment itself looked to be padded with something extra. Perhaps leather, metal plates, or even just hidden layers of animal hide, but judging by the jagged stitches, whatever it was had been an addition of her own handiwork.

She'd not paid much mind to Spiric and Grethard, allowing the pair to drop back out of earshot and consult in whispers. Curiktics, Grethard said, never felt cold. Channelling pure light from the infernal sun, they always retained some of its warmth. With bitter chills passing through his bones, Spiric could only wish she'd share that warmth, but she'd probably punch him in the face for posing the question.

A narrow silt in the mountainside served as their hideaway when the last tint of sun vanished from the sky. The entrance faced west, a few dregs of heat still remaining in the rocks, and Spiric shifted around until he found the warmest. Through dim starlight, he watched Grethard rummage through his pack, hopefully with the intentions of a campfire. Spiric would happily choke on the smoke if it would fire up his lungs.

'No fire,' Byreth hissed. It was like she'd read his mind.

Instead, Grethard pulled out the frayed blankets from the night before. He dropped the first at his side, then tossed the other to Spiric, missing by about five feet. Once he'd retrieved it, the speck of heat was gone from the rocky wall. He wrapped the blanket tightly around himself, huffing warm air down into his chest for what little good it did to relieve the shivers.

'You're welcome to share with Spiric if you like,' Grethard said to Byreth.

'I'm fine,' she said quickly. 'I've made this journey before. Don't get colder than this.'

'Suit yourself,' the old man grunted. He pulled the torch out of his pack next, giving it a quick shake, then setting it on the floor between the three of them. Green light lapped in waves across their bodies as the torch hummed quietly. It left their faces in darkness, spare for the occasional glint in their eyes.

'The ruin we came from, does it have a name?' Spiric asked. He wasn't sure who the question was directed to, but judging by the two of them, he'd get vastly different answers.

Grethard spoke first. 'We never gave them names in the Academy. We'd just designate them with numbers and nonsensical codes, but even then, that felt like too much to me. Official reason was to keep them as secret as possible, stop people from seeking them out and getting lost or dying or worse in them. But we were always scared to think about them. To keep them in our heads. Scared it would taint us, in a way.

'But after spending all those years in there alone, I now think a bit differently. The world we live on was built among the rotten bones of an empire far more complex than we can imagine, and the ruins are just shards that remain visible to us. So those places must've had a name once, but it's nothing we could possibly glean now, washed away by the sands of time and whatever tragedy befell those peoples.'

Spiric took it in with awe. What if the Hytharo were just the same, washed away by time, and he was just one life that was out of place? His trail of thought was interrupted as Byreth let out a derisive snort.

'What a load of lizard shit!' she said. She glared at Spiric, her eyes flashing in the torchlight. 'I don't know what kind of crazy things he's been telling you, but if it's stuff like that, you might as well forget it. That ruin is called The Lightning Cage and no one has been able to get into it, and we ain't seen anyone come out, neither. Been other ruins like that one, with poles in the ground that lightning will blast between if you cross 'em, but those have been cracked by walking 'round them long enough and throwing sand at it until you find a breach. I've heard of people doing whole laps of The Cage, and they all swear on their own lives that there ain't a hole. That's why I want to know how you got in, old man, and how the hell you two got back out.'

Spiric opened his mouth and hesitated. Byreth hadn't seen him yet, her darkened gaze fixed on Grethard, so maybe he shouldn't say anything at all. Mentioning the shadow dancer would be one thing, but saying that it *knew* him... Before he needed to summon an answer, Grethard spoke quietly.

'Some things don't have answers. Thirty years ago I walked in. Today we both walked out.'

'So then where the hell did you come from?' she shot at Spiric.

He glanced to Grethard, who gave a slight nod. Spiric told what he knew of the story, starting from being pulled out of the sand and making sure to leave out anything hinting at the shadow dancer. If Grethard was right about how people reacted to those things, he didn't want to see what Byreth would do.

'Come to think of it, I would have had to have walked into those ruins myself. And others would have, too! I... I remember they followed me like hungry dogs. Maybe there was a way past it after all?'

He could make out Byreth shaking her head. 'You really want me to believe you're from hundreds of years before? Really? This is *too* crazy. No, until you can prove you're the real deal, I ain't buying it.'

'Then how do I prove it? I need help remembering what happened to me, who I am, and it all has to do with the sh— I mean, the ruins, and you know about those, right?'

'You really want help from her?' Grethard muttered.

Byreth ignored the comment, waving for him to shut it. 'The woman I work for, Leerukhart, she's in the town we're heading for tomorrow. She'll know enough.'

'And where we're going, does that have a name?' Spiric said. 'Something ominous or doom-inspiring?'

'Kurkress is the town. It's not nice, but it's...' Byreth grimaced, a flash of teeth in the dark. 'It's close to a few different ruins, so enough drifters ended up there to make something of it. Enough structures and wreckage from the past to throw up shacks with, but not bad like ruins.'

'It was little more than a base camp last I was there,' Grethard said with a chuckle. 'Maybe I'll feel as you will, Spiric, when you see Breggesa.'

'I feel I'll be in for more of a shock than that.'

'What do you mean?'

He gave a small shrug the others didn't see. 'I can barely remember the world I came from, yet this one already seems so different. How will people treat me once they know what I am? What if I'm hunted again? I won't be able to escape, not this time.'

Something clattered at his feet, thrown by Byreth. He scooped it up, feeling a set of glass lenses encased in scratched metal. A loop of rough leather ran out of the sides of the goggles.

'You'll be able to just about look into the sun with those things. Doubt anyone'll see your eyes. No one'll know unless you can't keep your mouth shut.'

For the rest of the night Spiric did just that, his jaw set against the cold. Byreth and Grethard continued to bicker, and he tried to doze through it, but the prospect of civilisation twisted his guts, the need to hide a startlingly familiar instinct. He must've spent a whole lifetime before this cowering in the shadows. Would he be hunted again? Would they even recognise what he was?

The two questions swirled back and forth in his head until dawn light began to trickle into the cave. He twisted to avoid it, his mind begging for one more moment of false sleep, but the stiff creak of his bones brought him back to his senses. Through his gummed-up eyes he could make out the slumped forms of

Grethard and Byreth, both fast asleep. The old man was irritable at the best of times and Spiric didn't want to find out if the girl would lash out when he woke her, so he let them be, pushing aside his thin blanket and staggering to the cave's mouth.

A lemon-yellow sun peaked over the mountaintops, painting the rocks with an odd maroon light. He took a few more paces away from the cave, raising his stiff arms above his head to stretch them as he watched his shadow follow with exaggerated bounds. When he stopped, it continued to walk, shimmering through a haze. Spiric froze in place as it wavered further, truncating towards him before taking form, a dark silhouette rebelling against the dawn.

'You asked me to remember you,' Spiric said, his voice shaking.

The silhouette snapped into the shadow dancer's form. This time his expression was blank yet somehow more frightening for it.

'Have you?' the shadow dancer whispered back.

'No.' The word almost choked him. 'But I remember you buried me, somehow threw me forward through time. I need to know why. Why me?'

The shadow dancer gave a mournful smile. 'Because you were the last, Spiric. The last one I remembered. Not even myself.'

'You don't remember who you are, either?' Spiric hissed. He wanted to take a step closer, to really see the shadow dancer, but his legs wouldn't cooperate. 'At least tell me who I am! Surely—'

The shadow dancer smiled once more and shook his head. 'You will know who you are. You'll need to look deeper. Then you'll find me again.'

His last word was cut off as he simply disappeared. Spiric rubbed his eyes stupidly, certain he hadn't blinked, but the spot the shadow dancer had occupied sat undisturbed, almost as if they'd never been there.

A few minutes passed before he dared to relax, deciding to wander a short way from the cave, sitting down near one of the steeper edges and running his hands through the coarse dust on the ground. Below, smooth walls of burnt stone lined either side of the canyon, with a flat of pale and cracked clay filling the bottom, long dry from what once was a river.

The lack of water meant this was no longer his world. Even if Spiric could make it rain like Grethard had said, it would still be alien to him. His people, the Hytharo, were long gone. Coursing streams and blue oceans wouldn't bring them back. He'd have to get used to a new people, a civilisation that could never look him in the eyes.

The sky was tinged in dashes of pink as the sun continued its journey. Away from dawn, the mountains lost their lustre, the fierce umber that the early sun blessed them with subsiding to a drab grey.

Spiric looked over them pensively. Somewhere out there lay red mountains, the ones in that tantalising fragment of memory. He could remember the midday sun beating down upon him when he'd trekked through, so they couldn't be a dawn illusion like these ones. To the east, they hid The Lightning Cage. Thinking of the name made Spiric shiver. Had it been named that in his time?

'Gotcha!'

Byreth's victorious shout snapped Spiric away from his thoughts. He twisted around to look, almost sliding from his perch. She was stood a few paces away, holding some kind of two-legged creature covered in matted grey fur by the leg with one hand, pulling a small, serrated knife out of it with the other.

'What is that thing?' Spiric asked, trying to ignore the way his stomach turned as Byreth wiped the bloody blade on the dead creature's coat.

'It *was* a redfoot.' She waved it towards Spiric, showing off the red wrinkled pad at the bottom of its paw. 'Now it's dinner.'

Byreth busied herself tying the creature's legs together with a length of metal wire, complaining about how hard it was to catch one. Its entire body was only a bit bigger than Spiric's head. Hidden in the fur at its sides was a set of deformed wings, which it made up for with long muscled legs and a gnarly set of teeth. It resulted in an ugly little creature, a horribly fitting description to accompany its bottomless black eyes which had remained open in death.

*Just like the shadow dancer's.*

They wandered back to the cave together, Byreth spending the time boasting about the other creatures she'd managed to hunt on her own and the number of meals they'd made for. By the sounds of it, the redfoot was her biggest trophy yet, and Grethard's mumbled congratulations as he finally emerged from the cave only went to her head. As they set off north, she fantasised endlessly about hunting larger beasts Spiric knew he wouldn't remember the names of.

He just let her words wash over him, only half-listening in the event that she accidentally revealed more to her than swearing and killing things. She barely deviated over the day's walk and Spiric gave up hope that she had any other aspirations. Maybe swearing and killing were the only things that remained in this world.

## CHAPTER EIGHT

# KURKRESS

T HE SUN BOILED OVERHEAD as they crested what Byreth promised was the last ridgeline. Grethard was on his last legs and Spiric was sure he wasn't far behind as they crossed it. Mercifully flat rock lay on the other side, stretching off into the horizon in a gentle decline. The only pockmark on the land was the mining pit in the distance, ringed by walls of scrap iron and a spider's web of twisting rails which connected a trail of outposts and other half-ruined oddities.

'There's Kurkress,' Byreth said, pointing to the hole. 'Maybe an hour 'til we reach it.'

'I swear it wasn't there last time...' Grethard panted. 'Then again, thirty years and all...'

As they set off, Spiric donned the goggles Byreth had given him. It was like day had turned to night, but this was the most reassuring thing Spiric could've wished for. If he could barely see out of them, no one else would stand a chance at seeing in.

The outposts Spiric had spotted from the ridge turned out to be a series of rusted machinery emplacements. Contraptions bearing pumps, valves and a rat's nest of copper piping were arranged in every design imaginable, each one more disused than the last.

'What are these things?' he wondered aloud.

'You never seen the pumps before?' Byreth replied. 'Throw a fireball down a hole a mile deep and pray you catch enough water to fill a vial. I reckon you don't even need all this metal, though. Kretatic's excuse to get a cut of the water.'

'I don't understand,' Spiric said.

Grethard explained it a little better. 'If you ever see anything made of iron, a Kretatic can turn it into an arcanite, metal they can command, provided, of course, they have the right runes. I don't know exactly what they do with these machines to draw more water from the ground, but it must be something, otherwise they wouldn't be leaving the damn things everywhere.'

In the distance, Spiric could see the occasional pair of workers pushing a small handcart along the rails between the pumps. By their slumping trudge, they didn't look to enjoy it, nor that they'd been successful.

Kurkress itself was surrounded on most sides by a patchwork of corrugated iron and rusted-out sheet metal, their purpose defeated by the yawning gaps made from the fallen sections nobody had been bothered to repair. Despite the supposedly easy entrances, Byreth led them closer to a rickety guard tower that peeked over the top of the most stable part of the fortification. An old woman peered from it, a dark shawl covering most of her face, but Spiric could pick out the frustration in her eyes and she appeared to be pointing some kind of long cannon at them.

'Byreth! What the hell have I told you about sneaking out of the fence without telling anyone!?' she bellowed. 'Leerukhart is already on my ears for a missing hand cannon. Last thing I need is you skulking about out there while the Scythes are on the loose!'

'Can't call it sneaking if you're still missing bits of it, Petra,' Byreth shot back. 'Besides, I even managed to catch a redfoot!' She waved the carcass high, but the old woman didn't seem impressed. 'Hasn't been a sign of the Scythes since that village south of here got raided. Looks like they got what they came for.'

The old woman gave a disgruntled kind of nod. 'Then who are these strangers?' She motioned the long cannon at Spiric and Grethard.

For a second, Spiric was taken aback. He'd spent the whole

night worrying about what these people would do if they saw his eyes that he hadn't thought of what to say if they asked where he'd come from. Surely saying he'd just wandered out of The Lightning Cage would be far worse than declaring he was a Hytharo. His mind raced for an alibi, but before he could summon one Grethard had stepped forward.

'I'm a trader. From the east.'

'What've you come to trade?' Petra snapped back. 'Leerukhart doesn't like foreign traders peddling trash.'

'She doesn't like a whole lot more than that,' Byreth muttered under her breath.

Grethard either hadn't heard it or ignored it. He was holding the canister of water now. 'I have water.'

'Water!? That whole canister?' Petra exclaimed. 'And the boy?'

'He's family.'

For some reason, Spiric felt his heart swell. Even if it was a lie Grethard was telling out of sheer convenience, and even if he'd only met the old man a few days ago, the feeling of finally being attached to something in this new world was indescribable.

Petra glanced furtively between the two, and Spiric attempted to offer a friendly smile, though it didn't seem to help.

'Fine!' she spat down at them. 'But you all go straight to Leerukhart. She gets first pick round here!'

She gave a truncated wave to someone behind the wall

of scrap and a section of it began to grind open with the ear-splitting sound of iron on rock. Byreth trotted ahead happily, leaving Spiric and Grethard to follow.

'This is why I love you, Petra!' she called as she passed through the gate.

'It shouldn't be!' the old woman shouted back.

On the other side of the wall they were met with a few other lazily pointed long cannons, held by men and women similarly wrapped in rags and just as old as the gatekeeper was.

Beyond that, descending tiers of carved rock were lined with ramshackle rows of hovels and occasionally a more substantial building that Spiric could just see into, where metal glowed and people gathered. Sprawling iron catwalks crossed over the pit, suspended on wires that branched from massive pylons. At the bottom of the pit was Kurkress' bounty, a heaping pile of half-mined metal trash. Men worked in tandem with sputtering mechanical contraptions that acted as beasts of burden to excavate through the wreckage.

'Are those arcanites down there?' Spiric asked.

'Tah, and don't go messing with them,' Byreth grunted. 'Don't want to piss off the metal mouths.'

Spiric frowned at her. 'The what?'

'Kretatics, the ones controlling the machines,' Grethard said. 'And don't call them that to their face, either.'

Byreth began leading them across the network of swaying catwalks and rusted stair sets on a path she seemed to be making up as she went. It took them past workshops of clanging forges, rows of spits that spun charred meat, and the bloody butcheries next to them, where men covered in gizzards hollered out offers for the redfoot Byreth carried. She stopped to curse back at them. The price had been insultingly low by the sounds of it.

As they skirted around the pit, Spiric began to recognise what they were attempting to salvage from it.

'That's a skyscraper they're digging into, isn't it? Is that safe?' Foreboding curdled in his stomach, or it could have been the caustic fumes wafting up from the canisters of acid the miners were throwing around. What if he'd escaped one ruin just to fall victim to another?

'It'll be safe enough until they hit a fracture,' Grethard said.

'And don't bloody talk about that to their faces, neither!' Byreth snapped at him.

Spiric was beginning to wonder if he should even talk at all. They'd crossed the entire town by the time Byreth stopped them in front of one particularly large house. It didn't look any nicer than the other shacks, but it certainly looked sturdier. The metal exterior was embedded into the cliff walls, and Spiric could guess that the inside had been excavated to some degree, likely to the point of encroaching on the shacks flanking it. The slanted second story that cast shade over where they stood and if there were any windows, they were shuttered. Before they approached the door, Byreth turned and fixed them with a hard stare.

'I do all the talking, got it?'

Spiric found himself nodding immediately, but when he glanced to Grethard, the old man wasn't doing the same. He'd probably lived enough lifetimes to not be intimidated by teenage girls.

Byreth hammered on the heavy iron doors with a balled fist, then stood back, sucking in a deep breath as she stared at a slot embedded at eye-level. Spiric did the same on instinct, apprehension filling his chest.

A full minute passed, one where Byreth didn't dare knock again or even glance away, before the slot scrapped open, a pair of dim green eyes appearing in the gloom beyond.

'You're late by a day.' The woman's voice was low and rich, a statement of fact rather than an accusation. The eyes glanced between Spiric and Grethard. 'And a motley crew you've brought with you.'

'I'm sorry, ma'am,' Byreth muttered, using more manners than she'd shown Spiric in the past day. 'It will be worth it, I promise.'

She considered the trio for another excruciating moment. 'Fine. Shoes off, as always.'

The eye slot slid shut, and there was an unmistakable sound of a latch coming undone on the other side of the door, but it didn't swing open. Byreth gave the door a gentle push, shooting the two another deathly glance as it swung open.

'Say *nothing* until she asks you to.'

The inside was an impenetrable gloom, the drifting smoke of acrid incense carrying the low green light of the strange little orbs that hung from the ceiling. Spiric tugged his boots off as requested, placed them on the rack by the door that Byreth had pointed at, and savoured the feeling of the various furs underfoot.

The place was less of a home and more of a warehouse, one big room stuffed with ancient furniture, wrapped animal pelts, and an endless array of open crates and barrels, each one brimming with preserved food, shining gold pieces of scrap, and tangled heaps of fine garments that would look alien if worn in the soot-covered town.

A woman was draped on a sloping lounge at the other end of the room, an opulent-looking long cannon displayed proudly on the wall above her. Her clothes matched her weapon, a dark flowing shawl that glistened with strands of silver thread. Spiric followed as Byreth drew nearer, the woman only turning her pale, pointed face once they'd crossed the room.

'You're late by a day,' Leerukhart repeated. 'I don't like to worry, Byreth.'

Byreth said nothing, her head hung.

'What's your report? This had best be worth it like you said.'

'Nothing in the filters up north, or the dishes out east. The village down south still has no sign of life, but the Scythes haven't come back yet.'

Leerukhart raised a thin blonde eyebrow. 'And The

Lightning Cage?'

'It was still blocked out, but these two said they came out from inside.'

She glanced between the two, Spiric standing stock still at Byreth's shoulder and Grethard, who was skulking around the room with idle curiosity. A frown crossed her brow.

'When I took you in months ago, I didn't take you for gullible, Byreth.'

'She's telling the truth,' Grethard said mildly.

The woman gave a derisive snort. 'If the truth is impossible, then fine, I'm sure she is. Byreth, you said this would be worth—'

She was cut off as Grethard slammed the canister of water on the table beside her. Before she could ask how he'd crossed the room so quickly, the unmistakable sound of sloshing liquid filled their ears. Leerukhart glanced uncertainly between the old man and the canister before twisting off the lounge and weighing it in her hands. Doubt was replaced with shock as her eyes fixed Grethard's.

'You got all this from inside the cage!?' she exclaimed. 'You got *out* of the cage?'

Grethard smiled, holding out a hand which Leerukhart gingerly shook.

'I'm Grethard, and I've lived in "The Cage" for around thirty years, exiled by the Academy. I found Spiric in there a couple days ago, though he's lost his memory. We need help jogging it.

You seem like a well-seasoned merchant. A portion of this water could be yours for any items related to the Hytharo.'

Leerukhart's lips split into a wry grin. If trade was her language, Grethard now spoke it. She stood up from the lounge, her height matching Grethard's, and sauntered across the room. She fingered through crates and shelves as she spoke, meandering back and forth in an almost hypnotising manner.

'There isn't much that's written down about the Hytharo. Precious little of that has survived since they died out. Most of it is hoarded in the Academy's Breggesan archive. The few things out there fetch an extremely high price. One that would cause me to hesitate even at the thought of sale.'

From a small silver lockbox in the shadows, she returned holding a small, furled scroll of parchment between thumb and forefinger. Spiric stared longingly at it, fighting the urge to snatch it from her grasp just to see what was inside.

'What is it?' Spiric couldn't help asking.

Leerukhart stared him down, her eyes narrowing as she attempted to pierce through the goggles' tint. Thankfully, it held out.

'A recipe. All others may know how to craft their ink from heart; however, that knowledge for the Hytharo is one lost by time.'

'But you found it,' Grethard said. 'And your price?'

'More than the water alone. Thirty years in the cage, you must have some paralicts to show for it.'

The old man gave out something between a grunt and a laugh. 'I'd be a fool if I did. The water is easily valuable enough.'

She shook her head, waggling the scroll slightly. 'Not for something like this.'

Grethard shrugged in response. 'Well, you'll have to let me know when someone else comes along with that much water.' He scooped up the canister and looked to Spiric, jerking his head at the door.

'I'm sure the Scythes will have plenty,' Leerukhart replied.

Panic flooded through Spiric's veins. The woman had turned back to the lockbox, the click of it being opened sending a shock through his spine. He looked to Grethard, already picking his way across the room towards the exit. Did he not even care!?

'You ever seen what the scroll said?' Spiric whispered to Byreth.

'I don't even know how to read,' Byreth muttered back. 'Leerukhart said she found it when they first dug up Kurkress years ago when she showed it to me. I just saw the red rune at the top of it and thought it was weird, but I didn't—'

'It doesn't matter,' Spiric hissed. He heard the door scrape open. The lockbox clanked shut. The damn scroll was going to escape him!

Glancing between Leerukhart and Grethard one last time, he chose to do what an hour ago would've been insanity. With one hand, he whipped the goggles off and strode over to Leerukhart. She turned as he approached, only regarding

111

him with condescension. Grethard had noticed as well, giving a panicked shout from across the room.

'Spiric, put the goggles—'

'No!' Spiric snapped. He turned back to Leerukhart. She towered over him now, but the blood rush pumping through him made him feel like a giant. 'I need that scroll.'

She smirked, then plain burst out laughing, looking between Byreth and Grethard as she attempted to wipe the mirth off her face. 'After all that, a demand?'

'Look me in the eyes!' Spiric shouted. 'Look at me and tell me I don't deserve to know what that thing says!'

Still wearing a mocking grin, she brought her gaze slowly down to meet his. The smile all but fell to the floor, and with a screech, she recoiled, crashing into the metal crate behind her and almost toppling to the floor.

'It can't be!' she began to compose herself, struggling to contain the shock on her face. 'No, you have to be fake.' Her head snapped to Byreth. 'Bringing me frauds, I'll—'

'I'm real,' Spiric said slowly. 'The water proves it. I brought it from the ground in the middle of those ruins, so much that I made a lake.'

'A what?'

He stepped in closer again, forcing Leerukhart to take a step back. 'More water than you could ever imagine. Just think about it.' He let his words hang in the air, waiting a few more heartbeats before adding one more. 'Rain.'

'You could... you could bring it back?'

Spiric nodded. A lie, obviously. He couldn't know for sure, but it was what Leerukhart wanted to hear. 'Though I'd need that scroll and anything else related to the Hytharo.'

Leerukhart straightened up as she considered him, and out the corner of his eye, Spiric could see Grethard still frozen in place by the door.

'I'll accept that, but I still want payment.' She pulled a tiny glass vial from a nearby table and drew a pocketknife from inside her shawl. 'The most unique thing in the world, a few drops of your blood. The blood of something... something impossible.'

Spiric heard Grethard gasp as he thrust out his hand, forearm already exposed. Leerukhart gripped him with cold fingers, scraping the tip of the blade along his forearm until it rested right over the veins on his wrist. There was a sharp prick of pain and Spiric watched in sick fascination as blood welled up from the new wound. Leerukhart pressed the vial against it and flipped his wrist over, fixing him with a satisfied smirk as it began to fill.

'When you make it rain, Spiric, make sure to call a storm my way.'

When the vial was full she stoppered it quickly. Blood continued to flow from Spiric's wrist, but Leerukhart didn't seem worried by it. The vial disappeared into her shawl, her hand returning from its folds with a short twin-helix of metal. It writhed and flexed in her hand, each side sluggishly fighting to get away from its rival.

'A paralict from the undercities,' Leerukhart explained softly.

She held over his wounded wrist and it snapped straight, running parallel to his skin. The burnt and rusted metal began to glow like it were molten, but all Spiric could feel was a sporadic tingling against his skin. Soon the pain of the wound disappeared. The small pool of blood remaining began to quiver and bubble, flecks of it darting to the metal until it was all gone, leaving untouched skin.

Spiric inspected the repaired wound with a mixture of awe and uncertainty, his eyes still picturing the levitating droplets of blood. As promised, Leerukhart returned to the lock box, pulled out the scroll, and handed it to Grethard. He read it with wide eyes before he looked back up at her.

'We're going to need some reels.'

## CHAPTER NINE

# THE FIRST RUNE

I T TURNED OUT REELS were the currency of the land, and as Spiric walked out into the blinding sunlight, it was with a fat sack of them stashed under the less tattered part of his cloak. It had cost them half the canister of water, a measure that Grethard and Leerukhart had hotly debated, but if what the old man said was right, they now had plenty of both.

Byreth shooed off any other lingering eyes with deathly glares, having been assigned to escort Grethard and Spiric to make sure they'd "spend the reels well," whatever that meant. Spiric kept one of the coins in his hand, rubbing his thumb against the smooth surface. It was nothing more than a round of thin metal with a hole punched through it, though counterfeit was prevented by some kind of trick Kretatics performed on each coin. Spiric couldn't wrap his head around it, and judging by Byreth's eye rolls, that wasn't uncommon.

'May I see the ink recipe?' Spiric asked, cutting off Grethard's fourth attempt at explaining the concept. 'I want to see if I remember anything.'

Grumbling, Grethard handed him the scroll. 'Be careful with it. That parchment is probably older than you.'

Spiric laughed as he took it, but Byreth didn't seem to get the joke.

'I still don't buy your whole "I'm from the past" thing,' Byreth said, far more boisterous now she was out of Leerukhart's earshot.

'We're all from the past in a way,' Grethard said with a smile.

Spiric couldn't help giggling along with the old man. 'Would you rather I was from the future instead?'

She replied with a bruising punch to his shoulder that only made him laugh harder. Once Spiric had got a hold of himself, he unfurled the scroll. The ancient hand that had scribed this looked clumsy, as if it were made up on the fly.

*To a half-vial of water add equal parts crushed Treghit Root, Charus Blood and powdered iron, giving the root time to dissolve before adding the next two items. After resting until a dull purple is achieved, shake vigorously to turn the ink bright red. After resting once more until the ink turns blood red, it is ready to use.*

'Where am I supposed to even find some of this stuff?'

Grethard nodded. 'I'm not sure, it's certainly unusual. I was hoping we'd find it in the markets.'

'Treghit Root and Charus Blood, whatever that is.' He could only imagine what kind of massive beast he'd need to slay for the blood. 'Powdered iron should be easy to find, at least.'

'Some metal and two little plants!? Looks like you really do need me,' Byreth said. 'Better make it worth my time.'

What followed was a whirlwind blur of catwalks and stairs, cluttered stalls and bickering merchants. Charus Blood turned out to be an uncommon mountain flower with deep crimson petals, and Treghit Root was more a weed than anything, growing as tight spirals in fields far to the north. Grethard had the forethought to stock up on these, coming away from the dishevelled merchants with a pouchful of each.

'Now what?' Spiric said. The sack of reels was still almost full to the brim.

'Well, if you're going to Breggesa, you'll need provisions. Food, weapons maybe...' She gave Spiric's tunic a flick and a section of the fabric simply disintegrated. 'New clothes, too.'

'We don't need weapons,' Grethard said sharply.

Spiric felt himself shrug. 'I think she's right. I wouldn't mind something.'

The old man glanced down at him before looking out over

the town. 'You'd be ready to kill someone?'

'That's the thing,' Spiric said hesitantly. 'I think I have before.'

The smell of charred flesh bolted through his mind, gone as fast as it had come. He didn't relish it nor the violence it implied.

Byreth led them back through town, Grethard grumbling along behind them. By now, a few of the merchants had cottoned on to the spending spree and attempted to follow, plying them with fine fabrics or sweet goods. Where Byreth's barked curses didn't repel them, invoking Leerukhart's name did, and soon they were back at butcheries they'd passed on the way into town, leaving with a few satchels of cured meats and other hardwearing rations. Spiric had the bulk of it in a sack slung over his shoulder, the sheer weight of it making for a worrying tell of the journey to come.

Their next stop found them in caves that glowed from a dozen furnaces, most dedicated to melting down the cartfuls of scrap metal the miners brought in. An ornate sabre at one of the stalls caught Spiric's eye, and he didn't wait for permission to pick it up. As soon as it was in his grip there was a particular energy in it, like lightning was flowing through the hilt. It felt strangely natural, but the merchant seemed to think otherwise and snatched it out of his hand.

If a slight wobble of the wrist disqualified him from even thinking about having it, who the hell would even be allowed to buy one? In the end, he came away with a small, pointed mace, along with a leather sling to wear it at his hip. As the merchant had put it, the weapon required precious little skill to be a threat with, and the only way Spiric could hurt himself was if he threw it in the air and tried to catch it with his face.

It was an outcome Grethard managed to begrudgingly accept, and they continued back to the garment merchants. Every colour of cloth Spiric could imagine was there, and he lost track of time delving through the wares. The traders of each stall were happy enough to let him dig through, their eyes constantly fixed on the sack of reels still in his hand.

He soon settled on a new set of light trousers, a leather satchel that hung by his side, a pale shirt and a dark red tunic of tough leather, covered all with a long tan trench coat he was sure would blend into the sands. He was hesitant to trade in his old clothes, hemming and hawing over a sentimental bond he couldn't remember, but when he voiced it, Byreth berated him as to why the hell he'd drag them along. Besides, the merchant was offering what they said was a good discount in exchange for the worn garments.

When they turned to Grethard, he shook his head. 'I've worn these for thirty years, no point in changing now.'

Spiric went through the pockets of his old clothes one last time before handing them over, but turned up nothing.

'Damn, I was hoping there'd be a note or a message or something in there.'

At his words, Grethard slapped a palm to his forehead. 'But

there *was* a message! The axiom on your arm!' He rummaged through his pack again, this time pulling out a page torn from a book. 'I sketched the runes out the first night we met. I was sure they'd mean something.'

He dashed from merchant to merchant with the energy of a starved rodent, shoving the page in their faces and demanding they tell him what they knew. Embarrassed, Spiric tried to give an apologetic look to Byreth, but she was staring back at one of the garment stands. He glanced down at the bloody rip in her pants and couldn't help feeling partially responsible for ruining them. Giving her a nudge on the shoulder, he held out a handful of reels.

'Take it,' Spiric whispered. Byreth hesitated. 'I wouldn't have known how to make my ink if it weren't for you.'

'You just got lucky, is all,' she muttered.

'Yeah, lucky I met you.'

Byreth met his gaze with a smirk, made sure Grethard was still distracted with his interrogations, then snatched the reels and dashed back to the garment stand. She returned only a few minutes later, her torn rags replaced with a clean set of dark green overalls and a mottled travelling cloak that draped over her shoulders. Even the boots were new, the steel toecaps tapping on the rocky ground as she walked. With a wide grin, she flashed a few leftover reels in her palm and Spiric began to worry he'd given her too much.

But then he looked down at his own sack of reels, still bulging at the seams. It was a shame he hadn't gone down into those ruins with two canisters! Then again, what would he possibly spend it all on? Grethard returned a few minutes later, his questioning having turned up nothing.

'They just kept telling me to go north to Basarod or talk to the Academy if I was so damn curious about rune lore, but they're the last people I want to have a run-in with.'

Spiric took the torn page from him, focusing again on the set of five runes. Nothing jumped out at him.

'What kind of a message is it supposed to be, if it is one?' he asked.

Grethard let out a reluctant sigh. 'I was hoping you'd already know the basic concepts of rune lore, but I suppose we're starting from scratch with everything.'

Condescending as it was, Spiric resisted jabbing back, letting the old man continue.

'Each rune relates to a word, or a number of different words, depending on how it's interpreted, forming a statement known as an axiom, which you cast out to the world. This is why things like mental intent and theory are vital parts of magic.'

Spiric looked back to the sketched runes. 'So you're saying this *is* a message.'

Grethard shrugged. 'It could be any number of messages, depending on which rune is interpreted as what.' He glanced at Byreth, who was peering over Spiric's shoulder at the paper. 'Can you make any sense of it?'

121

'Five runes at once? Never found myself with that much ink spare, or a reason to use it.'

The old man cursed under his breath and snatched the paper out of Spiric's hands, stuffing it back into his pocket. 'Looks like we need the Academy after all...'

The bottom of the town's pit fell victim to sunset much faster than the rest of the land. Even with blue sky above, the lanterns around them were lit with fervour as Byreth led them back up to the food halls next to the butcheries. It was a communal space carved deep into the rock, filled with silent braziers and ramshackle chairs. Nestling themselves as far back in the cave as they could, Byreth threw the redfoot to the ground.

'I'll trade you a half vial of water for your shares of this.'

Out of the corner of his eye, Spiric saw Grethard open his mouth to argue, so he cut in.

'Done!'

Byreth grinned and pulled a small knife from her pack. 'I'll collect on that later, don't want the rest of the folks in here seeing that much water sloshing about. And I want my damn hand cannon back, too!'

'It sounded more like Leerukhart's hand cannon,' Grethard teased.

'Well, it ain't yours!'

Grethard laughed harder as he tossed it to her and Byreth stuffed it away in one of her many new pockets.

As she began to roughly butcher the best parts out of the

redfoot, Spiric watched the cave begin to fill. Miners, still covered in dust and soot, crowded around the nearby butchers who picked through the offered buckets of precious scrap metal and doled out cuts of raw meat in return. Arguments erupted like fireworks. Those satisfied with their lot made their way over to the braziers, lighting them up almost with a snap of their fingers and throwing their meat on the racks.

He turned to look at Byreth. The redfoot was split wide open now, tender pink meat on display and a pile of gizzards on the ground next to it. Tiny, six-legged rodents were already stealing bites from the latter, having the sense not to go for the good stuff. She held the palm of her right hand at the rim of the brazier. A single yellow rune slid into place, burning before manifesting as an orb of fire that rolled into the coals. They began to glow immediately, and Byreth didn't waste any time flicking pieces of meat onto the grill with her knife.

A thick layer of smoke soon blanketed the cavern, along with the wafting scent of spices for those lucky enough to have them. Babbling conversations flowed between the fire pits, filling the place with a tired buzz. Spiric couldn't help staring at the weary faces as they forced smiles and told the same old stories. He wondered how bad the rest of this world must be that people would be willing to stay in this desolate place.

'How'd you end up working for Leerukhart, anyway?' Spiric asked, still not looking away from the crowd.

She gave a bark of laughter. '"End up" is the right way to

put it. I tried knocking off some of the pretty things in that stockroom she calls a house once, real late at night. I was almost out the door before one of her damn arcanites had me caught. She said either I could work for her or she could clean up the mess, and I knew I was going to be that mess sooner or later.'

'You must've been pretty desperate to try stealing from her,' Grethard probed. He reached for one of the sizzling pieces of meat on the grill, but Byreth swatted his hand away.

'Didn't want to be, but that's what happens when you come out here with nothing else.'

'But why?'

Spiric's question had her silent for a moment and he worried he'd struck a nerve. He watched her prodding at the meat with her knife, a distant look in her eyes.

'I came out for my brother, Vehli, following him. Ma and Da wanted to act like when he left he was never even there in the first place, but I couldn't live with that. Said he was going to find a paralict where no one else had found one before. Make us all rich off it. Waited weeks. Took me more weeks to get this far. Iroka ain't close by and the only place that sounded like what he was looking for was The Lightning Cage. I skirted as much of the place as I could, but I couldn't find a way past the lightning. Real kick in the guts when you two wandered out like it was nothing.'

Byreth stabbed a hunk of now charred meat and took a vicious bite out of it. Burning vapour flowed from her mouth as she chewed openly, but it didn't seem to bother her.

'In thirty years,' Grethard said. 'Spiric was the first human I saw.'

'And all that long ago, you just walked in.' she said bitterly.

Grethard shrugged and leaned back in his chair. 'Not by choice. It was an escape from a world that didn't want me alive.'

*What if that's how I ended up there, as well?*

'Maybe you couldn't get in because you're still needed, somewhere out there, I mean,' Spiric suggested.

Byreth gave a dark chuckle. 'Not by my parents, that's for sure.'

Spiric decided not to press the matter. He couldn't even remember his own family, if he had one, to compare. Byreth filled the silence by distributing chunks of the redfoot on thin rusted skewers, saving the largest for herself.

'He might still be out there,' Grethard offered. 'Could've joined with other scavengers or picked up with the Academy for research.'

'Hope not, that's a death sentence. This Academy ain't the one you knew, old man. They'd throw bodies on a fire just to see if it would keep burning. Cut you to see if you'd bleed. Stuff they already know. That they don't need to be sure of, but keep "testing" anyway. In the name of learning and all.'

'So they managed to take over after all,' Grethard muttered to himself.

Spiric didn't try to ask what he was talking about. The

redfoot was an intense jaw workout with little payoff except for a full stomach. They didn't linger around the fire once they were finished. Another family of miners gladly took their place, pulling leftover scraps off the grill.

On the way out, Byreth haggled with the butchers for the price of the redfoot's pelt, coming away with half a dozen reels. Spiric patted his satchel, feeling the full sack of reels still there. If he couldn't find his memories, at least he'd live a rich life, as long as he could make more water.

With a very subdued offer of hospitality, Byreth guided them back to where she called home, a small hut nestled against the outer walls of the town. She tried to talk it up as best as she could, yet the phrase "it's not much," was peppered between every other sentence. When the place had first come into view, Spiric couldn't distinguish it from any other structure in the town. It was a patchwork of stacked rubble and scraps of corrugated iron pilfered from the walls.

'It's still better than Grethard. He didn't even have a roof,' Spiric quietly assured her.

A gravelly mutter came from behind him and he guessed that Grethard had heard.

The interior was a hopeless imitation of Leerukhart's palace of goods. Scraps of cloth paraded as rugs on bare rock floor, broken crates held nothing but scrap and trash, and a single orb of light wedged into a gap in the ceiling provided a dim glow over it all. They sat down on chairs that were suspiciously similar to those from where they'd just eaten, a rickety table between them.

Grethard was already unpacking, placing a few of the pouches purchased that day on the table, along with a few empty vials and the half-full canister of water. With a small smile, he handed Spiric the ancient scroll of parchment. His unspoken instruction was clear.

'We're about to see history, Byreth.'

She snorted. 'I don't care about that. I want to see him make it rain!' she exclaimed.

'And let everyone in the town know I'm a Hytharo? I'll stick to just the rune for now.'

'Very wise.' Grethard put his sketch of Spiric's runes on the table along with a beaten paintbrush. 'Pick one of those. But ink first. Tradition for a student to mix their own.'

'Can you really call him your "student" if the Academy kicked you out?' Byreth said.

Spiric suppressed a chuckle as he unfurled the parchment, re-reading the instructions three times before he set to work. He could feel eyes burning into him as he carefully filled a vial from the water canister. Spilling a drop was most likely a crime. When he was done, he filled another and handed it to Byreth, trying to ignore Grethard's stunned look.

'Payment for dinner and lodgings,' Spiric said.

He opened two of the pouches, first pulling out a spiral of the Treghit root. It was brittle, crumbling into powder in his fist. He funnelled it into the vial of water, turning it an odd transparent red. He continued to the Charus blood. It was a wild guess as to what "equal parts" consisted of with the delicate petals, but after shredding some between his fingers and dropping them in, the mixture started to look the colour of a fresh bruise. He added the powdered iron and watched it rest for a few moments, the liquid turning a dark purple. Sealing off the vial, he gave it a quick shake. The purple started to lighten and with a few more vigorous shakes, it turned a bloody crimson.

'Matches your eyes,' Byreth said.

Spiric picked up the brush and ran his eyes down the runes. He glanced at Grethard, who maintained a perfectly expressionless face as he observed. Perhaps he was waiting to see which rune Spiric picked on instinct, as if his blind choice would hint at something more. After meeting Byreth's eyes and guessing she was thinking the same, he tapped the end of the brush against the first rune.

The symbol itself was a simple one. A solid, central square with four matching siblings connected at each corner. Spiric couldn't tell why he was drawn to it, or if there was a deeper meaning to his choice, but was reassured by Grethard's nodding.

'Power rune,' he muttered. 'Good choice while we figure that out.'

'What does that mean?' Spiric asked.

'Runes mean a similar thing for everyone but manifest

differently depending on the people you've descended from and the intention behind it,' Grethard explained. 'For a Reythurist like myself, it would be a blast of air, for Byreth, a Curiktic, fire or light. And for yourself... well, I don't know.'

'You said you were a storm caller,' Byreth said. 'Don't know what that would mean for power.'

'Lightning.' The word escaped out from under his breath. The memory of the smouldering corpse lying before him in the depths of a skyscraper flashed through in his mind. Now he knew how he'd done it.

He dipped the brush in the ink and began drawing the rune on his wrist, well-worked muscle memory guiding his hand. As the ink dried, the stray lines began to take shape, forming a perfect set of blocks to make up the rune. He focused his mind on it and was able to force the ink to slide up and down his forearm just by visualising it.

'So Leerukhart had the real thing,' Spiric said. 'I wonder if she has anything else?'

'She was one of the first people to dig in Kurkress, nearly thirty years ago.' Byreth replied. 'Must've turned up all sorts of things from those-of-glass.'

'But a Hytharo scroll?' Grethard questioned. 'Why that among the ruins?'

'Because we would've hidden here,' Spiric breathed. 'And that scroll was left in case we ever came back. I just wonder if we left anything else.'

'Whatever it is, it'll cost you your head,' Byreth said.

'And how much would your head get us?' Grethard teased. 'Half a reel, the way she treats you.'

The reignited banter continued well into the night. Grethard and Byreth sparred equally, with Spiric occasionally getting a cheap shot in to keep things even. He kept glancing down at the new rune on his arm, checking in case it disappeared. Part of him wished it would. He couldn't help dwelling on what it could do, what it had once done, and why he'd be desperate enough to do it.

## CHAPTER TEN

# THE SCYTHES STRIKE

S PIRIC BARELY SLEPT THAT night. When he thought about it, he hadn't really slept much at all the past few days. Probably something to do with not having an actual bed. The light of dawn came in through holes in the roof big enough for Spiric to stick his head through. Still lying on the rock floor with his bunched-up cloak as a pillow, he could just hear the distant mutters of the night guards waiting for someone to replace them, counting down the seconds until they could say the sun was truly up.

The mutters suddenly turned to shouts and a clanging bell joining the racket. Spiric sat bolt upright. The other two were still asleep. He wrangled the goggles over his eyes and stood, listening hard. Somewhere in the distance, the shouts continued, far-off running footsteps, but nothing close. He felt his shoulders unwind a touch.

*Maybe it's nothing.*

But then a ground-shattering thump from just outside made the entire shack quake. Before Spiric could recover from the shock, there was a deafening slam on the door and it was flung into the room. The man who kicked it stood in the doorway, clad in dark blue robes with glistening silver hems, dust swirling at his feet. His face was covered by an angular mask of iron, every spare inch of the surface studded with a network of stubby, interconnected tubes. A strange, snapping rattle filled the room as they breathed, eerie enough it made Spiric's heart freeze.

'All of you, assemble outside on order of The Academy of Breggesa!'

Their voice was distorted, unnaturally amplified and echoing in Spiric's ears even after they'd stopped speaking. There was another shockwave of air and the man launched into the sky. A cacophony of swearing sprouted behind him as Byreth scrambled to her feet.

'Fucking Scythes! Of all fucking days!' She kicked Grethard hard enough to make him wake with a yelp. 'Get up, you old fart, and pack your things, we need to go! NOW!'

'But... but why do we—'

Byreth was suddenly in Spiric's face, his collar held tight in her balled-up fists. 'If they find out you're a Hytharo *and* you came out of The Lightning Cage, you will NEVER see the light of day again and they'll slaughter this entire fucking town to keep the secret!'

'What happens now they're in the village?' Grethard said quickly, hurling things into his burgeoning backpack. 'Can we hide?'

Byreth shook her head. 'They're going to turn the whole place upside down for even a trace of anything that came out of a ruin and punish whoever was trying to hold on to it.'

'Like Leerukhart,' Spiric said. 'She had those... those beads after she took my blood.'

Fear flashed across Byreth's eyes. 'Shit! We got to find her!'

Spiric tried to grab her and stop her from dashing off, but she was too damn fast. He sprinted after her, ignoring Grethard's yells behind him.

'Wait! What the hell are you even going to do when you get there!?'

Chaos fell from the sky. The blue-clad figures tore through the air from door to scrap metal door, kicking them in with ease and ordering the dwellers out with distorted shouts. Anyone stupid enough to get their hands on a weapon was swooped, pinned to the ground and interrogated on the spot. Spiric dashed after Byreth as she took to the catwalks, the streets below already frothing with panicked crowds.

The Scythes acted as shepherds, corralling the people along, packing them so tight they risked toppling down the cliffs. Grethard had barely caught up with them, but Byreth was still practically sprinting down the rickety steps. The catwalk ended abruptly, placing them atop the stony cliffs that overlooked the grand house of scrap. Four Scythes held a clearing in front of it, keeping the crowd back by their sheer presence while more of them forced people to press in. Screams rang from inside, the echoes casting a terrifying silence over all of them.

The door suddenly burst open and Leerukhart was thrown bodily out of it, landing in a heap. Her shawl was half-shredded, a mess of black hair covering her face as she scrambled away. One of the Scythes strode out after her, unmasked and with robes hemmed in gold instead of silver.

'Oh no,' Grethard murmured.

Out of the corner of Spiric's eye, he saw Grethard shrink back a few steps. But he couldn't look away from the unfolding scene. Whoever this Scythe was, he looked to be in charge of the operation. He was about Grethard's age, a pulled-back coat of iron-coloured hair contrasting with a skin like beaten leather. The only pale patch was around his clenched jaw, merciless retribution twisting his face into a rage.

'I don't appreciate a lie!' he roared in a gravelly voice that made the crowd recoil. He stepped forward, pulling Leerukhart back by her hair and holding something right in front of her face.

'Please, you didn't even ask—'

'Yet by not telling us you lie by omission! How long have you had this? How many lives endangered by it!?'

Spiric recognised what the Scythe had. It was the vial of his blood.

'Shit,' he muttered under his breath. 'What do we do?'

'With him there, nothing,' Grethard whispered from behind them.

'How the hell do you know who that is? I thought you'd been in the cage for—'

Grethard shushed her. 'That's Vorric. He was the one who chased me into exile.'

Spiric looked back down at the Scythe as he threw Leerukhart to the ground again.

'What else are you hiding?' He punctuated every few words with a sharp kick to her ribs. 'What else are you planning on spiriting off to a black market?'

She started coughing violently, splitting blood and who knew what else as she tried to get away. 'Inside... The lockbox... I promise, it's worth it... Just... just don't kill me...'

Vorric didn't seem impressed. He wrenched her to her feet, leaving her swaying for balance, and turned to the crowd. He held up a hand, making a single blue rune in his palm visible for all to see.

'It looks like I must set another example. The previous one is the village in the south, which had to be cleansed due to a corruption we could not root out. If you have not seen that, then see this now. Do not keep strange relics to yourself. Do not hide them. Do not spend a single breath to lie or it may be your last.'

Slowly, Vorric turned to Leerukhart. She was sobbing, trying to turn her face away as he held his palm nearer. It was no use. The rune burned white hot. The air around her gave a thunderous clap and she gasped, clutching at her throat as she collapsed. Twitching on the ground, blood began to flow freely from her mouth, her nose, and even her ears. Spiric felt his chest flip at the sight and he prayed it wasn't because it was a familiar one.

Grethard began cursing under his breath. 'Spiric, we need to go now. If any of us are caught, that's what happens to us.'

The old man was already pulling him back from the horrific view, but Byreth still hadn't moved. Spiric broke away from Grethard's grip and ran to her. A strange mix of shock and rage was frozen on her face. He tried to grab her shoulders, to bring her along with them but she wouldn't budge.

'Leave her!' Grethard shouted at him.

Spiric replied by shooting him a deathly glare before turning back to Byreth. 'You've got to come with us, to Breggesa! To anywhere but here!'

The Scythes were taking off again, scattering the crowd with force as they resumed their raid.

'But... but I've got nothing else.'

'Did you see what they just did to her!?' Spiric hissed. 'You want to hang around and find out what they'll do to you when they piece together you've been working for Leerukhart!? What about your brother!?'

This snapped her out of it. She met his gaze, blazing determination in her eyes. 'I know a way out.'

She dashed off again and they followed, leaving the frightened crowd behind as they dived through a labyrinth of shacks and hovels. People scrambled out of them as Scythes all but crash-landed into their rooftops, but with Byreth almost punching her way through, no bystander could slow them down. The town's perimeter walls stood ahead and Byreth kicked aside a piece of scrap covering a hole barely big enough for them to wriggle through.

On the other side, Spiric felt much more exposed. Barren rock stretched out in every direction. If a Scythe so much as glanced over the wall, they'd be spotted. Byreth skirted along the perimeter, following one of the ground rails until it ended abruptly at a beaten-up looking shelter where something with wheels was hidden within.

A complex hunk of pipes, gears and rotors sat between the front two wheels, two pairs of seats welded to the rest of the frame, the whole thing sitting precariously on the set of ground rails. If it were some sort of cart, Spiric could see no beast present to pull it. That didn't stop Byreth from scrambling in, her seat featuring about eight different levers in front of it.

'Where the hell did they get a buggy from out here?' Grethard asked as he climbed into the seat next to her.

'Heard they were everywhere after Revance fell,' Byreth said. She threw a few of the levers and the buggy's machinery gave a guttural roar, belching black smoke from both ends.

'Revance fell!?' Grethard exclaimed.

'What's Revance?' Spiric asked as he clambered into the seat behind Byreth.

'It's a walking fortress,' he shot over his shoulder.

'*Was* a walking—'

'Never mind that, just go!' Grethard snapped. 'The whole town can probably hear this contraption.'

The buggy roared louder and began to roll, jerking across the twin lengths of ground rail as it picked up speed. Each bump threatened to rattle Spiric's teeth and suddenly the surroundings were sweeping past at a blinding speed. Water pumps and other outposts flashed past in blurs of grey and rusted brown, their path dictated by the whims of whoever had first laid these rails. Between the clanking rattle of the wheels and the sporadic sputtering of the engine, he couldn't even hear the conversation the other two were supposedly having in the front.

He twisted in his seat, his guts chugging nauseatingly as he tried to focus on the receding town. After what those Scythes, and especially that Vorric, had done to Leerukhart, they were lucky to get away. But he couldn't help but feel for the people still stuck there. Were raids like that just part of the drudgery of daily life? Would it just keep happening until they'd all been driven away from this forsaken place?

At least they'd escaped. Or so he'd thought. A speck of movement darted up from the town like a vulture, catching high in the wind and gliding towards them. Spiric could barely fix his eyes on them. The blue figure was so hard to distinguish from the rest of the sky.

'They're following us...' he muttered under his breath. 'They're following us!'

Byreth didn't even look around. 'You better do something about it, old man!'

'I haven't got any axioms ready! What do you want me to do, throw rocks at them?'

Spiric looked down at his wrist, the red rune still glistening on his skin. One that would produce lightning. The Scythe was slowly gaining on them and he could almost make out the iron mask that hid their face. But they didn't seem in any hurry, content to just soar on the eddies and lows of the sky, watching them, waiting to strike. Stalking them from the sky.

His vision began to blur as he tried to focus on the distant figure, but tearing off his goggles did nothing to help. A pounding heart threatened to explode out of his chest, a misplaced fear driving faster and faster until a memory hit him like a tidal wave. Thunder clapped in his ears and suddenly he was no longer sitting in the buggy, but standing upon solid rock, high up in the mountains he was sure he'd just been in two days ago. His old traveling clothes hung off his shoulders, his companions replaced by a boy and a girl his age, both Hytharo.

Spiric tried to stare at them, to beg his body to move so he could grab them, force them to tell him who the hell he was, but his face kept turning to the sky. There, far in the distance, human vultures stalked them. Just as they had done for days.

The girl's voice came at his shoulder, hoarse and breathless. 'It's time to end this. Send them a message.'

'Agreed,' his own mouth said, the sound reaching his ears in an echo.

He looked down at his wrist. It was still dotted with runes. He recognised the five at the crook of his elbow as the ones he'd come through with, but his focus kept getting drawn back to the first at his wrist. Power. Lightning. As one, they pointed their hands to the sky and they made the runes burn in their palms.

Deafening thunder clapped again and he was back in the buggy, staring once again at the single rune on his wrist.

'I need to send a message.' They weren't his words. He still wasn't sure how he'd come to them. But they felt right.

The rune began to slide in the centre of his hand and he pointed his palm skyward, towards the vulture of a man that followed. He didn't need to aim, to visualise what he would create, because he knew he'd already done it before.

The skin on his palm sizzled as the rune burned white hot, his fingers twitching as sparks of blue energy danced off them. He held it, savoured it as long as he could. This was power. *His power.* And the Scythe would be the one to suffer it. It felt as if his arm would burst, but he knew that was right. That was how he'd done it a thousand times before.

Lightning, a brilliant arcing bolt of energy, exploded from his hand with a crack that broke the sky. It struck the Scythe square in the chest and an inhumane scream filled the air, one Spiric knew all too well.

The Scythe stalled in their flight for a moment, then began to plummet towards the ground, disappearing between rocks below. It was only then he realised Grethard was shaking his shoulders, breaking him out of his trance-like state.

'Spiric! What have you done!?'

He was breathing hard, still struggling to get his eyes to focus. 'I sent a message.'

'Sent a message!?' Grethard bellowed. 'Everyone in Kurkress would've seen that! They'll know what you are, Spiric! They'll know that you're—'

'A Hytharo,' he finished. 'I know. But they would have known anyway. They have my blood.'

Grethard stared at him, utterly speechless.

'Doesn't matter if they know. Let them come!' Byreth declared. 'All we need is to fix you up with a few more runes and you can shoot the rest of them right out of the sky!'

Spiric didn't answer her. They would have been followed anyway, he told himself. He had to strike that man down.

*But did I want to?*

## CHAPTER ELEVEN

# PAST LIVES

G RINDING RAILS SMOTHERED ANY opportunity of conversation as they rode on. The growing lump in Spiric's throat acted almost as a blockade any time he tried to break the ringing silence, any half-mustered words or thoughts snubbed when he wrenched his eyes from the rushing-by landscape to focus on the back of Grethard or Byreth's heads. It had been an hour since they'd fled Kurkress, yet neither had turned to look at him. At least Byreth had an excuse, constantly tending to the spluttering and belching engine set in the rail car's frame just between her legs.

He tried to speak again, but then the vision he knew the

others were replaying flashed into his mind, along with that scream of agony as the Scythe fell from the sky. He hadn't heard the thump of their body hitting the ground, but it was all too easy to imagine. It made his heart flip in his chest, a feeling that was becoming all too familiar. Perhaps the life he'd led before this had not been a gentle one. But was it that way by circumstance or by his own doing?

The gut-twisting sensation was soon given a physical excuse as the rails guiding the car began their descent through a stony pass. The sharp corners of the switchbacks threatened to tip them over the cliffs until the rails finally flattened out at the sandy desert floor. The buggy thundered on in spite of it, hanging onto the rails that were only just hidden by the dunes until it could do so no more.

When it reached its limit, the machinery gave one final shriek of protest as the buggy's path slid perilously sideways, its guiderail finally buried like everything else in this blasted land. Byreth grunted as she threw a few more levers, putting the thing out of its misery before swinging her boots into the sand. Grethard followed without a word and Spiric had no choice but to do the same, wondering how long it would take for the sands to swallow the rail cart. A day? Maybe a week? Would someone one day pull it out like what had happened to him?

They continued to walk against desert wind for another hour, the unpleasant whistle of it catching in Spiric's ears. At least he had the goggles. The grains of sand that blasted his face felt as if they were peeling off his skin.

The horizon soon birthed a shimmering tower, perfectly round and coated in glass. It was shorter than a skyscraper, rounder, too, but as the only feature of the land surrounding them, it seemed monolithic. Spiric found it nothing but ominous. He watched Grethard closely as they approached, but the old man didn't seem to hesitate a single step of the way. Either he trusted Byreth, or he knew it was safe.

Massive metal carcasses lay strewn around the tower. Long, rounded shelters that were blown open and consumed by the dunes. Whenever they passed one of the openings, Spiric could spy a strange white moss growing inside, almost completely filling the cavity. It looked as weightless as hair, yet the wind's gusts could not force it to move, only producing a strange, snapping crackle as it passed through.

There was a worn foot trail between the most overgrown, yet Byreth's path guided them far away from it, only intersecting once they neared the tower itself. It sat on a concrete block raised above the sand. A few squat grey buildings flanked either side of it, forming a strange courtyard. A few shade cloths hung between them, clearly not the addition of those who'd constructed the tower, but rather something much more recent, likely by whoever had been building the strange piles of pilfered scrap that lay underneath them.

Byreth stopped just short of having to step onto the concrete, her left hand drifting towards the rough holster at her hip.

'You expecting a welcome?' Grethard asked.

'Don't hurt to,' she replied. 'Wait here.'

Leading with her weapon, she stepped onto the slab, silently creeping towards the nearest grey building. Once she'd disappeared inside one of the buildings, Grethard rounded on Spiric.

'What the hell was that, back in Kurkress?'

Spiric had been bracing himself for this for hours, but he still flinched. There was a certain fear in the old man's voice that had caught him off-guard. 'I did what I had to,' he muttered back.

'What you—' Grethard sputtered. 'I've never seen someone as young as you so ready to kill! Byreth might be all talk, but I don't even think she knows what it is to take a life.'

'I do.' He paused, watching as Grethard drew a shuddering breath. 'When we fled Kurkress, I remembered more. Two other Hytharo and I were being pursued from the air, and together we put them down. We didn't have a choice, Grethard. Just like now.'

Grethard weighed him up, looking down his broken nose for a moment before he spoke. 'I'd worried that might've been the case. Your final moments must've been desperate. Killing does a strange thing to people. Once you start, you don't stop, for the next will save you from the last. Absolve the guilt, hide the crime or make wrongs right. It only ends when there is no more left to kill.'

His words put a pit in Spiric's stomach. The only thing he'd felt when summoning lightning was the thrill of rediscovered magic. What if Grethard was right? It only stacked on the doubts of his past.

'How do you know Vorric?'

A sad smile crossed his face. 'He was the last person I expected to see. He was the one to chase me into The Lightning Cage.'

'But why?'

Grethard gave a forlorn smile. 'Because like you, I didn't have a choice.'

Suddenly Byreth's voice cut through the air. She was finished with her sweep. 'You'll have to tell us more than that, old man! I just saw the only person who took me in cry blood and die. If this Vorric guy is after us, we'll need to know everything.'

The old man grimaced, looking between a blazing stare that Byreth gave him and Spiric, who found himself nodding as well. None of them wanted to meet that fate.

'Fine,' he muttered. 'But we go inside first. I worry they'll send more Scythes after us.'

'After what Spiric did? Not likely!' Byreth said. 'I reckon you've got them running scared.'

Grethard shook his head. 'Vorric is not a man to run scared. Come on.'

They headed for the cracked tower, Byreth explaining along the way that the other two buildings were too overgrown with filter moss to linger in, whatever that was. Sand hid in the corners of the metal antechamber inside, sloping into small dunes against overturned and abandoned desks. More piles of scrap lay in organised allotments, with harvested bales of what Byreth must have been calling filter moss sitting between them.

'What is all this stuff, anyway?' Spiric managed to ask. 'Means someone's been here, right?'

'As long as they aren't here now,' Byreth muttered. 'It's filter moss. Those vent masks that the Scythes wear? The pipes are stuffed with it. Lets them go in and out of ruins without breathing in too much tainted air.'

'Never heard of such a thing,' Grethard snorted. 'I've been in the cage for decades now.'

'They must've figured it out in that time,' Spiric muttered as he leaned in to examine a tuft of it. The air certainly smelt cleaner near it, but the fine fibres of it prickled into his finger like shards of glass when he touched it. 'How tainted does that make us?'

When he looked to Byreth, her jaw was set, making Spiric's expression droop.

'I don't like it down here,' Grethard sniffed. 'Can't see anyone coming.'

Following a narrow spiralling staircase, they emerged onto a wide platform, bound on all sides by windows of cracked glass that gave a view for miles and let the sun pour in from above. Rows and rows of slanted steel and glass panels ringed the place and everything else that wasn't nailed down was knocked over. Even the carpet underfoot had either been cut up and stolen or eroded by sand. The trio sat themselves around one of the flatter-looking steel panels, the closest thing they could recognise as a table.

'So... Vorric,' Grethard started. 'What do you want to know?'

'How he killed Leerukhart,' Byreth said. 'What did he even do to her?'

'Something I'd hoped I wouldn't see again. A Reythurist can manipulate air. Force it all into a compact space suddenly and the sheer pressure would make your brain bleed. Last thing she would have heard would have been a loud bang, then nothing at all. I've no idea how painful it would be. It would have been my fate all those years ago had he caught me.'

'But you escaped him, right?' Spiric said. 'There's a way that doesn't happen to us?'

'If we go back to The Lightning Cage, yes,' he replied. 'That's why I stayed there so long. It was the one place he couldn't seem to follow me.'

'Well, that's no good now!' Byreth burst out. 'We've got a bloody Hytharo to protect from a guy who'd kill you for so much as *seeing* a shadow dancer!? Why the hell did you tell him in the first place? You could have kept that all to yourself!'

Grethard's face grew pale, his eyes unfocused in the distance. 'I didn't have a choice. I wasn't alone when it happened. It was an expedition into a small subset of a ruin, far, far north of Breggesa with a crew of four others from the Academy. I'd volunteered to make the first dive, as we called it, and when I came back… I couldn't hide what I'd seen from them. Not after all I've heard.' He took a deep, shuddering breath. 'Let's just say Vorric wasn't the first to try to take my life.'

'But you survived that,' Spiric said quietly. 'I don't want to ask but—'

'I think you already know.'

A certain sadness pulled at the edges of the old man's face. A mourning he longed to forget. One Spiric could almost remember. He turned to Byreth, but she was still staring at Grethard.

'You deserve the truth, Byreth. If you're here, with us, I mean.'

She turned slowly to him. 'You've got to be…'

'I saw a shadow dancer, too. They spoke to me, asked me to remember them. That's why I'm out here, trying to backtrack on how I ended up like this. How they got me here. I'm sure that they're the key to the rest of my memory somehow. If I can remember them, they can tell me who I am.'

'I'll tell you who you are,' a voice drawled from the stairs. 'Trespassers!'

They spun in their seats, Spiric nearly falling out of his, to catch sight of a tall woman brandishing a long cannon at them with a glint in her green eyes that was all too ready to pull the trigger. The rest of her face was covered by a metal mask cruder of both design and craft than that worn by the Scythes. A set of thick, coarse furs covered the rest of her body, making her look deceptively bulky.

The gun's barrel swung to Byreth, the movement flowing in the woman's sleeves just enough to reveal a flash of skin. It shone strangely in the sunlight, tattered by a thousand tiny scars.

'What've I told you 'bout bringing people here, Byreth?' Their drawl wasn't purposeful and this time it came with a strange, crackling hiss given off by their mask.

'These ain't any people, Tetran!' Byreth said quickly. 'You heard what happened at Kurkress?'

She shook her head, turning her weapon's attention to Spiric and Grethard.

'Scythes,' the old man said.

'So Leerukhart...?'

'Dead,' Byreth answered.

The newcomer cursed softly under her breath before lowering the gun. 'Just as we got a good thing going there...'

Spiric leaned closer to Byreth, but not so much that it was noticeable. 'Is she safe?'

'What?' Byreth whispered back.

Spiric shot her another pointed glance, hoping that she'd now be as painfully aware as he was by his lack of goggles, but no matter how hard he glared, it only seemed to inflict confusion onto Byreth's face. Yet this soon caught Grethard's attention and out the corner of Spiric's eye, Tetran's, too.

'Spiric, what are you—'

'No way...' Tetran cut in, gobsmacked. 'Is he...?'

Before Spiric could begin to panic, Grethard let out a dramatic sigh. 'Well, good secret keeping you two, very subtle.' He motioned to another of the rickety stools as he looked to Tetran. 'Get comfortable, whoever you are. We've got a story to tell you because, like it or not, you're now a part of it.'

Thankfully, Tetran holstered her long cannon and obliged. 'A patchwork like me can't refuse another yarn. I heard about shadow dancers?'

'Like you wouldn't believe,' Spiric answered.

The usual introductions began, which were almost a repeat of what Spiric had said to Leerukhart and Byreth before that. It took nearly an hour, but Spiric felt it as a blur, just going through the motions of providing unfulfilling answers to suspicious questions. He couldn't help but wonder how many more people he'd have to explain it to.

'I reckon you're something out of the undercities,' Tetran said sagely when Spiric was done. 'I went down there once before. Saw things you probably wouldn't even believe.'

'Really now?' Grethard said dryly.

'Best paralict haul I ever had. Too dangerous a game, I've found. Filter moss is a more stable crop as long as you don't have pests like Byreth here blowing up the spot. But that's not what you look for, no? How the hell are you meant to find memories down there?'

Grethard was already rummaging in his pack as she said this, pulling out his sketch of the runes. 'You know what these mean?'

Tetran leaned in, theatrically squinting at the page. 'Means you need to talk to someone else.'

'We've been trying,' Spiric muttered.

'The Order of Reyat should have someone that can figure it out.'

Grethard gave her a blank look, and Spiric couldn't help doing the same.

'The Order of what?' Grethard said.

She frowned at them. 'You two been living under a rock?'

'In a cage, technically,' Byreth said.

## CHAPTER TWELVE

# RESPARK

'You reckon this is how I'm going to meet everyone?' Spiric asked.

'Hm?' Grethard raised an eyebrow.

The pair of them were standing in the shadow of the crooked tower, off to the side as Byreth and the newcomer, Tetran, toiled stuffing as many tightly compressed bales of filter moss as they could into the latter's beast of an arcanite without swearing at each tiny cut on their fingers. When she'd introduced them to it, Tetran had called the arcanite her "scutter," though through her thick accent Spiric couldn't bring himself to ask if it was that or "Scouter," so he instead just resorted to joining Grethard in calling it "that infernal contraption of yours."

The machine itself was like a barrel of burnt metal, clad in the same type of black leathers Tetran wore. Supported on six highly-articulated legs, it stood about as tall as Spiric, with the only thing that could come close to a head represented by the dozen or so glinting lenses welded into one end of it.

When Tetran wasn't by its side, it pawed at the ground under it or trotted around to find a better spot to take in the view. From the little Spiric had picked up from Grethard's reluctant teachings, this surely meant that keeping the machine running always occupied a portion of Tetran's mind, which might do well to explain the halting gait she sometimes broke into. Once she and Byreth had disappeared from view to grab another few bales of moss, Spiric found his voice again.

'I mean, is everyone going to be waving guns at me until I tell them I'm a Hytharo?'

'At least you're attracting something, even if it is trouble,' Grethard said with a shrug. 'In thirty years I didn't see a single soul but in only a matter of days I suddenly have three travelling companions and was in breathing distance of a man I'd happily call a walking nightmare.'

Spiric began pacing as restlessly as the arcanite, still staying within the bounds of what little shade the tower cast. 'Do you trust her?'

'Which "her?"'

'Tetran.'

Spiric stopped next to the old man, who leaned in with a lowered voice. 'Never trusted Kretatics. Not after knowing how far they'd go for some of their machines.'

'What, it's just a hunk of scrap metal, isn't it?'

Grethard shook his head. 'That may be so, but the means to control it is slightly more complicated. It takes focus. Mental energy. When I was your age, they had this way of making fresh corpses walk, using those empty minds to help them control numerous and larger arcanites than they could on their own. Just imagine, an empire of machines sprawling out of one man's mind, aided by a thousand bodies all shackled together. It was horrifying.'

'But that would have been years ago, right? They're not doing it now, are they?'

There was a longer pause. 'Not as far as I can see. But it was about control, Spiric. So many of them did this and when they ran out of corpses, the living were slaughtered for the sake of an endless demand.'

'So even if they don't do it anymore, you still—'

'It's about how far people would go to keep power, Spiric. She might be young, born after that time, but the legacy of what was gained from it still remains.'

Spiric glanced between Grethard and the newcomer's arcanite. It seemed like more of an old grudge than a reason to actually distrust her. While Grethard spoke, Spiric's mind leapt to her defence. If it was something before her time, something she was simply born into without choice, could she truly be blamed for it? It was a question he was already asking about himself.

With the excuse for further stretching his already well-paced legs, Spiric wandered off. It was mostly in the name of staying out of sight. The tower's shade may have been welcome, but they were still out in the open. With the way he'd seen the Scythes leap down from the sky, they'd be on them in seconds, no matter how much Grethard assured him that he'd feel them coming.

The rows and rows of filter moss-infested metal fuselages went on for a mile. Spiric's ears twitched as he reached the end of it. A small crackle was emanating through the air. Up ahead, a series of tall and rusted metal boxes flashed with tiny arcs of electricity. It travelled in a dance on the sagging wires linking the boxes together, licking at the sand below where they hung too limp, petrifying it and turning it to glass for a moment before it would crack into a thousand pieces. Spiric lingered at the edge of the chain-link fence surrounding the scene. It certainly wasn't keeping him out. The massive rents through the criss-crossed barbs practically invited him in.

The sparks converged on a small ceramic disc at the centre, making it jump with each shock, its dull orange colour flashing vibrantly for a moment before fading. Spiric observed it for a while longer, any thoughts of danger vacant from his mind. Would this be a spot where he'd need one of those masks Byreth had been talking about? He'd survived the undercity, surely this was no worse.

Sometimes when the disc jumped, it would break free of the sand, rolling as a balanced coin on its edge towards the nearest of the corrugated boxes, slotting perfectly into the divots and coiling up the sides of it before falling off, crackling with tiny bolts of white-hot energy when it crashed back to the exact spot it had started in.

'A respark, huh?' Spiric muttered to himself. Another involuntary word, just like when he'd first seen the skyscrapers. Maybe this thing was familiar.

He couldn't be sure if the disc was giving off lightning or absorbing it, but the more he thought about it, the further he strayed through the chain fence. Every hair on his body stood on edge as the flickering lightning welcomed him, shaking his hands with tingling arcs that reached up from the sand itself. He almost chuckled at it, then remembered what his own lightning had done to the Scythe earlier that day and to whoever else he'd encountered in his past life.

The respark lay at his feet now, embedded in the sand but still spinning as if it were powered by a restless motor. For the first time, caution warned in his mind. But this thing was all about lightning, was it not? That was his domain. His birthright. The way the last word had just popped into his head... it was less a thought and more... more a memory. But why remember it that way? Why would such a deadly force of nature be his to behold? The answers would come later, probably from the shadow dancer. It was time to stop thinking so damn hard about it.

Picking up the paralict was tricky business. Its uniform dull orange colour and smooth texture was a mirage that hid the sheer torque that it spun with, even while half-buried. It took both hands to clamp it down, and when he picked it up it came away from the ground with a sizzling tear of sparks.

Even in his hands it wouldn't stop, and he had to hold it at an odd angle so gravity would counteract its endless spin. As he walked back to the tower with his newfound prize, a seed of worry began to sprout. What if this thing wasn't deadly yet but would be tomorrow? Or the day after? Had picking it up doomed him already? He dismissed each question with the memory of his meeting with the shadow dancer. If what Grethard said was right, he was doomed to begin with, so why not add this curio to the mix?

Back at the tower, Tetran's arcanite trotted up to him, circling around his back before re-joining at his flank, an undulating pincer arm lingering close to his newfound paralict as if it were fixated on it. A short while later, Tetran came storming over, Byreth and Grethard following with confused looks on their face.

'Drop that paralict right now!' she shouted.

Spiric hesitated, the alarm in her voice not the congratulatory tone he'd been expecting. 'Why should I?'

The question stopped her dead in her tracks twenty paces away. As she eyed off the paralict, worry also began to grow on Grethard's face and Spiric did his best not to absorb it.

'Do you even know what you're holding?' Tetran said through gritted teeth.

He nodded unconsciously. 'It's a respark.'

'It will kill all of us if you don't drop it right this second!'

But Spiric kept his grip, letting silence linger. Grethard broke it.

'Why do you know it by that name?'

'And why hasn't it killed you, either?' Byreth added.

Spiric looked down at the ceramic disc. The orange surface had turned a violently yellow hue with tinges of red streaking through. It was practically yearning to be free, vibrating in his hands, its colour growing redder by the second.

He looked up again, and Tetran had risked a few steps closer, a hand outstretched and her eyebrows drawn together. It was only then he realised her face was now uncovered, her pale cheeks twisted in panic, only interrupted on her left by a thick black bar tattooed straight from her eye to her jawline.

'I don't care what you call that thing, but you got to put it down. They're meant to spin. They *want* to spin. Anyone stupid enough to stop them from doing that gets fried by a lightning bolt bigger than anything you're supposed to be able to spit out.'

Spiric looked back to Grethard and Byreth, who were

backing away. No matter how great a prize the respark felt, it wasn't worth risking them. He crouched down, planting the disc hard into the sand before leaping away. But little happened. Despite all the force it had been throbbing with in his hands, it happily resumed its idle pace. Only the edge of the disc touched the ground, the rest hovering above it at an impossibly tight angle. A single dancing arc of energy sputtered from its highest edge and to the ground, turning the sand under it to glass rubble as the respark's colour drained back to the faded orange.

'I think I used to play with these when I was a child,' Spiric said, still staring at the thing.

'You still are a child,' Grethard muttered.

He shot the old man a withering glare. 'The game was to see how long you could hold it still, then throw it at someone's feet to watch it spark off.'

Tetran walked over and tapped the disc with her foot, yelping as a bolt of static replied. 'These types of paralicts only show in places where lightning is constant. The Lightning Cage down south is probably full of them.'

'It's not,' Grethard said. 'I've spent thirty years there and never saw something like that once.'

'Starting to think you're the one chucked through time,' Byreth chuckled. 'Not having any regrets coming out?'

'Just a few,' he muttered back darkly.

## CHAPTER THIRTEEN

# DOUBT UNDERFOOT

I NSTEAD OF NORTH AS Grethard had originally intended, Tetran led them west, back into chalky mountains nearly identical to those between The Lightning Cage and Kurkress. White tinges turned to pink, then over the course of days, the rocks became a sunburnt red. There was something familiar about the mountains and Spiric tasked himself with constantly scanning the horizons, aching to hear that thunderclap in his ears that would show him just a hint more of who he was. Yet no matter how much he willed it, it wouldn't come.

Tetran seemed to know the route well, as did others. Then again, it didn't look hard to remember. A thousand footfalls had landed on every possible step of the trail, carving a winding and unnatural grove to guide their path. In the flat valleys and high ridgelines, oncoming travellers could be spotted from miles away, but it was difficult to discern good intentions from specks in the distance.

The first time they'd encountered the situation, Grethard had all but insisted on flying over to greet the travellers himself, but this was an eventuality Tetran had practiced well. They'd drawn to a halt, an overdue respite for Spiric and Byreth, and Tetran sent ahead her arcanite. It had jogged for a mile further, wandering near the travellers before returning, the fact that it had come back in one piece being good enough for Tetran to trust the oncomers.

Traders and rugged mercenaries formed the bulk of who they encountered. They mostly exchanged local knowledge and warnings of what had just happened further up or down the trail, but Spiric wasn't lucky enough to be privy to the conversations themselves. While the other three talked, he lingered a way off the path, doing his best to play a shy boy who couldn't bring himself to look a stranger in the eyes.

When night fell, they holed up in the hollows of small caves close to the path or, if they were lucky, abandoned trading outposts. These were often little more than a series of creaking metal pylons as thick as Spiric was, somehow planted into the ground and bent together into shape. The wind moaned against them, something creaking within its structure, but they never moved or shifted. When he asked Tetran where the long-gone builders of these places had found the metal, she always replied with a cryptic "you'll see."

That was almost all he heard from her each night. Most of her time was consumed by the respark. By day, the paralict was carried securely in the belly of her arcanite, stashed inside a hessian sack that dulled its static touch, and whenever it was out, she never dared hold it with her bare hands, instead commanding the arcanite to poke and prod at it as she murmured observations to herself.

On the first night, Spiric attempted to join her in her experiments, but they quickly grew dull and repetitive. Instead, he began hunting game with Byreth. They were rarely successful, to the point Spiric started to wonder if Byreth had actually killed that redfoot or just found one that was already dead and stuck her knife in it.

'You sure you know how to hunt these things?' Spiric said late into the fifth night.

They were crouched in a rocky crater with only their heads poking out over the rim, eyeing a spot about ten metres away where Byreth had stacked a small pile of Grethard's cured meat. The food was indistinguishable from gravel in both looks and taste, but maybe it would be bait for something more tender.

'Course I'm sure. Was born into this. Ma and Pa did it. Their folks did it. That's what my brother did, then he went off and started hunting something else.'

'Things like a respark?' Spiric whispered. A redfoot had stuck its head up from behind some scrub. This showed most of its squat little body and Spiric pictured it skewered and roasting over a fire.

'Yeah,' Byreth said breathlessly. She was also watching it, practically salivating.

The redfoot ambled out of its shelter, one of its legs dragging along behind it.

'I don't get it, though. Why would people want them so bad? The thing Leerukhart had healed me in seconds, but you could do that too, right? And I'm not even sure what the respark would do.'

Byreth punched him to keep him quiet. The redfoot was cutting a wide path past the bait, glancing sideways at it with one beady little eye. She let out her breath as it kept going, disappearing into another patch of mountain scrub. 'There're more than just those two kinds of things. They're nothing next to the stuff he was going on about.'

'Like what?'

Byreth scrunched her face for a moment then slid back down into the ditch. 'I remember this one hunk of metal he talked about that made things real slow 'round it, or one like a chunk of blue rock, but it just made everything quiet. You could scream at it, but you wouldn't hear it.'

'Be great to put that near Grethard at night,' Spiric muttered. The redfoot came back into view, but it still wasn't interested. It weaved in and out of sight between rocks, its incessant sniffing only just reaching his ears.

'But then there's a bunch of stuff that seems like it just kills you after a while once you touch it, but for some reason, people throw sacks of reels at that them,' Byreth shrugged, her tone going to a whisper as she pulled herself back up to Spiric's level. 'I don't get it, but if people are buying, I want to be the one selling. I reckon the only ones worth keeping are the ones that stop you from having to use runes.'

'Like Leerukhart's one?'

'Yeah, shame I didn't swipe that up.'

Byreth's words trailed off as the redfoot wandered forth from another hiding spot, its eyes now fixed only on the bait.

He glanced down as Byreth readied her knife. She'd done this the last few nights and had been outrun every single time. Even with this redfoot's injured leg, he was too hungry to let her try again. Before Byreth could jump, he grabbed her wrist, almost getting punched in the face for it.

'What?' she hissed.

'I've got an idea.'

The redfoot was nosing about in the bait now, all its other worries gone as it tried to figure out if it was edible. Spiric slid his left hand above the groundline, willing the rune into his palm where it burned white hot. Familiar sparks began to crackle across his fingers and the redfoot looked up at the sound, snorting in alarm.

The lightning snapped through the air, catching the redfoot on one of its working legs and sending the animal jolting into a tumble. Byreth pounced on the twitching animal, putting it out of its misery with a few grunting shanks.

'I didn't kill it,' Spiric breathed, something sick rising in his chest.

'Damn straight!' Byreth said. She pointed the bloody knife at him. 'Good thinking on stunning it.'

Spiric barely heard her. He was still thinking about the Scythe in Kurkress. If he hadn't been able to kill a squat little redfoot in one go, then he definitely wouldn't have been able to do so for a grown man. They would've plummeted to their death. His appetite for the redfoot was already gone, and the next thing that popped into his head made sure it wouldn't come back. Deep in the skyscraper, back when he was being hunted, a man had lain dead before him, two runes gone from his wrist.

He wasn't just a killer. He was an executioner, too.

Numb dread filled Spiric as they walked back to that night's camp and no matter how boisterously Byreth went on about how much of the redfoot she was going to eat, he still couldn't clear the feeling from his mind. He'd been grappling with the prospect of his memories showing him desperate fights where the death of those attacking him was either inevitable or accidental, but now a darker option appeared. Memories that saw him as a merciless warrior, going in for the kill even after victory was had.

The redfoot was quickly devoured, and while sleep usually followed, Spiric struggled to bring himself to rest. To even lay down his head. Instead, he sat below a ridgeline, just out of sight of the others in case they stirred.

The sky felt big tonight. Distant. The stars impossibly far away and uncountable. It wasn't what he watched. The horizon held his gaze, but it didn't hold his attention. His mind strayed far away from here, far from this time, but whatever his subconscious was reaching for, it wouldn't come. It wasn't forgotten. It was hidden. Something blocked his way and his will to smash through it was waning because he was afraid of what he'd find.

'You're troubled.'

Spiric spun from his seat, kicking up a spray of dust in his scramble. Tetran stood behind him, eyes fixed on the horizon too, her words not a question but a statement of fact.

'How do you know?' Spiric said.

'Got an eye for these things,' she grunted. With a few heavy steps she planted herself down next to him, still watching the horizon.

He returned to doing the same, less to see something, but instead to have a sense not to worry about.

'Besides, anyone coming out of a ruin comes out funny,' Tetran continued. She cast a sideways glance at Spiric, a vacant smirk on her face. 'Don't think I've been the same after my one venture, I can't imagine what you've been through.'

'It's not the ruins...' he said. 'It's what I am.'

'A Hytharo?'

Spiric hesitated for a moment. 'Maybe. Until I can remember, I can't say for sure. But I don't know for sure what I was. What the Hytharo were. Who we were.'

'You're legends,' she said, absent-mindedly chucking a pebble with a whip of her elbow. 'Myths. Tales. Stories. You made sure this world was quenched when you disappeared.'

He shook his head. 'But in our time, there's a chance we weren't and I'm worried what we were isn't something good.'

Tetran looked across at him, fixing him with a perplexed look, but he kept his eyes firmly forward. 'I saw you come back from your little hunt looking a bit more gaunt than usual. Thought you'd seen yourself another shadow dancer. Heard some of that lightning go off before, as well.'

'I didn't kill the redfoot,' Spiric muttered. 'I don't know if I did more than stun it.'

'So?'

'I've killed before, in my time,' he said slowly. 'I remember it. But I don't remember how much I wanted to kill. I mean, what if I really wanted to?'

A sigh came from next to him and suddenly the whole thing felt stupid.

'If it was like that, then you'd be joining a whole lot of people now that do just the damn same. I don't know if Grethard told you what happened to Revance, but that was less of a battle and more a massacre. The sands outside Iroka are an endless graveyard.' She gave him a punch in the arm, much gentler than the ones Byreth doled out. 'Pretty normal to be a killer these days, as long as you're doing it for the right reasons.'

Spiric looked over to her. 'How do I know if my reasons were right?'

Disappointingly, Tetran only offered a shrug. 'Never killed anyone myself. Stay out of fights if I can. Seems like a question you should ask Grethard. Now there's a man who has come out of the ruins all different. Wonder what he saw in all that time.'

'Apparently not a shadow dancer,' Spiric grunted. 'Not like what I've seen.'

There was a comfortable silence between them. A sleepless daze only interrupted by the distance clatter of the occasional pebble Tetran couldn't help hurling out into the distance.

'What'd they look like?' she eventually asked. Her tone was forced into being only casually curious, but there was a certain excitement in her.

'You really want to know?'

She nodded. 'They're the reason I said people don't come out the same. They get afraid, then everyone gets afraid of them.'

He paused for a moment, holding back his answer. 'What... what do you think you saw?'

A chuckle escaped her. 'I ain't sneaking that past you, am I? Well, I reckon I saw one. The one time I went underground, of all my luck. Stuck above ground since then. Less stuff, but

I ain't seen it again. It was like a shadow. A body without a body, just standing darkness that seemed to look right at me. Reckon you're the only one I've ever told about it. Telling folk is a sure-fire ticket to a killing, I'm sure Grethard would'a told you as much. But I keep wondering. Keep wanting to go back.'

Her face had tweaked into an earnest grimace.

'I don't think that was it,' Spiric eventually said. 'The one I saw, they looked human, but they moved like they were flickering. They recognised me, so I've been trying to remember them, but I just... there's nothing. They were the one who buried me, they're following me, but I don't know why and the more I think about it, I'm not sure they know, either.'

Tetran let out a long, low whistle. 'Looks like I've just been running scared all these years for nothing. Maybe I should ditch you lot when we get to Basarod in a few days if you're getting stalked by a real one.'

Spiric looked over at her, ready to say something scathing, but held his tongue. Her smirk was back.

'Should get some sleep,' he muttered sheepishly.

He dusted himself off as he got up, but Tetran didn't join him.

'Shout if you wake up remembering more about that respark!' she called after him.

Spiric didn't answer back. He almost didn't want to remember more than he already had.

*Almost.*

## CHAPTER FOURTEEN

---

# THROUGH RED MOUNTAINS

---

'**Y**OU WORKED OUT WHAT this thing is good for yet?'

It was a question Byreth asked every morning of the journey and every time Tetran shook her head as she silently ordered her arcanite to swallow the respark in its central cavity. The answer always sent Byreth into a frustrated huff as they set off walking. This usually gave Tetran enough space to linger by Spiric and quietly ask a routine question of her own.

'You remember anything more?'

It was a question Spiric berated himself with each morning as well, just to silently shake his head and swallow his pride. But today, Tetran flashed a cheeky grin back at him.

'Don't worry, Basarod's tomorrow. They'll have answers for us.'

At least Grethard had given him space, maybe a little too much. They'd barely spoken since they'd added a fourth to their motley crew, but Spiric knew that wasn't the cause of his quiet. Dust was hanging in the air now, an omen, according to the old man, that they were nearing the end of the mountains. It filtered the blue sky into a permanent beige-yellow hue, where even Spiric's now well-worn goggles couldn't keep out all the silt.

In the late afternoon, Tetran was babbling on about the high iron content in the hills surrounding them. Her lecture only stopped as she led them up what felt like the steepest one she could find, falling silent at the very top.

'And there it is...'

When Spiric joined her side, the same words flashed through his mind. Burnt clay sloped down before them into an enormous basin, the walls streaked with rings of ochre, yellow, and orange, a cross section of eons of sand and rock compressed into one tapestry. Its walls arched into red mountains, their crested peaks already causing a sunset.

At the very lowest point lay another golden dome. It was almost a perfect replica of the one Spiric had explored in The Lightning Cage, but instead of orbiting shrapnel, it was surrounded by a ring of rusted steel. A lattice of tall bars sprouted from the ground at 45-degree angles, crossing over each other like soldiers closing their ranks. Sections were missing, leaving those they were meant to support creaking and flexing as the wind toyed with them. Yet no matter how hard it blew, sand never crossed the iron boundary.

Spiric kept staring, unaware of the tinny pitch that was filling the air and the unsettling questions being hurled at him from somewhere far away.

Thunder cracked in his ears and the hazy sky was replaced by a red dawn. He was walking in the opposite direction, away from the iron lattice. Over his shoulder it stood proud and whole, its structure complete as an enclosure that arched over the golden dome. Silent lightning flickered across it, racing in laps and waves around its perimeter.

Three Hytharo now walked with him, but Spiric still couldn't make out their faces. Looking at them was like trying to stare into a sun that dazzled with shame. He glanced back again, this time spotting the bodies that lay just beyond the ironworks. He counted a dozen. He knew there was more. Voices reached him next.

'I still don't believe what we saw in there,' a girl's voice said.

'It was him!' his own voice came out. 'It was Arallak! I'm sure of it!'

'But he's dead! We saw—'

'It doesn't matter what we saw,' another boy's voice spat. 'It matters that he took one of ours! Will he come for the rest of us? We're being hunted as it is.'

'We just need another place to hide,' he growled through his gritted teeth. 'Another ruin. Anything.' He glanced back west one more time. Figures already dotted the mountainous horizon.

His last words echoed in his ears as the sunrise retreated from the sky, placing him square back where he'd been. His legs could only quaver under him. A sense of pure disgrace coursed through his veins like thick tar. But he'd heard a name.

*Arallak.*

Each syllable echoed in his mind as he turned it over and over. Could it be the shadow dancer? Who had they taken from them, and why? Spiric leaned forward, forcing his legs to stagger.

'What is it!? Did you remember something?'

He couldn't tell who the question had come from, or who was grabbing his shoulders, trying to right him, but he shook them off as roughly as he could. The trail of the memory was still there! He could chase it! Just for a small moment longer! Just for one more glimpse of that name.

*Arallak.*

The shadow dancer's face flashed through his mind once more, enough to turn his gut feeling into a surety.

'I was here.' Spiric said. 'We were here.'

He looked up. Grethard and Tetran were arguing a few paces away, words flying so fast that he could only barely make out the phrase "give the boy some space!"

Byreth was on his left, her hand lingering in the air, ready to grab him if he fell, but aching to twitch away as he turned his head.

'You okay?'

Spiric tried to speak, but the words got caught on his tongue, leaving him nodding like an idiot. He waved Byreth's hand away and tried to straighten up. The slight movement left his head spinning and before he knew it, Byreth had threaded an arm under his own and around his back, her strength almost enough to scoop him off his feet.

'You look just like you did when you shot down that Scythe,' she muttered. 'Seen something that bad, huh?'

He nodded again, slowly this time. Even with her support, his head felt as if it was revolving like the respark. 'There was four of us. Well, five before that. The shadow dancer must've taken one, the same way I would have been taken, I'm sure of it.'

Byreth glanced across him. 'You seem pretty sure about a lot of things for a kid with only a few scraps of memory.'

'He had a name,' Spiric continued, 'Arallak.' He was only saying it so he wouldn't forget again. 'We knew him. I... I said I saw him die.'

'Shadow dancers were alive? Like us, even?'

He didn't have an answer. He had to know more and the glinting dome was calling him. It was where he'd met the shadow dancer last time, but would the others be willing to risk it with him? Spiric looked over to the other two. Their bickering had died down to snide remarks, which ceased once they caught his eye.

'Are you alright, Spiric?' Grethard asked. At least he seemed genuine. There was a hunger in Tetran's eyes to shoot out more questions.

Before he could answer, Byreth hefted him off her shoulder, letting him wobble on his own feet for a moment as he regained his balance. 'He'll be fine. Said something about feeling like he'd know more if he went down there. Right?'

'Yeah, that's right,' he said hastily.

Tetran's curiosity erupted into protest, of fears of what lurked down there, but the other three held their gaze silently and she quickly realised she was preaching to the choir. 'Fine,' she muttered. 'But if I get hit by lightning...'

Byreth snorted. 'By that thing? Never been touched by even a spark.'

'It has,' Spiric said quietly. 'And I think I had something to do with it.'

The lattice of metal loomed before them like a half-completed bird's nest, its sheer bulk injecting caution to their descent into the basin. Standing before it, Spiric wanted to ask if this place had a name like the rest of them but held his tongue. He already knew it was a graveyard. He stared at the dome through the net of metal that separated them. The gaps easily big enough for a man to walk through.

'You don't have to come with me,' Spiric said slowly.

'Didn't have to do a lot of things with you,' Grethard said with a chuckle. 'And yet here we are.'

'With your lead, Spiric,' Tetran said, motioning him forward.

Not even the smallest of prickles breezed against his skin as he stepped through the boundary. Flat rock turned to squeaking soft sand underfoot, his boots sinking in a few inches with each step. Enough had gathered over the eons to cover the corpses from when he was last here, yet the wind was yet to disturb it.

He tried to keep his eyes away from the golden dome as he approached it, sweeping his gaze left and right over the ground, waiting for the shadow dancer to appear from nothing. More squeaking footsteps followed behind him. The others had made it through.

Out of sheer paranoia he led them on a lap at the fence's perimeter before approaching the dome. Sections of the lattice were stripped away to the point that some of the metal hung impossibly suspended in the air. Spare for the ringing still filling Spiric's ears, the place was silent.

*Dormant.*

The gleaming hexagons of the dome were steadfast. Spiric had pondered the problem for a few silent minutes as Grethard observed him, looming at his shoulder. The others were too afraid to touch the dome, leaving Spiric alone to run his fingertips over each tile's polished surface. He eventually settled on the simplest approach, which was to shove his fingers between the narrow gaps around each tile and attempt to pry them apart.

He was sure there was a give, a slight hint of movement, that the dome would open for him because it was fated to do so, but after a few minutes of trying, he was forced to concede. He was a fifteen-year-old boy foolish enough pit himself against the craftsmanship of a civilisation he couldn't even begin to understand.

A cry of frustration brewed in Spiric's throat as he leaned heavily against the dome. He was close, so close to answers, but giving up now seemed the only option. The golden metal surface was almost ice cold under his palm, a calming wave that washed through his body as he slumped his head against it, praying for it to just let him in.

'Is there anything else you remember, Spiric?' Grethard asked gently. 'If you even got into this thing in the first place?'

'I must have!' he cried out. 'Why else would we have come here?' He turned to rest his back against the metal, letting his body slide down it until he was sitting in the dust. 'We needed to hide. We were being hunted. Both by people and by the shadow dancer. What good would we have done ourselves coming all this way just to put ourselves in this cage?'

'What do you mean, "we?"' Tetran asked.

' The other Hytharo and I.'

Her gaze lingered on him for a few moments longer before she summoned her arcanite to her side. It rummaged in its belly with its creaking metal arm and pulled out the hessian sack the respark was stowed in. Without waiting for him, it dropped it in his lap.

'What good will this do?' Spiric said as he produced it, letting it spin hopelessly against the smooth sand.

'I remember you said it was something your kind played with,' Tetran said. 'It might not be much to go on, but you look clean out of ideas.'

With a few fumbling grasps, Spiric ferried the respark to the join between two of the hexagons where they met the sand. The smooth edge of the disc took to the gap as soon as it made contact and, without wasting a single drop of its momentum, it began climbing, leaving behind a trail of hissing yellow sparks. Each time it reached a junction between the tiles, it turned right, taking a drawn-out minute to return to the ground. Spiric scooped it back into its sack, stowed it in his satchel for the time being.

The path the respark had taken was now glowing orange with heat, the colour crawling into the centre of the tile, but when Spiric placed his hand on it, the metal was still ice cold. He gave it a slight push, a test, not even expecting anything from it, but the man-sized tile complied, silently folding away to lie flat on the ground inside. Only darkness lay beyond it, a cool, drifting breeze emanating from the cavity that made Spiric's breath catch in his throat.

'Torch,' he said without taking his eyes off the darkness.

Even with his goggles pulled off and resting around his neck, he could only see a metre inside. There was the sound of rummaging behind him and he held his hand back to take the metal rod.

A few shakes had it glowing brightly and Spiric wedged it in his satchel, its lit end still poking out. He clumsily drew his battle hammer with his right hand. The damn thing had hung uselessly at his waist for the past week, bouncing and bruising his hip, yet wielding the heft of it now was even more uncomfortable. It was like he couldn't find the right section of the haft to hold it by. He compensated for it by raising his left hand. After his hunt with Byreth, he'd secretly reapplied a few more copies of the power rune, one of which now sat ready at his wrist.

'Spiric, let me send the 'scutter in first,' Tetran hissed. 'You don't know it's safe.'

'No, I've done this before,' he breathed back. It was a lie, at least for now, but maybe whatever he found in here would make it the truth.

Into the darkness he went, one slow step at a time, Byreth's hand on his shoulder as she followed, the others close behind. Unlike the other dome, this one still had its guts. He was surrounded on all sides by pristine consoles of metal and glass that were just taller than him, forming a maze of narrow alleyways. A dull, flickering orange glow ebbed over the top of them. As Spiric picked his way through the labyrinth and towards the centre, it began to glow brighter, the temperature dropping until each of his breaths misted in front of him.

On what had to be the other side of the dome's innards, the maze finally gave way, confronting him with a bottomless pit nearly ten metres across and ringed by a narrow catwalk, its guard rails not even reaching his knee. Spiric took a step out onto it, half expecting it to groan under his weight, but it took him without protest. Staring down into it, he discovered the source of the glow.

*Another respark.*

It floated deep down, orange streaks across its surface revolving slowly as it turned and tremored, raising and lowering itself along the depth of the shaft, giving and taking the orange light as it did so. He circled the catwalk, the others too wary to follow him.

'How far down does it go?' Spiric asked.

'Got a torch to throw in?' Byreth said. There was something about her words that made his ears twitch, but he ignored it.

'Too dangerous,' Tetran said. 'You'll set off that respark.'

Byreth snorted at her, swaggering out onto the catwalk. It was almost like she was showing off. 'What, you think you know everything about them, after poking at one for a few days straight?'

As they bickered, Spiric pulled the smaller respark from his satchel, half-unsheathing it from its sack and gripping it just enough that it could still gently revolve without slipping from his fingers. Its spin matched the one below, along with the gentle swirls of crimson that crossed its orange surface. He frowned for a moment, then tightened his grip, grinding the respark to a halt. A deep screeching of twisting metal filled the air as the massive respark halted in its path.

'What have you done!?'

Grethard's gasp caught Spiric by surprise and his grip fumbled, letting the respark loose a volley of tingling blue sparks. But that wasn't all. The larger copy below boomed with energy as it vomited a blinding torrent of lightning up the shaft. The last thing he saw was the bolt spider-webbing its way across the roof of the dome, the faces of his companions frozen in fright.

## CHAPTER FIFTEEN

# THE HUNTER DESCENDS

T HE AIR SMELT BURNT, but thankfully not of flesh. Through his hazy vision, Spiric searched desperately for the others, but there was no sign of them. Down below, the enormous orange disc spun lazily as before. Had the respark somehow stolen them? He squeezed the respark again, counting under his breath as the sound of grinding steel filled his ears. He clamped his eyes shut as he let go, another crash of lightning echoing in the dome.

A single figure now stood their place, a black cloak draped across their shoulders. Spiric felt his throat clamp. Only one word escaped him. One name.

'Arallak.'

The sound of the name made the dangerous grin flicker from the shadow dancer's face. His hands twitched at his sides. Was he remembering something from his past life the same way Spiric did? He willed his legs to run, do to anything, but the shadow dancer blocked the entrance to the catwalk.

'You remembered me?' the shadow dancer eventually said.

Spiric shook his head. 'Not all of you. Only a name. The other Hytharo I was with... It was as if we knew you.'

Arallak frowned, his head cocked slightly. 'Why? Why would you know me?'

'Because you hunted us, just as you hunt me now.' The venom rose dangerously in Spiric's voice, but he couldn't fight it. 'What have you done with my friends? Where are they?'

The shadow dancer's smile returned and a familiar mix of fear and fury rose in Spiric's chest.

'I removed them for a few moments. A similar journey to yours.' He paused, taking a silent breath as he stared down into the pit. 'You are being hunted. That much is true. But you are not my prey.'

It was Spiric's turn to hesitate. 'I think you may have once been one of us,' he said quietly. 'A Hytharo. But I don't understand—'

'How I became a shadow dancer?' Arallak finished. 'I've had eons to ponder the question. To embrace the strange magic this privilege has cursed me with. It's a fleeting immortality, Spiric. Time marches forward without hesitation or pity for those it inflicts its will upon. A shadow dancer's power is that of rebellion. Under our will, we may only choose what is present and what is not, at a cost to ourselves that is far greater.'

'I've lost everything except my life,' he said. 'What more could you have to lose than that?'

'Time,' Arallak replied bluntly. 'For you, the end of days is a distant dream, but for me, it is a certainty. I will still exist to witness what lies beyond it. An eternity of nothingness so vast that all these eons that still stretch ahead of me might as well have already come and gone. It has brought me to treat every remaining moment of this present as something that is both infinite and instantaneous.

'I may only exchange these precious seconds to inflict my fate on those still living, forcing them to hurtle with me towards the end, yet I would give anything to know what I have lost.' Arallak's expression turned grim and the ebbing crimson light of the respark glimmered in his downcast eyes. 'That's why I follow you now, Spiric. To know why I would make a sacrifice so great. Why our people were forgotten.'

'It's been a thousand years since the time of the Hytharo,' Spiric's jaw was clenched and he had to fight the instinct to strangle the respark in his hands. 'I thought I wanted to know. But all I've remembered these past days is death by my hands. It made me start to wonder what the Hytharo were. Do you think that's something I want to remember?'

'How else do you expect to know who you are?'

'Who I was,' Spiric spat. 'And who I was, I will never become again.'

Arallak was motionless. The scraping of the respark in the pit below was ringing in Spiric's ears. When the shadow dancer answered, it was barely more than a whisper. 'Then you must find a way back to your memories, for you will never be sure if you've changed until you've reckoned with your past.'

'And what do I do until then?' Spiric said out of frustration. 'What about my friends?'

'They'll return. But remember, you are still hunted.'

The runes on Arallak's cloak shimmered as they blinked out of existence, the rest of the shadow dancer's silhouette fading along with them. Once again, Spiric was alone, left with more questions than answers.

Arallak's explanation of shadow dancer magic had been cryptic at best, but it still didn't explain the juddering way he moved or when he was bound to reappear from thin air. As uneasy as he was, Spiric would just have to take Arallak's word that the others would eventually return.

By green torchlight, he found his way to the exit, the respark still in his hands. The relationship between the two copies of the paralicts should have mystified him, but the shadow dancer had already left him with so much to ponder.

The afternoon sun turned the ground into a chaotic glitter

and Spiric regretted not donning his goggles. A grid of shadows lay across it, wavering in the afternoon's heat haze. He squinted up at the iron lattice, his eyes adjusting slowly as he tried to figure out if the respark's explosive reaction had changed that as well. The joins between the intersecting beams seemed thicker than he remembered, but maybe that was just the sun.

Out of the corner of Spiric's eye, one of them twitched.

Spiric didn't even have time to flinch as nearly twenty figures leapt from the heights of the lattice and swooped towards him. They hit the ground with deafening booms that sprayed a blanketing screen of dust. He backed away blindly, only making it a few steps before his back hit the dome's exterior. Another blast of air came, slamming him hard into the metal as it dispelled the obscuring dust cloud, revealing the figures which had him trapped.

*Scythes.*

Their magnificent blue robes fluttering in the settling air, their iron masks glinting with the reflection of the golden dome they had Spiric pinned against. Even from a distance, the chorus of their breath, filtered through their vent masks, formed a sinister rhythm of hisses and clicks.

One more stood before Spiric, not wearing a mask but instead a face that was just as jagged and angular. Spiric recognised him instantly, the cruelty in his dark blue eyes straining to be unleashed. The only thing he'd seen Grethard truly afraid of.

'You've come a long way from Kurkress,' Vorric said quietly. His voice was menacing, an echo of the roaring dictates Spiric had first heard from him moments after he'd executed Leerukhart. 'I must admit, your slaying of one of my men was rather enraging, but your method had my curiosity outweighing it.'

'I knew you'd follow me,' Spiric said, stalling as best he could.

'The tenets of The Academy of Breggesa dictate observation above all.' Vorric slowly paced past Spiric, paying him little mind as he ran his hand along the open seam of the golden dome's entrance. 'I only ordered direct intervention once you entered this structure. Our records have it as sealed and dormant since we first found it, but it took you only seconds to find your way in.

'An extraordinary feat, but then again, I should expect that from an extraordinary being.' He turned his head, expression completely blank as he stared deep into Spiric's eyes. 'I've seen many things in my studies and travels, though I never expected a Hytharo. Where are your companions?'

Spiric wanted to bluff, to say they were inside, ready to strike, but even then they'd be outnumbered four to one. If he hadn't been screwing around with the respark, Arallak wouldn't have needed to throw them forward through time. An idea struck him and he clamped his hands down on the respark.

'They're gone,' Spiric eventually said. 'Only I survived.'

Vorric returned to where he'd first stood, his back to Spiric as he looked across the lattice works. 'You didn't need to survive,' Vorric said, his voice starting to rise. 'It took the Droughtlands generations to adapt to your extinction. In the eons since, we've thrived with the Hytharo existing only as a myth. Without the abundance of water they brought we could finally bring magic under control. Well, almost all of it. The Academy of Breggesa now works tirelessly to protect the living from the anomalies that vomit forth from the fractures left by those-of-glass. Not that they appreciate it.'

'You protect them by killing them,' Spiric said.

Vorric regarded him with a sour look before continuing.

'We spend a great deal of time preventing lustful treasure hunters and misguided scholars from stumbling into the shards left by their civilisation. It's rare we see someone stumbling *out*. More dangerous than a paralict, you carry an idea that would encourage others. One which would threaten the delicate equilibrium that formed in your people's absence. It cannot be risked. This is the mantle that has been passed to me as I lead the Academy forward, a duty I will carry out to my last breath.'

The respark was shuddering in Spiric's hands, the faint grinding of its larger sibling reverberating out from the dome, but the Scythes hadn't noticed the sound.

'So you want to kill me?' Spiric grunted, struggling to grip the respark. He pressed it close to his chest in order to free his left hand, holding it out to flash the red runes in his palm. But bracing the respark like this made it crackle in protest, his entire body tremoring from the pent-up energy.

Vorric glanced back at him, eying the runes with little concern. 'I've no idea why you're so brave for one so young and so alone, but I will admit it worries me. You killed one of my Scythes without a second thought. But if we could master this land without you, I can assure you we will master it against you.'

'Then you'll have to catch up, because I think I've already had a thousand years to do it.'

Sparks began to lick off the respark and around Spiric's chest, wrapping across his body like chains as they snapped into the air. The other Scythes looked worriedly between themselves, their stances shifting, aching to retreat. Vorric glanced down at the paralict, barely raising an eyebrow as his jaw shifted into a leer.

'That paralict isn't large enough to harm either of us. Much like you.'

'I know,' Spiric replied. 'But the one inside is.'

Before Vorric could even think about leaping into the air, Spiric hurled the respark as hard as he could into the sand at his feet. A pair of devastating eruptions crashed across Spiric's body as the resparks exploded within moments of each other.

In front of him, lightning bloomed from the rapidly fragmenting respark, snaking past Vorric's body as tendrils of blinding light. The last thing Spiric saw before his vision simply turned white was the shadow it cast of him, an impenetrable darkness that lay beyond the boundless energy before it also vanished. A silent pain wracked his body from behind as the second respark went off, blinding his thoughts until he could feel no more, his consciousness once again buried in sand.

The cold that came with it was relieving. No worries, no cares. No blasted shadow dancer to do the bidding off.

It was too good to last and Spiric swore he was going to kill whoever was now sending scorching bolts of pain across his chest. Sensation came back in his arms next and his attempts to thrash out were restrained with far stronger hands. There was a burning agony as his throat roared, screaming until his vision burst into life.

Blazing sun and bloody destruction surrounded him, charred bodies scattered across the sand. Byreth and Tetran were crouched over him. Their hands assaulted him with harsh grips and jets of cauterising fire. Their mouths shouted the whole time, but no sound reached his ringing ears. It was a high pitch, so high it went low again, a sound that couldn't be real.

More feeling came back. His body was slumped against the dome, the sand under him sharper than usual. His hands were buried in it, but they weren't dry. Spiric looked down slowly. The front of his tunic was drenched with blood, Byreth's hands belching fire as they darted across jagged gashes, each pass summoning puffs of smoke. Smoke that carried the smell of burnt flesh.

It kindled a burning rage in his heart and when he blinked, he found the spark of it.

The haze in the air was suddenly replaced by a clear blue sky, albeit one that was punctured by the smoke columns of battle. He was no longer hunched and dying against the dome, hidden away in a valley, but standing proud, a fortress wall his perch as he surveyed the siege lines upon the plains before him. Soldiers clad in crimson robes like the ones he now wore stood at his flanks, leaning through the crenelations of their bastion and raking those below with showers of lightning.

Spiric edged forward and the fury roared within him. The bodies of his warriors were scattered across the rocky switchbacks that led up to the fortress gate, their blood painting the golden sands. The invaders trampled them with utter disregard. Massed in their thousands, they were a human wave, their momentum unperturbed as their vanguard was slain.

Spiric looked to his wrist where rune patterns he couldn't remember were sliding up in his palm. He thrust it forward with well-trained vigour and lightning lanced out, forming into a ball of energy that hung above the invading throng for a moment before detonating. The clatter of their fallen spears was drowned out as their comrades rallied furiously to take their place.

Spiric went to strike again, but a hand on his shoulder held him back. When he turned, it was a familiar yet long-forgotten face, one that made his next breath fill his lungs with passion and zeal.

'The gates are breached, Spiric!' she said. 'The catacombs are our only way out!'

'No!' he snapped. 'We have to hold the city! Arallak's sacrifice won't be in vain!'

The girl stared at him, confusion reigning over her. 'Who...?'

Spiric opened his mouth too, but words never appeared. He couldn't remember.

A wrenching breath punched into his lungs and he was on his back, whatever he was lying on clanking as it carried him. The night sky was above, stars glimmering in a rhythm that matched the crackling pain in his chest. He tried to move, to roll over, but his groan at the thought of it prompted Grethard to appear, hands clamping down on him as the old man silently mouthed his name.

'Spiric!'

Arallak's voice pierced through the veil and Spiric was on his feet again. Prideful nerves flooded his body, but the shining silver breastplate covering his spotless crimson robes steadied him. A grand avenue now surrounded him, leafless trees with rust-coloured bark entwined overhead, casting shade over smooth sandstone slabs. Arallak stood to his left, dressed as Spiric was, stern determination on his face as he met Spiric's eyes.

Only now he had red eyes.

'She is a treasonous criminal,' he announced to the crowd. His face was restrained into expressionlessness. 'We have every justification. It is a trial by combat, a symbol of their so-called rebellion against Hytharo might.'

'What if I can't win?' Spiric whispered to him.

Arallak's sad grin curled across his lips. 'It's our duty to win, little brother.'

Spiric turned slowly to look down the avenue. The crowd that gathered on either side of the road donned regal robes similar to his or were rugged, wrapped in rags that weighed on their shoulders far more than the garments themselves should.

The woman twenty paces opposite him was the epitome of this. She may have only been a few years his senior, but she looked as frail as an elder. Animosity flashed in her yellow eyes just as a rune burned in her palm. But Spiric never gave her the chance.

The flash of lightning blinded him, and suddenly, a pair of yellow eyes were looking down at him, dim against the starry night sky. His body was rocking again, the cool metal under him leaching at his body heat.

'Stop squirming!' Byreth hissed, 'At least until we get through the gates!'

Spiric could only let out a low moan in response, already fading back into the waves of memory. A feverish argument reached his ears before he went. One voice was unfamiliar, the other belonged to Grethard.

'You call this a levy!? This is strong-armed theft!'

His vision warped, the night turning back into day, a wafting field of unharvested wheat before him. The woman he'd just fought stood before him, her fists clenched, the same burning hatred in her eyes. But now she was less frail, only restrained by the hunch-backed old man that grasped at her shoulders. Rage and hubris swirled into him as Grethard's words came out of her mouth.

Spiric felt his face twitch. He wanted to taunt her, to goad her to fight, to put her out of her prideful misery and make a final example of her. But then she cooled. Whatever that crippled elder had whispered in her ear calmed her rage and a part of Spiric wished he could've heard it, too. Anything to put out the fire that Arallak had instilled in him, the never-ending rage that would have him follow his brother's footsteps. But Spiric's indecision was something he'd become skilled at repressing. He had no choice now. She still wouldn't pay the tithe.

Spiric turned to the dozen of his red-robed guards and nodded once. With a practiced grace, they lowered their torches, touching them to the edge of the field. The two farmers didn't flinch. There was nothing they could do. Flame took to the field as a single wave, sweeping its hell to the horizon in seconds. When ash finally fell from the air, Spiric drew one last breath, readying the words he was sworn to.

'If you wish to banish us, then you banish the rains.'

They were words he didn't want to say. But it was his duty to say them. They were the words that echoed across The Hytharo Empire. The words that gave them unquestioned power.

The scene flashed with blinding fire and he was back in the

avenue, the woman now collapsed at his feet. An ornate sword was in Spiric's grip, its very tip at her chin. She was breathing hard, a crude dagger lying discarded and useless at her side. He blinked and suddenly his blade was thrust into the sky, his other hand braced at its pommel as he pushed a rune into it. Lightning lanced out from the blade and over the heads of the gathered crowd as he roared the words again, another grandiose display of his raw power.

'If you wish to banish us, then you banish the rains!'

The crowd cheered. Spiric revelled in it. The fame of his first execution would be a rite of passage that counted him among the highest of the Hytharo. It was an intoxicating ecstasy, blocking out those in the gathering that cowered among the jubilation. Spiric turned as he drank it in, not seeing the look of pitiful disdain flash across Arallak's face as he turned his back and disappeared into the crowd.

Darkness crawled in from the edge of his vision, until Arallak's retreating back was the only form he could see. As he tried to focus on it, his red cloak billowed, flickering to black until the two forms separated, walking at each other's side across rippling and burnt sand. Spiric followed them, barely able to make out the words they whispered.

'I want to take up your offer. This has gone too far. It's a suffering too great to witness.'

'Then what do you propose?' The other voice was low and soft, a man's that seemed to echo through to Spiric out of order.

'I propose what you propose. What you told me you've done before.'

They both stopped and faced each other, but Spiric couldn't make out the other man's features, something holding him back from drawing closer. Beyond them, a wall of black stone cast them both in an almost perfect silhouette.

'You'd want to be forgotten?' the black-cloaked man asked.

Arallak nodded, a grim tone taking over. 'I want all to be forgotten. Our sins and their suffering at the hands of them, erased as one.'

A moment of silence let his words drift.

'The cost to both of us will be devastating.'

'A cost others have paid a thousand times before.'

## CHAPTER SIXTEEN

# FRAGMENTATION

A DELICATE CLATTER OF clay on metal tweaked in Spiric's ears. Far off, someone muttered under their breath, but he didn't care about it. It was like he'd lived another lifetime after his last moments outside the golden dome. But it wasn't another lifetime, was it? It was his. The faces of those he'd remembered flashed through his mind in an instant, gone as fast as they'd come, except for Arallak's.

*Because he's my brother.*

The thought jerked Spiric awake and he tried to thrash, but something restrained him. His vision was blurry, but he could see the thick leather straps tight at his wrists and shoulders, his bare chest covered in blood and raw flesh. He tried again to free himself, but more bindings across his legs and at his neck bit into his skin.

An old man suddenly appeared in his view, his pale face contrasting against the dark stone ceiling as he began making a shushing noise, his yellow eyes focused on Spiric's chest.

'Three more, my boy, just three more and you can flail all you like.'

'Three what!?' Spiric grunted. 'Where am I?'

The man grumbled to himself as he leaned closer to Spiric's chest and a sudden, precise burst of pain made him gasp in agony. They straightened up, inspecting a tiny shard of rock held in a pair of bloody tweezers.

'Two more fragments of what appears to be a paralict that you've done something impossible with.'

He dropped the piece into a metal bowl somewhere off to Spiric's right and stooped back closer to Spiric's chest. 'I thought I would prefer you to be awake and your friend asleep, but it looks like you're both determined to make a racket down here.'

Another strike of pain and Spiric ground his teeth against it, holding his scream out of spite. He twisted his head, catching sight of Byreth in the corner of the cluttered subterranean room. She was slumped in a chair, out cold and half-hidden by a table laden with strange surgical tools.

'What have you done to her!?'

There was a clink, then a creak as the man straightened up, wincing as he tried to hold a hand to his lower back.

'I wore her out. I told her to go with your friends, but she was determined to remain at your side. All questions, she was, and when she ran out of those, she never stopped talking. Nearly had to tie her down because she kept trying to help.' He glanced down at Spiric's chest, a pitiful grimace flashing across his face. 'She did her best, I just hope that her best has not harmed you for good. Whatever happened to you requires an experienced hand to properly mend, but you'll have some scars from it.'

'She saved me?'

The man nodded. 'A day of firsts, by the sounds of it. A Hytharo detonating a respark, killing more than a dozen Scythes and then surviving thanks to the ministrations of what I could only describe as a keen and foolish novice. It's certainly unusual.'

'I've got used to it,' he said darkly.

The man removed one more piece, the largest by the feel of it, and held it in Spiric's sight.

'A souvenir, perhaps?'

Spiric shook his head quickly. The man shrugged and pocketed it, then began working on the many restraints that held him down. As he was slowly freed, he went to sit up, but a stiff pain in his chest stopped him.

'At least you are still eager,' the man said. 'But you'll have to temper yourself a little while longer. I almost had to piece you back together like a puzzle. The last boy I saved in a state like this went on to destroy Revance. I only hope you won't go on to be involved in a similar catastrophe.'

Bitter memories lingered in Spiric's mind. 'I fear I already have.'

The angst was short-lived as Byreth's corner of the room exploded into a clattering avalanche of instruments. She emerged from it, shaking a fist at the man in an almost comical way.

'Dammit, Greely! I told you to wake me when he came to!'

'And I told you it was rude to ask things of people they do not want to do,' the healer snapped back. He turned away from Byreth as she untangled herself from the mess she'd made, cursing under his breath as he offered Spiric his tunic.

His hands shook as he took it, his fingers barely able to close around the firm leather.

'A weakness that may only be temporary. We can only hope. I've seen some lose a certain sense of touch after brushes with a respark or other similar energies. You'll need your strength according to the tall tales Byreth has regaled me with.'

'They weren't tall tales!' Byreth snapped as she made her way over. 'They're true!'

Greely rolled his eyes as he set about gathering the tools off the floor. Byreth took the opportunity to help Spiric get his tunic on. As gentle as she attempted to be, it simply wasn't something in her nature. Not that Spiric expected anything else.

'I tried to stitch up all the leather, but I probably did about as good a job as Greely said I did on your chest.'

Dark splotches stained nearly every inch of the tunic's front and Byreth's rough needlework had practically turned the garment into a rough shawl. He tried to get to his feet, but Byreth shoved him back onto the cot.

'You're lucky to be alive, you know that, right? Quit squirming around and tell us what the hell happened before you pass out again.'

Spiric shook his head, another wave of dizziness stunning him for a second. 'Once the others are here.' Talking was hard enough now he was sitting up and he couldn't imagine being able to do it more than once.

Byreth stared at him for a while, almost too long, until she reluctantly yielded. 'Back at the dome, when we were in there, you just disappeared when you started messing around with the respark, the big one down that hole along with it. The air was just suddenly smoky, kind of like after you throw a couple runes around and by the time we'd found our way out of the dark in there, you were just... bleeding out in the sand. I don't know what you did to all those Scythes, but the state they were in...'

This was something he could recall perfectly. The scene outside the dome overlapped with his memory atop the fortress walls for just a second, fused together by the stench of burnt flesh.

'I thought you were a goner for sure and all Tetran cared

about was finding the respark you had. I didn't even think I could save you, there was no chance but Grethard... he was yelling at me like you were his only son. It took me and Tetran almost an hour to piece you back together as well as I could, but even then, it wasn't going to hold for long. I thought... I thought...'

'But you did it,' Spiric said, drawing a painful, shuddering breath. 'I'm alive.'

She nodded, kneading at her tired eyes with balled-up fists. 'I'd given up on that. Grethard wanted to try carrying you here to Basarod through the air, but it would've torn you apart. We just had to chuck you onto Tetran's bloody arcanite like dead weight and leg it. It took too long as it was, then the bastard at the gate wouldn't let us in until we coughed up a fortune, then we had to go in—'

'Through the catacombs,' Spiric finished.

Byreth cocked her head at the word and from the other side of the room, Greely did the same.

'Precious few know this place by an ancient name like that,' he said slowly. 'Byreth told me the tale of your... displacement, but I didn't think it possible.'

'I've been here before.'

Greely continued tending to the wounds on Spiric's arms, muttering questions under his breath the whole time, not even giving him a chance to answer. Another painful hour passed before Greely had finished his ministrations and by then Byreth had fallen asleep again.

'I need to speak to Grethard, the old man I was with.' Spiric said.

A moment's pause was followed by a glum nod as Greely glanced towards the door. 'All in good time, young Spiric. But there is another who sees it more important to speak to you first.'

The iron door burst open as if on cue, the sound of the reverberating clang enough to wake Byreth and almost knock Spiric from the bloodstained cot. Four guards wearing chainmail over grey robes burst in, long cannons slung across their back as a pair each roughly picked up Spiric and Byreth, despite Greely's futile cries for calm.

Spiric tried to protest, to struggle, to flail with what little energy he had left, but he might as well have been a child throwing a tantrum for all the guards cared. With a firm grip on each arm, they hauled him through darkened sandstone corridors. At the first junction the guards that were struggling to restrain Byreth split off, her vigorous protests echoing behind Spiric as he was hauled away. The walls were occasionally interrupted by breaches that leaked sand or carved alcoves that held daises bearing stacks of skulls.

*Hytharo skulls.*

Their last stand had been a failure. He'd survived, but from the memory of the masses pressing at the walls of the fortress, it wouldn't have been for long if not for a way out. But now whoever these guards were seemed to be retracing those steps with unnerving accuracy.

The tunnels grew more and more familiar as vents began to pour light over their heads. Whoever wanted this badly to speak to him could only be interested in one thing. The one thing that he and his people had lorded over so many others.

*Rain.*

## CHAPTER SEVENTEEN

# VICEROY

I T WASN'T MUCH LONGER until the guards relinquished
him. They'd roughly shoved him towards one last door they
didn't seem to have the guts to barge through before turning
their backs, almost like they were about to stop another rush of
intruders.

Spiric glanced at his wrist. He still had a few runes left, but the
flash of anger begging for him to use them cooled quickly. The
smell of burning skin still haunted him and this tunnel already
stank badly enough without him adding to it.

With his left hand he pulled back the rusted latch, a stinging
twinge of pain shooting up his arm as he did so. Blazing sunlight

washed across his skin as the door swung outwards on its own weight, leaving him blinking for a moment as his eyes adjusted.

A set of stone steps lay ahead of him, each one so narrow that he had to walk on the balls of his feet as he ascended. He almost wished the guards had been ordered to carry him up these, too. They curved tightly to the right before he was exposed to the full force of the setting sun.

It didn't matter that he was half-blinded by it. He knew exactly where he was.

The sandstone crenelations of Basarod's fortress walls were awash with the sunset's brilliant orange glow. While time had taken its toll, the masonry was still perfectly interlocked. He lingered near them, daring himself to look over the edge, to where he'd spat deadly volleys of lightning only yesterday.

*At least, it felt like yesterday.*

With all his will, Spiric tore himself away from it. A woman sat a dozen paces away in an ornately carved wooden chair, its twin opposite her as she beckoned him with a wave, almost purposely not meeting his eyes.

Spiric approached and as much as his aching chest pleaded him to, he didn't take the seat.

'Where are my friends?' he said, his voice still sounding weak.

'They are not important,' the woman said dismissively.

She still didn't look at him. The other side of the wall bore no barrier to the yawning drop into the town and she continued to stare into the heart of the clustered network of stone terraces and tight alleyways. Her hair hung short and loose in curling blonde locks that dazzled in the sunlight, held in place by a thin silver circlet, the beads and jewels embroidered into her ever-folding white robes complementing the effect.

Her skin was the thing that drew Spiric's attention. It was pale, paler than his, to the point it was hard to see where the fabric ended and the nape of her neck began. All others he'd seen so far in this land looked to have been bronzed by the sun from their first steps.

'I wouldn't be alive if it wasn't for them,' Spiric said.

A small huff escaped the woman, almost as if he'd somehow missed the point. 'Do you like these chairs?'

The question seemed bizarre to Spiric as he lowered himself into one. 'What's special about them?'

Only now did she look at him, her brilliant green eyes piercing his soul. 'They are of wood.'

'So?'

She smirked slightly, shaking her head without breaking her gaze. 'Something you may be familiar with, almost dismissive of, but practically impossible to find in our time. Just like you. I wanted to see how you would treat it. Most would be in awe at the grain of it, the craftsmanship poured into such a rare commodity. I wanted to see if the stories I had been fed by the exiled scholar calling himself your teacher were true. That you were from another time. And it looks as if he was right.'

'His name is Grethard,' Spiric said, keeping his voice cool.

'I do recall him saying,' she replied. 'I was only a child when I heard of his exile. He was one of the last scholars insane enough to search for a shadow dancer before the Academy clamped down on it. Not a particularly subtle man. Barging into the halls of Reyat and waving around a page of runes, asking about Hytharo myths. I found out quickly of your presence with one of the healers down in the catacombs. It piqued my interest, to say the least. A boy out of time, out of sand, and long outside his people. I had to see who you are. Who you had been.'

Her last words lingered in Spiric's mind. For her, they were two separate questions, but these new memories had confirmed his quiet worry that the answer would be one and the same.

'I need to know who you are first,' Spiric replied, stalling. 'If I can trust you.'

Another sigh escaped her lips, a prelude to a well-worn answer. 'I am the Viceroy of Basarod, Arch-Mesos of the Order of Reyat and Honorary Apex of the League of Revance. My name is Voss-Ela, and all your naked eye can see from this citadel has been mine and my family's domain to protect for twelve generations. Not since the disappearance of the Hytharo has one with red eyes set foot in this domain. Not until today. Both your past and your future will have an incalculable effect on this place and the people that call it home. This is why, today, you are far more important than those that brought you here. Why I must understand how you came to be.'

It took a while for Spiric to digest all these titles. Eventually a voice in his mind that sounded eerily like Grethard's was urging him caution, in spite of the old man having done the complete opposite himself.

'There's not much I remember about my past. Flashes of it have been coming back as the days go by.' He glanced again at the crenelations. 'This place was our last stand. There were so few of us left that, were it not for these walls, we would've been overwhelmed by those that hunted us down.'

'Mythos states they were hunting for rain. Desperate for it as the Hytharo dwindled to nothing. Between what little the Order of Reyat and the Academy have uncovered over the years, the act of bringing rain must've involved some form of sacrifice on the Hytharo's part.'

'Arallak's sacrifice won't be in vain.' The phrase escaped him as a whisper, a confirmation that the memory was real.

Voss-Ela had caught the words. 'Was Arallak the last Hytharo? The one that locked water into the air? Or the first? Folklore calls them the Rakel-Nyn, but I always thought it more a title.'

'I don't know,' Spiric said quietly. 'But he was my brother.'

She let the silence between them linger, each moment a tempting tendril that jabbed at his mind, waiting to grab another detail. His eyes lost focus of his knees as all the memories flashed through his mind again, but he kept his mouth bolted shut.

'Could you undo it?' Voss-Ela eventually said. 'Bring rain

again?'

'You would ask that sacrifice of me so soon?'

She tilted her head slightly, ready to deflect his question. 'It's natural for me to ask. Do you understand what you mean to us? Men and women have sacrificed their lives here and across the land to research every strange manner of paralict that has been pulled from the ruins of those-of-glass, to explore every untested combination of runes in the slim chance of producing a single drop of water. But with you... With rain... You could be the great equaliser. Reels would no longer control the land. Magic would not be constrained to those who lay claim to the water, or the pumps used to extract them. People wouldn't have to labour as they currently do. Imagine what we could create, Spiric!'

'An empire.'

'An empire?' Voss-Ela repeated, this time perplexed.

'Do you know who the Hytharo were?' Spiric shot at her. 'What this world was before we all disappeared?'

There was another pause as she gathered herself. 'Do you not remember?'

'I think I've remembered enough,' he said. 'But I want to know what you think it was like.'

'That's the problem, Spiric. We don't know. Whatever wiped out the Hytharo took along any record or recollection with it. It was as if they wanted to be forgotten.'

'We did. Our sins and their suffering at the hands of them,

erased as one.' Spiric drew a long breath, one that filled his chest and made the fresh scars across his skin tense and tingle. 'The Hytharo ruled by their control of rain. It was the great equaliser, setting everyone under the Hytharo. We controlled whose fields would grow, which plains would be flooded, which people were allowed to survive, all under a levy, one we enforced with lightning and death. So, you would have to tell me, would this happen again?'

Voss-Ela slouched in her chair, staring at the last moments of the setting sun with a single thin finger at her lips, deep in thought. 'Are you familiar with molten flux? There was an era not so long ago where the substance was almost as valuable as water. A catastrophe not so long after extinguished the flux from this land, but those who gained extraordinary wealth from it still possessed their fortunes, along with the control that came with it. Some remain to this day, having inherited the fortune of their forebears to continue to shape the society around them. An unfortunate consequence Basarod must still deal with.'

'So if I were to make it rain, I wouldn't be allowed to live. My capacity to control the rain would have me controlled by someone else.' Spiric paused for a moment, the next words on his tongue already feeling like a foolish blunder. 'Someone like you.'

She glanced across at him, her next question coming quick. 'Can you make it rain?'

'I wouldn't even know where to start.'

It started as a low snort, nothing more than a giggle, before Voss-Ela dissolved into a riotous cackle, almost sliding out of her seat as she clutched at her sides. 'You've been leading me on! Oh, for mercy's sake, here I was expecting you to stand up and open the skies on top of us!'

A small chuckle escaped Spiric. He couldn't help joining her. In a way, he'd been expecting just as much of himself these past few days. As Voss-Ela collected herself, she had to wave away the pair of guards who had appeared at the stairway, her gaze returning to Spiric with a warmth that hadn't been present before.

'I suppose we would need to help you rediscover just that. We can leave whether or not the return of rain and the Hytharo is a good idea once we have the means to answer that very question. It will take time and study, though with the Order of Reyat at my disposal, it may only be a matter of days. Besides, you'll need to use this time to rest. I've never heard of anyone tangling with nearly two dozen Scythes and being the sole survivor.'

She circled a finger in the air lazily, and it was soon followed by the sound of clanking coming up the rampart. A sleek machine appeared, a construction of finely twisted silver rods and thin plates of bronze, striding on six elegant legs.

Spiric eyed it off as it approached, unconsciously rising from his seat. The seemingly headless mechanical beast didn't even come up to his waist, but there was a certain power about it, like that of a tensed coil.

'My arcanite will lead you to my guest residence where your companions are also quartered. It will also collect you in the morning to bring you to the Halls of Reyat. You will be free to wander the city and I shall see to it that you are all well looked after. All I ask in return is to be an observer of any studies or research you may undertake here. Never before has the world had a second chance at the Hytharo.'

'I can only hope things turn out differently.'

'If it saves Basarod from coming under siege like it did in your time, then we can share the same goal.' She reached into her robes and produced a thin leather pouch, barely the size of her palm, and held it out to Spiric between two fingers.

Inside were a pair of copper-rimmed glasses, the perfectly rounded lenses so deeply tinted they reminded him of the shadow dancer's eyes. They were a much finer instrument than Byreth's goggles and when he donned them, they didn't dull the world one bit.

'Please do me a favour and keep a low profile. Maybe teach that madcap you call a mentor how to do the same.'

'I'll... I'll do my best,' Spiric stammered. The chances of him teaching Grethard something new were about the same as another Hytharo appearing before him.

The arcanite set off without warning, forcing Spiric to catch up with something between a limp and a jog as they descended the ramparts. He had to assume it was under Voss-Ela's control, as it seemed keen to lead him through the heart of the city rather than force him back into those suffocating tunnels.

The streets couldn't be more than a metre or two wide, enclosed on either side by two- or three-story terraces of fine bricks, each one pressed so close to their neighbours that they swelled from the pressure. Balconies of wrought iron loomed overhead, most occupied by steadily burning braziers that wafted charred meat into the air.

The thoroughfare bustled with Basarod's people, filing into the city from the enormous gate with dirt painted across their faces and bales of hay or some other crop of dried long grass slung across their back.

It was almost like being back in Kurkress, but instead of catching snippets of snide complaints and mutinous murmuring, there was an aura of good spirits, almost jolly despite the hard work they were returning from. Those who disappeared into houses just as soon reappeared and were quickly invited into someone else's.

When blocks of market stalls presented themselves, they were a riot of colours, the variety of hues matched by all the different wares that were getting constantly replaced. For a moment Spiric thought he'd even seen someone sell a book! He'd assumed the act would be too bizarre for this new age to occur in public.

Despite the chaos of the streets, the arcanite found no trouble cutting a path through. Most people stared after they'd leapt out of the way, but their eyes were more drawn to the arcanite than the blood-spattered boy limping after it.

One of the clothing stalls he passed had what looked like an exact replica of his tunic, but when he reached for his satchel, he realised it was gone. He could only hope the others had it because the tunic could do with a replacement, unless Byreth also knew of a way to wash out blood without water.

As the arcanite led him closer to the centre of the city, the buildings shifted from sandstone to marble. From tight clusters to well-spaced blocks of land, each on its own tier of a hillside leading up to a castle of pure white stone at the top. Lampposts of ornately moulded bronze now lined new pathways, flameless globes of orange light casting an infinite sunset into the night.

Spiric was out of breath when the arcanite finally cut off the street and walked up to the double doors of one of the residences.

*Of course it had to be right at the top of the hill.*

It was practically next to the damn castle. His chest was aching as if his scars had torn open. It was a shame that rulers like Voss-Ela didn't keep their quarters right next to the city walls. Maybe he could request that in exchange for making it rain, as well.

Reaching for the door handles was a futile exercise as the arcanite had already managed to twist them with its two front legs. It led him only a few steps inside before it stopped dead in its tracks and folded itself into a neat metal box, right in the middle of the entryway.

'At least I can't trip over Tetran's bloody arcanite as easily,' he muttered to it.

He moved over it carefully, the smooth marble floor slippery beneath his feet. More orange lamps lined the hall, smaller than on the lampposts but just as bright. The space was so large that each footstep echoed off the chiselled stone slabs underfoot, with passageways branching off from both walls, the back of the hall dedicated to a mezzanine that led straight to a balcony.

A thick layer of dust coated the floor that was interrupted by trails of bootprints that wandered from room to room. Even one of the couches that was pressed against the wall bore a few footprints.

Spiric took a few more steps forward before the sound of another pair of boots reached his ears. There was a particularly metallic clank about them, and his suspicions were confirmed when Byreth appeared from one of the hallways, her expression bursting into an almost overjoyed grin when she recognised him.

Before he could say a single word, she'd dashed across the hall and thrown him into a crushing bear hug, so tight he could only grunt in pain.

'Byreth!' Spiric sputtered. 'Let... go!'

She gave him one last squeeze before relinquishing him. 'We all thought you were dead.'

'The others are here?' Spiric gasped, still regaining his breath.

'Yes, we are. And we've been waiting quite some time.'

Spiric looked up to see Grethard at the mezzanine, leaning on the railing with a stony expression. Tetran was next to him. At least she looked slightly relieved to see him.

'You had us quite worried.'

## CHAPTER EIGHTEEN

# BY INVITATION ONLY

'I 'VE REMEMBERED MORE, GRETHARD. More than I think I ever wanted to.'

It was early the next morning and the sun still awaiting its first call to action. Spiric had found Grethard perched against the railing of the balcony that opened into their temporary lodgings, the old man's crinkled eyes still set on the darkened horizon to the east as he joined him. Fields of hardy grey crops lay before them. How they'd taken root in the loose dunes of this land was beyond Spiric, yet the denizens of Basarod were already among the rows tending to them.

'Surely that's a good thing, is it not?' Grethard replied. 'We set out in search of your memories, after all.'

Spiric nodded, a slump settling across his shoulders. 'That's what I'd thought too. But now I wish I'd never tried in the first place.'

Grethard glanced down at him, still not turning his body away from the view. 'Not liking what you've found?'

'I was a murderer. A tool for a tyrant. An executioner.'

To Spiric's surprise, the old man didn't waver.

'I had worried as much. A people of good deeds would not go to whatever lengths the Hytharo appear to have taken in order to be forgotten.'

Grethard took in a shallow breath, glanced at him once more, then turned away, idling towards one of the wrought-iron chairs scattered about the balcony. Spiric moved to join him, lowering himself into the seat just as gingerly as his mentor had.

'Byreth told me you were hauled off to speak to someone. I assume it was with our sponsor who's provided us with these lodgings?'

'Yes. Voss-Ela. Leader of Basarod, the Order of Reyat, and something about Revance, I didn't catch the rest.'

Grethard let out a low whistle. 'You certainly got the attention of someone important. I can only guess what she wanted from you,' he added sardonically.

'Rain. Just as everyone else has.' Spiric could barely hide the exasperation from his voice. 'I told her I couldn't remember, but I'm not sure if she fully believes me.' He looked up, the disappointment for their host apparent on Grethard's face. 'She agreed to help me,' he quickly offered. 'At least for what the runes meant.'

'Do you trust her?'

He was about to say he did, but then a worm of doubt appeared in his mind. Of the idea of being under the thumb of yet another ruler.

*Why is that feeling so familiar?*

'I trust you.'

A raised eyebrow was the only response Spiric received before Grethard began probing his new memories. Reliving them a second time was more painful than the first. Every answer Spiric gave prompted Grethard to ask why he would have acted in a certain way or how he felt about being in that situation. Despite the analytical nature of the carefully worded questions, Spiric soon found himself comfortably mulling over them in the silence the old man provided after posing them. It was like he wasn't interested in the answer himself, but in helping Spiric find it.

'So Arallak was your brother,' Grethard mused. 'The most likely reason he saved you. But it doesn't explain the others you were with. Why save them? If that's what you think he was doing.'

It was another matter that Spiric hadn't considered, another drop of fuel driving the incoherent yearning to find Arallak again. 'I'm not sure. I still don't understand how he would've made *us* forget our pasts, as well. Or even why?'

'Meddling with memory is something beyond the magic of the living, but if you saw him meet another shadow dancer...' Grethard trailed off, unable to meet Spiric's eyes. 'A deal with a shadow dancer is always a dangerous thing.'

'Like the one I've made myself?'

The old man chuckled. 'I think the difference is that he needs you. Make sure to keep it that way.'

'But he's my brother.'

'Does he know that?'

'No.'

'Then you'd best tell him.'

'Whose brother are you talking about?'

Byreth's sharp voice almost cut Spiric's nerves in two and he twisted to see her coming up the stairs of the mezzanine inside. While she was bleary-eyed, being half asleep hadn't affected her hearing.

'My brother,' Grethard said calmly. 'Spiric reminds me of him from when I was a boy. His age, in fact.'

'And where is he now?' Byreth said. She pulled up another metal chair, not flinching from the jarring scrape of its metal feet as it was dragged across the floor.

'Dead for all I know,' he said with a shrug. 'Didn't get a chance to tell him where I was going when I was exiled.'

A dour look crossed Byreth's face that only Spiric saw. Grethard had already pottered off, muttering something about breakfast, though where he'd find that in this bustling city was beyond Spiric. It left the two of them stewing in a tense silence Byreth had no intention of breaking.

'I hope your brother's not dead,' Spiric said.

'Why the hell do you even care?' Byreth snapped back. 'You're a Hytharo! All this travelling, this house, everything is for you. Why would my stupid brother even matter to you, compared to all that!?'

'Because all my family is dead,' he said softly. 'Long dead. I can't even remember their names, let alone have a hope of finding them. You've still got hope. I only have echoes, and sometimes... sometimes I feel like finding your brother might be like finding mine, because I know nothing else in this world.'

Byreth wouldn't look at him, her tone still surly. 'You don't mean that.'

'I do. Just so I can find something that's alive.'

The sun gained a few more inches on the horizon before Spiric's next question.

'Why did he want to get into The Lightning Cage, anyway?'

She gave a derisive snort. 'Same as anyone else, looting.'

'But if no one else could get in, well, aside from Grethard, why did he think he stood a chance?' Spiric mused on the question silently for a while before adding: 'Did he say anything else, leave anything behind? Maybe he was going to a different place?'

A slow nod took her head like a metronome as she chewed her

lip. 'Yeah... "A place where time stands still..." Some waster said it to him and then he wouldn't shut up about it. I've still got no idea what it meant. I've just been looking for places like that, but found nothing. It's what led me to Kurkress, then Leerukhart got her claws into me.'

Boundless speculation ensued, fuelled by Byreth's unending supply of grim rumours about the Scythes of the Breggesan Academy, only stopping when Tetran interrupted them. Voss-Ela's bronze arcanite stood at her side, its front legs tapping the ground in an eager rhythm.

'It wants us to follow,' she said. 'I doubt the Viceroy is a patient woman.'

'I hope she doesn't mind I'm still wearing this,' Spiric said as he stood up, flakes of dried blood wafting from his slashed tunic. At least he'd been able to keep his travelling cloak to throw over it, though it hadn't completely escaped the bloodletting. 'Did anyone get my satchel? I wouldn't mind buying a new set of clothes.'

'Buy new!?' Byreth guffawed. 'Is wasting reels a Hytharo thing?'

Spiric glanced at the rough workings of Byreth's garments as they walked to the front door and resisted the urge to laugh back.

'If they don't like looking at you, it's on them to do something about it,' Tetran said.

As if it were waiting for her cue, a hatch on top of the

bronze arcanite's body sprung open and it trotted to Spiric's side, showing off a perfectly clean outfit.

'It's like she heard you!' Byreth chuckled.

'Kretatics can do that,' Tetran warned. 'Metal can do a lot more than just walk.'

Spiric ignored her, gingerly pulling the garments out of the arcanite and trying not to get his fingers caught in the rapidly spinning gizmos that made up its guts. 'It's kind of her, either way. I'll have to pay her back.'

'I doubt she would've needed to pay for them in the first place,' Byreth muttered.

Spiric got changed in the privacy of his own bedroom after waving off Byreth's offers to help, regretting it with every twinge of pain brought by the act of disrobing and then dressing himself. A polished metal wardrobe was the closest thing he could find to a mirror in the room, but the hazy reflection allowed him to assess his new garments well enough.

The only thing Voss-Ela hadn't thought to send over were a new pair of shoes, so he hoped his once-regal travelling boots would look the part. They still bore the stains of his run-in with the Scythes, but this served to tastefully darken their appearance.

Next was a pair of darkened crimson trousers, the length of each leg so long that he had to tuck them into his boots to avoid tripping on the hem. The pockets at either side of his waist were either unfinished or bottomless due to some unfamiliar tradition, yet Spiric could not discern the point of the latter, unless it was to allow him to scratch his thighs or backside more directly.

A weaved belt of tanned leather held the trousers in place. It had been made for a man twice Spiric's size, judging by the fact he had to loop it around his waist just as many times. At least the white shirt covered this. It had yellowed slightly from age, but it was a sure sight better than his ruined tunic.

It ran long down his torso, its hem stopping a few inches before his knees with a split on either side to stop it from turning into a dress. Putting it on had been a puzzle in itself. Instead of each side buttoning up in the middle, it was a complex dance of folding one end of the fabric into the opposite side's hip, then blindly operating a series of hooks to keep it together.

The final outer seam ran up his right side, tapering off at his breast to meet at his neck and forming a small collar there. It was sleeveless and hugged at his form, exaggerating what little muscle he held in his shoulders as if his figure was meant to match Byreth's.

Before leaving, he decided to throw his travelling cloak over the outfit, despite the stains it bore. It was only marked on the inside, and at least this would hide the runes still prominent on his left arm, along with the freshly welted scars the respark had given him.

When he stepped out into the main living area, he found Grethard instead of Byreth and Tetran. Before Spiric could ask the question, Grethard was already answering it.

'Apparently it's just us today.'

Spiric glanced past him and spotted the two guards from the day before waiting at the manor entrance, Voss-Ela's contraption tapping away impatiently next to them.

'So where did they—'

'They said they had business in the city,' Grethard whispered, quiet enough that the guards didn't catch on. 'Better to lie low,' he added with a wink.

The bronze arcanite's path was shorter and much more direct today. A wide, stepped road led up to the palace atop the hill, trafficked by nobles clad in fine garments. They stared and sniffed at Spiric's ill-fitting clothes, and from behind Voss-Ela's glasses, he stared back. None of them even flinched, meaning his red eyes were hidden.

They snaked through grand marble archways that stood free of any structure, markers of the Viceroy's status at every steep curve of the stairs. The palace's grand entrance was blockaded by a scrum of finely dressed advisors and petitioners, each one waiting their turn to debate the worth of their supposedly far-flung journey to the enormous guards that braced against the well-reasoned throng.

With vigorous use of elbows, the pair of guards escorting Spiric and Grethard cut through, handing them off with relief to those charged with protecting the palace and disappearing back to their more mundane duties.

The bronze armour of these guards had been forged with similar intricacy as that of their arcanite escort. They were led by a man who towered naturally over the crowd, his dominating presence matching his etched-in scowl, not a single hair present on his exposed head. He waded through the assembled ranks of his soldiers and pulled Spiric and Grethard through to the much calmer antechamber as Voss-Ela's arcanite followed.

'Apex Shiro, Palace Keeper,' he said, forcefully shaking Grethard's unwilling hand. There was something in his tone that made his title sound more like an arduous curse. 'Not often Voss-Ela has me waiting for a guest. Can you share why she invited you?'

Grethard snatched his hand back, his knuckles cracking as he massaged them back into place. 'If she's not told you, I feel we may not be at liberty to say.'

Shiro grimaced and gave a sharp nod. 'Clever answer.' He turned his attention to Spiric, his deep blue eyes drilling through the tint of his glasses. The man raised an eyebrow and Spiric's heart leapt.

*Can he see my eyes?*

'I can feel your heart racing through my feet, as if you're hiding something.'

Spiric glanced up at Grethard before answering. 'Like he said, if she hasn't told you...'

Shiro gave out a frustrated sigh and it seemed to make him shrink by about a foot. But the man quickly recovered. He led them deeper into the palace, pushing through a second set of impossibly heavy doors with a grunting effort.

From the outside, Spiric had perceived the palace as a squat structure, its grand qualities embodied by its fine stonework rather than its burgeoning size. But within, the latter was represented by the enormous plummeting staircases that drove deep into the ground for six tiers. Tall archways, replicas of those lining the path outside, flanked each landing, growing higher and higher from their base at each tier to support a ceiling that stretched out into the distance.

The palace was already situated high over the lands below, but the cavernous hall between Spiric and the open air made it feel so much higher. There was no wall at the opposite side of the cavernous chamber, only pillars on either side that were as thick as houses, which stretched up the entire six floors that the stairs had descended, perfectly framing the view in its archway. Enormous red dunes rolled across the foreground, so immense they were mountains in their own right, receding to the horizon until they were as insignificant as the creases of a bedsheet.

Something nagged at Spiric as he savoured the sight. It was either familiarity or vertigo. He couldn't tell. He'd stood in Basarod in his past, he had the memories to prove it, so why couldn't he remember this sprawling vista?

*Maybe this place was built after the Hytharo.*

The thought hadn't left his mind when a flash of darkened skies crossed his vision, the silhouette of a dark shape towering over the lands beyond. Bright day returned as Grethard's hand clapped down on his shoulder and wrenched him from his vision, an unplaceable grief lingering in his throat.

'They make us come up that big steep path only to have us go all the way back down?' Grethard grumbled.

Apex Shiro nodded. 'I'd rather traverse the Spine Mountains than patrol this palace, but that doesn't pay reels. Whoever built this place was long before our time, maybe even long before all that damn sand was out there, too. The slightest breeze and the staircases are covered.'

'What do you do in a sandstorm?' Spiric asked.

'Accept that we will be buried.'

## CHAPTER NINETEEN

---

# AN HONOURED GUEST

---

Apex Shiro led Grethard and Spiric's ascent, the sound of his clanking armour almost drowning out the ringing nerves growing in Spiric's ears. Down below, a small amphitheatre sat in the place of the last landing. It curved between the bases of the two pillars, each row looking down at the marble-slabbed clearing in the archway. The seats were jammed with robed spectators, their circulating murmurs breaking rhythm as they noticed the newcomers.

Their fresh and youthful faces began to twist into fruitless squints, and the attention made Spiric's guts lurch. Was he supposed to put on a show for them? The amphitheatre's clearing formed a perfect circle, almost completely deserted like a waiting stage, half of which stretched beyond the palace's shaded bounds as a grand balcony. The morning sun drenched this outer portion, making the marble almost blinding to look at.

Impatient and impertinent whispers reached Spiric's burning ears and he clenched his jaw. His hands twitched at his side as they passed through the crowd, aching to rip off the glasses and glare at those who were set to doubt him.

As they reached the bottom row he took a deep breath, his heart still throbbing. This pre-emptively injured pride wasn't his.

*It's nothing but a memory.*

Across the clearing was a small stone dais, surrounded by a crumbling wall of stone that was only knee high. It held a pool of sand, a sheet of stone rising through it, upon which sat Voss-Ela. She lounged in one of her treasured wooden chairs, the shade cloth positioned over it being her only mercy from the battering sun. She waved a single hand out from under the canopy, sunlight flashing her bright skin impossibly white, and the crowd crumpled into an unwilling silence.

Spiric felt a small nudge at his shoulder. He thought it was Grethard, yet the old man was already wedged in among the gathered crowd. It had come instead from Apex Shiro and its meaning was clear. He was to go alone.

The murmurs returned with a vengeance as Spiric walked

towards the dais.

'—just a boy? Basarod's streets are filled with boys like that!'

'—has to be political, a prince or some other kind of—'

'—the one Greely got dragged away to work on? I've not seen him since...'

Voss-Ela motioned her hand again, but she'd lost power over her audience. Another wave. Still no effect. Her wrist fell limp in frustration, mustering one last effort to flick in the direction of Apex Shiro.

'BE SILENT!'

His piercing roar made the ground beneath them tremble. Now, not even a whisper dared disobey. Spiric had stopped dead in his stride, half his body still in the shadow of the colossal archway, half beginning to prickle in the harsh sun as he regarded the quelled gathering. An expectation was written across their faces that teetered on the cusp of dissatisfaction. He looked back to Voss-Ela, and she lazily motioned him forward.

The sudden vastness of the sky above made Spiric unsteady on his feet. In the dim shadow that hid Voss-Ela's face, he could tell this was exactly the effect she desired. Surrounded by blinding light, the power of her throne could not be observed and examined. Being seen in this way was a plight endured only by those who approached her, their intent starkly illuminated for all to see.

He stopped short of the low wall surrounding the dais. His satchel sat in the sand on the other side, the leather shimmering in the sun's heat yet hidden from those gathered. Spiric to snatch it. He instead locked his stare with Voss-Ela's, her green eyes barely glimmering in the shade she was lording over him.

'Behind you is nearly the entire Order of Reyat. Exiles and dissenters of the Academy of Breggesa who have gathered in my city for nearly two generations. I am the first of my line to lead them and my offer to you will be their services. All I ask in exchange is for your destiny to be fulfilled.'

'But you haven't told them what I am. Why I'm here.'

Voss-Ela smiled, then shook her head.

'I think they'd have trouble believing me. They don't see me as one of their kind. A leader tends not to be one ready to learn, according to them. A view that only compounds with their recent struggle to accept me as the Arch-Mesos. Let them see you for who you are. To discover your worth by their own methods. It will prove yourself worthy of them. Prove me worthy of them. Then they shall help.' She nodded to his satchel. 'Your personal effects. I apologise for their confiscation. I would not have been able to marshal this opportunity for you if I had entrusted you and your inks with free reign in my city.'

He returned the smile and removed the glasses she'd given him. Halfway through, he let the motion slow, giving his two remaining power runes time to glint red in the sunlight. It was small, but Spiric had been watching for it. Expecting it. Voss-Ela had flinched.

'I hope I've earned your trust,' Spiric said softly, 'and that one day you will find mine.'

A sharp grimace came to her face, but Voss-Ela didn't let the expression linger long enough for the crowd to see it. Spiric took his satchel, the super-heated leather searing into his grip as he turned away from her. Once he was back in the merciful shade, he stopped, looking each member of the assembled crowd dead in the eyes.

The whispers came, accelerating to murmurs and then into a perplexed babble. Apex Shiro and the rest of his assembled palace guards looked just as confused, the Apex glancing between Spiric and the Viceroy, unsure if he should quell the crowd. As the racket grew louder, some even got to their feet to consult a neighbour in the next row.

The only person who was motionless was Grethard. He was still hunched forward in the front row, his expression unreadable. For every step of this journey, he'd warned Spiric against drawing attention, yet Spiric could remember that first day he'd proven himself a Hytharo. The way Grethard looked at him as a prize. A ticket to redemption. Only now the old, exiled scholar wasn't the one presenting Spiric to the world.

This small resentment of being a tool in someone else's ambitions had played in the back of Spiric's mind since they'd met. He hadn't been able to shake it, no matter how much Grethard had gone on to guide him and protect him as his own. Spiric glanced back at Voss-Ela. She was savouring a grin as the crowd threatened to dissolve into a riot. The destiny she promised was not his, but her own.

'Enough!' It was a woman's voice that cut through the commotion, old and pitching into a shriek. 'Enough of this!'

The assembled scholars resumed their seats and the shrill voice's owner emerged from the front row. She must've been twice Voss-Ela's age and three times that of her surrounding peers, a thinning crop of white hair fraying in every direction while a well-worn squint of pale yellow eyes homed in on Spiric. She would've been taller than him if not for the hunched stoop that necessitated a gnarled ivory cane.

The crowd's attention was fixed on her, each blow of the cane against the floor a thunderclap in the silence. Her garb was similar to what Spiric now wore, though a fine silk shawl took the place of a tattered and bloody travelling cloak. When she drew up to him, she brought with her a huffing breath of rotten poultry and even more rotten gums. Spiric pushed down a gasp of repulsion, trying not to retreat.

'Red eyes...'

More muttering took to the crowd, and Spiric resisted the urge to say something. He'd let this woman decide for herself before he showed his hand.

But instead, she sidestepped him, drawing Voss-Ela into her sight.

'What trick do you play, Viceroy? What are you attempting to pass off as discovery this time?'

'Mesos Braiyth, this is no trick!' Voss-Ela snapped back.

She was on her feet, her face now illuminated in the sun. 'As Arch-Mesos you have appointed me to direct the Order's studies, so today I direct you to this boy, for he represents something not a single one of us has seen before, the opportunity of a lifetime, as if the Rakel-Nyn had returned to walk among us.'

This was Voss-Ela's flourish, but it barely elicited a short round of whispers. Once it had quelled, the attention returned to Braiyth and she relished it in silence, fixing the Viceroy with a sickly-sweet smile.

'Don't think we are so easily fooled, my child.' Mesos Braiyth began to pace, addressing the crowd as if it were her own. 'We may not be able to return to great Breggesa, but word travels of each development and innovation they proclaim. The Academy has apparently refined their crystal works to produce hair-thin lenses of stained and coloured glass, small enough to be placed upon one's eye and not bring them blindness. I would hate to think you've been fraternising with those that would have us executed, if only for this cheap stunt.'

Spiric couldn't hold back a quiet chuckle.

*If she's worried about glass, she won't like where I was found.*

But he hadn't been quiet enough. Braiyth wheeled around to face him, her cane now brandished as an accusatory sabre.

'You find it funny because it's true, boy?'

He did his best to remain diplomatic. 'It's actually quite the opposite.'

'Bah!' Braiyth grunted, mercifully lowering her cane.

This elicited a small titter from the crowd, though it might've been at Spiric's expense. She hobbled over to him, her free left arm now exposed, the yellow runes upon it rapidly rearranging themselves.

'You will find that I am not one to be so easily fooled.'

She burned the four-rune axiom in her open palm to produce an orb devoid of light. It hovered an inch over her hand and she held it close to Spiric's temple. The skin on his neck began to crawl, but he did his best to hold the old woman's scowl. After a few uneasy seconds, she pulled away.

'No glass,' she announced to the crowd. 'Yet this may be some other form of magic.' She turned to Voss-Ela, her sickly-sweet smile returning to her face. 'I thank the Viceroy for our direction of study, it should keep us busy for an hour. If we are lucky.'

Voss-Ela scowled back, not saying a word as Braiyth hobbled away. Some of the crowd began to leave their seats, their once-excited murmurs now darkened with discontent. Spiric met Grethard's eyes, and the old man finally gave a reluctant nod.

'You're wrong!' Spiric cried out.

Mesos Braiyth stopped and turned, but she was the only one to do so.

'You know, you're the youngest person who's ever said that to me.'

'I can assure you I'm not.'

The old woman cackled back at him before she composed herself. She turned to the retreating crowd, beckoning them back with both arms.

'Come on then, everyone, let us see what amazing feats this boy can perform! He might just reach out for the skies and summon a storm into this very hall! Come! Show us, boy!'

Spiric unleashed a wide leer, the expression feeling alien on his face but so familiar in his mind. 'I would like nothing more.'

He turned his body, reaching his left hand back to the sky, just as the arrogant old hag had requested, and shifted a power rune into his palm. Spiric savoured the sight of her mirth turning to astonishment as sparks began to crackle in webs between his outstretched fingers.

Braiyth's shock infected the crowd as he let the power coalesce, holding it back until he was sure all were watching. It was worth the burning tingle that enveloped his entire arm, a sensation strong enough to make his heart pound faster than it ever had.

Spiric unleashed it, sending a jolting fork of energy into the sky over Voss-Ela's head along with a clap of thunder that echoed twice through the hall. The scent of scorched air lingered, further proof that what Spiric had done was as real as can be.

But the burning in his arm hadn't gone away. He looked back at it, ready to see it engulfed in flames, but instead it was twitching and jittering, the uncontrollable motion spreading quickly to his chest and legs before his body was suddenly no longer his to control.

As he fell, the last thing he saw was Voss-Ela standing on her ruling dais, frozen in a silent scream of utter defeat.

## CHAPTER TWENTY

# EXCITED DELIRIUM

G RETHARD'S WRINKLED FACE APPEARED in Spiric's vision, but the old man's signature combination of stomping boots and disgruntled muttering was incomprehensible. He didn't waste any time, snatching up Spiric's hand to bend and flex his fingers, asking if he felt anything. Spiric had to keep shaking his head, panic rising in his throat with each despondent answer.

'Looks like some kind of excited delirium,' Grethard announced as he kept testing Spiric's fingers.

'What's that?' Spiric croaked back.

Grethard shrugged and lowered his voice to a whisper. 'Don't know. I just made it up in case you die in front of all these people and I need something to explain it.'

The rest of the crowd resumed their babbling, though it felt like they were miles away.

'I'm not going to die, am I?'

'I wouldn't be so sure. Very deadly condition from what I've heard.'

Spiric choked out a chuckle, but before he could take a shot back at Grethard, Braiyth's voice cut the air like a battle axe. She was standing nearby as she brandished her cane, this time at Voss-Ela.

'Viceroy Voss-Ela, you go too far! A Hytharo may be one thing to attempt to bring before us, but with the presence of this man—'

'Mesos Braiyth, remember yourself this instant!' Apex Shiro barked.

'Grethard is a prodigal son!' she bellowed back. 'A cursed one at that! You all know why! His crimes were the catalyst that warped the Academy into the blood-soaked abomination it is today. What necessitated the Order of Reyat. There are few of us left alive who had the chance to explore the undercity, but we went in understanding the consequences we must submit to if something down there tainted us. But he didn't. He chose to fight.'

Spiric looked to Grethard, unable to hide the confusion on his face. The old man couldn't meet his eyes, his face cast grimly down. He helped Spiric to his feet as the crowd began to murmur again. Grethard looked over them, then turned to Braiyth. His voice was quiet. A confession only to her.

'It's a regret I've carried for thirty years in exile, made worse by the doubts of what I saw. I searched to find a shadow dancer again, just to be sure, and it wasn't until I found Spiric that—'

Braiyth made a good show of ignoring him, eventually cutting him off. 'Viceroy, these circumstances are unacceptable!'

Voss-Ela was still standing on her dais, now fully exposed to the sun. 'Circumstances that must be ignored in light of the opportunity we have. This is the chance of a lifetime!'

'A lifetime due to be cut short for all of us if we continue to harbour a man who crossed the sight of a shadow dancer!'

The crowd gasped and writhed in a panicked wave, the palace guards struggling to contain the bodily commotion as skittish academics retreated up the stairs. As Apex Shiro roared for calm, Braiyth's voice cut above his.

'Whatever opportunity you have blundered us into, Voss-Ela, holds only peril. By now the boy is tainted, too.'

Spiric was still wobbling on his feet, leaning heavily against Grethard for support, but a raging and focused fire ignited in his heart as he locked eyes with the insolent Braiyth.

'I was tainted long before Grethard saved me!' Spiric shouted. It was barely heard over the crowd, but he didn't care. Shock was back on the old woman's face. 'A shadow dancer is what holds the key to my lost memories! A shadow dancer is what pulled me through time to today! A shadow dancer who was my brother, who asked for our cruel empire to be wiped clean from this world's memory, the one who sealed water, our power, into the air itself so we could never become tyrants again! His name is Arallak and we all owe our lives to him. The least you can do is to help me remember his.'

Now the palace was silent. A silence that was deafeningly final. The academics who'd made it halfway up the hall's many stairs now froze in place. An old part of Spiric, one from when he stood as the executioner for an empire, relished the fear in their eyes.

'I... I... I don't believe you.' Braiyth's voice finally had a quiver of fear, but she still stood defiant.

'Why?' Grethard snapped. 'After everything this boy has been through, why is nothing good enough!?'

'A good scholar is a sceptic, something you know nothing of.'

'Then believe me.'

Arallak's whisper emanated from a flash of darkness at the centre of the clearing. It was carried forth by his shadowy figure for only a moment, lingering just long enough to catch a glimpse of the silver runes embossed across his cloak before he disappeared.

Spiric thought there'd be chaos, that the guards might just execute them all right there and then, but all remained still.

'There. We're all cursed,' Grethard barked. 'Unless anyone

wants to start the grand and honourable sacrifices, I suggest we cut the politics, because I've heard that when a shadow dancer *asks*, you *do*.'

'Is that true?' Spiric whispered.

'Doubt they'd know better,' Grethard muttered back.

'He's right.' Voss-Ela had finally left the dais to join them in the shade, a furious determination written across her face as she surveyed her subjects. 'Grethard, the Order of Reyat is at your disposal. We may only have hours before word of what has transpired here leaves this city, so we must work fast.'

'What about the shadow dancer?' one of the crowd shouted from the back.

'He saved me,' Spiric said quickly. 'But he has no memory of it either. I need to know why. And why I would end up here. Why now.'

More gossiping, but at least the crowd was drawing closer, those who'd retreated again descending the stairs.

'You have your studies,' Voss-Ela declared. 'If what the Hytharo has told me is right, everything we know of his people is a work of fiction, so your research must begin anew. Mesos Braiyth, take Grethard and begin.'

'And the boy?' she replied.

'He shall stay. My healers must check he has not injured himself by his... excited delirium.'

'Yes, Viceroy.'

Whatever bile Braiyth was about to spit back at Voss-Ela

was swallowed as all memory of her challenge was washed away in the babble of other academics. Some surrounded Grethard, greeting him as either a forgotten myth or a cautionary tale. No matter how the old man tried to shrink from the most attention he'd received in a lifetime, he was suddenly being swept along in the gaggle, down the various passages branching off the great hallway and out of sight before Spiric could say goodbye.

It left him in the company of Voss-Ela and Greely, the latter being the only one to remain seated as the others left. He pushed heavily on his knees as he rose to his feet, the creaking groan that escaped him echoing through the emptying hall.

'Looks like the secret's out,' he said as he plodded over to Spiric. 'Are you sure all these theatrics were wise?'

Voss-Ela nodded slowly. 'At the very least, Braiyth won't be able to complain any longer that I have nothing to contribute. I've presented them with a Hytharo.'

'I believe Spiric deserves most of the credit on that. After he fell, I thought that would be it.'

'I'm fine,' Spiric muttered as Greely began prodding and gently twisting his arm.

'Of course you are,' Voss-Ela replied casually. 'A dying man couldn't make a speech with that kind of vigour.' She paused, gazing out at the dunes. 'The shadow dancer wasn't a trick, was it?'

'No. If it was, I would've had him stay longer.' Spiric paused for a moment, wincing as Greely examined the scars on his chest.

'Grethard never told me what seeing a shadow dancer does, at least nothing more than driving someone mad.'

Voss-Ela grimaced back. 'Try not to think too hard about it.'

'But I want to know more.'

Greely glanced up at him, shaking his head ever so slightly.

'I want to know more,' Spiric repeated, his tone deliberately stony.

From inside the layers of her robes, Voss-Ela pulled a single reel, holding it between thumb and forefinger, close enough for Spiric to make out every scratch and imperfection on the worn iron ring.

'If I drop this, you expect it to fall, yes?'

Spiric nodded, at a loss for how a basic concept like gravity could possibly be connected to his question. She let go and, predictably enough, it hit the marble floor with a sharp clink. She stooped down and picked it up, again holding out for Spiric to inspect.

'Will it fall again?'

'I can't see why not.'

The coin was falling before he could say anything more, landing almost exactly on the same spot as the first time. Voss-Ela collected it once more.

'Again?'

Spiric shrugged, then nodded, but Voss-Ela didn't release the reel.

'What if it didn't?' she asked. 'What if it simply hung in the air, flew to the sky, or morphed into something else entirely?'

He felt himself frown. 'Why would it?'

'The most dangerous question,' Greely muttered. He'd finished giving Spiric a once-over and seemed satisfied enough to wander back to the amphitheatre's first row of seats.

'Why would something defy all expected and known quantities of this world?' Voss-Ela said. 'It's a question the Academy of Breggesa had been trying to answer up until the Scythes took over. The ruins of those-of-glass and paralicts from the undercities were the prism through which their research was observed. The question begs another, doesn't it?'

'But surely you could find out, right? Some kind of magic, some combination of runes—'

'And if it's not? Just as is the case with so many things we've found, things you've likely encountered while in The Lightning Cage, of which have no explanation, where either we don't yet have the means to understand, or there is nothing possible to understand, what we observe has no reason to it, no obedience to our expectations. Ponder this enough, see this enough, and the second question comes to mind.'

Voss-Ela let her words hang in the air, the single reel still held in front of his eyes. Spiric couldn't tear his focus from it, the Viceroy's implied second question emerging in his mind.

'Why would anything act as we expect?' he said.

She snatched the coin from his view and hurled it out into the endless sky. 'That thing could arc and fall into the sand like we all know it to, but what if it only did that because we thought it would? What if we all had an unshakable belief that it would sail off into the sky, lost eventually among the stars that come by night?'

'A magic unbound by runes,' Spiric muttered. 'Just like those-of-glass.'

It had been the first way Grethard had described those who had built the ruins, a shard of a memory that was suddenly bound with that of the shadow dancer in his mind. He'd seen the black runes held in Arallak's hand, but he seemed to have had no worry or need for ink and for water like Spiric or the others did.

'Exactly,' Voss-Ela replied. 'If there were no runes, if magic just vomited forth from our minds in whatever form we believed it to take, how would we know which aspects of the world are fixed down and which are a construct of what we believed to be around us?'

Spiric was still struggling to wrap his head around it. 'But we still need runes. You just tasked nearly a hundred of your people to try and understand mine!'

She shrugged. 'Means to an end. We all believe that the runes are the key. You said so yourself. By the sound of it, you figured out how to use them without even being able to remember what they do. No one really knows how the runes carry power. We've spent centuries theorising on the properties of the water —a branch of research made all the harder by the actions of your brother locking it in the air— or if it's something to do with the ingredients the ink is created with, but the theory that's only whispered about, the most dangerous one, is the one that harkens back to whatever it is that those-of-glass wiped themselves out with.'

'So, if I try hard enough, believe hard enough, I could create lightning without a single rune? Just imagine it into the world?'

'Who's to say that's not what you're already doing?' Greely said from his seat.

'But you'd need to believe it,' Voss-Ela said quickly. 'Just as you would believe that reel would fall to the ground. It would have to be an undeniable reality in your mind. So true it would overcome the doubt of those around you, even the thoughts unknown in your own mind.'

Her eyes bored into his as her pause made the air tense.

'Without a shadow of a doubt,' she continued. 'That's why it's not good to spend too long in a ruin, to venture down into undercities, to bring back the paralicts they hide and most of all, to see a shadow dancer. Because everything you see that defies your reality gets you one step closer to defying it yourself.'

'But it's all a theory, isn't it?' Spiric asked hesitantly.

'It's not. It's rare, but it happened enough it was given a name. Pure resonance.' Voss-Ela drew closer, her voice sinking to a hissing whisper with each step until they were almost nose to nose. 'A single moment of burning unreality in the mind that strikes upon it. A moment where anything is possible because everything is suddenly impossible.'

'Then what happens?'

'You become a shadow dancer.'

## CHAPTER TWENTY-ONE

# LONG SHADOWS

SPIRIC BURNED OUT THE rest of the day back at the manor he was temporarily calling home, languishing in a mixture of restlessness and exhausted nerves. With his injuries still fresh, the walk back up the palace steps was so strenuous that Apex Shiro had abandoned his post as palace guard and all but carried him home. Once there, Spiric didn't have a choice in heeding the enormous man's warning to stay put. He could barely take a few steps without a shooting pain ricocheting around his ribcage.

Byreth and Tetran were still absent, so he passed the time imagining what they were seeing or discovering in the sprawling city of Basarod, quickly replacing his boredom with envy. So far he'd only seen a snippet of the city, an image he suspected would continue to be carefully curated by Voss-Ela and his other minders. If he'd been to this city before, then his memories surely were contained within their walls, and minute by minute, Spiric fought the urge to hunt them down. It was starting to look as though sitting still was not one of his natural talents despite it being exactly what Greely had prescribed.

The healer had requested that Spiric stay in Basarod at least a week, promising daily check-ups to make sure he recovered properly. He could only hope that more Scythes wouldn't capitalise on this advantage.

A flash of the respark's explosion danced through his mind and his wounds singed at the thought. It had been such a terribly overwhelming force, so why did he have the faintest memory of using them as playthings?

If the shadow dancer, Arallak, *his brother*, showed his face again, then Spiric wanted answers. More than just the spiteful fragments of who he had become under his instruction.

The way Arallak had stood resolutely by Spiric's side as he'd carried out his "duties" made him shudder. Maybe he didn't want to see him again. To be done with it all and move forward, as ignorant and innocent of his history as everyone else seemed to be. But then a few more of Arallak's words floated into his mind.

*"You will never be sure you've changed until you've fully*

*reckoned with your past."*

Spiric swore under his breath. Alone in the manor, he'd resorted to leaning heavily on the balcony's railing, watching his long shadow grow even longer as the sun drifted behind the mountains at his back. He'd been staring into the dark shade he was casting like a sentinel, waiting for Arallak to step out from it as if it were a simple doorway. But after what felt like hours he still hadn't appeared, leaving Spiric tossing up between a path of ignorance or exposed guilt.

He cursed again, a directionless mutter. 'Maybe Arallak's right.'

'I'd hoped I wouldn't have been.'

Spiric managed to keep his reaction to little more than a flinch this time, but when he turned to Arallak, he hadn't been watching him. Instead, he stared pensively into the distance as Spiric did, but Arallak's form did not cast a shadow to match.

For the first time, a certain sadness lingered in those deep black eyes, and Spiric almost felt pity for him. It was wiped away as he pictured them red like in his memory, when he'd been by his side as Spiric meted out the Hytharo's version of justice.

'You've remembered more,' Arallak said softly.

'I have,' Spiric replied through gritted teeth. 'Brother.'

Arallak finally turned to him, grief stricken across his face. 'Our people consumed themselves and others just to grapple desperately for control, for power, but because of me, because of what I've done... I'm so sorry. You carry our legacy. Been hunted for it. The terrible nature of the Hytharo. Not lightning, not storms nor rain, but...'

'Power.' Spiric finished for him.

Arallak nodded, turning back to the horizon.

'But more has come back than just that,' Spiric said, unable to keep the bitterness out of his voice. 'More pieces of what I am, what I came to be... What you made me.'

Arallak nodded again, repressing a slight shake in his shoulders. 'And you shouldn't ever forgive me for it. I see no reason to. I still can't recall anything about you from before. About us. Our family.'

The last word hung in the air as a thick haze that clouded Spiric's vision and thoughts. A family. Of course they would've had a family. But how would he even begin to remember them? Even if he did, they were all gone now. Long gone.

'What turned you into a shadow dancer?'

The question was carefully chosen. For all Spiric knew, Arallak could disappear before the words were out of his mouth.

'I still don't know.'

'Still?' Spiric burst out. 'I remember standing on the walls of this very city, a city under siege as dozens of Hytharo killed dozens more each and I refused to flee. I said that your sacrifice wouldn't be in vain. I even saw you talking to another shadow dancer and you were human, alive. You wanted us to be forgotten. No matter the cost.'

'I asked for this.' Something had clicked in Arallak's mind, his stare intensifying by the moment. Both his hands were white-knuckled on the balcony railing as the metal slowly sizzled beneath his pallid flesh.

'You asked him to do what he'd done before,' Spiric pressed. 'I don't know what that means, but if you want any more of my help, I need to know who that shadow dancer was and exactly what you did.'

He didn't get an answer. Arallak was gone. All that remained was a smell of burnt metal that smoked from the warped railing. Spiric's breath was uncontrollably quick as the scent invaded his mind. He wanted to curse, to rage, but it would come as a scream his wounds couldn't afford to be strained by. He could only stare into the long shadows below, his own a solitary line. Another grew next to it, and Spiric resisted the urge to turn to its owner as he forced the last of his composure onto his face.

'That was him, wasn't it?' Byreth's voice said. 'Arallak? I really saw him?'

He let out his breath. She was probably the best person he could've wished an intrusion from. 'You and just about everyone in the palace today.'

'I'm not afraid,' Byreth said abruptly. 'I've stalked enough ruins that I've probably got one of my own stalking me, too.' Spiric's last words finally clicked in. 'Wait, the entire PALACE? What the hell happened in there?'

Spiric shrugged and shook his head, anything to buy himself

a few extra seconds. Trying to find the words made the whole thing seem so stupid and so risky.

'The secret's out. I thought that Voss-Ela was going to help me, but she just showed me off like I was some kind of trinket to all these people that already don't listen to her. Scholars, like Grethard was, but I've got no idea if they can even help me. They didn't believe me until Arallak decided to make an appearance.'

Byreth began to swear under her breath and Spiric learnt a few new words from it.

'If everyone knows, won't they come for you? Just like... well, you know...'

'Maybe, but they'd think twice after seeing what I could do with a few runes.'

'Then what about the Scythes?'

Something bitter curled in Spiric's chest and his day-old scars prickled. 'They're dead. I killed them.'

'Nearly killed yourself! You got lucky. *I* got lucky! Still got your blood under my fingernails to show for it.'

'I'm sure I've had a lot more blood under mine. At least you were doing something good. I don't even know if saving me was worth it anymore.'

Spiric glanced across to see her fuming.

'You don't get to throw your life away, you know that?' she shot. 'I can do that with mine, hell, it's what my brother did. But you matter to this world. You must've mattered in yours if a fucken' shadow dancer saw fit to bring you this far.'

'But I don't know that! I barely know who I am! What if you're right? What if I was just lucky and I never mattered in the first place? All I've remembered is the slaughter of the innocent and the desperate by *my* hands. I shouldn't matter! I wish I didn't!'

Before he knew it, Byreth seized two fistfuls of his shirt and hurled him to the ground. His body crumpled as he writhed in pain and his chest felt like it was about to burst open.

'Fuck you, Spiric,' Byreth spat at him. 'At least you get a choice. You fucken' matter. I've spent the entire day trying to find someone who'd even have a hint of where my brother ended up and they wouldn't give me the time of day. Tetran wouldn't even help me! You showing up was the best thing that's ever happened to me, you know that? I'd still be stuck with Leerukhart if you hadn't come this way. And I don't care if you've gone around killing folk. I sure as hell know Grethard probably has. No other way he could've just ended up where he was.'

'But I wasn't fighting people like Scythes,' Spiric choked out as he propped himself up. 'You don't get it, it was anyone. They were just asking for more rain. Just to survive. You wouldn't even understand...'

'I don't need to!' Byreth shouted back. 'I ain't seen you going around killing folk now that weren't about ready to do the same to you. Maybe it's 'cause you've forgotten why you'd do it, maybe they aren't even your memories, but right now you are Spiric, a boy who climbed out of the desert and just wants to know how he ended up there. I'd only start to worry if you found that out and didn't fucken' learn from it.'

Weakly, Spiric chuckled. 'That sounds a lot like what Arallak was saying, actually.'

'Looks like he fucked up a perfectly good balcony too and I'm not going to be the one tellin' it to Voss-Ela.'

Byreth offered him a hand and he shook it, their friendship slightly repaired as she hauled him back to his feet with ease. 'What else did he say, anyway?'

'He said he was sorry. For everything he'd done, but neither of us know exactly what it was.'

'Still figuring that bit out, huh?'

Spiric nodded. 'Yeah. I don't know what I'll find, but you're right. I'd better learn from it.'

It didn't take much longer for the sun to set while the pair swapped stories of the day. Byreth had briefly been helping Tetran shop around for new parts for her Scouter, but she could only watch someone haggle over sprockets for so long before she decided to wander off and do her own thing.

Since Basarod was just about the only city that wasn't under the thumb of the Academy of Breggesa, Byreth had been hunting for paralict brokers. From what Spiric gathered, absolutely no one trusted a kid who'd just rolled into town and was asking around for an introduction to the most dangerous black market in the Droughtlands.

'I didn't even have enough reels to try and bribe my way in, either. Spent all the ones you gave me getting past the city guard the other day and they wouldn't take yours while they were covered in blood.'

'Sorry for bleeding all over them.' Spiric glanced back to the chair he'd left his filthy satchel on. He'd look like a madman carrying that thing around now. 'You've got plenty of time to keep looking. Greely wants me to stay for at least a week while I get better.'

'And I'm guessing people shoving you to the ground and yelling at you ain't helping?'

They shared a giggle.

'I'll ask him next time.' Spiric paused for a moment. 'Can I help, you know, find your brother?'

'Got me this far, didn't you?' She sucked her teeth for a moment as she thought. 'Everyone I talked to was real jumpy 'cause they'd heard of Scythes on the loose. You might've taken care of some of them, but they'll probably be a whole lot more coming for payback. Word of a Hytharo and the shadow dancer that's following him probably going to make 'em more nervous once it gets out.'

'It worked with Leerukhart,' Spiric offered.

'Yeah, and look how that went for her.' She sighed, pausing a moment. 'I'll tell you. It ain't right now, but I'm sure I'll need you soon.'

'I want to help,' Spiric repeated. 'I'm sick of it being all about me.'

Byreth snorted derisively. 'You better get used to it!' She leaned into the railing, recoiling with a yelp as the burnt metal singed her arm.

'Looks like Arallak left you a little present,' Spiric said with a smirk he couldn't help as Byreth rubbed at the already reddening patch on her skin. The mark was already blending in with the patchwork of other scraps and scars on her arm.

She squinted at the twisted section of the railing. 'Looks like he left you something as well.'

He leaned in to join her, his heart starting to race. Before, the railing had been machine-smooth, but now an axiom was imprinted in each warped section of metal where Arallak's hands had been. There were four runes in each, both ending in a power rune, the axiom on the right looking almost familiar. For a moment his mind flashed back to the memory of him being on the walls of Basarod, of the lightning he'd hurled over the siegelayers below.

'Runes?' Byreth said in confusion.

'My runes,' Spiric breathed. Finally, the shadow dancer had given him something useful. But Voss-Ela's last conversation was still playing in his head. What if he didn't even need them? The thought didn't last long enough to take hold and was interrupted as Byreth started wildly theorising to their purpose.

'Are these the rain ones? You think you can do it now? Maybe it's more lightning! Would make it a lot easier to fight the Scythes coming for us! Or even something else, do Hytharo do other things?'

'Byreth—'

'I mean they call you storm callers, right? I know sandstorms are wind, no idea what rain looks like, but maybe that?'

'Byreth—'

'I guess that's what Reythurists already do. But they don't have dibs on that, either! I've heard of Kretatics somehow making machines that can spit lightning or Curiktics that can shunt air just by fire alone!'

'BYRETH!'

'Sorry.'

'Tomorrow.'

'Tomorrow,' she said resignedly.

Tetran returned from her ventures in Basarod soon after. Lounging in the main room, Spiric and Byreth exchanged a silent look to keep everything that had happened between them secret. The Scouter arcanite followed her in. It was so waylaid by pistons, twisted joists and racks of springs that each shuddering step it took cracked the marble beneath it.

'How'd you buy all that?' Byreth blurted indignantly.

'With... reels?'

'I thought you barely had any. That's why I burned all mine to save Spiric's life!'

'For which I'm very grateful and will pay you back,' Spiric interjected.

'Doesn't help that you didn't ask, neither,' Tetran said pointedly. 'You just pushed past the Grethard and threw everything you had at that guard. Didn't even try to haggle.'

'He was DYING!'

'Still could've asked,' Tetran said with a shrug. 'If it makes you feel any better, I picked up a little something for you.'

She rummaged through her haul, then pulled out an ornate-looking hand cannon and tossed it to Byreth. She fumbled as she caught it and Spiric had half a mind to jump behind the couch he was lying on before the damn thing hit the ground.

'One of my parts guys wanted to offload it, so I've got no idea if it's stolen, but if you keep that to yourself you shouldn't get into trouble.' She tossed over an ammo pouch next and it sailed past Byreth by about five feet. But she'd made no effort to go after it. She was still enamoured by the weapon.

'This ain't Revance pattern,' Byreth said slowly.

'What's that mean?' Spiric asked.

'It shoots more than once before you need to stop and put more slugs in.'

'But what's special about that?' Spiric asked.

'Most guns were drawn up to be made for the Fortress of Revance,' Tetran explained. 'Cheap and dirty, but it went bang and probably wouldn't break, despite acting like it was about to. Revance bought most of them, but near the end of the flux catastrophe it was like they were just making too many of them.'

Spiric frowned, trying to remember what he'd been told about the fortress. 'Didn't that get destroyed ages ago? Greely said so.'

'Which means that anything "Revance pattern" is either older than all of us put together or has been pumped out of a workshop that hasn't been refitted for about as long,' Tetran said. 'You can buy one of 'em for a firm handshake if you go far east enough. Folks usually just need something to wave around and make some noise with, so they aren't going to spend big to buy something better. Barely could if they wanted to. It ain't worth the reels to be competing with that, so anything good like what Byreth's got is about as rare as water.'

Spiric thought back to the little warhammer he'd bought in Kurkress. It was almost primitive compared to these things, but at least it was simple. Byreth was still engrossed with the weapon, prodding and spinning every part on it that she could budge without a rhyme or reason to why she was doing it.

'Don't come complaining to me if you lose any fingers,' Tetran said sternly. 'Don't know why a Curiktic would want one of those things when you're a walking fire spout.'

'Irokan tradition.'

She brandished the cannon, looking down the barrel of it at a spot a few feet to Spiric's right. 'Plus, it's good to have a backup for when you run out of runes.'

Tetran smirked. 'And just how many fights have you been in, let alone ones where you ran dry for runes?'

Byreth stayed silent, sheepishly tucking the hand cannon into her tunic before getting up to grab the scattered munition pouch.

## CHAPTER TWENTY-TWO

# UNDERSTANDING
# INTENTION

D AYS PASSED BEFORE SPIRIC managed to properly see Grethard. He caught him in the antechamber of the manor one morning, a full week after their arrival, yet Spiric barely had time to say hello before an eager academic was pounding on the door to whisk the old man away. If they were this excitable, surely it meant progress, but how much longer would Spiric have to wait before they even told him a hint of what they were doing?

'I don't get it,' Spiric said, his stride just a bit too long for comfort as he followed Grethard up to the palace. 'If it's just five runes, five words, how can it be taking this long to figure it out?'

'The same words can form markedly different axioms all by their intention, boy. If we came back to you with only one understanding, we would have failed in our attempts to paint the entire picture.'

Grethard and the academic —who was jabbering by now— disappeared into the writhing crowd at the palace doors. Instead of slinking off, defeated and resigned to another day of pointless waiting, Spiric turned on his heel and marched back to the manor, gracing it only long enough to heft Grethard's empty and discarded rucksack over his shoulders and don a cowl deep enough to hide the brass glint of Voss-Ela's gifted glasses.

The previous day, he'd scribbled down the pair of axioms that Arallak left on the railing. Then, once the scrap of paper was safely stored in his satchel and he was sure no one was around, he'd attacked it with a few blows of his warhammer. But his attempt to erase the imprint in the metal was futile, likely work best left to a Kretatic.

But Spiric wasn't going to wait around for one to turn up to finish the job. He was sick and tired of waiting, which was why he was going to do some rune research of his own.

The market stall stocking the tunic he'd spied the other day after his first meeting with Voss-Ela was his first stop, where he bought two of the garments, to the merchant's confusion. He followed up with a sturdier rucksack, doubling back to drop

Grethard's at the manor, then enough dried supplies to fill it to the brim, including a new vent mask and enough filter moss to stuff in its tiny valves. He was certainly going to take Greely's advice of going for a few casual strolls, but not in the way the kind-hearted healer had thought.

Journeying out of Basarod took nearly half the morning, mostly due to his own caution or paranoia, depending on if he was actually being tailed or not. He would double back down busy streets, loop around hillside town blocks and loiter aimlessly at market stalls, every third step accompanied by a quick glance over his shoulder. At least one of Basarod's iron-clad guards was posted at every street corner, so uniform in appearance that Spiric couldn't be sure if a face was new or one that pursued him.

On the other side of the walls, Spiric lingered just beyond the city gates. The sparsely trafficked trade routes stretched north, and fields full of dusty workhands lay east, leaving just about anywhere in the mountains to the west as a prime location to let ring the cracks of thunder his practice would require. But there was one place he had in mind, just to make sure of something that was still playing on his mind.

The steep escarpment soon had him overlooking Basarod to the east, but the west only bore rocky plateaus like those he'd spent the past few weeks travelling through, not a single sign of civilisation on the horizon. At least he'd be alone.

Walking further, he began to suspect this might've been the

path Byreth and Tetran had hauled him along, maimed and bleeding, after his last meeting with Vorric. Not that he could remember that part of the journey. Further ahead, the rocky ground dipped suddenly, giving way to the enormous crater that hosted the steel lattice.

Each long, curving beam was warped and frayed, twisting away from its centre and split from the support of their nearest twin. Far more than a week's worth of rust gripped them. The formerly dull grey was now an even duller orange, the powdered debris given off by it turning the sand a kind of burning red that looked hot to the touch.

The golden dome at the centre had suffered most. The massive hexagonal tiles were rippled with cracks and deep gouges that all but vanquished the smooth sheen of the other day. From the top of the basin, Spiric guessed that some of the dents were deep enough for him to fit his arm into.

But what had caused such damage? The respark inside was the thing that had apparently detonated, so why did it look like it had been pelted with stones from the outside? Even where the dome met ground, more tiles had fallen inwards until it looked near ready to collapse.

But Spiric wasn't deterred. Not entirely, at least.

He negotiated his way down the steep hill with caution. Every second step with his left was causing him to wince from his wounds and he tried not to think about the difficult journey back up.

Spiric donned on his new vent mask as he drew closer to the lattice, making a mental note to go back and thank the merchant for improving the fit of the metal to his cheeks with a few precise hammer blows. The curled copper lip of the mask's rim now adhered so tightly to his face that he probably didn't even need to secure the leather strap supposedly holding it in place.

The surrounding ridgeline offered a merciful shade as the basin flattened out. Wispy hazes of tiny mites thrived low to the ground. They kicked up from the sand of Spiric's footsteps, swarming around his ankles, carried by a blur of tiny cadmium-coloured wings. The twisting, travelling hive only abandoned him once he came within a metre of the metal lattice.

A rival cloud of bugs lay beyond it, rising in a chaotic dance as Spiric stepped into their territory. They washed over him as a single wave, crashing and breaking against the bounds of the lattice behind him, a few of them prickling as they caught in his palm. He held them close to his eyes, turning them over on his fingertips as he recognised what they really were.

*Rust.*

The tiniest flecks of it. It crunched softly as he curled his hand into a fist, turning to fine sand that flowed between his fingers and scattered to the ground. A soft breeze snatched at them, reforming them into the rust mites they'd once been and they raced to re-join their swarm, indistinguishable from the mites they mimicked outside the lattice.

Looking up at the interlaced iron beams, he could see more rust swarms trickling from them, taking to a lively, twirling flight before they hit the ground, their purpose now a calm orbit of the pylons' boundaries. An endless cycle, eating away at both the iron above and the ground below. Maybe it was what had eaten all the scorched bodies as well.

Due to the fallen tiles, the golden dome now bore more entrances than walls, yet Spiric circled it just as he'd done last time, searching for his first point of entry. Dull pale sunlight flowed in tendrils out of the new gaps, and he made sure to steer clear of the strange light. It was only as bright as the thought of dawn, but it was somehow enough that it blurred what lay beyond it, much like the light-bend Grethard had led him through in The Lightning Cage.

Spiric found his original entrance and hesitated at the threshold. This one didn't issue the same rippling light as the others. Inside, the strange rows of metal consoles were gone. Only a pool of sand remained, dotted with twisted scraps of metal and sloping to the centre where a void stretched down. A mirror image of the dome in The Lightning Cage.

*A place where no one will find me.*

Spiric shrugged off his rucksack and dropped it into the sand, which was quickly joined by his travelling cloak and the Viceroy's tinted goggles. Without the filtering glass, the world was almost too colourful for a few moments.

A stiff leather plate had been weaved into the back of the

rucksack, likely so the contents wouldn't dig into his spine, but now upturned, it now served as a mobile worktop. On it he'd laid out his inks, brushes, various scribblings and notes he'd snuck from Grethard over the past weeks and the page of his own making that noted Arallak's axioms.

His own wrist currently bore one last power rune. It flashed redder for a second and his entire arm tingled. Spiric knew what he was risking by tinkering with axioms in such a desolate place. If he passed out here, he might never be seen again, but wasn't that the fate Arallak had wanted for them?

As if it had a mind of its own, the rune crawled into his palm, spurning a curiosity Spiric already couldn't resist. He held his hand towards the ceiling, not even pausing to savour that initial crackle of energy, and clenched his eyes shut as he forced the rune to burn.

The ensuing thunderclap deafened his ears down to a blunt ringing. It was surely something that would've been heard as far as Basarod. Then again, who'd be stupid enough to come into this place to investigate?

*Aside from me.*

The tingling in his right arm subsided after a few seconds, settling as a warm fuzzy feeling, like he'd just stuck his arm in a bale of freshly harvested hay. Spiric waited a few more minutes to see if that would also disappear, but recklessness got the better of him as he glanced at the paper he'd sketched Arallak's axioms on.

One of them looked almost familiar, just out of reach, but Spiric decided to focus his attention on the other set of runes first. He had an odd feeling about just *how* familiar the former would be. If it was the axiom he'd used in his past life to defend the city that had become Basarod, then he didn't want to take the chance of relearning something so deadly.

The new axiom introduced two unfamiliar runes, the first and third of the sequence, while the second was one he'd seen Byreth use before. The fourth and final one was a power rune, which was a staple for Spiric by now. As he reached for a brush, Grethard's words from their brief conversation that morning ran through his mind.

*Axioms are about meaning and intention.*

Was this the meaning of the runes? Grethard and Voss-Ela had both said each one could take the place of so many different words, but how was he supposed to know which one to use? That second rune, the one he now thought of as Byreth's rune, was what he'd seen in her palm just before a jet of flame shot out of her fingers when she'd haphazardly cauterised her wounds the day they'd first met.

But that rune couldn't be one that produced fire, Spiric decided, as that's what she'd use a power rune for. A frown cut deeper into his forehead as he leaned closer to his own notes. What was important about it to her? It mended the flesh. Bound it together. Maybe this rune was some kind of attaching function? The idea felt right in his mind, an echo from another life, so he trusted this gut instinct and moved on to the next question.

Why would he want to attach lightning to anything? It would just disappear the instant it hit. Perhaps one of the other runes was to make it remain in the world, but what would it remain as?

The third rune stared back at him. He recalled seeing it among the many dormant axioms that had lined Voss-Ela's arm, yet he didn't have a chance at discerning their purpose now. But what if he didn't have to? A few of the Viceroy's words drifted through his head, so clearly she might've been standing next to him, watching intently, for all he knew.

*"Overcome the doubt of those around you, even the thoughts unknown in your own mind."*

As he pondered the statement, he couldn't help but wonder if the reverse was true. What if he already knew? Had known? That the meaning of this rune was locked away in a memory he was yet to glean, but one present enough in his subconscious that it would give meaning to an axiom he still didn't understand? More of Voss-Ela's words came to answer the question.

*'Try not to think too hard about it.'*

The paintbrush was suddenly in his hand, and four runes were quickly scribbled onto his arm. The axiom crystallised in seconds. Each rune stacked in his palm, burning hotter and hotter before he hurled the force across the dome. Blinding blue-white energy sprayed from his fingertips, but this time it arced wide, forming in the air as two spheres of crackling light linked by a rope of writhing lightning. It hit the sand and, to Spiric's utter amazement, remained there.

Their presence was a threatening hum that made the hair on his still outstretched arm stand on end. Spiric pulled a pebble from the surrounding sand and tossed it underarm, lightly enough that it bounced a few times before making contact with the beam that linked the spheres. It set off another thunderous flash, and when his vision cleared, the axiom was gone, its legacy only marked by the jagged burn marks on the sands opposite, already fading in the constant shift towards the void between it and him.

Spiric gave himself a few more moments before he sat down again, waiting for the tingling in his arms to fade. He'd just deciphered the runes. At least enough for them to be usable. It had only taken him a few minutes, to boot. So why was it taking those scholars days to do the same? Grethard's voice returned in his mind, replacing Voss-Ela's.

*'If we came back to you with only one understanding, we would have failed in our attempts to paint the entire picture.'*

An anxious pang of regret made his shoulders slump. He'd discovered the axiom, yes, but like Grethard had said, it was just one interpretation of it. What if there was something he'd missed that Arallak was trying to tell him through the runes? Surely he could never know now, because in his mind this axiom and the runes that it was composed of would always produce a singular and definitive result.

He swore under his breath. The other axiom sat tantalizingly on the page. Three more unknown runes. Three more he would lock himself off to. Begrudgingly, he began packing his things, donning Voss-Ela's glasses last of all as he left the dome and began the arduous journey back to Basarod. His curiosity now seemed a curse, and the less he knew, the better, no matter how much Arallak wanted him to remember.

## CHAPTER TWENTY-THREE

# A FORGOTTEN
# TRANSLATION

B Y THE TIME SPIRIC was overlooking Basarod, his shadow was long enough to reach the city walls. The gates were a throng of labourers and travellers clambering to enter, unwilling to be corralled into an orderly line by a trio of heavily outnumbered guards. Beyond the city, an orange cloud loomed over the desert, spanning from horizon to horizon as it ate away at the ground.

Being stuck out in a sandstorm this vicious would likely have him end up buried again. Spiric hung back, not wanting to be jostled in the crowd, and spotted a familiar figure emerge from it. It was Tetran's arcanite.

Spiric stared at it, his head cocked, and a moment later Tetran appeared a few paces behind it. Both she and the arcanite were waylaid by heavy cloaks and more supply bags than Spiric could count, each of the machine's steps almost causing it to buckle under its load.

Once clear of the gates, they set off north. A barren and deserted trail lay before them, one that would be consumed by the sandstorm long before she reached any kind of shelter.

'Hey Tetran!' Spiric called out.

He could barely hear his own voice over the nearby babble, but she only regarded him with a glance before turning her back and forging on. Spiric jogged after her, his legs screaming at him to just let her go.

'Tetran!' Spiric shouted again.

He received another glance, but little more until he caught up to her. Even as he doubled over to catch his breath from the pathetically short sprint, she kept moving.

'Where... where are you going?' he managed between gasps.

'Back on the road, Spiric. Like I was always meant to.'

He caught up to her stride again. 'At night?'

'I usually do. Made an exception for you, though,' she said with a wink. 'You might be "once-in-a-lifetime," but everyone's life still goes on. I got contracts to fill. Moss to deliver. Places to see. People to be.'

Spiric's mind was still grappling for any reason he could give to persuade her otherwise. 'But you saved my life, I haven't even repaid you—'

'I've got a box of respark shards and enough notes on that thing that anyone I sell it all to won't say otherwise.' She stopped for a moment, the arcanite ahead of her gratefully collapsing onto its haunches as she put her hands on her hips. Her eyes stayed on her boots, only meeting Spiric's after a long pause. 'I feel like we talked about this already, ain't we? You're something out of this world. The kind of thing I've already gambled my life on, then wasted years wondering if I'd come up good or not. Not saying I don't like you, or if you're a danger or anything... I'm tryin'... I've had enough excitement, you know? Precious few people you're going to meet in this world know when to walk away, but I pride myself on being one of 'em.'

'Wish I could be, too,' Spiric said darkly.

Tetran guffawed. 'I always hear people say that! Nothing stopping you! Those fancy glasses work well enough, why not just walk back to The Lightning Cage where Grethard found you and just be an exile like him as well?'

'That's not what I mean!'

'I know... But I also see you ain't going to be good and satisfied until you get to the bottom of who you really are. I don't envy that. Not one bit. But I can't come on that journey with you because I already got a pretty good idea of who I am.'

Spiric frowned. 'You're saying Grethard and Byreth don't?'

She smiled softly. It was the first time he'd seen her expression that gentle. 'They're still looking for a few pieces of themselves. Right or wrong, they think that you might be able to help them find it, or they can help do the same for you. Why do you think I gave Byreth that fancy hand cannon? It sure as hell wasn't a freebie.'

She took a breath, glancing around for an eavesdropper that wasn't there before continuing.

'There's going to come a day for you two when that old man is gone and whatever's been hunting you down ain't going to be fended off by fire an' lightning. That day you'd better pray that metal will save you instead.'

He didn't know what to say to this. It was something he'd tried not to ponder on, lest it make the possibility more real, but Grethard had already spent far too many of his years. Byreth and Tetran had been the only other two he'd met who hadn't instantly revered or feared him for what he was. Now with one of them leaving, he almost couldn't be sure the other would be enough.

'You think we'll meet again?' Spiric asked sheepishly.

She sighed, looking back to Basarod one last time. 'If I ever hear thunder in the distance or rumours about red eyes watching the locals, I'll be sure to pay a visit. Until then, we both need to follow our own separate ways. I just hope mine is a damn sight safer than what yours looks to be.'

There were very few words they could share after that, but Spiric still watched her go into the distance, the night swallowing her and her arcanite before the horizon could. He trudged back to the gates, one of the last stragglers through before the guards resigned themselves to the strenuous task of hauling the massive iron doors closed.

Inside, the city was far more alive than Spiric felt. Tetran's departure was an abandonment he was strangely familiar with. Maybe another memory would crop up as he made his way back towards the manor. The last time seeing his family? Maybe the last time he saw Arallak? Or even something from before he fled with the other nameless Hytharo?

But nothing came. He was exhausted when he reached Voss-Ela's generous guest house. There was a depression in the sand washed up against one of the walls that looked good enough to curl up in until morning.

For once, Spiric didn't want to see Grethard. There was no way the old man could know, but it felt as if he'd inadvertently gone out and ruined all the research and study he and all those other faceless academics were undertaking.

One of the runes he'd used today he knew was part of the axiom he'd been found with. What if his own mind had suddenly made something... anything... impossible? At least Grethard wouldn't be back from the palace yet. The sun had only just set, so it would be hours until he'd be forced to confess his blundering to the old man.

Spiric pushed through the front doors and was instantly proven wrong.

A wash of light, warmth, and noise engulfed him. On the pair of couches in the centre of the main room, seated from left to right, was Mesos Braiyth, Viceroy Voss-Ela, a slightly out-of-place-looking Grethard, and an extremely out-of-place Byreth.

The rest of the space was filled by a dozen of Voss-Ela's palace guards and maybe twice as many academics.

Without a word being said, an uncomfortable hush fell over the room. All eyes met his as he gently removed the tinted glasses.

'You've had us worried,' Voss-Ela quipped.

If only Byreth was by his side to offer a quick lie.

'I would have told someone, but—'

Voss-Ela shook her head, cutting off Spiric's attempt at an excuse. 'It wouldn't have made a difference. I was watching the whole time.' She pointed extravagantly to the glasses in his hands and its pair of unfolded arms snapped into place. 'I'd never give a gift that wasn't also for my benefit. I'm surprised you didn't realise. I'd picked you as sharper than that.'

'For gods' sake, he's just a boy!' Grethard snapped. 'I promise I had no part in this skulduggery, Spiric.'

If the glasses had been some kind of arcanite of the Viceroy's, she would've seen everything while he was wearing them, what he'd just said to Tetran and the axiom he'd used inside the golden dome.

Spiric couldn't help cursing under his breath, something Voss-Ela would probably pick up through the damn glasses as well. Had he been wearing them when he'd spoken with Arallak the other day? He couldn't be sure.

'Would you rather we tail him like a prisoner?' Voss-Ela said to Grethard. 'The Order of Reyat's first principle is to acquire undiscovered knowledge and knowledge of the undiscovered. By *any* means necessary.'

She picked the emphasis on the word as she met Spiric's eyes again, sending a shiver through his spine.

'But this is no interrogation,' Braiyth said firmly. 'We only have theories, but with what the Viceroy has seen you do today, we've decided that it can wait no longer. I loathe to admit it, but we need help, Spiric. Your help.'

The old woman stood up, waving her cane at one of the closest scholars who dashed to the centre of the room with a bar of chalk in hand to sketch out the five runes of Spiric's original axiom. Each one was about a foot across and hollow, drawing the attention of the entire room.

'What we bring to you now is the results of days of interpretations; however, for this to be of any use, I need you to be open to each different one. Has Grethard ever taught you the practices of intention when it comes to axioms?'

Unsure of the answer, he looked to Grethard, who nodded slowly. 'I think so,' Spiric said. 'I feel like I figured out a bit of it for myself today.'

'And that is?' Voss-Ela asked.

'That... that intention is just as important as the runes themselves, maybe even more than that. Intention changes the meaning... the effect... completely.'

Mesos Braiyth nodded. 'You might as well have read that from a book.' She paced the length of the runes, stopping at the first that was the furthest from Spiric.

'Grethard shared with us his account and some of your own words of what happened when this axiom was used.' She paused for a moment, eying Grethard from her peripheral. 'I can't say I've heard anything like it, but I hadn't met a Hytharo until days ago. This gleaned us one meaning of the axiom, which we suspect translates into a single statement: water rising, skyward and raging.'

'But how did I know what to do with the axiom in the first place?' Spiric asked. 'I didn't know what it was, what it did, even who put it there. If I didn't know, how could I use it?'

Braiyth nodded slowly. 'The matters of your lost memories make this study a unique one. I've heard of old and now banned experiments by the Academy of Breggesa to take ignorant children and teach them almost a new language with runes, an attempt at a different sort of magic. But it never succeeded.'

'Because they couldn't believe enough to overcome the

doubts of their teachers.' Spiric said. 'Or even, without thinking it, they weren't sure of it, right?'

Voss-Ela smiled at this, but Braiyth ignored it and went on.

'Another something you discovered today?'

'In a way,' Spiric said sheepishly. 'Please, go on.'

There was another moment's pause before she continued. 'Grethard and yourself have said you've been regaining memories of a life where you've used these runes before. Our suspicion, and really the only way to make our theories work, is that this blocked memory is enough to impart intention in moments of peril or panic.' She stopped for another moment, fixing Spiric with a quizzical look. 'You've said that your memories are of the last days of the Hytharo, correct? A time after water had been locked in the air.'

'From what I've seen.'

'That leads to a rather interesting question about the runes of this axiom, one that we believe shows that your particular usage *wasn't* the original intention.'

'How so?'

'It needed water, did it not? A massive, pre-existing source of it. Something that wouldn't have existed in your final days and definitely not for any moment after. So why would this be the original intent? No, we believed it as something else. However, what that "something else" might be is the subject of... lively debate.'

It was only then that Spiric saw Grethard staring daggers at

Mesos Braiyth. Next to him, Byreth joined in, likely just for the hell of it.

'What else could it mean?' Spiric prompted.

She couldn't quite meet his eyes, an almost exasperated expression crossing her face. It was more aimed at herself than anything. 'It was the first thing we asked as well, but the answer to your question lay with each rune individually.'

'Grethard once told me that there could be dozens of meanings in a rune.'

'Something I heard repeated many times when I asked of their progress,' Voss-Ela commented.

She received a few withering scowls in return but brushed them off. Mesos Braiyth paced back to the first rune, and Spiric moved to stand opposite.

'Power rune.' It was probably the last useful thing he'd be able to say when it came to these runes.

Braiyth nodded charitably. 'Power. Yes. Common to all. A simple purpose that confers function without modification or assistance. Anything else added to it tends to be guidance. It often represents the main element of a person's magic in its rawest form. A Kretatic; magnetism in metal. A Curiktic; fire or light. A Reythurist; the air itself. For us, these are known and dwelled upon constants. For you, we begin making assumptions based on what we've witnessed and what shaky information legends glean.'

'Lightning, then?' Spiric added.

'Storms and water by our guess, as well.' She moved to the second rune and Spiric followed. 'This is frequently employed by Kretatics to create their arcanites. Gives the bound metal life. A birth for it. A capacity to grow as it gathers more pieces. From this "growth" we decided on "rising" being the key meaning here, but you see many substitutes, no?'

'I used one of these today,' Spiric admitted. 'It made the lightning almost... almost solid.'

A murmur of interest swept the crowd, but Braiyth had already moved on. 'This third one is what Reythurists use to take flight. For them, a power rune alone will cause a compression or explosion of air, but this one is what can send it skyward. At times it even just means "up." It's one of those tricky runes that is more intention than concrete meaning.'

They moved to the fourth, Spiric losing track of the echo of a thought as they went.

'This one is even more vague, but in a way that is convenient to us. It binds different axioms together. Imbues one with another, spreads it across the plane or even into a material object. "And, of, all," if it were words off our tongue.'

The final rune now stood between them, and Spiric prayed something would click into place.

'The last is another with a tendency to be seen on Kretatics. It accompanies the second on its way into an arcanite, gifting it with autonomy, intelligence or sometimes self-determination, all at the cost of the controller's mind. It draws the most study as it represents a way to inject purpose, emotion, even sentience into an axiom. Almost as if it could think like us.' She turned and looked, almost begrudgingly, at Grethard, whose face was now pleasantly neutral. 'Your teacher's early theory, by chance.'

'It was a deluge of liquid that carried him to the dry sand straight to my side,' he said. 'He could've ended up anywhere, and I don't believe in that kind of luck.'

'From this alone we found ourselves debating numerous possible translations,' Braiyth continued. 'It could be a lightning storm of old that grows above from nothing, with enough purpose to attack a city. A walking being of pure energy, gifted with a soul almost like an arcanite. Wilder still, it could've just been the means to undo whatever the final Hytharo had done and convert the air back to water.'

Spiric could tell the last meaning had been saved just for this moment. The crowd was leaning in, wide-eyed and waiting for that final secret, but he had nothing to give them.

'But what if I never knew any of this in the first place?' Spiric countered. 'In this life or the last? No hidden memories to give intention. What if it really was pure resonance?'

'A shadow dancer was the one that confronted you, correct?' Voss-Ela said. 'Would they not have already experienced it? Felt it enough to believe they'd know it if they saw it again? Could your blank slate of a mind have been willed hard enough to overcome that?'

'For gods' sake, Viceroy!' Braiyth huffed. 'It's like you want to lose him to a shadow dancer with questions like that!' She composed herself and turned back to Spiric. 'The axiom must be the key. I don't for a moment believe in a thing called coincidence. Look at it again. See if they fit in with any of those memories you keep finding.'

He already felt like he'd stared at the written axiom for hours but still took one more protracted glance down the line before shrugging to the Mesos. 'The runes alone, maybe. But it's like you said. All five of them like this, they could mean something completely different when read together.'

'What if they were never meant to be read?' Byreth burst out. She was overflowing with pride from being able to contribute such a clever-sounding question.

'Of course the only one in the room that never figured out how to read would say that,' Grethard muttered.

His prize for the remark was a punch from Byreth that came hard enough to fold him over like scrap paper. It elicited a small gasp from the crowd, but they quickly learnt from the example Grethard had so unfortunately set.

'What could you mean?' Voss-Ela asked her, hiding an amused look as Grethard gasped quietly for air.

'A secret. Smuggled. One never meant to be found. Not until it was meant to be.'

She paused, only picking up again once Voss-Ela nodded her on.

'What did this mean to the Hytharo, Spiric? Not just the

people, but the world they built? Why put something that had to be stashed in the sand like a sack of stolen reels on your arm, only for it to be dug up now?'

Spiric was glancing rapidly between her and the runes on the floor, that long-gone thought now crashing into his consciousness.

'A meaning to the world they built,' Spiric murmured. 'To The Hytharo Empire.' He strode back to the first rune, Braiyth hobbling to follow. 'Power almost always means lightning to me, but The Hytharo Empire was one of slaughter and cruelty. That was where the power came from. Bathed in blood.'

The last word resonated in his mind, and he moved quickly to the next one.

'But The Hytharo Empire could not grow on its own. Not on pure violence.'

'A sword is only as good as the peasant that toiled to have it forged,' Voss-Ela said.

A second word clicked into place. *Forged*. Spiric moved again, not wanting to lose momentum.

'You said this one could be vague, right? What if skyward wasn't a physical instruction? A place where the sun and the stars dwell.'

'Of gods?' Braiyth chided. 'Don't be ridiculous!'

'No one else could have toppled the Hytharo! We'd best ourselves if we fought with each other. Even a shadow dancer wouldn't see fit to wipe them all out, would they?'

It was a question the room didn't want to think too hard about answering, so Spiric launched onwards.

'What if an act of a god was needed to do this? A ruling power wiped out by an ultimate one?'

'There's no such thing!' Braiyth said sternly.

'Then who gave us magic?' Spiric shot back.

'The last people that walked this land who were also arrogant enough to wipe themselves out with it!'

'And who to them!?' Byreth called out, eliciting a hubbub from the academics.

Spiric didn't wait for the next answer to come, skipping ahead to the final rune. 'To give it purpose, a reason why the shadow dancer brought me into this time.' He paced around it for a moment, then met Braiyth's eyes. 'You know, I remembered more about him. About when he was alive... He'd talked with a shadow dancer, too. He wanted us to be forgotten. Wiped from memory.'

Spiric paused and the room held its breath. All except for Byreth, who was on her feet and grinning like a maniac. 'It's not an axiom at all, is it?'

Her energy was infectious, and Spiric could feel it thumping in his chest. 'It's a message.'

His vision blurred, Byreth's place somehow simultaneously occupied by Arallak, who stared back with blood red eyes, his mouth moving in concert with Spiric's.

'A warning of what caused our downfall.'

Their voice was a harmony only Spiric could hear, a sinister invocation perfectly matched between the span of more than a thousand years.

'The Blood Forged God of Memory.'

## CHAPTER TWENTY-FOUR

# A VEILED THREAT

EVEN THESE WORDS HAD been a revelation to Spiric, leaving him as stunned as everyone else in the room. However, it didn't take long before the scholars began to do what they did best. The manor hall was soon a rabble of smouldering debate. Groups clashed like opposing waves before breaking off into separate arguments that split again into smaller duels as they quibbled over phrasings, interpretations, exceptions, and potential mistranslations. Others were arming themselves with chalk and scrawling complex patterns of runes into the floors, the walls, anything within reach.

It quickly drained any exhilaration from Spiric. The words

he'd spoken just moments ago with such conviction suddenly meant nothing to him. Had he or Arallak, or anyone else for that matter, really tangled with a god? And what the hell did "blood forged" mean?

Soon Spiric was getting dragged from place to place, bombarded with questions and pulled away before he had a chance to stammer out his ignorance. They even got him to copy the runes from earlier today back onto his arm for what little good it did, aside from wasting more precious ink.

Even Grethard had a difficult time pressing his way through the crowd to eventually extract Spiric up to the mezzanine, which, aside from Byreth, was mercifully empty. He could feel the old man's eyes on him. He, too, would have questions, but at least he knew to hold his tongue.

'I saw Arallak again.' Spiric said. 'When I said it. Just for a moment.'

'He don't like hanging around, does he?' Byreth said.

'You think he said it to you at one point?' Grethard asked.

Spiric let himself shrug. He wanted to give a definite answer, just a single one for the night, but he knew it would be a lie. 'He could've said anything. I need more time with him. To talk. Really talk. And it won't happen here. There're too many people.'

'I hope you're not thinking of leaving.' Voss-Ela and a flanking pair of guards had found them, appearing at the stairs without warning. 'Your safety is only guaranteed under my watch and I am blind beyond the walls of my city.'

'You only let me leave because you were spying on me,' Spiric retorted.

'It was a calculated risk,' she said coolly. 'One I shall not take again.'

'So, he's a prisoner now?' Grethard said.

'Yeah, what about us?' Byreth added. 'Want to lock us up, too?'

The Viceroy paused for just a moment too long. It was answer enough.

'I can't make it rain,' Spiric said as firmly as he could. 'Not for you. I'd just make things the way they were from the time I've come from.'

Voss-Ela's brow twitched, but she remained composed. 'I keep the Order of Reyat in my purview to learn from the mistakes of history. Why would the fall of this empire you talk of need to leave behind a warning?'

'Maybe it worked too well,' Spiric said. 'Enough that it was forgotten as to why the Hytharo needed to be felled in the first place.'

'So you're a tombstone, then? A monument?'

'To make sure it never happens again.'

The Viceroy glared at him, calculating her words. 'You don't trust me?'

His options were a lie and an insult, but Grethard stepped in to save him.

'It's a question you shouldn't have to ask, Arch Mesos, and I worry that you felt the need.'

Her attention snapped to the old man and even he couldn't resist flinching under the withering glare she now harnessed. 'That was a frequent adage of my mother, coincidentally.' With a deep, composing breath, she looked back to Spiric. 'It's been clear to me that we never trusted each other in the first place. We never had a reason to.'

'Even less've one now,' Byreth muttered.

'Time will fix that,' Voss-Ela snapped. 'Until then, caution must take its place. Do try rest easy tonight, Spiric. Eventful days are to come, I'm sure.'

Before he could stammer out a half-hearted goodbye, she and her troop of guards were down the stairs and herding the still-bickering academics out of the manor. Spiric had to hold himself back from chasing after her, from demanding they sort the unfinished business of his very well-placed mistrust.

'What the hell does she mean by "Eventful days are coming," anyway?' Byreth said after the house was clear.

'She meant for you to be thinking just that,' Grethard said darkly. 'I remember talkers just like her before I got kicked out of the Academy. Everything they say comes with an escape they can back out of. Nothing is nailed down until they've got what they wanted out of you. You're right not to trust her, Spiric. Her running away like that pretty well admits that she knows it, too.'

Spiric found himself leaning heavily on the banister that ran the length of the mezzanine. The walls and floors were thick with chalked-out runes. The marble floors were scuffed by a few dozen sets of boots and indiscriminate trails of dust crossed each other like a pile of dead worms. With the sandstorm still brewing outside, it would probably get much worse.

'I've got what I wanted now,' he said. 'That's what she's thinking, right? Now I know the meaning of the axiom.'

'Might as well leave tonight,' Byreth said. 'Catch up with Tetran and all. I reckon she saw this coming.'

Grethard rubbed his rough stubble, the action polishing a grimace onto his face. 'Don't think it'll be that easy for us now. Caution, she said. She'll be watching. We'll need to lie low.'

'Lie low!?' Spiric said. 'I can't stop now! We've been going for weeks on only the axiom and now we finally know what it says and—'

'What about what they mean?' Grethard asked sharply. 'There's a combined thousand years of scholarly knowledge at your disposal and you just want to go gallivanting off into another ruin to find that damn shadow dancer of yours to ask him instead!?'

It was like a light had flicked on in Spiric's head. A smile began to creep over his face, and Grethard let out a low groan.

'I think that's the best thing. He was there, after all. For all we know, he could've been the one to put the axiom on me!'

No matter how Grethard tried to argue it, Spiric never once felt himself swayed. It was like a shining, golden path had opened in his mind. One singular, definitive journey which would hold every answer he could ever want at its end. Byreth's goading only made this feeling surge in his chest, much to Grethard's chagrin.

It took an hour for the old man to give up, storming off to bed as he insisted that Spiric would feel very differently about things come the morning. But despite all this, Spiric simply couldn't believe him. The only thing he was right about was calling it a night, but when he looked to Byreth there was a manic gleam in her eye.

'Thought the old fart would never turn in.'

'What?' Spiric said.

She nodded towards the front door. 'You in the mood for a late-night walk? Got someone I need to get you in front of.'

'I've been in front of half the damn town already, who else—'

Byreth shushed him suddenly, glancing between him and something in the corner of the room behind him. Spiric turned slowly to where she was looking. It was in the darkest part of the mezzanine, where even the chandelier in the main room couldn't reach. He watched it a few moments longer, his trust in Byreth's surreptitious glances waning quickly, but just as he was about to give up he caught the slightest glint of metal.

He froze, straining to make out the tiny figure squatted in the corner. It was an inch tall, a bronze box supported by four spindly legs. It was practically inanimate, yet Spiric couldn't tell if it was a trick of the light the way each of its tiny legs trembled.

He turned back to Byreth and nodded. Without another word, they split off to their rooms to collect their belongings. There was no telling what Byreth had in store for him, so Spiric stuffed everything he could into his recently purchased travel pack. By the time he was done, he was set for at least a week out in the wastes.

Byreth was already waiting for him at the front door, two sets of cracked goggles in her hand. While not nearly as stylish or comfortable as what Voss-Ela had provided, it did its duty of keeping his eyes clear of sand as they set out into the raging gale. His pockets and boots were filled in seconds as they walked, and each blast of wind forced him to slide back a few feet as the carried dust caught in his layers.

The tight alleyways and towering city walls in the lower reaches of Basarod eased the storm into a dark, swirling haze where the few others that braved the streets looked more like shadow dancers than human, stepping forth from a wall of darkness and disappearing just the same.

'Where are we going?' Spiric bellowed over the gale.

'Paralict trader,' Byreth grunted back. 'Finally managed to track one down, one that would talk to me, at least, but he said that unless I had the goods, he ain't telling me anything. Said it's too risky or something.'

'And let me guess, I'm the goods?'

A punch came from Byreth, striking the same spot on his bruised shoulder that it always did. 'You're more than that, you know that. But I gotta show him I ain't running straight back to the Scythes, and I figure the kid who killed twenty of 'em would be proof enough.'

'So not the Hytharo thing?'

Byreth shrugged. 'Might help.'

They trudged silently onwards for a few more moments.

'Tetran didn't care about it,' Spiric said. 'Caught her coming out of the city.'

'Shame that. Guess she got what she came for.'

'She knew when to quit.'

'You saying I don't?'

Spiric shrugged, but it was barely perceptible with how hunched he was against the wind. 'I don't know. But she said that cannon she gave you was to protect me if it comes to it.'

'As long as you pay for the ammo.'

'But you think you'll stick around? Even when we find your brother?'

Byreth chewed on the question, taking too long to answer. 'Depends how much of him we find. Come on, this is the place.'

The brick-lined alcove was a welcome respite from the sandstorm as Byreth pounded on the rusted iron door. It was a patchwork of excessive plating and riveted like a bank vault that opened out to the street. A hidden slot high in the door swung open, only large enough to reveal a pair of bleary eyes. A man's voice came from behind the door, coarse and shrill against the gale.

'You woke me up for more lies!?'

Byreth grabbed Spiric's wrist and yanked it up to the peephole, displaying the four red runes.

'He ain't a fake!'

'That's just red paint, that is!'

Spiric swore under his breath. It was just Leerukhart all over again. Despite the man's bickering doubts, the sound of rusted latches began sequentially scraping. The door only swung open a foot, and the pair of them squeezed through before it was slammed shut, leaving them stuffed in a tiny antechamber with a crookedly-stood man shorter than Spiric was.

In the confines, Spiric had the choice of either toppling onto Byreth or letting the step built into the outer door continue to dig into his shin as the man's hands ferreted across another set of homemade locks on the next door.

It had barely opened, and the man was already skittering down the flight of stairs it revealed, leaving Spiric and Byreth to stumble after him as they found their footing. The low ceiling of the next room taunted at their heads as a few sputtering oil lamps placed precariously among the piles of mismatched junk glowed weakly. Miniature dunes of sand flowed underfoot, maybe a day or two away from flooding the room despite the double doors.

As Spiric wearily picked his way through to a nearby stool, he almost got the impression that this was expected, even by design. Fraying tarps lay draped over most of the crates and the wares piled therein, those at the back of the room already half swallowed by the drift. He glanced in the nearest box, but instead of seeing paralicts like he imagined, it was simply stuffed with charts and navigational instruments.

'You want to see him or not?' Byreth said.

The man had already busied himself at the other end of the room, fidgeting with odd little trinkets before stuffing them into a half-buried box. At Byreth's question he spared Spiric a quick glance before returning to his work.

'He don't look like a Hytharo,' he shot back.

'You've seen one?' Spiric said, an unexpected hope leaping into his chest.

The man just cackled back. 'Half o' Basarod reckons they have! Just another thing from the Viceroy to get us riled up. Seen Scythes circling the town for weeks until a few days back. I reckon she's done a deal with them and this "Hytharo" talk is just distraction from the fact she said she never would!'

'So you are a paralict trader,' Spiric said. 'That's why you're worried, isn't it?'

'No shit,' Byreth shot with an unusual amount of venom.

The man snorted. 'First right idea she's had. It's why all this needs to get buried before the inevitable happens.' He turned to him slowly, his jowls darkened by a nearby oil lamp's shadow to make them look even more out of place on his wiry frame. 'Name's Korbis. And I'm a broker, not a trader! There's a difference!'

'Doesn't seem like one, apart from the word.'

'Brokers don't hang on to 'em is the difference,' Byreth explained. 'They just figure out where the damn things are and then sell the location to someone else. Never have to hold on to anything in case they get caught.'

'Then what this all this stuff?' Spiric asked.

'It's to be forgotten about is what,' Korbis snapped back. 'Else I get little snitches like you going and blabbing out me being a trader not a broker to the Scythes!'

'Well, there isn't a point worrying about them,' Spiric said indifferently.

Korbis stopped what he was doing, turning with the final trinket in his hand. A grin showed mismatched teeth as his jowls began to wobble. A sputter turned into a giggle as the tiny gadget was dropped and forgotten, the hand that held it curled into a shaking, pointing finger.

'What, and you took care of them?'

'Sure as shit he did!' Byreth shouted back. The room rumbled with her voice. 'Twenty of 'em!'

Her outburst was met with a mirth-filled howl as the man doubled over.

'I've heard some tall tales in my time, girl, but none as

dim-witted as yours! Rolling 'round Basarod claiming you got a Hytharo!'

Spiric watched as Byreth shrank under the mocking barrage.

'Why even lie about it if you're going to aim that high!? Couldn't even find a boy who looks like he wants to play along! I'm starting to guess you ain't even got a brother, do ya? Just looking for a free tip on some corpse's loot!'

'You say another word about my brother and I'll turn this little pit into a fucking furnace!'

Korbis' mirth turned to a scowl, the grin barely remaining as his yellow eyes glinted. 'And toast your little friend? You'd be doing me a favour.'

The room grumbled again, a few thin streams of sand trickling from overhead. The storm had to be getting worse. Korbis uncurled his hand, revealing a yellow power rune in his palm. 'I'd need to get rid of you, anyway. Now it just looks like you got caught as the thief I thought you'd end up as.'

As soon as Spiric saw the rune he leapt to his feet, his own palm out, willing a rune to be ready. Korbis shifted his aim to him in a flash.

'You're committed to the act, boy, even if that is just a bit of dye. Now you're going to lose everything just for being a cheap fake.'

Spiric ripped the cracked goggles from his eyes and stared straight into Korbis' determined squint.

'Say it again!' he roared. 'Look me in the eye and say it again!'

Korbis went to. His mouth even moved. But no sound came out. Even with the storm grinding above, there wasn't a breath. Spiric kept his palm raised as he negotiated the junk piles and closed in on the broker. He backed away, hitting the rock wall at the back of the room of the shadowy as all the fight leaked out from his beady little eyes, replaced only by shock.

'She's right, you know. About the Scythes.' Spiric could feel a malicious glee slipping into his tone, and deep down he relished it. 'Nearly died fighting them. What makes you think you stand a chance against me?'

Korbis was stuttering and stammering before Byreth appeared at Spiric's side with the hand cannon pointed firmly at his face, kicking his mouth into a high-pitched, incoherent babble.

'Dunno why you'd like your face the way it is, but if you don't want me to change it, tell me where my brother is.' She poked him in the eye with the muzzle, causing him to release a yelp. 'Now!'

'I never said it's ya brother! Just a redhead, just like you! They're rare, they are! That's why I stuck around when you started yapping about a Hytharo!' He pointed between them nervously. 'I mean, fancy that, a pair of rare things like you two in the same little room!'

'Get to the point!' Spiric spat, the anger from his past life flaring in his veins.

'Well, it's like I said! He was young, older than you two, but young! Full of shit and energy and wanting to replace all that with reels! Gave me what few he had for anything I could tell him before he went racing off to go find it!'

'Find what?' Byreth said. 'Where?'

'A paralict! They call 'em ephemerals! If I hear about them being spotted I always sell them for cheap because no one comes back with them! Sometimes they don't come back at all!'

'You sent him to die!?'

Korbis screeched and ducked, narrowly avoiding the butt of Byreth's hand cannon as it sailed past his head. 'I don't know if he died! It's not like they have any reason to come back an' talk to me, they've just got to find someone to sell the damn things to!'

Spiric grabbed Byreth's arm before she went in for another swing. Something was bothering him. 'But why can't people get them? The ephemerals?'

'It's about where you find them.' Korbis said with a deep breath. 'Never seen it myself. Folk say you find 'em in a place where time stands still. That's what he was on about, anyway. Sometimes you can see them plain as day if they feel like showing up, but just around them... It just stops things, you know?'

Spiric's mind leapt to the dangers Grethard had hurled him into when they'd first met. 'Like a wall or something?'

Korbis shook his head rapidly. 'Not like that... people just... stop. Again, I ain't never seen it but everyone who's come back to me telling me about—'

The jabbering was cut off as the room quaked fiercely and a muffled hammering came from the outer door up the stairs. All three of them snapped to it as the brutal knock sounded again.

'I'd best get that,' Korbis whispered. 'Might be another Hytharo.'

Byreth took another swing at the broker and Spiric felt no inclination to stop her. Korbis yelped and fell like a corpse as she shoved him across the room, her hand cannon trained on him. 'Send them away or I'm going to find out just how well this shooter works.'

Korbis nodded nervously as he scrambled for the stairs, leaving Byreth to pull Spiric back into the dark corner of the room. Nestled between tarps, Spiric quickly snubbed the nearest oil lamp as the inner door scraped open.

It wasn't even a second later that an explosion of wind torn the outer door clean from its hinges. Korbis' limp form suddenly came careening down the stairs and landed in a crumpled pile as an ear-popping gust extinguished the rest of the oil lamps.

Spiric made to get up, to help the pathetic bastard, but Byreth's left arm wrapped around his still-tender chest and clenched tight, pulling him closer in despite of his pained gasps. Slowly, he felt her right arm reach over his shoulder. Only the glint of her hand cannon's barrel was visible in her hand, along with the faint green glow that radiated from the stairs.

## CHAPTER TWENTY-FIVE

# STORM, SAND AND FIRE

T HE LIGHT GREW STRONGER with each jump of Spiric's accelerating pulse. The axiom in his left wrist was ready, his left hand outstretched just beyond Byreth's hand cannon. The only thing left to see was who'd unleash death first. He knew Byreth had never killed another person before. He wasn't sure how many he had.

The source of the glow came into view, flashes of orange from further up the stairs throwing enough light for Spiric to pick out the angular iron of a Scythe's mask. The metal itself shimmered green like Grethard's torch, making it impossible to make out the rest of its wearer. It looked as though the mask itself floated. A ghost returned for vengeance. Spiric couldn't give them the chance.

The runes rushed up his arm as a blood rush surged through his veins. Blue sparks began to crackle at his fingertips. The mask turned to him in idle curiosity. There was no expression beyond it. No human Spiric could see. The twin spheres of energy burst forth and split, a single chain of lightning connecting them as the room flashed bright before it broke across the Scythe's chest with a gash of white flame.

But in that blinding moment, Spiric saw this was no normal foe.

The lingering motes of lightning danced weakly across the thin bands of interlaced metal wire that encased the Scythe and their deep blue robes. They twinkled and died as they failed to penetrate the mesh-like armour.

The Scythe hadn't even flinched.

Before Byreth could fire her hand cannon, a vicious explosion of wind came in reply, racing around the walls of the chamber as a wave that swept up Spiric and hurled him forward. A gauntleted hand caught his throat, wrestling him to his knees, and suddenly the glowing mask was in his face, the blue eyes behind it lit for only a fraction of a second as they stared into his.

'So you *are* real,' the Scythe whispered to herself.

He struck out with an awkward kick, his boot clanging of

the Scythe's strange armour. He was shoved to the floor for his trouble, landing hard on his back, pinned under the Scythe's weight as a knife glinted in their free hand. She raised her arm to swing but was caught mid-motion as a blazing flash of yellow light filled the room, accompanied by a sound louder than a thunderclap.

The Scythe's grip slipped from his throat, and Spiric scrambled away desperately as another yellow blast billowed over his head. This time it illuminated Byreth, her arm thrown back as the hand cannon vomited white smoke. A third flash, this time giving sight to the torrent of gore erupting from the Scythe's back as they spasmed from the shot. One more, Byreth finally standing over them, a spray of fresh blood coating her arm.

His ears were screeching. Someone was yelling from far away but still not getting through to him as what he prayed were Byreth's hands wrenched him off the ground. A ball of light had appeared in her hand, her bloodied face close and silently yelling, but Spiric could only gawk at the corpse next to him. Grisly craters the size of his fist had punctured deep into the Scythe's body, the mesh armour around each wound bent straight into the lifeless flesh.

'—miracle you didn't—'

Spiric couldn't stop staring at his blank palms. Why hadn't the lightning done anything? In his head, Vorric's last words were overlapping with Byreth's frenzied speech.

'—they know where we—'

'—*if we could master this land without you*—'

Maybe it had been the armour. A walking metal cage. But how did that even work?

'—looks like—'

'—*we will master it against you*—'

How had they even known that they'd need it? No one else knew of the way his axioms destroyed people. He'd killed all the Scythes at the dome.

'We—'

*Hadn't I?*

'Spiric!'

Byreth's voice finally cut through as she shook his shoulders. There was a panic in her eyes, the same kind after Leerukhart had been executed. The same he'd glimpsed as she'd desperately worked to staunch his bleeding outside the dome.

'We need to hide!' he said.

'Been trying to tell you that, but you ain't listening!'

'But if the Scythes are here—'

'Doesn't matter!' Byreth pulled Spiric's pack from the scrambled debris at his feet and shoved it into his chest. 'Runes! As many as you can!'

For a moment he stood there dumbstruck. 'But they don't work.' He was staring at the corpse again. Somehow that armour had protected them from his lightning and if there were more Scythes out there, they'd be equipped the same.

'Distracted them enough that I could blast 'em,' Byreth said. Her hands were shaking as she forced four more slugs into her weapon. 'They're going to need something a lot thicker to stop Tetran's little gift here.' She snapped the cannon's mechanism shut and unsteadily levelled it at the stairway.

His racing mind and similarly trembling hands flushed any thought of fancy or complicated axioms from his mind as he hurriedly applied more runes to his arm, repeating the power rune again and again until he realised he'd emptied half a vial in his haste. He just had to hope they didn't run into more Scythes wearing that strange armour.

'What am I meant to feel, anyway?'

Spiric looked up, confused, as she nodded at the Scythe's corpse.

'Killing someone,' she added. 'You said you'd done it enough. I want to know what I felt right now is...'

Byreth trailed off, instead focusing on her own arm. She was applying runes of her own, the vial in her jittering hands down it its last drops, each brushstroke accompanied by a shuddering breath.

'Depends,' Spiric eventually said. 'I've had memories of it being a triumph. As if I was finally taking what's mine. But they were before... They're faint. They feel wrong. Like it was someone else doing it. But the first one I remembered after meeting Grethard... must have been right before Arallak buried me... I was alone. Alone and afraid.'

'Alone and afraid?' She nodded grimly. 'Yeah, that sounds about right.'

'You saved me,' Spiric offered reassuringly. If not for her, that knife would've been in his throat. He didn't want to think about it.

'Might have to do it again. You ready?' She forced a grin for him then looked towards the stairs. Another red glow flashed from it. Carried in by the gale were distant booms of fire and the braying havoc of a town under siege. It was a sound he'd heard here before.

'Doubt staying here is a better choice.'

Despite it being not nearly as impressive as Byreth's hand cannon, he wrestled the small warhammer out of his bag, the heft of it in his grip somewhat comforting. He lugged his pack onto his shoulders and pulled his cracked pair of goggles over his eyes before nodding to Byreth.

Up on street level, fearful mobs formed fearsome waves of bodies that thrashed to escape the city. Sand-flecked wind howled in their ears as they sheltered in the ruined alcove of a doorway as earth-shattering thuds, signature of a Scythe's touchdown, sporadically pieced it, followed closely by distant wails and screeches.

Byreth bellowed something, the words lost to the storm, and hauled Spiric bodily onto the street, where the human current swept them up. Byreth's free arm was threaded around his back in a crushing grip, keeping them together as she used the butt of her hand cannon to bash a path through the chaos.

'—need to get out of the city!' Byreth roared at him, only half of it coming through.

'What about Grethard?'

She waved the hand cannon towards the inner tiers of Basarod and Spiric gasped, buying himself a mouthful of sand for his shock. Fire licked up the sides of the white palace, radiating an angry dark orange across the sky as what could only be the flitting shapes of Scythes dashed around it like overly cautious night flies.

Larger motionless shapes hovered above it all, pouring gouts of fire down upon the city, the victims below conflagrating in burning pyres that momentarily licked the dirigibles' metal shells.

More Scythes crashed into the crowds around them, crushing their victims and slashing rapidly at their throats with jagged short swords. Spiric was shoved from every angle, hands and bodies alike forcing him to his knees, burying him in a stampede as Byreth fought desperately to haul him up. He could hear her swearing, feel her fighting valiantly, but it wasn't enough.

Her grip slipped.

In an instant, he was on the ground, barely able to scramble to all fours before another blow from above flattened him. He tried swinging his hammer, catching shins left and right and doing nothing to slow the crush. Spiric could only scream in pain until the trampling ceased, holding in terrified gasps as he realised that he was free.

Figures still fled and screamed ahead of him, leaving corpses and casualties in their wake. He pushed himself to his feet with a groan, throwing aside his broken goggles as he turned, searching desperately for Byreth. A single Scythe stood there, robes flapping beneath coiled armour and the open city gates burning beyond them. They cocked their head at him, spotting Spiric's hammer just as he realised he still had it in his grip.

His next breath filled his lungs with rage. A rage he now knew the source of. A rage he finally knew how to use. Spiric kicked into a staggering charge as the Scythe advanced, a dagger in their hand. His hammer led him on a wild, clumsy swing that sailed straight past his foe, carrying him a few paces too far before he could gather himself.

The Scythe hadn't capitalised on it. They could've had him dead, but they were just standing there waiting. Toying with him! Another distant rage caught Spiric and he charged again, priming his hammer for what he thought was a vicious backhanded swipe. He unleashed the blow, caught in confusion as the tip of the mace flew through the air far slower than he expected before his heart sunk.

The Scythe had stepped back. They watched the weapon

skim harmlessly past their hips and then caught it in their free hand, easily wrenching it from Spiric's grip and hurling it into the darkness.

Before he could even flinch, the same hand snatched his neck into a chokehold, their thumb pushing his jaw up, exposing his throat as their dagger drew closer and closer. Spiric's fingers scrabbled at the gauntlet holding his neck, choking and gasping as his desperate kicks bounced off the Scythe's coiled armour.

The knife scratched against the skin at his collarbone, but it didn't dig in yet. The Scythe was hesitating, wondering if they should execute the only Hytharo they'd seen in their life. Spiric didn't let them finish the thought.

His hands found a gap in the gauntlet, his fingers touching that tiny bit of exposed skin not covered by the Scythe's coiled armour. Behind the mask, Spiric saw a pair of blue eyes go wide. His axiom burned and arcing coils of blue lightning ricocheted along their body, caged by their armour as they convulsed and thrashed, dropping Spiric before slamming into the ground themselves.

Spiric stumbled into a run, his vision swimming with each step. Now was not the time for memories, Spiric thought. He already wanted to forget what had just happened, he wasn't prepared to see what in his past resembled it! But he didn't have a choice.

Darkness flickered into bright day as the bloodied corpses on the street flashed in and out of sight. The retreating crowd of Basarod's terrified residents turned to a charging horde as Spiric's palm rose to greet them, axioms showering them with lightning and filling the air with the stench of burnt flesh.

Spiric's throat cut loose a war cry, and the survivors turned back into the panicked mass. A hand clapped down on his shoulder and spun him. The dark storm lifted as he turned, sunset blazing over the city walls as he was met with a black-haired woman, her skin pale and blood-spattered, her eyes just as red.

'Spiric! The catacombs are about to fall!'

'No!' Spiric barked back. 'We stay and fight!'

She opened her mouth, words lost on her tongue as her eyes glazed over. 'For what?'

He didn't have an answer. He never had one. What had the question even been? His mind began to fog as he turned to look up at the palace. It was then he saw it. What they were fighting.

A monolith of black obsidian and the size of a skyscraper was suspended over the city as an executioner's insatiable blade. Its surface was smooth, etched and carved with elaborate precision to create channels and rivers that coursed vertically up its length. Blood flowed through the grooves, defying gravity itself as droplets of it sprang from the grounds of the stricken city and rose towards it like a twisted rainstorm.

It absorbed light just as it absorbed blood, its very presence blotting out the burning blue-orange gradient of the sky beyond it, looming closer, threatening to crush the white marble palace.

A single figure floated above the city in defiance of it. A tiny, pathetic speck of humanity that was dwarfed by the goliath before it. But then lightning burst forth from them. Enough to engulf the entire form of the monolith. More, more than natural, more than possible. It halted the monolith's fall, but blood still flowed to the god's obsidian hide.

Spiric's vision swam as he turned back to the woman who held his shoulders. The flecks of blood on her face were gone. Her own now flowed freely from her ears, nose, mouth, anything it could get out through, anything except her eyes.

They were blank.

Her irises gone.

*Hytharo no more.*

The grip shook him again, and suddenly the blank eyes were yellow. The darkness had returned and Byreth's face was illuminated by the fires of Basarod. She was yelling, swearing, yanking at his collar, but Spiric couldn't move.

'I saw!'

Byreth screamed something back at him, but he didn't care to hear it.

'I saw it! What wiped us out!'

A pyre of pure white fire lit up the sky, a light so bright it would shame the sun itself as a shockwave of scorching heat slammed into them. Sharp, thunderous booms cut through the air close behind it and the palace was no more, the inferno it fed now threatening to consume the entire city as more Scythes whipped through the air to fan the flames.

'Catacombs!' Spiric roared. 'It's the only place to hide!'

They ran.

Ran for the walls on which Spiric had first met the Viceroy of the burning city.

Ran as he should've done a thousand years ago when he'd first seen The Blood Forged God of Memory.

## CHAPTER TWENTY-SIX

# BURIED MEMORIES

F EW OTHERS HAD MADE it to the catacombs. Perhaps it was Basarod's guarded secret that the cowering families, huddled in the dark and dusty corridors, prayed the Scythes wouldn't find. Spiric couldn't catch his breath as he led Byreth through the tunnels. If he were to stop for only a moment, there was the chance one of the new refugees would look at him, see his red eyes, and know that it was his fault this cataclysm had engulfed their homes.

They had to keep their heads down, anyway. Looking ahead would only fill his face and lungs with the fine powder raining from the ceiling. Flickering glow orbs guided their way intermittently, Byreth's own held orb filling in where the others had failed. Sometimes a distant boom reached them, another piece of the city levelled, and larger rocks would join the downpour.

'You sure you know where we're headed?' Byreth hissed.

He nodded back at her. 'I've been here before.'

It was a blatant lie, but Spiric hoped it wouldn't be for long. All he needed was one more flash of a buried memory to guide the way. It had to be down here somewhere. How else would he be alive now if he hadn't escaped? There was no other way to reckon with it.

They stalked further, the tunnels growing emptier and emptier as they twisted and dipped more violently.

'Spiric, this don't look right,' Byreth said quietly.

'I know, I just... I'm sure—'

They rounded a sloping corner and one final stretch of tunnel lay before them, dead straight and a dead end. There was only one glow orb at the end that cast a pitiful light on a blockade of rubble.

Spiric looked up at Byreth, trying to twist his face into something that looked apologetic, but he was only met with her dark suspicion.

'What did you see up there, Spiric?' she whispered.

'The Blood Forged God of Memory. From my time, I mean. It was huge. Like a skyscraper of nothing but black rock that had taken to the air and was about to crush the city. I was here with the other Hytharo, fighting on the streets as it bore down on us... drawing even our own blood into the air.'

'But I don't care about no god right now! How did you get out?' Byreth snapped.

Spiric found himself shaking his head, the confusion too hard to cut through. 'But I was here —on the streets I mean— with other Hytharo... I saw the life drained out of them but... but... but why didn't it happen to me? How did I live?'

The tunnel rumbled. The air around them shrieked and made them both stagger as an unnatural wind billowed past. Words followed, each syllable coming as a clicking snap in his ears.

'I've long wondered the same thing, Spiric.'

Byreth righted herself before he did. She was waving her hand cannon wildly in any direction she could point it. Spiric dived for her, slamming his palm over her mouth before she could let loose a stream of cursed threats.

'That doesn't sound like Arallak,' Spiric whispered.

Byreth shrugged him off, mercifully keeping her voice low.

'Then who is it?'

The tunnel began rumbling again, and this time Spiric had the good sense to clap his hands over his ears. A few rocks dislodged overhead and Byreth grabbed him just in time to narrowly avoid being crushed. The strange clicking whispers came again.

'A fate evaded for too long.'

'But I killed you,' Spiric muttered under his breath. 'I saw you die.'

'Who are you—'

A billowing cloud of dust signalled another blast of air. The clicking followed, cutting Byreth off.

'And I you.'

Byreth was pulling him down the tunnel now. The dead end wouldn't take them much further, but at least she was trying. Spiric was struggling against her grip, straining to hear the voice as the catacomb quaked around them.

'It appears we both have found the means to dodge death.'

'How!?' Spiric demanded.

'Quit making him talk so much,' Byreth hissed. 'There's going to be a cave-in if he says anything else!'

'She's right,' the voice said. But there was no clicking to go with it. No gust or shaking ground.

A single figure stepped around the corner, clad in blue robes and wearing a delighted scowl on his angular face. It was Vorric. He was identical to when Spiric had last faced him. He stalked towards them at a slow, calculated pace, both his hands hidden behind his back.

'I could bury you here. These catacombs hail from the days this city held the Hytharo. Long ago, when it was known by the name "Andias." But from what I've heard of you in these last moments, you've only just remembered this. You've been buried once before, haven't you? A treasure to be preserved for a time beyond your people's strife.

'But your return is not welcome, Spiric. This goes beyond the matters of balancing this land. You were never meant to live. From your own words, I think you've now realised this. No matter how you run or hide, you are a walking anomaly, and your streak of survival must be purged from memory.'

Vorric had covered half the distance, close enough in these silent grave-tunnels that Spiric could hear a whisper without the aid of magic, but he couldn't help shouting back in rage.

'Then what of yours!?' There was venom in his voice, and he relished it. 'Nearly twenty Scythes died last time you tried this and somehow you didn't! Is that why you've come alone!? Guilt for leading your own people to their deaths? Because I can *definitely* tell you how that feels!'

Vorric faltered, his advance paused for the moment while his face cracked into a chuckle. 'Simply means to an end. Means which tie our fates together. You already know how I survived, don't you?'

'Shadow dancer,' Spiric breathed.

Vorric took another step forward. 'It appears we're both anomalies.'

'Yeah? Well, I'm not!'

Spiric felt a shove at his shoulder, hard enough to send him tumbling to the ground as Byreth swung her hand cannon level to Vorric. The air split with a colossal boom as a gout of fire engulfed the hand cannon, consuming her entire arm and everything in front of it.

But Vorric was quicker. His right hand moved as a blur, swatting the metal slug off course with an instant gale, and it whizzed past him, ricocheting down the catacombs. The ceiling quaked once more, finally giving out after so much punishment.

A sandstorm erupted overhead. Rocks and dust flooded down as one, smothering Spiric and choking his sputtering breath. Something landed on his legs, and he tried to kick it off, but it held on tight as sand began to bury them.

He squinted through the chaotic haze. Byreth was huddled on his lower half. Another figure stood over the both of them, unphased by the pelting rocks that seemed to pass straight through his elaborate black cloak.

'A place where time stands still,' Arallak said, his voice clear despite their surroundings. 'It's what we were asked to find. You told me she'd know the way.'

The shadow dancer placed his hand on Spiric's head and darkness swept through his vision. The sound of grinding rocks was silenced, the smell of shifting earth vanquished. Whether he was asleep or buried, Spiric couldn't tell, but he knew it to be deep.

# ▰ ◀ ▮▮ ▀ ▝▖

The sensation in his body returned slowly, starting with the ringing of his gun-shy ears. It was a series of incessant far-off bells and, no matter how he scrunched his eyes and tossed and turned, it was impossible to dismiss. Eventually, he found a piece of his sleeve not ruined by the cave-in and wiped his vision clean.

The catacombs were now a cramped rock tunnel. Any sign of it having once been carved by human hands was gone, spare for a lone, dim light orb a few metres down the way. Byreth was still a heap across his legs. Spiric grunted as he kicked her off, eliciting a similar sound from her.

She awoke with a start, scrambling to her feet and slamming her head into the now low ceiling. Back on all fours and swearing, her stream of curses was cut short by a loud, dry retch. A much wetter one followed, and every single vein in her neck bulged as the sickness enveloped her.

'Shit... I'm going to be hungry after that,' Byreth slurred.

She crawled a few feet away from the quickly evaporating puddle of vomit and collapsed on her side, looking at Spiric with wide, bloodshot eyes. All the freckles on her face had been erased by the clinging chalk dust, making her look almost ghostly. She waved vaguely at the rest of their surroundings, striking her wrist on a jagged rock and swearing again.

Byreth didn't need to ask her question. Spiric was already wondering the same thing.

'Arallak was here,' he said quietly.

Spiric didn't continue. Something was rumbling inside him that wanted to add to Byreth's receding mess. It was like being poisoned, but Spiric forced it down by swallowing hard.

'He must've... Oh, I don't know. I'm sick of trying to make sense of all this.'

'You an' me both.' Byreth propped herself up to sit, pulling her legs close. 'Any sign of Vorric? You think he's dead, for good this time?'

Spiric glanced around them and shook his head. 'He's got a shadow dancer on his side. It might be that he's survived the same way we just did.'

Byreth tried to rub the dust from her eyes but only succeeded in adding more. 'How stupid does a shadow dancer have to be to die and work for Vorric?'

It was a good question. Spiric pondered it for a moment. 'Maybe it's the other way around.'

'What?'

'Vorric works for a shadow dancer. One that doesn't want me alive.'

'From what I hear they don't want anyone alive.'

Spiric shook his head. 'No, but this one, listen to me, maybe doesn't want me alive because of something Arallak did. He saved me, but what if he wasn't meant to? You heard Vorric just then. It's like he *knows* something. When you were dragging me to Basarod, one of the memories that came to me… I saw Arallak talking to another shadow dancer. What if this one—'

'Has waited around who knows how many years and generations and whatever else, just to snub you out as soon as you poke your head out the sand?'

'When you put it that way…' Spiric grumbled.

He wished Grethard was here to take his side. The old man had a special gift for helping his vague and fanciful thoughts make sense. Though where he was now was a conclusion Spiric didn't want to come to.

'It won't even make sense, anyway,' Byreth continued. 'Can't that other shadow dancer just come and… I don't know, do whatever weird shit they do to kill you if they want you gone so bad?'

Another good question. It took Spiric longer to explain it away. 'Arallak said his magic costs him time. The last thing an immortal has left to lose. Maybe killing is too costly for them. That's why everyone talks about them driving people mad.'

'Or someone else does the work for them,' Byreth muttered to herself. 'Whether they've seen one or not.'

'Like what happened to Grethard. What got him banished.'

'Well, that's good, then!' Byreth clapped her hands on her knees and stood up, carefully stooping under the cave's low ceiling. 'Now the only thing we need to worry about is the entire muscle of the Academy of Breggesa.' She held out a hand to him. 'You want to keep sitting around here or what?'

'At least no one is trying to kill us,' Spiric muttered as he clasped it.

As he found his wavering balance, he quickly checked his travel pack, which was still mercifully on his back. Nothing seemed broken in there, but he could only imagine the shattered glass of broken vials stabbing through the leather.

Byreth led the way with her hand cannon and Spiric followed, praying she wouldn't have to use it again. His ears couldn't take any more punishment. What was once a wide, well-carved passageway was now a claustrophobic hollow, seemingly excavated by hand. It continued like this for far, far too long, to the point that Spiric was certain they'd be trapped down here for good, but small slits of bright sunlight streaming in from above eventually allayed his fears.

It was further still until they found an opening big enough for them to consider. It was only a short scramble straight up, but he and Byreth found themselves staring dumbstruck at the blinding light it gave.

'How long have we been down here?' Spiric asked.

'You smell that?' Byreth said after a deep, theatrical sniff.

Spiric joined her, but everything still smelt like freshly turned rock and something less desirable.

'What?'

'No smoke.'

'What?' Spiric said again, dumbly.

'Remember? How everything was on fucking fire before we came down here?'

'Ah,' Spiric said. 'I'd forgotten about that with everything else.'

She punched him in the shoulder and as much as it hurt, it was worth it to see Byreth nursing a set of bruised knuckles from the cave-in. She didn't wait for him to say anything else witty before she was scrambling up the rocky walls to freedom.

Spiric emerged from the ground next, blinking from both dust and harsh noon light. He could barely make out Byreth. She was already a fair way away, calling for him to follow. The ground around him was covered in a strange white powder... no, it was ash. Layers of it came up to his ankles, flickering into the air at the slightest breeze.

He pulled his tattered shirt to his face just as the wind picked up, carrying the cinders on past ruined walls and rubble-filled streets. The charred remains of the neatly packed buildings sat in collapsed piles, as if they'd simply fallen in on themselves. Further ahead, the hill where the palace had proudly stood looked bald. Only a few low walls had been sturdy enough to remain and mark what once was.

'Ruins within ruins,' Spiric muttered to himself. 'Worlds upon worlds.'

What if this was what Basarod had once looked like? After that time it had been called Andias, as Vorric had said. Not a single body lay in the street. Not even a footprint. Had Basarod already been forgotten? He voiced the question as he caught up to Byreth, who replied by calling him a moron.

'Forgotten? How can it be forgotten if it's still here to see? You're the only one forgetting things!' she berated. 'Forgetting yourself! Why don't you "remember up" what the hell we're meant to do next?'

Without rising to the goad, Spiric decided that from now on, he'd wonder more quietly.

'We find Grethard,' he eventually said.

Byreth made an exaggerated play of looking around and shrugging. 'And where'd you think he'd be?'

He pointed to the ruins of the palace. 'Up there if we're lucky. Maybe Arallak did the same thing to him as he did to us.'

'If we're lucky,' Byreth repeated darkly.

Secretly, Spiric was already agreeing with her. As they strode through the wastes of the city, he knew there wasn't even the slimmest of chances that the old man would arise from a nearby pile of rubble with a quip at the ready. But that wasn't who he was looking for. If this had once been his city, his own home, maybe he would see a flash of a much more familiar face.

## CHAPTER TWENTY-SEVEN

# NOTHING BESIDE REMAINS

B ASAROD WAS NOT A city suited to an empty street. As the thought crossed Spiric's mind, he found it rather dull-witted. Not many cities seemed charming when the nearest buildings were pulled-in wrecks that had long stopped smoking.

Spiric and Byreth's path up to the palace had initially been a purposeful one, but their stride had lost enthusiasm as vistas of destruction unfolded behind them. A silent agreement arose between them that they'd given up looking for Grethard. Finding any living soul would do.

This quickly turned into a fool's errand, something Spiric

barely wanted to admit to himself as he picked through the dozenth of the larger surviving structures they'd so far come across. Calling it more significant than its surroundings was a generous guess. The tallest remaining wall barely met his nose. The rest of it was a gathered pile of rubble twice the size. Yesterday it had been a trade hall of three stories, home to a maze of fabric-decked alleyways and frenzied bartering, but not even a hint of discarded merchandise or wares remained among the broken slabs.

They lingered in the former trading quarters of Basarod until any hope of scavenging a few undiscovered scraps faded.

'Can't believe there's nothing here,' Byreth said with a heavy breath as they hiked up the hill towards the palace. 'Even the bones must've been taken. How long do you reckon we've been gone? Weeks?'

'Months, even,' Spiric replied. The answer to this exact question had been brewing in his mind all afternoon. 'Long enough for Vorric to excavate the catacombs to look for us and the Scythes to lose interest.' He couldn't help double checking the sky was still clear to be sure. 'Even long enough that looters arrived and picked the place clean like vultures.'

'But how did Arallak do it? Hide us, I mean?'

'Same thing he did to throw me forward through time, I think. I'm fairly certain it's what happened to you and the others just before I blew myself up with that respark.'

'But I don't remember that!'

'You wouldn't, would you? It's day one moment, then the next... he said it was like he was just removing you from time. You still end up where you were, just later on.'

Byreth thought on it for a moment, an expression Spiric still wasn't used to seeing on her face. 'Can he put us back, then?'

'We are back.'

'No! I mean... before.'

'I don't...' Spiric trailed off. It was another good question to ask Arallak. 'He would've done it by now. It would've saved all this mess from happening.'

Byreth nodded. 'I'd give anything to be here when my brother came through. I'd have a chance to beat some damn sense into him.'

For a moment Spiric chuckled. However, on spotting her clenched fists and white knuckles out the corner of his eye, he silenced himself as best he could.

'Arallak did mention him, in sorts, just before he saved us,' Spiric said carefully. 'He said you'd know where to find him.'

'But did Arallak mean him or my brother?' Byreth snorted to herself. 'Either way, I've got no idea where to start looking.'

'In a place where time stands still,' Spiric said. 'Arallak said he and I were once asked to look for it and that you'd know the way. I think he means us to find your brother. Maybe he had something to do with all this!'

'Be bloody typical if he did,' Byreth muttered murderously.

Spiric couldn't hold back his mirth, and soon Byreth was

chuckling with him, the grim surroundings of the razed city forgotten for just a moment. They continued on to the inner reaches of Basarod, the piles of rubble they passed growing smaller and smaller as they approached the bones of the palace.

The manor they'd called home only the night before was gone. Even the foundations had been torn from the ground. Spiric and Byreth stood at the lip of the clay pit for a moment, not wanting to ask the question of what had happened to their sardonic old companion.

The only place left to explore was the palace itself. The marble walls were charred and scratched. The blinding white sheen was now just a dull grey that wouldn't shift no matter how hard Spiric rubbed at the flaky film coating it. Piles of cold white ash surrounded what remained of the entrance like drifting dunes that wafted away ahead of Spiric's footsteps as he crossed the threshold.

The grand cathedral that encased the palace had collapsed. Anything that had risen more than a few metres from the ground now lay as debris on the enormous staircases that led down to the dais. From the massive landing at the top, Spiric paused to survey the devastation. They were architectural corpses that baked in the sun, seeming to decay the same as flesh would.

'Something wrong?' Byreth asked. She'd already taken to entertaining herself by kicking some of the smaller fragments of tile down the stairs and watching them clatter along the length of it.

'No... But something isn't right, either.'

'Yeah, everyone's dead, ain't they.'

'So where are the bodies?' Spiric asked. 'The Scythes couldn't have done something with them all. There must have been thousands of people in this city. You said you hadn't even seen a bone, let alone a corpse. Who's... who's...'

His sentence trailed off as he heard a clatter far below. One that Byreth hadn't caused. He glanced at her. She was instantly alert, the hand cannon aimed down at the dais without a care for the fact the shot would probably miss anything further than the first landing.

It was torture to wait. It felt like hours, just straining for the slightest flash of movement down below. Could the Scythes still be here? Could they have really waited all these months? But then, down at the dais, a figure rose from the distant throne. The shade cloth that hung over it, now tattered and flapping in the wind, cast their shape into indiscernible darkness, but Spiric had already convinced himself it was the shadow dancer.

He blinked, and suddenly a second figure had joined them, their forms now both cloaked in gloom not by a shade cloth, but by a night sky in the desert beyond. Once again, red robes hung from Spiric's shoulders as he stood atop the pristine stairs.

An unbearable envy rose in his throat as he watched the pair converse, their voices somehow so distant yet so close to his ears. It was as if each word was spoken twice, making it difficult to discern who each voice belonged to.

'I've long thought you right, my prince. I've pondered the difference between a birthright and a blood price,' one voice whispered. 'Yet I always thought your lineage taught it one and the same.'

'They do,' the other said, sounding like a boy's voice, just a bit younger than the first. 'And that's why I know it to be a lie. I'm glad I can confide this in you.'

'And only me. My brother may be your guardian, but he has been taught exactly how he should be.'

The envy turned to boiling rage, and Spiric felt his fists clench. It was him they were talking about. Him! Which meant that the first voice was Arallak.

'As have all around me. I worry I will never have a chance to rectify my own legacy. The timing of my birth between my sisters is akin to a curse upon my potential to rule. What good will an old man be who agitates for his own abdication?'

'As good as dead,' Arallak said back to the prince. 'Lest you engage in those tactics you fear?'

There was a pause. A long pause. Long enough for a flash of the present day to creep back into Spiric's vision, the figure now walking up the stairs towards them. But the night returned before Spiric could even squint at them.

'I could dream of nothing more worthless,' the prince replied. 'Hytharo bloodshed shall only bring Hytharo bloodshed. I make no shame in admitting that I would not be a victor in a struggle for this damned throne, and I shudder to think of which one of us would.'

'Only one who would happily carry it on,' Arallak said. 'One who would believe it their birthright.'

'I wish I had been born at a more opportune time,' the prince muttered, each word already seeming familiar to Spiric. 'A far future where I could have a chance to right this.'

'A future further trailed with the oppression of all at the hands of our few?'

Another flash of day, of Byreth shaking him, yelling in his face as scuttering arcanites surrounded them.

'A price I would be willing to pay if only for a chance to pay it back. To erase the sins of the Hytharo from this world.' The prince took a long breath. 'It is yet another sin to speak of it, but I hear rumour of a place that might make this possible.'

'You want me to find it?'

'Yes. Find it. I feel it my only option now, so I may one day return and reclaim this bloodied throne. A place of skyscrapers in the west, surrounded by a crown of white thorns. A place where time stands still.'

The bright sun returned as a burning betrayal filled Spiric's guts, the figure standing before him taking the form of Voss-Ela. Her skin looked thrashed and beaten, by hand or by sun. Her once-royal face was marred by an aged bruise that surrounded a hollowed eye socket. Her robes were in a similar state. Gone was the methodical and almost precarious layering that would befit the leader of the great city, each cloth now an obscuring shawl that hid whatever had turned her stride into a stagger.

The previously glimpsed arcanites turned out to be just as unthreatening. There were only four of them, rusty little creatures composed of only enough parts to make two of their regular form. Byreth, her hand cannon stowed again, gently kicked one with the steel tip of her boot, causing both it and Voss-Ela to violently flinch.

'I would prefer if such tests of metal were avoided,' Voss-Ela said. Her words came out as a sour rasp. 'After all these months, they are the last beings I control in Basarod. Or what is left of it.'

'It used to be called Andias,' Spiric said vacantly. Suddenly, one of the viceroy's words snapped back into his mind. 'How long did you say?'

She scrutinised them with her one good eye. 'Months. Months I've lost count of, and yet it looks as though the pair of you haven't experienced a day of it. I've wondered for many cold nights if you'd been able to escape the Scythes. They razed the city in search of you. I could never help the bitter thought that if they'd found you they would have called off the slaughter.'

'They wouldn't've,' Byreth said. 'They'd say we're all tainted.'

Voss-Ela gave a dejected nod. 'A conclusion I gave into myself.' She paused, her battered face mustering a scowl that she fixed on Spiric. 'I regret to say I now know your pain, boy. They saved me for last. It was only after they were sure I knew not of your escape, or where you'd gone, that they finally relented. They still circled high above for weeks and I wondered why they'd left me alive. But now I realise I live for the same reason as you. A monument to my own hubris. I was so foolish to parade you around.'

'I'm sorry,' Spiric said quietly.

She shook her head. 'It's not your sorrow to have. I think that's why they left me. Walking among the grave of my home is a pain worse than death. Just as you said.' She looked back down the stairs and Spiric spotted the makeshift camp set up in the ruined amphitheatre at the lower landing. 'Come. You're still my guests. I'd trade a meal for a tale of escape. It's not the type of thing I've yet heard since...'

Voss-Ela couldn't bring herself to finish her sentence and began making her way back to the camp. Spiric and Byreth followed, slightly more at ease but still glancing to the sky. Even if the months had been as lonely as the viceroy said, Spiric couldn't shake the feeling that he was still being watched.

'Do you know what happened to Grethard?' Spiric asked as they descended.

The answer was somewhere between a grunt and a laugh. 'The old man turned out to be quite the fighter, from what Vorric said. He seemed as intent on hunting him as he did you, Spiric, yet he appears to have been just as fruitless. He may have escaped. Maybe engulfed in the blaze. Or cut down without a thought by one of the other Scythes. If he did live, he's smart enough not to linger here.'

He glanced to Byreth a few steps behind.

'The Lightning Cage?' she mouthed silently.

He shook his head. Grethard had said he'd only kept his exile there for fear of a shadow dancer, but after everything Spiric had told the old man, maybe it was something else.

*Maybe it was Vorric.*

'If you do happen to find him, send him my regards. Even if he were only a passing associate, he may be all that's left of the Order of Reyat.'

'So... so no one else...'

'Survivors? None.'

It was only as they reached Voss-Ela's camp that the length of their supposed absence set in. The improvised luxury of it certainly explained how the rest of the town had felt so picked clean. The tent which sheltered them from harsh sun was composed of many market shade cloths with a heaping collection of singed cushions inside. The centrepiece of the camp was a battered bronze firepit that crackled with an enduring flame which spouted from half-crushed light orbs.

The skewered lizards and scorched weeds Voss-Ela was clumsily tending to reminded Spiric of his first night in Grethard's company. She handed Spiric a warm metal bowl of the two, presented in the most appetising form she could manage. She then pointed out to one of her arcanites, baking in the sun on the stone balcony that overlooked the desert.

'The lizards aren't clever creatures. In the mornings, their feet find the sun-touched iron appealing to their night-cooled blood, but by the time they've soaked their fill of warmth, the soft skin around their claws has fused to the metal.'

Byreth picked up one of the skewers from her own bowl, examining six charred sockets where the joints had been. 'Explains why they look like stabbed snakes. What do you do with the legs?'

A grim smile crossed her face. 'Bait for the next lizard.'

They ate quietly and carefully. The lizards wore a tough hide wrapped around far too many bones, so what little meat to be gleaned from it was savoured before having to start scavenging for the next mouthful. Even the strange weeds, which Voss-Ela said she'd scavenged from the ruined fields around Basarod, were a chore to get down. Spiric could only handle a few at a time before they were all stuck between his teeth, but Byreth's gnashing jaw seemed to have no trouble.

As fair a trade as it was, Spiric then launched into a recounting of his and Byreth's last few hours. Voss-Ela listened with a silent stare, not even flinching when Spiric told of their rescue at the hands of the shadow dancer or even what he'd seen of the Blood Forged God of Memory.

'And then, just as we met here, I remembered more. Arallak was talking to another Hytharo. A prince... A prince I was supposed to protect... Who asked him to find a place "where

349

time stood still." Somewhere to wait until a better time to claim the throne to put a stop to the brutality of The Hytharo Empire.'

'Which is why he told you to find my brother!' Byreth burst out.

Spiric looked over to her, and there was a mad twinkle in her eye as she paced around them, jabbering away.

'Because that's what Vehli was looking for! Korbis the broker said so! That's what he said the ephemerals do! What if Vehli and your prince were looking for the same thing? Maybe Arallak found it and managed to bring the prince there before your big memory god came and wiped everything else out!'

'You think he could be alive?'

'You've been telling me the same damn thing about my brother the whole time!' Byreth laughed. 'Maybe that prince remembers you! Who you are!'

Spiric couldn't help a grimace. 'I hope he doesn't. I haven't liked what I've remembered so far.'

Voss-Ela interrupted them, a puzzled look on her face. 'So this god of memory made you forget everything it touched, and by the sounds of it, killed everything too... But you said you saw it... I don't understand how you escaped, let alone how you're now remembering these things.'

Spiric went to wave a hand dismissively at the question but held himself back. Voss-Ela still had a certain imposing aura about her, though this didn't stop Byreth.

'Put it down to shadow dancer nonsense,' she shot. 'We can always ask Arallak next time we see him.'

'Which won't be until we find where your brother is,' Spiric said. 'I remember the prince saying it was to the west. A set of ruins with a crown of white thorns.'

Voss-Ela nodded slowly and looked over her shoulder, out across the desert. For Spiric, there was a strange familiarity about the motion.

'I know of this place, but it's not as near as you'd hope,' Voss-Ela said. 'You'd get lost trekking straight through the sands. Following the edge of the mountains will be safer but will take weeks and you'll be chancing encounters with scavengers and what few bandits remain in this area.' A sigh escaped her before she continued. 'With nothing left to offer, Basarod is no longer the merchant hub it once was. The few that visited found themselves disappointed in the small welcome I could give. Despite the Scythe's efforts to suppress the tales of your presence, Spiric, word still got out. Some have come looking for a Hytharo, and I made sure to answer with the same warning you gave me.'

'Maybe it was Tetran,' Byreth said, adding for Voss-Ela's sake; 'She was a trader that took us through the mountains from Kurkress to here. She'd left in the day before the Scythes came.'

Voss-Ela scowled, but her face softened quickly. 'She could've tipped them off, but then again, anyone could've.' A hand emerged from her shawls, and she buried her face in it. 'I was such a fool.'

'Today's genius is yesterday's fool,' Byreth recited with a bit too much confidence.

'Grethard say that to you?' Spiric asked.

'Nah, made it up, but he probably said something like that at one point.' She cracked her knuckles. 'I ain't going to say the same thing to my brother when we find him.'

Spiric also held his tongue at this. He was starting to think that a family reunion between the two might be a touch more violent than it should be.

'Stay the night and rest,' Voss-Ela said. 'Going by what you've told me, I would hazard a guess that blood rush is the only thing keeping you awake. Your destination is a long journey, and I should be able to find you charts to assist in it, among other things.'

'And what will you do?' Spiric asked.

'The same as you'll one day have to, Spiric. Mourn and rebuild.'

## CHAPTER TWENTY-EIGHT

# BOUNDLESS AND BARE

Voss-Ela only journeyed as far as Basarod's demolished gates with them the next morning. Their farewell was a muted one. It barely hid the unspoken advice to not return to this place. As he and Byreth trekked up into the mountains, Spiric found himself wondering if Arallak had once imparted the same sentiment.

The distant conversation he'd glimpsed between Arallak and that faceless prince had shown his brother was just as intent on protecting him as Spiric had been the prince, yet try as he might, he couldn't summon the slightest memory of the royal.

The incline was too steep for he or Byreth to exchange a word. After the exertion and terror of it all, a single night's rest had barely been enough to scrub his body's weariness. It was a silence only punctuated by their sharp and heavy breathing, but the absence of Byreth's chatter at least gave him time to process.

At the time, Spiric had been more than happy to accept Byreth's explanation of his escape from Basarod, or Andias, as it had been called then. But Voss-Ela's question which had prompted it still lurked at the edge of his consciousness. If that enormous block of blood-streaked obsidian had been supposed to erase all it touched from memory, then how was he now still seeing fragments of his past life?

The blank and fading face of the black-haired woman flashed across his vision again. Her eerily white eyes lingered longer than the rest. There was still no escape Spiric could remember. He couldn't even comprehend the possibility of it. Yet there were so many more memories that seemed to take place after it; that seemed so *real*. The terror of being alone and hunted and of his hands being forced to kill just didn't match up to the wanton slaughter he'd so gladly taken part in. Something about seeing that god had changed him.

The mountain ridge soon crested underfoot, the last of the desert floor's sand only carried up by the occasional violent gust of wind from where Basarod's still smouldering ruins lay. They surveyed it silently for a while as they rested. It was a sorry sight.

'Ruins within ruins, worlds upon worlds.'

Spiric only just caught Byreth's whisper.

'Funny how true that seems to be,' she continued. 'I wonder how far back it goes.'

'To before those-of-glass?'

'What?'

He shrugged. 'Grethard said it to me once. Said that's what they called the people who built all the skyscrapers.'

'Yeah, well, I just wonder what they buried to build what they did.'

'I dread to think it, but likely something more dangerous than they could even produce.'

The obsidian tower blinked into his mind again, the timing of its appearance being far too convenient to be a coincidence.

Along with whatever else they'd managed to stuff into their burgeoning packs, Voss-Ela had saddled them with a dozen furled maps and charts. The expeditionary wing of the Order of Reyat had long ago scouted Basarod's surroundings and found the city to be a lonely port in a desert the size of an ocean, a metaphor which Spiric had little success in explaining to Voss-Ela and Byreth.

The encircling mountains sectioned it off from the greater desert plains that hosted the cities of Breggesa, Kyrea and Iroka. The only entrance into the region that didn't require climbing was a distant pass that was simply known as Saltgate. The undulating trail which led to that particular valley was a trade route marked by golden domes that intermittently dotted the landscape like foreboding sentinels.

Beyond Saltgate lay the second half of their journey. The only knowledge of the path that Voss-Ela provided took the form of rumours brought back by those desperate enough to travel it. But she promised what they sought would lie at the end of it. Ruins that were surrounded by a crown of white thorns.

Between them, words weren't wasted as they walked, for there were precious few hours temperate enough to travel. The thin air did little to filter the full force of the midday sun, forcing them to shelter in cramped but cool caves that were pockmarked with makeshift firepits or scrawled and long-faded graffiti.

The nights found them in a similar spot, though for the opposite reasons. With each passing day of travelling north, the wind picking up from the desert floor grew more bitter and piercing. Only a fool would consider attempting to traverse the craggy mountain path in these conditions lest they be blown clean off into the sky. Many nights, Spiric found himself restraining Byreth from becoming one of them.

In the evenings, without the relentless pace she was setting to burn off her energy, Byreth had instead channelled it into wondering aloud any stray thought that crossed her mind. It often centred on questions of Spiric's past that he was still struggling to find answers for.

At first he'd gladly taken part. But soon he couldn't help but sit and grimace as Byreth continued to rehash every word anew. In these long nights, Spiric missed Grethard's wisdom the most, especially how the old man knew when to stop talking and snore instead.

Eight days had passed since they'd left Basarod. Eight of the most mundane and dull days Spiric could remember. No appearances from shadow dancers, no new memories revealed, not even any new methods of wielding lightning to be toyed with.

In a rare show of caution, Byreth made the threat of her much talked up beatings if Spiric summoned so much as a flicker of electricity, lest they risk the sound or flash of light attracting unwanted attention.

Even the day when the border crossing outpost of Saltgate appeared in view, Spiric couldn't muster a single spark of excitement in his heart. Without a pair of tinted goggles between them, he'd reluctantly agreed that Byreth would be the only one to stray across the path of any kind of civilisation they encountered. He could see her point. Staring at his boots the entire time was a sure-fire way to be spotted as a stranger worth investigating with rumour of a Hytharo in everyone's mind.

Spiric could only stand and watch as she approached Saltgate. Despite all the days of walking, her stride still carried the confidence it once had when she'd walked him and Grethard into Kurkress. Then again, most of their remaining precious water was sloshing in her pack, a small fortune Spiric prayed she'd trade wisely for the rest of the supplies they'd need.

Once she was a speck on the rocks creeping towards the

distant outpost, Spiric sighed and began cutting a much less pleasant route out onto the desert floor. His path was lengthened by the need to keep Saltgate from view and the undulating sand dunes seemed to double the number of steps he needed to take to gain ground.

Each footfall felt exaggerated as his boots sunk into the soft sand, and his hips were burning with the exertion of it when he reached the cliffs on the other side of the outpost. A chilly wind signalled dusk and Spiric secreted himself in a cave that overlooked Saltgate from a distance, only emerging to wave Byreth in when she finally trekked up an hour later.

'Have I got stories for you,' she grunted as she hefted a bulging sack of supplies off her shoulders. She slipped a hand into a pocket and tossed him a fresh pouch of food before finding one for herself.

'About damn time,' he said as he ripped it open. The evening meal was a much heartier affair than those of the past week, even if it was just a few more twigs of cured meat washed down with a handful of grain that turned to glue when chewed. 'What did you hear?'

'Heard all sorts of things about a Hytharo,' Byreth managed around her own mouthful. 'They know you're out there, Spiric. I didn't even have to ask, they just told me when they heard which way I was coming from.'

'How much did you tell them?' Spiric blurted in a panic.

She shrugged. 'From Kurkress, nothing much else. They said

everything south o' here is dead quiet. Not even the Scythes have come through since. Heard tell that Breggesa came down hard on them for wrecking a city with nothing to show for it.'

'But the point was to "show nothing," wasn't it? They were trying to wipe the place off the map.'

Another shrug. 'Well, it didn't work, did it? People up and down the place claiming they'd seen the Hytharo, even that they'd seen more than one! I was half tempted to join in for the fun of it. All these tales of people pulling water from their fingers or something... They just about accused me of being you when I told them how much I had.'

'But did you hear any more of what happened to the Scythes? Of Vorric?'

'Tried asking about that one, but the answers I got were as real as what they said about you. Disbanded, broken up, fed to something or other, or executed.'

'Vorric wouldn't have been,' Spiric said. 'He's got his own shadow dancer.'

'If there is one,' Byreth shot back. 'I'd be worried if he felt ballsy enough to tell us the truth about it. Last thing we need is that.'

'Most of what happened is "the last thing we need."'

For the first time in a while, they shared a meagre chuckle. The night that followed was quiet for once. Spiric found himself lulled to sleep quickly and when he awoke the next morning, Byreth had already returned from one last venture into the outpost, another smaller sack of supplies in one hand and a beaten-up pair of boots in the other. It was only when Spiric brushed the tarp they'd been using as a blanket aside that he figured out why his feet had felt so damn cold for the past hour.

'It ain't much, but I paid one of the hunters to stuff a bit of redfoot fur into our boot soles. No idea if yours'll fit right, but I ain't going to carry you the rest of the way.'

With a muttered thanks, Spiric stuffed his feet into the boots, trying to ignore the odd squishing sensation around his toes. The fit was tight, but not uncomfortably so, and they set off soon after. The mountain bluffs around them grew more frequent, providing midday shade and a few more walking hours.

After another day had passed, Spiric finally received Byreth's blessing to begin experimenting with his axioms. Camped down for the second night, he began adding more runes to the few still on his arm, experimenting with different combinations and looking to Byreth for what little advice she could give.

Even if Grethard had been by their side, it was more an exercise of rediscovery than practice. The few axioms he knew were corroborated with the knowledge Basarod's scholars had quibbled up for him, and then cross-referenced to the few memories of Hytharo magic that he'd glimpsed.

Five nights and three entire vials of ink later, Spiric could barely feel his fingers for the sheer quantity of lightning he'd forced through them. They tingled as he walked in the day, and even the simple task of eating had become a clumsy and ham-fisted affair.

But it was worth it.

He could now bind his lightning to rocks and the rare hunks of scrap metal found along the way, wield it as a length of chain, even have it encase his own body like a carapace. The next person to threaten him would be in for one hell of a surprise, Byreth had said, as long as they weren't wearing the cage-like armour of the Scythes. With only one vial of his red ink remaining, she once again forbade his experiments. Spiric couldn't bring himself to say it, but it was for the best.

It didn't stop him from feeling powerful. Almost invincible. Like he used to feel. Any intention of tamping down this sentiment was brushed aside. If Voss-Ela's maps were right, their journey's end lay waiting for them the next day. Whatever he was to find there, whatever he'd face, he'd need to do it with confidence.

*No matter how unnerving my past is, I must face it.*

When they made camp for the night, it was at the foot of the last ridge of their mountainous path. It was growing dark as they'd set down, the gravel underfoot only painted by dim stars. Stray curiosity drew them to investigate what lay beyond.

Atop the summit, the view of lone and level sands stretched out until the horizon took them, a pure, dull white under the last hints of dusk. Not a single dune punctuated the land, leaving the gleaming structures that stood alone in the flats as the only thing Spiric could focus his eyes on.

Skyscrapers, like that of The Lightning Cage, were held in a cluster by a ring of gigantic white spines, their smooth metal surfaces creased into mosaics of oblique shapes and angles that curved each pinnacle's end out over the desert. They overshadowed the silhouetted shapes which they guarded, twice the size of all but the one sitting in the very centre.

Its presence was undeniable, like it grew taller each day just to spite the massive barbs that surrounded it, its obsidian skin a stubborn contrast so dark it didn't even hint at the starlight above.

'That's it,' Spiric said quietly to Byreth. 'That's what I saw.'

'It's huge. How did—?'

'I don't know. But maybe... Maybe tomorrow I'll remember.'

## CHAPTER TWENTY-NINE

# LONE AND LEVEL SANDS

WITH THE TIP OF the first spire's shadow only a few steps before him, Spiric brought his tired legs to a halt. Byreth stopped as well and trudged over to him. With no trail or so much as a rock to avoid, they'd kept a dozen or so metres apart as they'd crossed the flats. There wasn't even a breeze to drown out their whispers, so Spiric often found himself straying far from Byreth if he wasn't keeping his eyes on her. Every time he marched purposely back to her side it was only minutes until she was again a speck in the distance.

'Vent masks?' Byreth suggested. It was the easiest day of

walking they were likely to ever have had, but she still sounded out of breath.

Spiric could only gasp and nod, swinging off his pack and pulling out his own. He checked each tiny valve on it for filter moss as he tried to remember the rule-of-thumb Tetran had imparted on him for how long each would last before he needed to switch which one he was breathing through.

His mask had five valves on it, yet one was already empty from his trip back to the golden dome. He swore under his breath as he put the mask on, unsure if Tetran's timings had been in minutes or hours. He'd feel it if he needed to switch. The air here was strange enough as it was.

The twin rhythms of faint clicking filled the air and he nodded to Byreth. They set off again, the same foreboding he'd felt at the final border of The Lightning Cage filling his mind as he watched the spire's shadow retreat with the motion of the sun.

The twisting surface of it and its cousins had turned from last night's uniformly grey surfaces into a patchwork gradient of dark shade and blindingly pure white. Spiric couldn't make out the borders that separated these angles, but he swore there was an occasional flicker of movement along them.

The spaces between the spires' trunks were filled by thrashing clusters of angular glass. They clashed like competing weeds, any gaps in their façade looking like wounds that'd been carved out by an enormous yet precise blade. They ranged from narrow crawlspaces to wide swathes of open ground, yet they treated them with suspicion all the same.

Every opening or path was tested with a hurled handful of sand, a trick Byreth's brother had once taught her, each one responding in ways he and Byreth least expected. The only commonality between them was the growing growl of frustration Spiric found rising in his throat.

'Didn't you say Grethard was throwing you into these things from the second he met you?' Byreth asked as they skirted around another wall of glass.

'You want to do the same now?' Spiric snapped back.

The last opening they'd attempted had belched a spurt of green flames back at them, almost taking off his eyebrows. They'd joked about running out of sand to throw, but the prospect was growing more likely by the minute.

'None of these things are like that. All the fractures Grethard showed me we could at least see coming. A wind tunnel, or... or a light-bend.'

'What's a light-bend?'

Spiric shuddered at the thought of it. 'I was going to say it was a place where nothing looks right, but...'

He waved up at the nearest stretch of glass as he passed it. Portions of its surface were bent inwards like punctured skin, but instead of revealing the same dusty and oddly decorated innards Spiric was used to seeing, it only showed a vacant blue sky or even more layers of glass panelling.

'I mean...' Byreth said slowly. 'This doesn't look right, does it?'

'Problem is it looks solid, so unless you or Grethard forgot to tell me that Curiktics can walk through walls—'

'*Looks* solid.'

Byreth turned to him, something either smug or manic written across her brow. Taking a few cautious steps back, she scooped up a heaping fistful of sand and hurled it at the glass, where it simply vanished.

'What if we've been doing this all wrong?'

Spiric shook his head and turned to march off. 'Grethard still wouldn't do it, he wouldn't know what's in there and neither do we.'

He'd only made it two steps before Byreth had grabbed him and spun him back around. 'Then how would he find out? You knew that old bastard better than me, but he wouldn't just walk away from something like that, would he?'

'Sure looks like he walked away from us,' Spiric muttered.

Despite the months that had supposedly passed, there was an odd resentment that had plagued Spiric for these past weeks. One he'd tried to push down, to excuse, to rationalise away. None of it had worked.

'He didn't walk away from us,' Byreth said firmly.

'Then where is he!?' Spiric snapped back. 'He waited thirty years alone in The Lightning Cage for a shadow dancer he wasn't even sure he'd seen, but he couldn't wait a fraction of that for us? He just gave up, didn't he?'

'He didn't give up,' Byreth retorted. 'You and I both fucking know what happened to him, but I just thought you didn't want to say it! I've been thinking this whole time you were holding on to him the same way I'm holding on to my fucking brother, but he's gone! Got it? They're both gone!'

Something was seething in her, a rage that barely veiled grief.

'Thought you'd know this by now,' she continued. 'Cost of waiting like that. All that time. It's what you told me that prince of yours said. That he'd give up everything else just for another chance. Even if you found Grethard... or your memory, what do you get, huh? You ever thought about what's at the end of that road for you?'

It was a question Spiric had wondered for months. 'I don't want to give myself the hope.'

Byreth's voice grew softer, something Spiric hadn't heard before. 'But then you get to move on, right? You find out why, then you never have to ask yourself that question again.'

Spiric met her gaze, a sad one rare enough to match her voice as it was now. Maybe she'd never hoped to find her brother alive from the beginning. It was all just a lie to make the task less complicated for those she'd shared it with. But all along, the only thing she'd been looking for was the truth of why he'd left her behind.

'If we find him in there, your brother, I mean...' Spiric said quietly.

'Then I'll know he did as he said and that'll be enough.'

Spiric savoured her words. Deep down, it was the same way he felt of Arallak. Of himself. That all this wasn't a lie, a trick, a plan gone wrong. Just a means to make things right, even if all those wronged were long, long gone.

'Let's try it,' Spiric eventually said. 'I think you're right.'

She held out a hand and he took it with a firm grasp. They approached the glass until they were face to face with it. Byreth went to step in, but Spiric held her back for a moment, one last thing on his mind.

'Grethard told me Curiktics could see straight through light-bends.'

'Yeah, well, he told you all sorts of things, didn't he?'

With one massive stride, Byreth disappeared through the glass surface, yanking Spiric along with her. Her grip almost crushed his bones, but without it he would've been immediately lost. The sky turned iron grey, tainted with frozen trails of rust-coloured lightning. He couldn't help but gawp up at it until his head started to spin.

*No, I can be distracted like this, not now!*

Spiric focused again on Byreth's grip and snapped his eyes to the horizon ahead of him. It tilted at a strange angle, enough to make him topple sideways before it reset itself, its centre now giving birth to the obsidian monolith beyond. The sky's ochre bolts drained into its summit, flowing down it like liquid before engulfing it entirely.

He lost count of his steps as he watched it dissolve, leaving behind only the silhouette of a man. It was gargantuan in the distance, but Spiric blinked to suddenly find it at his height, only a few feet ahead. It silently walked past on his right and he twisted to follow, only to be met by an army of shadows marching rank and file at his heels.

'Byreth! They're—'

But she was suddenly one of them as well. Spiric tried to lurch away, but the thing's grip was too strong! It pulled him still harder as he tried to pry himself loose with his free hand, a black sleeve materialising around the shapeless figure's arm. Suddenly embroidered silver runes on finely woven black cloth were spreading across the figure's body.

All that remained was the blank face, tantalizingly withholding what Spiric was dying to see. His heart already knew who it could be, but he had to see him to be sure. Maybe he just had to say his name and all would be clear.

'Arallak?' Spiric whispered.

'No.'

The blank face was gone, replaced by one sharp and pearlescent, framed by swept and silken onyx-coloured hair and a pair of pitch-black eyes that drilled into him. There was a curious hunger about their grin. The kind worn by a man who'd never once eaten and had just laid eyes on a meal. He wrenched at Spiric's arm one last time, and the boy tumbled forward with a scream.

He hit the ground hard enough for it to daze him and he could only kick and thrash before his hand was finally free. He scrambled to his knees, holding his aching shoulder.

The blue sky had returned. Byreth was doubled over before him, swearing as her hands clutched at her now maskless face. Spiric checked his own, finding only the creases the straps had left on his cheeks.

'What the hell happened to them? Spiric, we need to get out of here, to—'

She couldn't summon another word, her eyes set on where they'd just come from. Behind them were more ruins, as endless and sprawling as their path ahead. Something in Spiric's gut warned him this wasn't another light-bend.

'We have to keep going,' he stammered. 'Whatever took our masks is probably a far sight more dangerous than the air they were protecting us from.'

'How do know!?'

'Because I just met them.'

## CHAPTER THIRTY

# A PLACE WHERE TIME STANDS STILL

THEY SET OFF THROUGH the low dunes in silence, the grid-like nature of the ruins reminiscent of The Lightning Cage. The glass here had fared far worse than the illusional walls that had linked the white spires, both of which were now nowhere to be seen. Standing around fifty paces from their neighbour, each skyscraper was uniform in their broken-down appearance.

Shards lingered in the metal frames, while the rest mixed into the encroaching sand dunes. Running up the four corners of each one was a series of hexagonal golden tiles, and at some points the thick plating seemed to be the only thing holding the structures aloft from the sands.

When they first strayed closer to one of the skyscrapers, Spiric had seen movement deep in one of the rooms exposed by its broken windows. A flicker in the dark behind a barricade of steel racks loaded down with strange instruments. He and Byreth had debated vigorously in panicked whispers until she threw caution to the wind, spending a single rune to hurl a bolt of light at the figure.

It remained formless.

Featureless.

Just like what Spiric had seen in the light-bend. He added it to the lengthening list of bizarre phenomena that Grethard would've called fractures. The strangest of all, however, was the shadows. All but their own rebelled against the sun. It was only after they'd passed more than a dozen crumbling skyscrapers that Spiric realised where their allegiance lay.

'They point to Memory,' he whispered.

He'd stopped in one of the informal avenues filled in by the dunes. It was perfectly straight, wide, too, but not wide enough to give him the full view of the monolith, its blackened face standing as a dead end.

'To what?'

Spiric raised a finger, and Byreth followed it. The sun shone in from the right, but not a single shadow crossed the avenue. They lapped across their neighbour like falling pillars leaning on one another, forming a dark border around the street.

'Why do they do that?' Byreth wondered aloud.

'I don't know,' Spiric replied. 'Ours don't—' The words caught in his throat as he looked down. Their shadows were stretching ahead of them. 'We shouldn't linger here.'

'They are,' Byreth whispered.

A figure stood a hundred metres away, barely a speck against the black wall beyond. It could've easily been another one of the walking shades they'd seen —Spiric had counted more than a dozen— but this was the first in the full blaze of the sun.

'Do you think it's Arallak?' she asked.

The face of the shadow dancer he'd seen only an hour ago flashed across Spiric's mind. 'If it wasn't, they'd have killed us by now, right?'

The pair followed their shadows, watching them grow longer and longer with each step towards the monolith. To his relief, Spiric soon recognised that familiar grim expression Arallak wore. Byreth's pace slowed as they both drew near and Spiric had to take her hand to reassure her, only now remembering she'd not properly met the shadow dancer yet.

'So you're...' Byreth stammered.

'I am,' Arallak said.

'It's been a while,' Spiric said, keeping his tone even.

'Seconds for me,' he replied. 'I came straight here after we met at Basarod.'

'And was it you who took our vents?' Byreth asked.

Arallak frowned. 'I... You won't need them here. I know the air is safe. This place...'

'We've been here before, haven't we?' Spiric said. 'We were in Andias. And that...' He nodded to the monolith. 'That thing destroyed the city. It would've wiped out the Hytharo.'

Arallak shook his head, a moment of pride crossing his grimace. 'Putting an end to a time of suffering.'

'Which time?' Byreth muttered.

Spiric ignored her. 'But my life wasn't meant to be saved, was it? The prince, the one who asked for a place where time stood still...'

'Yes,' Arallak said quietly. 'It's what allowed me to lead you both here.' He looked to Byreth and she quavered under his gaze. 'You have my thanks for aiding my brother in his journey. I can only repay you by helping you find yours.'

'You mean he's—'

'Come,' Arallak said, cutting her off. 'His is a tale best told by sight, not words.'

Arallak set a gentle yet somewhat faltering pace, a stark difference to the uneasy probing gait he and Byreth had been forced to adopt. He took them through the ruins, quiet hallways where even their breath didn't make a noise and the pad of their footsteps was muffled by settling dust.

The eerie, faceless shadows paid little mind to the intrusion as they passed. Some stood in doorways to watch and others huddled as close to the corridor walls as possible.

'What are they?' Spiric whispered.

The shadow dancer stopped next to one of the shadows at the sill of a broken window. Spiric could only make out their posture as some kind of crouch and imagined them peering down at something below the sands lapping at their invisible feet.

'The same as I, really,' Arallak said indifferently. 'Memories. Echoes of them, at least. Those taken from life so quickly they didn't even realise it had happened. Either they expected a tomorrow or the way they died was one they could not comprehend. And so, an echo remained.'

'They thought they would live... like... like it was pure resonance,' Spiric said slowly. 'The magic of those-of-glass.'

'The remnants of it.'

Arallak's hand snapped to grab Byreth's, who was reaching to poke it.

'I don't want to discover what touching it would do, however. Best not to understand it.'

'Is this what happened to my brother?' Byreth asked as they set back out onto the sands.

He shook his head. 'This doesn't happen to people of our time. Only those from before.'

'Of those-of-glass,' Spiric said. Lingering questions still followed him. Once their path was meandering through the dune-swept streets, he felt it was safe enough to ask them.

'I've never seen them before, except...'

'We don't know why they exist as they do. And maybe the echoes themselves hold this knowledge. It may be the fact they don't is the only thing keeping them there.'

'I saw them in a light-bend once. Twice, actually. The day I met you as well, but this time, today, one of them seemed to turn into a shadow dancer. One I've not met before. But do they turn into shadow dancers? Or would you turn into one of them?'

'I don't think it's something we should rush to find answers to.'

'You're right,' Byreth said abruptly. 'I want you to tell me how you know about my brother.'

Arallak glanced over his shoulder at her, an eyebrow raised for only a moment before he faced forward again. 'It's an insightful question. One that even Spiric might be able to answer when we get there.'

'Get where?' Byreth badgered.

'Here,' Spiric said as he stopped.

A skyscraper reached high before them, sunken and slanting. Enormous dishes sprouted from its sides like stray blades of grass. They were pure white, spare for the rust, with faintly concave shapes. It was the tallest of its surroundings, aside from the obsidian monolith itself, but the two hundred metres of vacant sand separating them made the comparison difficult to comprehend. When Spiric looked up at the skyscraper again, it was leaning just a bit further over their heads.

Arallak motioned towards the only broken window at

ground level. A musty orange haze lingered inside, rising and falling in a gentle rhythm from the decaying carpet. The only thing in the near-empty room was a jagged rock which lay a short way in, untouched among shattered glass.

Spiric estimated it was about the size of his hand, but when he looked down at his own, the rock was suddenly in his grip. He looked up. Only Arallak was there, his red eyes filled with grim determination.

'This isn't right,' Spiric felt his mouth say. 'Even if it's here, he'll never make it this far.'

'But you saw it,' Arallak replied. 'That's the most important thing. That you'll remember it.'

Spiric hesitated, then took a few steps back and threw the rock. It hit the glass, pausing for all of three seconds against it before passing through with a crash. The window shattered in a halting and staggered order, the next piece of glass falling only after the previous one had hit the ground.

'I don't think I could ever forget something like that,' he said.

Arallak nodded. 'We can only hope.'

Spiric looked up. Arallak was once again clad in black and Byreth was by his side.

'We've been here before,' Spiric said.

Arallak nodded. 'After you.'

Questions ached in his throat as they silently ascended the structure, and he sensed Byreth suffering just the same. But neither dared risk asking them. Ten levels of stairs, ladders and scrambles up piles of rubble took them to the rooftop. Exhausted, Spiric wondered how the hell they were going to get back down before the whipping breeze hurled them off first.

The final climb placed them on a narrow catwalk that skirted the edge of the building. The gentle screech of rubbing metal was constant in Spiric's ears as the scaffolding around them wavered at their presence. Rows of skyscrapers stretched to the horizon where the tips of the enormous pylons they'd passed on the way in were little more than studs poking into sight. Spiric cursed under his breath, trying not to think about how they'd get out of this place.

The centre of the rooftop was occupied by a raised dish. It was triple the size of those sprouting from the skyscraper's flanks and faced straight up to the sky. The decayed edges had peeled off at the rim and were hanging down like webbed vines.

Spiric tested the metal with his boot, and to his surprise, it waggled as loose rope would. While it could be used to clamber up to the catwalk running above them, he turned to Byreth first.

'If this is what I think it is... And I don't even know what I think... Are you going to be okay if we—?'

'Find him?' Byreth finished. 'I dunno. One way to find out.' She turned to Arallak. 'So this is it, your place where time stands still?'

Arallak nodded. 'Approach it with caution, Byreth.'

Byreth started muttering something murderous as she began climbing the frayed metal. Spiric went after her, straining to pull himself up onto the catwalk and envious of Arallak, who simply appeared up there, but the boy kept his focus on Byreth. Her grip was white-knuckled on the flimsy railing, resentment burning in her eyes as she stared into the shallow metal pit below.

'A place where time stands still,' she muttered. 'Looks about right.'

A man stood mid-step about four paces away from them, halfway to the centre of the dish where a perfectly black sphere hovered an inch off the ground. It ticked every few seconds, wobbling in place before settling with a gentle pulse of light. A shimmering heat haze filled the dish, but no warmth emanated from it. Its metal surface was blindingly white and untarnished. Not even a speck of sand had found its way onto it. Any that came close hovered as static dust in the air, marking the bounds of the heat haze.

*This must be the ephemeral the paralict broker mentioned, which means...*

The man was about a foot taller than Spiric. Most of his form was hidden by a mottled brown travelling cloak, but a shock of long red hair escaped from either side of the hood. Spiric looked back to Byreth, who was now almost doubled over, her posture slumped and head resting against the railing.

'That's him, isn't it?' Spiric asked quietly. 'Vehli?'

Byreth nodded slowly, still not raising her head. 'How did you know?' she whispered. 'How?'

He felt his mouth go dry. It was a question he couldn't answer, but he wanted nothing more than to take it on. His jaw was locked and any jabbering word that wanted to escape was trapped.

'Because Spiric told me,' Arallak answered. 'Before we first came here so long ago. It was something he remembered.'

'He remembered the future?' Byreth snapped back.

'It's why he needed to be saved. To be placed here. Because of what he is. A helixic.'

'That's meant to mean something to me?' Byreth said.

Arallak shook his head and looked to the obsidian monolith. As high as this rooftop was, the form of Memory still towered over them. 'It's the way he remembers things. It was the only way to preserve what had to be forgotten. The only way to leave a monument as warning to what The Hytharo Empire was. To what destroyed it.'

'Because these memories were unaffected by the Blood Forged God of Memory,' Spiric said, the realisation dawning over him. 'It erased everything it touched. Everyone. Even you. But not this. And you knew this. You knew before you died because we stood here and... and I must have remembered this, this moment, right now!'

Arallak nodded. 'Exactly. You told me of a brother lost and a sister who found them. That in this fracture he would be trapped. A memory convoyed from beyond the time of The Blood Forged God of Memory, immune to it because it was yet to happen.

'When I died... when I became this... This was the only place I knew. I watched for a thousand years until these circumstances came to be and this man was trapped here. *I* had remembered it. I saw it as a sign. That I knew I was right. So I came for you. To save you. To play my part in realising what you had told me so long ago.'

Spiric looked back to the monolith as well, biting his tongue. But how had he escaped? He'd remembered so sharply, so clearly, that he'd stood in Andias as it fell to the god.

'Why me?' Spiric said weakly.

'Being a helixic? I wondered that myself,' Arallak said.

'And there were others with me when we fled,' Spiric said. 'You think they...?'

Arallak could only shrug. 'It's a gift I appear not to have received. Everything I've pieced together has been from the fragments of memory you've given me.'

'Why'd you need to do it all, anyway?' Byreth asked. She seemed to be looking for something to distract from the frozen image of her brother. 'Spiric said you wanted everything forgotten, right? Wiped out. Clean sweep. Nobody would've known about your empire. We all would've just moved on.'

'Only to do it all again? Voss-Ela told me the story of the Flux Catastrophe. It sounded like history repeating.' Spiric said. 'Ruins within ruins, worlds upon worlds.'

Byreth snorted. 'That's what Vehli said and look at him now.

He's stuck in there. At least I know he went out and did what he said he was going to.' She let out a long, cool breath. 'Our folks just thought he ran away for the hell of it.'

'He's not stuck,' Arallak said. 'That's not the nature of this fracture.' He selected a tiny piece of shrapnel from the ground and tossed it towards the centre of the dish. It penetrated the heat haze with ease. For a moment, it flew at a walking pace, crawling down to a halt before it, too, appeared still.

'To your brother, it has been mere seconds. But each step towards the centre takes longer and longer to us. If you were to stand in front of him for an hour as he is now, you'd only be a flicker of movement.'

Byreth muttered Arallak's words under her breath, chewing on them as she hatched a plan. 'So I could get him out?'

'I have no idea how long it would take,' Arallak replied.

'But I *could* get him out?' Byreth said more firmly.

'You'd risk reemerging in another time. It could be months. Maybe more.'

She looked to Spiric. There was no manic gleam in her eyes. No catharsis. Nothing but grim resolve. The question didn't need to be asked, but it made his heart twist anyway. She would risk everything in this world, everything she'd ever known...

'I gave up my time to do what was right,' Spiric said. 'I found my brother. Now you find yours.'

Byreth looked away, only meeting his eyes once she'd found the right words. 'You'd better remember me.'

A smile broke on Spiric's face. 'I think I already have.'

He wanted to say more, he wanted to tell her every excruciating detail of what he was going to remember, what he'd miss of her, but the words wouldn't come. They couldn't come. They weren't something Spiric could even comprehend. But as Byreth cracked one last wry grin, he knew he didn't have to. She unbuckled her holster and handed it to Spiric, the hand cannon strapped loosely in it.

'Don't want to risk keeping it,' she said awkwardly. 'Might use it on my brother once we're out the other side.'

Spiric felt a sheepish laugh escape his lungs, and he struggled to breathe in to replace it. Before he could do anything else, Byreth had pulled him into a rib-crushing embrace, pressed so close that he barely needed to hug her back.

'Don't ever forget who you are to me,' she whispered in his ear. 'You are Spiric. My Spiric. This Spiric.'

He tried to nod, but her grip was too tight. When she let go, it was like she'd taken all the words with her. Spiric could only watch as she skirted past Arallak, around the catwalk to the edge of the dish. She readied herself, beaming at him one last time, that manic glint finally back in those yellow eyes before she leapt over the railing, her boots hitting the ground in a desperate sprint.

Spiric gulped fruitlessly at the lump in his throat as her pace crawled down to nothing in only moments. She'd set herself on a collision course with her brother, her arms already primed to tackle him from the side.

'Take me forward,' Spiric said with a shaking voice. 'To when she comes out.'

'I can't,' Arallak replied.

'Lizard shit you can't!'

'You are not done here!' Arallak said. 'You told me this yourself!'

'I'm going in after her!' Spiric spat.

He moved to skirt the catwalk, to follow in Byreth's path, but Arallak blocked him, his hands firm on his shoulders and fury in his eyes.

'Let me through! We were going to throw a fucking prince in there, so why not me!?'

'Why go now!?' Arallak snapped back. 'What is there to gain from following her now!?'

Spiric tried to throw a punch at his brother, but his fist just couldn't connect despite Arallak's unwavering stance. He let Spiric swing a few more times before shoving him back, moving to place himself between him and the dish.

'We both know you were destined for so much more. She's found her fate. Why would you follow her without finding yours?'

'Because she was my friend,' Spiric roared. 'She didn't use me! She helped me! She saw me as a human, not a Hythaio! Everything I've remembered, everyone I've met... I was just a pawn in someone else's plan. With her... with her I had a choice.'

The anger faded from Arallak, that familiar sadness taking its place. 'You did. You're right. It was what I should have given to you. And I failed you.'

Spiric let himself slump to the floor of the catwalk, not caring that Arallak sat down by his side. He couldn't bring himself to say another word. He could only watch Byreth as she edged her way closer to her brother and further away from him. He would wait for her, he resolved. Even if it was a thousand lifetimes, even if it were the end of days, he'd wait for her.

## CHAPTER THIRTY-ONE

# ECHOES OF
# THOSE-OF-GLASS

A N HOUR PASSED IN a silence Arallak had mercifully preserved before Spiric turned to look at him, but the shadow dancer had disappeared. He couldn't blame him for leaving. Solitude was what he needed. Byreth had made less than an inch of progress since he'd sat down, but at least she'd found the answers she was looking for. It was time he did the same.

*Helixic.*

The word was the first true thought he'd had in his mind since he'd sat down. It was what Arallak had called him. The reason why he'd remembered both his past and his future. But the why and the how of it was another matter entirely. He cursed himself for not asking Arallak before he'd vanished. It had been stupid to just sit there and mourn, Spiric thought as he'd descended the skyscraper. Byreth was not of his people or of his time. They were never meant to have met, but that did little to subdue the hollowness in his chest.

Spiric had abandoned his pack on the lower catwalks. There was no point hauling around another few weeks' worth of rations if he was planning on making camp on the lower levels of this ruin. Who knew how long he'd need to survive here? He'd need to hunt for more food, but what little he'd learnt of hunting from Byreth amounted to dumb luck and pointless trap-setting.

It kept crossing his mind to simply go in after her and follow her path, but Arallak's seed of doubt had long blossomed by the time the shadow dancer had left his side. There was something about this place that Spiric was yet to remember and he wanted to find it before it found him.

He sat for a moment on the lowest floor of the skyscraper, his legs dangling out the window in the sun as he cautiously fiddled around with Byreth's hand cannon. When his finger brushed against the trigger, the image of the Scythe's corpse in Basarod with their torn and punctured flesh flashed through his mind. The mechanics of the weapon were beyond his understanding, Byreth's, too, come to think of it, but its purpose was sickeningly familiar. Nothing more than a tool of death. Just like him and the rest of the Hytharo.

Standing up, Spiric slotted the hand cannon into the holster gingerly. At least he could savour the relief of travelling light for once. Aside from the weapon, he'd only brought his small satchel with him. He'd stuffed it with only a few bits of dried meat, Grethard's old green torch, Voss-Ela's compass, some scraps of paper with half a pencil, and his last vial of ink along with a frayed brush.

As he trudged aimlessly across the dunes, he could barely get his ears to focus on the eerie whistle that always seemed to ring in places like this. It was so high it went low, similar to the kind of sound that split painfully through his head just before he remembered some other atrocity.

His wandering feet took him between the ruined skyscrapers as he searched for the source, marking a perimeter around the sandbar that separated the monolith. More of those shadowy echoes watched from buildings, but they didn't move to approach him.

Just the prospect of walking across that barren plain filled him with trepidation. It looked a long journey, but the sheer size of the monolith before him looked as though he were already at its face. Its form was immune to shadow. Its breadth wider than Spiric's eye could see. Before, when he was with Byreth, he'd tried not to focus on it. After all, it was a thief of memory, what if he were to forget her?

But now he could truly make out the surface of the giant. The channels of its walls were free of the blood that had once flowed upon it, yet the erosion of time had failed to chip at it like it had the skyscrapers. Dozens of thin, shallow grooves made up a coursing wave that flowed up half of the face before rounding at its peak and coming back down. Gashes and cuts dashed across these paths, but no matter how deep or jagged they seemed, they looked just as purposeful as the patterns they interrupted.

Spiric had to get closer. To touch it. To feel it. To find his answers. As the black mass engulfed his horizon, Spiric could now recall from where he recognised it from.

*'The cost to both of us will be devastating.'*

*'A cost others have paid a thousand times before.'*

It was Spiric's memory. A memory that had been stolen. Of Arallak and the shadow dancer and he and Spiric had sought out to wreak this destruction. The blackness that had surrounded the view of this grim exchange had not been the clouded ink of a half-formed recollection, but this place, this thing before him.

At its face, Spiric reached out with a calm hand, his fingers brushing across the grooves before slotting perfectly into them. The ringing in his ears grew further still, confirming in his mind that it emanated from the monolith. Was this something to do with being a helixic like Arallak had said? Under his touch, he felt more layered hollows, another miniature echo of the overall pattern.

'Ruins within ruins,' Spiric whispered softly.

'Worlds upon worlds,' a voice whispered back.

Spiric couldn't find the energy to yelp. He looked across his right shoulder, his left hand still pressed to the surface of Memory. A shadow dancer stood with him, his pale hand pressed to the black wall just like Spiric's. His garb was identical to Arallak's, but it was not his brother. He was taller, a touch broader, yet just familiar enough.

'I've met you,' Spiric said. 'In the light-bend.'

'As I have you, in times before this,' the shadow dancer replied. He looked down at Spiric, the hungry grin stretched across his face. 'Yet I don't remember a time when we met today.'

He found himself suddenly two steps back, his feet acting long before his mind could initiate it. The shadow dancer's broad carved face suddenly leapt through his mind, invading the recollection he'd just summoned.

This was the shadow dancer Spiric and Arallak had found.

The one who'd roused The Blood Forged God of Memory.

'I should know your name,' the shadow dancer said slowly.

'I am Spiric,' he replied. 'Should I know yours?'

'You already do. I am Onassis.'

Spiric's jaw locked in place. The ringing in his ears increased its pitch, crashing as waves just as his first memory had done. But now he understood it. This was no ordinary recollection. This was what he was.

A helixic.

One final crash thrust through him and his vision was pure,

the low, rumbling heat of the desert back in his ears.

He was once again in Andias, in the grand palace before its destruction. The endless desert lay out before him as he stood on the balcony that overlooked it. On the horizon, a black shape hovered just over the sands. If he were to hold up his thumb, it would only just cover it. Closer still were clouds of dust, hiding the march of the thousands of men and women and the desperation that drove them to war.

The sun was warm on what little of his skin was unhidden by sweeping red robes. Where Spiric had once seen Voss-Ela's throne now lay an agonisingly flowing fountain carved of gold and copper. But he didn't seem surprised at the presence of the water that ran through it. Nor did the five others that stood around it. The only face he could make out was Arallak's. He looked nervous, but his words were rehearsed.

'My brother Spiric has worked tirelessly to find those like him. A bloodline who will carry the record, the true nature of our cruel empire, so it may never happen again, if it is ever reforged. In a short time, you will be the last Hytharo.'

'Then what of rain?' his own voice said. 'Those that may come to lay siege to us seek our blood, but it will never quench their thirst. Our empire was built upon what we thought we were blessing this barren land with, as much as we all regret it.'

Arallak was quiet for a moment, his eyes clenched shut as he thought. When he opened them, they seemed to flicker black. 'For our rule to truly end, rain can never fall again. It must be sealed among the air we breathe so that magic may not tilt the balance of what should be.'

'But how?' another voice said. 'One of our kind and of our cause would've done it by now if the axiom existed to do so. It is impossible.'

Arallak winced, recovering to a grimace as his eyes flashed black. 'It's not impossible. It's happened a thousand times before.'

The fountain began to froth before them, the water boiling and instantly steaming off into the sky. They looked back to the grand stairs in time to see the cascades that ran alongside it follow suit. They all turned back to Arallak, whose eyes once again flickered to black.

'Can you know for sure that we shall survive?' his own voice asked. 'That your plan will work?'

Arallak grinned back at him, his teeth gritted beneath it. 'No. But that's the only way it could.'

Darkness engulfed Arallak's form, and then Onassis was stood in his place, his hand still pressed to the wall of Memory. It took Spiric a few moments to realise he was back in the present. There was a curiosity on the shadow dancer's face, almost as if he knew what Spiric had just seen.

'You... you said you should know my name,' Spiric said slowly. There was a trepidation in his voice that he couldn't hide, but his gut was telling him to hide as much as he could. 'Why?'

Onassis removed his hand from the monolith and hid them both behind his back. 'The same reason you know your own.'

Spiric felt confusion dancing across his face, enough to make Onassis chuckle. The sound of it made something flare angrily in his chest. He didn't come all this way to be mocked!

'Tell me!' Spiric spat.

Onassis smiled wider. 'I don't need to.'

Spiric's vision began to haze, blackness creeping in from his right.

'You already remember.'

There was another crash in Spiric's ears. Suddenly the wall of the monolith was on his right, clear sand to his left and for just a second he was looking at himself, shock and fear straining on his face. Then it reversed, Onassis taking his place, before it all merged, black walls on either side, the vision of his own appearance blended with that of Onassis.

'Because I'm a helixic,' both their voices said.

Spiric was back in his own body, already stumbling and falling to the ground, his legs kicking and scrambling to get away.

'But I was the first,' Onassis continued.

'But I saw—'

'Through me. That is the true gift of the helixic. A memory. One outside of body, outside of time, outside of...' He looked up at the monolith for a moment. 'The old magic. The magic I could not destroy.'

Spiric found his feet, leaning heavily against the black wall as Onassis drew closer. He revealed a hand, his open palm to the sky. From nothing, water began to flow. It dripped through the gaps in his fingers, spattering to the sand and darkening it for the first time in eons. Saplings sprouted rapidly from the damp, their stems splitting in half and twisting as a pair, re-joining into a single bulb that bloomed into four thin petals of a violent white, their majesty lasting only a second before cringing decay took them. Then they were gone. Dust among the sands.

'I've not shown the wonders of my hand for more than a thousand lifetimes,' Onassis said vacantly. 'I've not encountered a circumstance such as yourself.'

'A thousand lifetimes?' Spiric couldn't hide the disbelief from his voice. 'But how can you be—'

The rest of the words wouldn't come. They didn't need to. The question had already been answered. The memory of Arallak came to his mind again.

*'It's not impossible. It's happened a thousand times before.'*

It rang through his head again and again as Spiric stared at the spot in the sand where life had once bloomed. No shadow dancer magic could've done that. It was something more.

*Pure resonance.*

The magic of those-of-glass, bound only by what their minds believed as fact. What they were sure of as the world around them, as sure as they were of the past they'd experienced.

*A past which Onassis had lived more than a thousand times*

*over.*

Spiric looked up at the shadow dancer. The hungry grin was back on his face, but the surroundings faded and flashed. Visions of rocky caves, of burning fire and showering rains. Of black, star-studded skies and endless armies that marched behind him. This man wasn't bound by the life he lived and breathed. He was held by the memories of the helixics that had met him, from the birth of this world to the very end of it. He was remembered as being present not just because of himself, but by others, others who saw him for what he was.

Spiric could only point wordlessly at him, his finger shaking as he tried to find the words. This was no shadow dancer. He was no man. He was a constant that this world revolved around. He had seen every bit of it, lived every moment.

'You're a god,' he finally stammered. 'A walking god. This magic... these runes...'

Onassis nodded. 'My invention. Every time.'

'But how?'

'The same way I live, Spiric. Because it had been done before. By my hand. Everything around us is as it should be, except for you. There is no way to count how many times I have walked across this world from beginning to end to beginning again. I am imprisoned in my duty to create and contain the magic that is both the birth and death of myself and this world. Nearly everything that occurs is a surety. Any deviation I make from it risks catastrophe, the complete destruction of reality.

'That's why The Blood Forged God of Memory exists. To snatch from all the minds affected by my meddling the vision of my mistakes. It is a risk to use, erasing all it touches. If it were to wipe myself clean from the slate...'

'It would destroy everything,' Spiric finished.

'I fade from this world as the shadow dancers do when it commences its duty. I can only return if I am sure that there will be one in my place that can quell it.'

'Which is what Arallak did. Once it was over Andias, he was the one to meet it, wasn't he?'

'It is a rare thing for me to say, but I don't know. Each time this world lives, there are only two times where Memory must be called to action. Two times where the world moves without my witness. Two times where the angst and unrest of the world risk more than pure resonance, as you call it.'

'Once to destroy the people I came from,' Spiric said.

'And once to destroy mine,' Onassis finished grimly.

'Those-of-glass?' he asked.

Onassis nodded.

'But if this happens every time, every... every lifetime, why don't you know my name? Of this happening, right now?'

'Because you are anomaly, Spiric. In all these lifetimes... The Hytharo never made it past Andias.'

Spiric frowned for a moment. It sounded like something Vorric had said to him.

'So you'd kill me? To wipe me from your world because I was

never meant to be here?'

Onassis shook his head with a chuckle. 'My interference bears a great risk. Were I to do that now, by my own hand, it would create a memory to be seen by every helixic that will come after you that depicts a death that was never meant to happen. It would seal a fate I'd need to relive in every successive cycle of this world. A risk of further anomaly. A chance at a changing fate. An uncertain future without my guidance. That's all I need to provide. Guidance to those that would correct it.'

'To Vorric,' Spiric said with a gasp. 'You saved him! You saved him both times!'

'Indeed, I did.'

'But then haven't you interfered?'

'Not with the way things are meant to be. Not with the true record of this world. The one held by the helixics. Your journey so far is little more than a grain of sand among the dunes and will be just as easily buried. After that, you will be forgotten, just as Arallak asked me to do so long ago.'

A high-pitched whistling filled the air as Onassis finished. Spiric turned and looked to the sky. Dark blue specks darted across it, leaping between the tops of ruins like they were steppingstones.

'You called them here, the Scythes,' Spiric said breathlessly.

'Brutal as they are, that doesn't give them enough credit, I think. They've been tracking you for longer than you know, Spiric. And now you've finally run out of sand.'

## CHAPTER THIRTY-TWO

# ERASE TRACES

B LUE-ROBED FORMS THUMPED DOWN into the dunes around Spiric, spraying him with sand and clouding his vision. Once it had settled, he was left staring into the grizzled and merciless eyes of Vorric.

The months had not been kind to him. The iron-coloured hair that had once been neatly slicked back was now only held out of his eyes by a mixture of dirt and gunge. It ran down his face as blood from a wound would, gathering in the deep, scarring wrinkles that cut across him and accumulating in the matted filth of what had once been an elegant beard. There was something in his eyes, something that looked hollow and broken, with only the faintest flicker of victory beyond them now that he'd cornered his prey.

Spiric glanced to his side. Onassis was gone. It was just him with his back up against the massive wall of Memory against Vorric and the four Scythes at his flanks. They were spaced out ten metres from each other with their iron masks pointed at anything but Spiric. Despite the cage-like armour they all wore, there was still something that worried them. Spiric knew exactly what it was.

'You've seen better days,' Spiric said as coolly as he could. The nerves that had wracked him last he faced Vorric were still there, but they were much quieter.

'And yet somehow you look as though you're seeing them right now,' Vorric shot back. 'If I didn't know better, I'd be envious. But I know how you escaped me last time, Spiric, and I know you no longer have the means to do it again.'

Spiric found himself nodding slowly, but it wasn't in agreement. 'But you do. I met to him.'

Vorric's face twitched and Spiric knew his gamble had paid off. The moment the word "anomaly" had come out of Onassis' mouth, he was almost certain that was where Vorric had learned to call him by that name.

'You're afraid,' Spiric said slowly. 'That's why you've been hunting me. Scared of a change that hasn't been predicted for you.'

'I can sense that you are, too,' he replied. 'I'm not here to kill you. We're long past that now.'

'But you still wiped out Basarod. You murdered every single person there without a second thought, just for the hope of finding me, but now you have...'

Vorric smiled slowly. 'The problem is you'd remember it, Spiric. Onassis taught me what you are, and now I understand. You're more than just a lost boy from another time. You're the means to rewrite history, something far more dangerous than I ever imagined. If it were anyone else, I would have given up searching for you long ago.

'It's cost us everything. Breggesa and The Academy believe that I purged Basarod without cause and decided it cannot be without consequence, so I've found myself in a position similar to yours, Spiric. Far too dangerous to be left alive, yet far too important to lay down and die. I may have failed at what I originally set out to do, but I can still mitigate any damage you may cause. Taking you to Breggesa will at least be proof of what needed to be done. Then can I put an end to the risk you pose.'

'I don't think I could cause any more damage than you have,' Spiric spat. 'Basarod is gone, and I've got no doubt you did the same to Kurkress as well. I've seen what happens when people decide to destroy anything left in their wake instead of attempting to make it right. It's my past. Now it looks like it's your future.'

'That's yet to be determined,' Vorric growled back.

A bark of laughter escaped Spiric, one his old self would've been proud of. 'That's not what your master thinks! I don't know what you are to him, but it can't be more than a minion, can it?'

The other four Scythes were looking uneasily between themselves, but the burning hatred in Vorric's eyes made Spiric press on with glee.

'A slave to a shadow dancer! That's what you've become. The exact thing you said you were setting out to squash. You only do it because you're scared of him, of what he might do if you don't.'

'Shut up!' Vorric snapped. The wind whipped with his words, leaving them to linger in the air.

'There's nothing noble about what you do. You're no protector. Just an enforcer of a dogma laid out long before you were ever born to question it, same as I was. At least I ended up doubting it. Doing something about it. But what have you done? You're just killing everything and everyone you've told yourself you need to because you're afraid of what happens if you start to understand it.'

'I know what happens if I "understand" it, boy! It would wipe out the world as we know it!'

'A world of your violence and slaughter?' Spiric retorted. 'It's what I was sent here to warn of. It's what The Hytharo Empire aspired to be. At least Breggesa and your precious Academy decided they'd had enough of it. I just hope they decided to do to you and the rest of your Scythes what you've done to so

402

many.'

Vorric smiled, a dark malice intoned in his words. 'Once they meet you, they'll see I was right.'

A single step forward. That was all Vorric took. His boot landed in the sand, and he halted abruptly, his eyes snapping to the sky. The other Scythes followed suit, scanning their surroundings for something Spiric couldn't see.

He felt his own hand drifting towards the holster at his hip where Byreth's hand cannon weighed heavy, but Vorric was still a good twenty paces away, too far for him to close the distance and jam the barrel straight down the bastard's throat.

The air itself began to warp, crying out as a distant howling of wind caught on a rock that refused to budge. It was a sound more unsettling than anything Spiric had ever experienced. Soon the air was compressed into a relentless weight that needled at his skin, scoured his eyes and grated in his lungs. The wailing only got louder and louder, bringing Spiric to his knees as it felt like his skull was about to burst.

Vorric remained the only one standing, shaking with exertion as he yelled at his allies. Axioms ran up his arm, burning in his palm and blasting wind back against the oppressive gale. It clashed, hitting Spiric like a tidal wave and slamming his arched back into the wall of Memory as a snippet of Vorric's shouts made it to his ears in barely more than a whisper.

'It's him. He's here.'

The cacophony ceased suddenly, and something slammed

into the ground in front of Spiric. It threw up another dusty haze that left Spiric coughing, and he didn't have a chance to discern what had caused it before he was scooped bodily into a tight grip. Another blast of wind made the ground lurch away and he was airborne. If there was even a breath of air left in Spiric's lungs, he'd be screaming.

The flight ended with a tumbling crash a few moments later. By the time Spiric had gathered his senses, he realised Grethard was standing before him. They were in one of the rooms of the shattered skyscrapers. It was far above the desert floor and filled with angular chairs that had been thrown about the room either by panicked hands eons ago or the harsh winds which had battered the room since. Everything in sight was torn, beaten, and worse for wear, Grethard included.

'You're... you're...' Spiric stammered.

'Still alive? I wondered every night if you were as well.' Grethard whispered back. He placed a finger to his lips as Spiric went to say more. 'Don't let them hear you. That trick won't work again. Been tracking Vorric ever since Basarod. Following him in the hopes that he'd be following you.'

'But why didn't you come before?' Spiric said in disbelief.

Grethard shook his head. 'I tried searching for you. When Basarod was attacked, I found yours and Byreth's beds empty, so I'd hoped your shadow dancer brother had found a way to save you.' He paused for a moment, a flicker of grief in his eye. 'I tried to stop them, Spiric.'

'No one could've,' he replied. 'They were ready for me. Their armour protects them from my lightning. None of us stood a chance.'

'Nor did anyone after. I don't know how much you know if it, but the Scythes have been a renegade force since Basarod. Breggesa disavowed them and they've been on a rampage ever since to evade capture. What you just saw is all that's left of them. I'll try stop Vorric, but you need to run, Spiric.' He jabbed a finger to a nearby set of stairs that led down to darkness. 'Hide underground. Vorric may not fear much but he'll fear a shadow dancer.'

Grethard stood up to make for the edge of the building, a rusted dagger in each hand, and Spiric barely managed to grab his robes.

'No!' he hissed desperately. 'He doesn't! There's a shadow dancer on his side! The first shadow dancer, the one that gave Arallak the means to wipe out the Hytharo! One that knows all the future and the past and that I'm not meant to be in it!'

'Not meant to?' he turned and crouched down, taking Spiric's hand in his own gnarled one as he spoke softly. 'But you're here. That means you're meant to be. In all my years in exile I didn't realise it, but we are not our past, or what our past intends us to be. This is who you are, Spiric, and you get to choose how the things that led you here will lead you forward. If that's what Vorric wants to wipe out, then he'll fail. I should know. I tried to hide from my past and look at the precious little good it did me. Can't keep living lives in cages, now can we?' Grethard straightened up again, offering Spiric one last wry smile. 'If you meet that other shadow dancer again, you tell them just that.'

'But you don't under—'

'I understand, Spiric. It's what you taught me.'

Before Spiric could say another word, Grethard had slipped out of his grasp, hesitating at the frame of the broken glass wall that led out to the open skies. The air shimmered around him for a moment, a trembling that carried through the cracked tiles of the skyscraper's floor before it formed into a blast of air, launching Grethard into the sky and out of sight.

Spiric scrambled to his feet and dashed to the edge of the floor. He made it just in time to see Grethard land with an echoing thump far below, the impact simply crushing one of the incapacitated Scythes. The old man's body whirled like flowing water, reaching the next man before he could react and sending countless sprays of blood across the desert floor as his daggers went to work.

Spiric pulled out Byreth's hand cannon as he sprinted for the stairs Grethard had pointed to. His axioms would be useless against the Scythes. He leapt down each flight like they were a long cliff, doing his best to ignore the crunching pain in his ankles that came with each landing.

Halfway down and the stairs abruptly stopped, but Spiric had already swung himself around on the metal banister with far too much momentum to avoid the fall. He plunged for what felt like the length of the rest of the building and smacked into the debris-strewn floor with his entire left side, knocking the air from his still breathless lungs. A sudden wave of nausea resounded through his bones, and he was only dimly aware of just how hard his head had bounced with the impact.

As he picked himself up, he thought he was hallucinating. This skyscraper was one of the unnervingly decapitated ones, the entire upper portion floating ominously above the rest. From a distance, Spiric had assumed there was an invisible force holding them in place, but now he saw he was only half right.

Razor-thin columns of radiant white light connected the floor to the ceiling like the last strands of sinew in a torn piece of meat. There were maybe a dozen of them, perfectly vertical and clustered towards the centre of the rubble-strewn floor. Even from a metre away, they gave off a heat that prickled on Spiric's skin, the warmth stabbing to his core as he threaded his path between the first pair of beams towards the unblocked chute across the floor.

The next few beams held shattered glass at their feet, a tripping hazard that Spiric barely had time to consider. The sound of howling wind was picking up again and a dash of a figure shot up past the outside of the building. Another two followed it, then they all came crashing as one tumbling mess in the collapsed stairwell Spiric had fallen down.

Despite his age, Grethard was first to his feet, a gust of air blowing in from the desert sky and carrying him terrifyingly close to the light beams Spiric had just crossed. The two other combatants rose to their feet as well, both masked Scythes, their armour bent and dented but still holding, their bare hands readied with blue runes. Spiric raised the hand cannon, but Grethard's hunched back blocked a clear shot and Spiric wasn't even sure if the old man knew he was there.

'Grethard! Be careful of the light!'

The old man whirled around in shock, almost touching the beam as he pivoted away at the last moment. One of the Scythes seized on the stumble and charged with gusto. But Spiric was ready for her.

He squeezed the trigger just as Byreth had shown him and a gout of brilliant flame vomited forth with a deafening blast to accompany it. The weapon's metal frame kicked back violently, feeling like it would have shattered his wrist if he wasn't grasping it so tight, but Spiric's target had fared worse.

A puncture the size of his fist burst into the woman's thigh and she collapsed, her momentum carrying her straight into the first beam of light. A sickeningly loud clicking sound filled the room as she passed through it, drowning out her abrupt and brief howl of pain as her torso was sawed in two by the colliding light.

Her mask slipped, the shock on her face excruciating as her eyes met Spiric's, the light blinking from existence as she stopped halfway through it. A massive rend across her torso spilled bloody bones and burning gore as she managed one last silent howl, but it was drowned out by the sound of grinding rock far below. The skyscraper shook with it, the upper half dipping a few inches closer to their heads before stabilising.

Grethard had gathered himself, stepping nimbly through the remaining light beams to Spiric's side. The remaining Scythe circled warily, keeping himself next to something big enough to leap behind so he didn't fall victim to the hand cannon next.

'If you've got that...' the old man muttered.

'She fine,' Spiric said quickly. 'Found her brother. Said she wouldn't be needing it for a time.' He had to stop himself from chuckling at his own joke,

'There's a great deal for me to catch up on,' Grethard replied. 'I agree.'

The pair of them whirled around at the sound of Vorric's voice. He was stood at the opposite side of the floor, right next to the chute down, his hands behind his back and his stance somehow unflustered.

Spiric only looked for a second, spinning back to the remaining Scythe, levelling the hand cannon as he risked a few steps closer. He and Grethard now only had a few tight feet of space to defend themselves in. It was so cramped that the cannon's lengthy barrel only just poked between two of the beams of light.

'It's been a long time, Grethard.' Vorric spat the name from his mouth like it was rotten meat. 'You never did learn not to engage with that you did not understand.'

'Then how were we ever meant to learn at all?' Grethard replied. 'All these years I've spent in exile, hoping that I could one day be forgiven for my greatest regrets, and it's only now I realise it was a life wasted.'

'It wasn't "learning," Grethard. It was crime. You risked a taint upon us all with what you saw.'

'What, a shadow dancer!?' Spiric shouted over his shoulder. 'Like the one you work for?'

'The difference is that I recognise my role in this world, boy. Nothing more. Nothing to disrupt the ledger of how things must be, unlike you. I'm sure by now you appreciate the power of a single dangerous thought, don't you?'

'Like the thought you had when you decided to destroy Basarod?' Grethard growled. 'At least my crimes were a mistake. You...'

'I did what needed to be done!' Vorric screamed back.

'That's what I told myself a long, long time ago,' Grethard retorted. 'Right after I'd finished off my own damn expedition team. I took the air right out of their lungs, a trick I can see you've picked up.'

'And I always intended to return that favour, no matter how long I had to wait,' Vorric said. 'There's only one way this ends.'

'You don't know that!' Spiric said quickly. 'Your shadow dancer sure doesn't. That's why he's scared of me, because for the first time there's something he doesn't know about and it sounds like you're terrified of that, as well.'

The other Scythe was still drawing closer, his left hand outstretched with a burning blue axiom at the ready. Spiric had seen what it had taken for Vorric to pluck a hand cannon's slug from the air, so he couldn't risk the resulting havoc while they were so close to the beams of light. He might've been lucky enough to escape the collapsing tunnel, but if the skyscraper were to do the same...

'That's why I have to put a stop to you, Spiric,' Vorric said. 'Because you have no idea where the unknown will lead you.'

'I think it'll be better than anywhere you can lead me,' he muttered under his breath. A stupid idea had hatched into his head, one worse than the exploding respark had been and likely just as destructive. The second Scythe was only a metre from him, ready to tread through the two remaining beams of light that separated them, his hand almost touching the cannon's muzzle.

'I can promise you we won't lead you far, boy,' the Scythe muttered.

'Especially not you,' he replied.

Fast as a whip, Spiric flicked the cannon barrel right, sheering the muzzle clean off as it crossed through the first beam of light and set off the ominous clicking that followed. The Scythe lurched back in surprise, not ready for anything except the cannon going off in his face as Spiric swung it back left, nearly shearing the cannon down to the trigger as the clicking grew louder.

No longer blocked by the beams, the Scythe leapt forward, not even bothering to use his axiom as he reached with both hands to grab Spiric's neck, the rush of victory gleaming in his eyes under the mask.

But Grethard was faster. Somehow, without a word between them, he'd cottoned on to Spiric's plan and whirled backwards, shoving Spiric out of the way and parrying the tackling Scythe into the next four beams. Sickening sizzles and splatters followed as bits of the once-Scythe slid in all directions across the floor, the clicking morphing to a rapid-fire drumbeat as the ground beneath them quaked.

The upper ceiling lurched, sagging heavily over their heads. Grethard grabbed Spiric by the collar and jettisoned them out the closing gap with a blast of air. The top half of the building thundered downwards, billowing dust as it imploded before the surviving hunks toppled into its neighbour, carving massive rents in its flank as they fell.

Spiric spun through the air like a thrown ragdoll, his vision swapping from the orange sands to blue skies at a nauseating pace before there was another yank at his collar, not enough to stop his fall, but instead send him hurtling sideways down the shallow side of a dune.

He skidded to the bottom of it in a cloud of dust, scrambling to stand with legs that felt like they were on backwards. He'd landed at the foot of another skyscraper. It rose barely two floors above the dunes, but by the way the sand washed into it, it was much deeper than it let on. Only sand lay beyond the broken glass, a swirling pit like the inside of the golden domes.

A low moan came from somewhere next to Spiric. He turned in panic and began desperately digging up Grethard from the crater he'd landed in. He worked with both hands, the fine sand soon coming away in wet, bloody clumps as he found the old man's leg.

A gash that was nearly a foot long and caked with dust ran down his left hip. Spiric tried to press his hands to it for what little good they'd do to staunch the rush of blood, but suddenly Grethard's own were batting his away.

'Get up! Grethard, we can get you to Byreth,' Spiric pleaded. 'She can fix you up, she'll know how, she—'

Grethard just shook his head weakly. 'We both know she won't make it in time.'

Spiric let out something between a sob and a laugh. It couldn't end like this, buried in the sand just as he'd found Spiric. It didn't make any sense. He wasn't going to watch Grethard die. Not again. Not after losing him at Basarod.

'Vorric's coming,' Grethard whispered. 'I can't hold him.'

'Then I'll just blow him away with this,' Spiric said, holding up what remained of the hand cannon.

Grethard barely chuckled. 'You'll blow yourself away. More like Byreth than I remember. But you need to do what she wouldn't. Hide.'

'No! Not again! I've lost too much because I ran and hid! I won't lose you!'

Spiric felt himself whimper as he held Grethard's shoulders. A faint smile crossed his battered and scarred face. Grethard placed one gnarled, bloodied hand on Spiric's heart and finally met his eyes. His gaze was hazy and distant, but Spiric told himself that's how it always had been.

'But Spiric,' he said, 'hiding is how you found me.'

Grethard pulled his hand away, revealing a shimmering blue axiom in his palm and before Spiric could do anything, a barrelling wind swept down from above, whisking him away from Grethard and down into the sands of the ruined skyscraper.

Spiric kicked, screamed, thrashed, anything to fight it, anything to get back to him, but the frothing dunes consumed him with hunger, twisting around his body like flowing water until his head sunk below, his last sight of his grizzled old mentor eclipsed by a blue-robed figure as they landed by Grethard's side.

## CHAPTER THIRTY-THREE

# THE DEPTHS OF MEMORY

C RINGING IN EVERY KIND of pain imaginable, Spiric was a coughing and blinded mess. Whatever Grethard had done to him in his last moments was like being sucked down a vortex of knives. The sand had folded around him at a rapid pace, barely allowing him a chance to catch a breath as it yanked him deeper, threatening to crush his body like a twig if he didn't conform to its whims. It spat him out after what felt like an eternity, leaving him with the final insult of dropping him the last two metres onto hard stone.

Spiric had no idea how deep he'd been buried, let alone how

to get back to the surface. Shifting the sands like that was one of Grethard's Reythurist tricks that he'd spoken of, but Spiric had never been able to persuade him to demonstrate it.

There was no way he'd be able to replicate the feat with an axiom of his own. Even if he did manage to find his way to the surface, he'd then have to deal with Vorric. Considering he was also a Reythurist, the order of the two problems might end up rearranging themselves before Spiric had a chance to tackle them.

Despite Grethard's last words, hiding was the last thing he could think of. Byreth and her brother were still up there. Trapped in that strange temporal phenomena, Vorric could still find them.

Even if Vorric could be dealt with, a thought Spiric shuddered to surmount, he'd then have to face Onassis. A god who deemed him not to exist. Spiric swore under his breath. Where the hell was Arallak when he needed him? Not that he could ever rely on the shadow dancer to turn up in the first place.

Spiric eventually got to his feet, a few strained grunts helping him along the way. The chamber he'd landed up in was almost pitch black, the only hint of light coming from a faint orange glow somewhere off to his right. He strained his eyes to focus on it for a moment but only made out the glint of the glass it was filtering through.

Grethard's torch was in his pouch, but something in his gut stayed his hand when he reached for it. Instead, he risked a few steps towards the light, sliding his boots across the sand-strewn stone floor and only stopping when he stubbed his toe painfully on something jagged.

'Damn it all,' he whispered.

There was no point stumbling around in the dark. If something wanted to kill him for shedding a bit of light in the gloom, they could join the queue. He pulled out the torch and gave it a few shakes, ignoring the stabbing pangs of remorse as he thought of the old man's fate. Both times Spiric hadn't even got to say goodbye. Not properly. Not at all.

A sudden, wrenching grief overcame him, bringing him to his knees as tears welled up in his eyes. They felt alien yet familiar as they went trickling down his face, more flowing with each shuddering sob his body spat out as he tried to wipe them away and stem the flow.

It was simply too much. He didn't need to be a helixic to remember this kind of pain. So much had already been taken from him, yet there was still so much more of it to discover. Doubt had cast a long shadow over his path for weeks and weeks, but it was only now, only in this dark moment, that he was truly ready to give up.

'Not yet, Spiric,' a voice said softly. 'Not far yet.'

He opened his eyes reluctantly. Arallak was knelt before him, illuminated by the pale green glow with an ethereal hand halfway to Spiric's shoulder. It wavered for a moment, then he withdrew it.

'None of it was your idea, was it?' Spiric said softly. 'To throw me forward, I mean. It was because I saw it.'

Arallak's expression was blank, but he reached out and finally held his shoulder, his cold hand a breeze against Spiric's cloak.

'What you saw gave me hope. That things wouldn't have to be the way Onassis dictated them to us but hope that we could be free of it.'

'How?' Spiric spat. 'Everyone's dead and gone and forgotten. What's there left to change?'

'We can still change the next time, Spiric,' Arallak paused a moment, his words then becoming more measured than ever before. 'I'm sorry I had to leave before. Onassis is a terrible and terrifying force to face. I would be trading an hour of my life for only a second of his to stop him, but I saw you confront him. To try and understand him. A feat braver than anything I could wish.'

Spiric shook his head. 'I didn't understand anything. It would take a thousand lifetimes to figure out what he is and he's already had a thousand to do it.'

'He's had so much more than that,' Arallak replied. 'We may end up changing nothing for our people in our past, for the world now, but we can still change the next one. Imagine if there were a world where we remembered The Hytharo Empire was never cruel. Never an empire.'

'But it was.'

Arallak grinned. 'Who says it has to be that again? Onassis

told you what the helixic were, didn't he? People born with a memory outside of time.'

He chewed on the thought. Arallak was right, wasn't he? That was how Spiric, in his own past, had somehow remembered the Vehli atop that tower. How he'd known that he'd make it through to the future, beyond the fall of The Hytharo Empire and beyond the wrath of The Blood Forged God of Memory.

'So then I could make new memories,' Spiric said slowly. 'I can. I did! That's why we found the others like me before the fall, wasn't it? The Hytharo helixics. So that next time we live, next time it all happens again, we can stop it!'

Arallak smiled even more broadly, and Spiric couldn't help doing the same.

'You can save our people, Spiric,' he said. 'Not now, but one day you will remember a way to save them.'

'But what about Onassis? What do we do about him?'

'I don't know, but neither does he and that's our advantage,' Arallak said. 'I must hide for now, but I'll make sure harm does not befall you.'

'Wish you could have done the same for Grethard...'

'As do I. Make sure his sacrifice was not in vain.'

Then Spiric was alone. He still had so many other questions, but he didn't have energy to waste in angst over them. They'd be answered in time. If not now, then in the next life. Maybe they already had been and he just had to remember them. The prospect was so confounding it made his balance wobble.

The torch responded to another few shakes and the strengthening green glow lit up the surroundings. Shining grey marble spanned out at Spiric's feet, covered by miniature sand dunes that grew thicker and taller towards the walls of the chamber, eventually flowing out through broken glass into darkness. Pieces of sleek furniture poked through the dust with their smooth white surfaces eroded at their edges.

A glass barrier, maybe about waist height, was the only thing that disrupted the movement of the sand, running from one side of the room to the other. Beyond it were the bounds of the skyscraper. This was marked by the enormous pillars of steel that held up the structure. It seemed quiet. Safe, even. But the ceiling above couldn't look more wrong.

Sand covered it, exactly as that underfoot, red and blown into the same sweeping patterns that Spiric was so used to seeing on the surface. The sight pressed like a weight on his shoulders as if it were all about to fall in on him. Spiric hastened to cross the low barrier and get away from the impending collapse, but as soon as he was outside, his guts flipped again.

'Oh. Of course,' Spiric breathed, unable to keep a note of annoyance out of his voice.

The undercity was truly cavernous, the surrounding skyscrapers acting as massive support struts for the darkened ceiling which, to Spiric's exasperation, were also made up of the dunes he'd just fled.

Two more forms sprouted at the cavern's centre. One was The Blood Forged God of Memory, the exact same obsidian block as it was above ground. The other came from above, the convergence of the enormous white spires from the surface connecting as one massive pylon.

From where Spiric stood, the skyscrapers had to be a good fifty metres from each other, separated by a clear plane of pitch-black stone that was swept by cursory layers of red dust. But high above, they melted into each other, stretching until Spiric felt he was about to fall backwards if he gawped up at it any longer.

Somewhat closer to the ground, rows of high metal posts gave off a strange, yellowed glow from arched peaks. Thin sheets of metal were affixed halfway up their lengths, printed with the symbols of a language long forgotten, their arrowed sides pointing in all directions. The more Spiric squinted at the writing, the faster it seemed to flicker and twist, one set of gibberish being swapped for another in a dreamlike fashion.

Lacking any other guidance, Spiric began following the blackened rock paths, weaving between the strange contraptions strewn across them. He guessed they were some kind of buggy, like that Byreth had bemoaned their lack of for the past two weeks, but the chassis of these contraptions was far sleeker than anything the Kretatics of this land could produce. The metals themselves were beyond comprehension. Even their wheels, each bearing six or eight of varying size, were wrapped with some kind of strange, darkened animal hide around their circumference.

He leaned to a glass window at one of the machine's sides, holding Grethard's torch closer and closer until the shape of a seat appeared beyond, along with a darkened figure sitting in it. Spiric leapt back, Byreth's blunted hand cannon fumbling in his grip as he struggled not to scream.

But nothing happened.

He bent forward again to get a better look at the figure. They were little more than a shadow, entirely featureless, just like the ones he'd encountered with Arallak and Byreth above ground. Echoes, he'd called them.

As Spiric slowly scanned his surroundings he picked more out, watching from the windows of skyscrapers, huddled at their entrances, or slowly wandering through the alleys between them, none of them seeming to pay any mind to this new mortal invader.

Occasionally Spiric caught glimpses of the blackened walls of Memory through the gaps of the skyscrapers, but he was unable to find a way towards it. The alleys were blocked by huddles of echoes, or strange fractures that seemed to peel the ground away before him, or even peculiarly clear paths that simply didn't look right.

The road beneath him wound and twisted, intersecting with its fellows by only coincidence before leading him like an artery to a much wider swathe of space that cut between the grid of skyscrapers. It was a hundred metres wide, buried by sand to the point the decaying wheeled contraptions only poked through the surface of the dunes.

The form of Memory was at the far end of the road, its faces only dimly lit by the surrounding light poles. Spiric looked down the other way, but saw only rock and shadow in the distance. He squinted. Perhaps it was a swarm of echoes. Lost souls that never managed to flee the city. Was it Memory they were fleeing from? Or something that necessitated the monolith's existence?

Memory loomed larger as he approached, the ceiling of the undercity's hollow raising until light could no longer reach it to compensate. But before Spiric could get anywhere near the obsidian face of it, the ground simply stopped. The remaining sand on the path had drained away, leaving only cracked black slabs of stone that led to the edge of the void. With measured steps, Spiric came right up to it, the toe of his boots only a hair's breadth from nothingness.

The pit was vast, as vast as the clearing Spiric had crossed when he'd first approached the monument above ground, yet there would be no approaching it now. The walls of the hole were perfectly smooth, as if long ago super-heated and burnt away. Severed tunnels dotted the circumference of the pit. Hanging bands of white metal sprouted from them like reeds as they reached desperately up to join the enormous root of the structure that led to the white thorns on the surface.

Beyond the broken tunnels, the only thing that continued was the form of Memory, though Spiric could not see how deep. As he stared, an echoed voice rang in his mind, bypassing his ears and the ever-present ringing that still pestered them.

'How far down does it go?'

'Got a torch to throw in?' Arallak's voice replied.

Spiric looked around, but his brother wasn't there, yet that odd whisper lingered in his ears and he felt compelled to reply with words he knew had already been said.

'Not... Not yet.'

It was only then he realised he did have a torch. Grethard's torch. He gave it a few more shakes, the reliable green glow rolling up as it always did, before he tossed it into the void. It spun as it fell, coming nowhere near Memory as it faded from view until a minute later, maybe more, it was gone. Spiric held his breath as he waited for anything, even just a faint clink of metal when the torch hit something, but the undercity was silent.

'I came here before,' Spiric muttered under his breath. He looked to his left, and Arallak was once again by his side, staring mournfully down into the void to hide his face.

'What drove us so deep?' he asked. 'Why weren't we afraid to come here?'

The mournful gaze was transferred to him and, for a few moments, Arallak simply couldn't find the words to answer.

'I was more afraid of what you'd become, Spiric. The prideful rage I'd taught you festered like no mortal wound ever could. I felt I'd failed you. This quest was to search for a way to end your turmoil, yet when I started to understand the nature of what you were, that this wouldn't happen a simple once, but that every memory and every lifetime would be of anger and pain, I knew I had to find a way to change that. To plunge to the depths of your memory and erase a past you were destined to be burdened with every time you were born into this world.'

Spiric found himself shaking his head at this, his feet backing away back from Arallak. There was no wisdom hidden behind his blackened eyes, no mystery to be unravelled. He sought the same thing Onassis did, only by a different intention.

'But I can't forget,' Spiric said slowly. 'I never can and I never should. Isn't that why you saved me, why you threw me through time to here? So that things like The Hytharo Empire could never happen again? So we could change it?'

'It's what I've told myself. But it's like you say, ironically enough, we can't forget our past, as such I cannot forget my intentions.'

'I would have to agree.'

Spiric looked up at the sound of Onassis' voice. The shadow dancer was hovering ten paces out over the void, the air below him as solid as the crumbling rock on which Spiric stood. Beside him, he sensed Arallak's stance change, his hackles raised.

'We were never meant to meet again like this,' Onassis continued. 'I always found a sense of finality to what should have been our last encounter.'

'Then what should have been?' Spiric asked. Out the corner of his eye, Arallak flinched, but he didn't relent. 'How was this was all meant to go?'

'Spiric, don't taunt him,' Arallak hissed.

'It isn't a taunt. I deserve to know!' Spiric spat. 'I've probably already remembered it.'

Onassis considered him for a moment, then spoke as if he were giving a statement of record. 'Your final moments are within the walls of the city of Andias, along with the rest of the Hytharo you both wished to erase. You dealt the same death and destruction as your legacy taught you, but at least this time it was in an attempt to repel your foes from the incoming form of The Blood Forged God of Memory and the annihilation it carried.'

'But how could you know?' Spiric shot back. 'You said yourself you cannot be present while Memory is.'

'I didn't need to be. I know because you remembered it.'

'What about Byreth?' he said. 'If you know everything, where would she have ended up?'

'Dead attempting to breach what you now call The Lightning Cage.'

'And Grethard?'

'Still in his exile.'

'Kurkress?'

'Razed. Unlike Basarod.'

'Which was destroyed by the hands of your puppet!'

'An action rendered necessary by your delineation. An action I did not interfere in, other than to save Vorric's life so he may correct your reckless trail and return all our fates to what they must be.'

Then something clicked into place in Spiric's mind.

'An action now impossible because I've already made new memories. The ones that led me here.' He tore his eyes away from Onassis, facing Arallak instead. 'It's because you believed me, wasn't it? Because you trusted me.'

But Arallak didn't return his gaze. His was still locked on Onassis, his gritted teeth finally mustering words.

'What of the prince?' Arallak growled. 'Of the one who asked for a place where time stood still.'

Onassis didn't answer. He regarded Arallak with a curious look which turned into a wry, triumphant grin.

'Dead in The Lightning Cage after the fall of Andias. Hunted by those not aware the Hytharo were no longer needed for rain due to your sacrifice. It was a shame. He was never a fighter. Not like Spiric.'

Whatever sound came out of Arallak's mouth next was something more terrifying than the tales of the shadow dancers could ever amount to be. It was a slow, open-mouthed, guttural gasp. A rattling breath of the dead as he looked slowly over to Spiric, a final sadness on his expression that his face would never be free of.

'I'm... I'm so sorry.'

'What? What do you mean?' Spiric said quickly.

But before Arallak could explain, the ceiling of the cavern began rumbling. Torrents of sand fell like rain as a far-off section of the upside-down dunes split in two, and the figure of a man came shooting out.

They darted across the undercity in a whirlwind of dust, weaving between the glass walls of skyscrapers as they barrelled closer and closer to reveal the howling, raging, blood-spattered form of Vorric.

## CHAPTER THIRTY-FOUR

# THE FOREST

SPIRIC TURNED AND RAN, all thoughts of being on the cusp of grand revelations spanning across lifetimes lost and forgotten as panic washed and blended with the blood rush suddenly pulsing in his body. The dust-strewn road exploded into hazy clouds around him, and the bone-shaking shockwaves sent his hurtling path leftwards into a side street. Spiric dodged through the narrow alley, dancing between the forms of idle echoes before bursting out onto the next glass-flanked avenue.

He hadn't even cleared the backstreet when the air snapped dark and Onassis materialised before him, catching his shoulders with both hands and halting him completely. Spiric thrashed against his grip, the howling wind already pitching in his ears, but he was powerless against the shadow dancer. High above, Vorric was plunging towards them.

'What happened to not interfering?' Spiric spat.

Before Spiric got an answer, Arallak appeared at Onassis' flank, his face frozen in panic, and for a moment, Spiric couldn't tell if his eyes were red or black.

'A second for an hour?' Onassis asked.

'As many as it takes,' Arallak replied.

Arallak's hand darted to Onassis' shoulder and then they were both gone. Spiric staggered sideways, barely regaining his balance before a crashing tackle sent him sliding across dune-covered stone. Vorric wrestled his weight down on him, further pinning him with the help of his iron-coiled armour, the razor-thin barbs biting into Spiric's chest as he screamed in pain.

He could barely feel the axiom burning in his palm; it might've just been his imagination, but he plunged his hand between the coils anyway. They tore and ripped at his knuckles, lightning and blood bursting out as one as his fingers scrabbled at Vorric's robes. The air was filled with a wail of pain and the smell of burning flesh, Vorric never breaking from Spiric's eyes as he screamed before finally relenting, lurching aside and almost taking Spiric's mangled left hand with him.

The echoes began to wander over as Spiric clambered to his feet, following inquisitively as he rushed into the nearest skyscrapers. The marbled floor had all but collapsed in here, giving way to a wide tunnel below that Spiric only saw as he tumbled into it. Dust and gravel rained down along with him, blanketing his crumpled form as he begged it to move.

The air was cold and silent. A red glow emanated from a narrow glassy strip that ran the length of the rounded ceiling which stretched forever forwards. But Spiric wasn't alone.

As he rose to his feet, dozens of echoes around him mirrored his action, watching him intently. They lined the walls of the tunnel, their presence bound between the stone and the twin steel rails that continued parallel to the distance. Further along, Spiric spied more of them, crouched and huddled, waiting for something.

He began with tentative steps along the smooth stone, flinching as more echoes rose to greet him as he passed. They hadn't moved before. Hadn't paid him any mind.

Not until he'd used an axiom.

He looked at his palm, the bloodied, prickling scratches across it glinting in the light as he pushed a rune into the centre. The nearest echo leaned in curiously, its blank face almost touching Spiric's. He snapped his palm shut with a wince of pain and the echo retreated in turn, its form blending indiscernibly with its brethren.

Spiric kept walking, tense minutes passing, only stopping when he realised the sound of his footsteps was not alone. He spun with his bloodied hand out, an axiom ready despite the echoes, but it was Onassis. Forcing out a snarl, he closed his fist and turned to keep walking, but the shadow dancer was already by his side.

'A strange irony that you find sanctuary with the echoes,' he quipped.

It was only then Spiric noticed how they shrunk away from Onassis' presence.

'You both remain because you can't believe that there could be a world where you do not exist, and yet you... you still live.'

'It's because I remembered it,' Spiric spat back. 'I saw myself in these ruins before the Hytharo fell.'

Onassis seemed to chuckle, an out-of-practice noise his expression didn't abide by. 'But was it yourself that you saw?'

'I know what's real!'

Spiric lashed out with his good hand, but it was a futile blow that whooshed through the empty air where Onassis had once been.

The tunnel twisted, dipped, and rose as he continued on, keeping count of his steps until he forgot them and began again. Time was lost in the strange red glow, and it was only when orange light began to flicker in the path ahead that Spiric realised he was no longer flanked by the echoes. The light widened as the ground rose under him, the ventricles of additional tunnels merging with his as more of the twin rails appeared at his feet.

They were no longer parallel, instead writhing over each

other's paths like a freshly cut bag of snakes, the metal sometimes reaching up to the ceiling like vines before looping back over and plunging into the ground. Spiric stepped carefully to avoid touching the metal. Whenever his path gave him no choice but to draw close, he swore he felt it vibrating through the cool air.

Arallak was waiting for him at the end of the tunnel, his feet on the border of the shadow that its mouth cast. Spiric stopped ten paces away, holding his nerve as his brother cocked his head.

'Who am I?' Spiric asked slowly.

For a moment, Arallak paused, the flash of a humoured grin dancing across his face. 'A question I've asked you so many times before, times when you were always sure of yourself.'

'Tell me,' Spiric growled.

'You're a warrior. You're Spiric. You're exactly what you need to be to defeat Vorric.'

'And Onassis, too?'

Arallak hesitated. 'I'm what I need to be. I can't defeat him like you can Vorric, but I can buy you time to find a way. Just as I threw you through time, I can do the same to him, even if it takes me to the end of this world.'

'You'd be exchanging an hour of yours for a mere second of mine.'

Spiric turned, the dim outline of Onassis' form on the edge of his sight down the tunnel, yet his voice was crisp as if it were in his ear. He looked back to Arallak, the grim determination on his face mirroring what Spiric felt on his own. He walked towards him, keeping an eye back over his shoulder to make sure Onassis remained where he stood, for what good that did, and stopped by his brother's side.

'How much time can you buy me?'

'I don't know. However much a thousand lifetimes can afford me.'

Spiric choked on his next words. 'Will I see you again?'

'In another life.' Arallak smiled down at him, placing a single hand on his shoulder. 'A life where we can make things right. Until then... Thank you. For being my brother.'

Arallak walked into the darkness, but Spiric still hadn't processed the words. The weight of his hand still lay heavy on his shoulder while he watched him go. Every emotion crashed through his mind like a vicious storm, churning with his pounding heart until he felt nothing but the dull, stinging throb of his own maimed hand.

He expected to see something. To hear something. Even as pathetic as the scuffling of two sets of wrestling feet, but nothing came from the darkened tunnel. His brother was gone without even a trace, as if he'd never had one. His only legacy was the future. One where Onassis would return at a time impossible to foretell. A time where Spiric would have to face the shadow dancer once again.

It took all of Spiric's willpower to wrench his eyes from the dark pit of the tunnel. Vorric was still out there, he chided himself, and no matter how insignificant and petty that struggle now felt, it was one that would hunt him down.

A nearly boundless yard of flat stone and twisting metal lay beyond the mouth of the tunnel Spiric had emerged from. Additional tunnels sprouted a hundred metres away to his left and right, spewing more tracks into a grand amphitheatre that sat at the edge of the pit surrounding the pillar of Memory.

In the abandoned centre stage, the metal had a life of its own, leaving the ground with sharp curves to point to a sky that was blanketed with sand, splitting and splitting and splitting again as branches and leaves to form the canopy of a steel forest.

Echoes walked among their smoothened trunks, gathering and marvelling at the very largest in the middle. Enough rails had converged like roots to form a thick structure free of rust, the surface polished to pure white as it stretched up to rival the skyscrapers, splitting off into colossal branches that reached outwards before disappearing into the ceiling's dunes.

'So that's what the thorns came from,' Spiric said to himself. Not that it brought him any closer to understanding the thing's true purpose.

By the looks of it, the echoes had studied it for an eternity, though their ever-curious stances showed they were no closer, either. Childish wonder lured Spiric to the base of it, dodging between echoes as he approached.

Up close it seemed almost too small, but as he stared up its length, it warped and swelled in his vision. He tore his eyes away again. It was almost like Vorric was right. Perhaps some things were never made to be understood. Just trying to make sense of it has shot a piercing pain through his temple, the last thing he needed on top of his achingly battered body.

Or at least, second to last. The air snapped as Vorric darted overhead, weaving between the branches of white steel before touching down in a distant clearing. The ground shook with the sound of crunching stone and the trunks of the steel forest hummed with it, sending more reverberations back into the tunnel to turn the labyrinth into a massive pipe organ.

At the edge of the steel forest, Vorric stood hunched. His entire body heaved as he struggled for breath, but it didn't lessen the murderous hunger in his eyes. A grin split his lips as he leered at his trapped quarry, but for the first time, Spiric didn't feel fear. Arallak's words still rang in his head.

He was a warrior.

He was who he needed to be.

Spiric began slowly strafing away from the gathered echoes as Vorric approached. There was a stagger in his step, but it wasn't a weakness Spiric could yet count on. His coiled armour still embraced him, smoking and blackened, Spiric's own blood clinging to the side of it. The echoes followed him, closer than they followed Spiric, but Vorric paid no mind to them.

'You should be careful of them,' Spiric called out. 'Unassis isn't here to save you anymore.'

Vorric's stride faltered for only a moment before he

summoned a surge of wind and rushed towards Spiric, smashing him to the ground before he could dive to the side. As Spiric pulled himself to his feet, Vorric hovered ten feet in the air, keeping his distance as more echoes gathered at his feet.

'It was never about my protection, Spiric! It was about protecting the living from the dead. From the abomination of forgotten magic. Isn't that what you thought of the Hytharo?'

'No,' Spiric managed with a gasp. The impact had knocked the wind out of him, but he struggled on. 'Magic wasn't the danger. Never was. It was you. Bastards like you!'

Vorric swooped again. Spiric ducked, almost in time and only copping a grazed face for his troubles. He climbed to his feet once more, cradling his stinging cheek with his already bloodied left hand, the mass of shadows under Vorric now a writhing blob of darkness. It frothed with tendrils that only just failed to reach him.

'It's a pathetic accusation! Look at this place! Would it all have happened had they controlled their magic like we do ours?'

'Who says we control it?' Spiric spat out with a mouthful of blood. 'Onassis? He told me he's the one who put it into runes, but he hasn't been able to stop pure resonance, has he? What happens when he's gone?'

'He is eternal!' Vorric roared back. 'He is the anchor that our world clings to!'

'Then where is he!?'

The question echoed through the cavern, punctured only by

the low hum of the wind that suspended Vorric.

'He's gone,' Spiric sneered. 'And if he's gone, what do you think is keeping us all here?'

Vorric dived, crashing into Spiric and crushing his throat with both hands. Spiric kicked and thrashed feebly as darkness encroached on his vision. His hands clawed at Vorric's, but he couldn't find a way under his iron grip before his fingers started to go numb as well. Time grew sluggish as his thoughts did the same. Even a blink seemed to take an eon.

All he could think of were runes. Runes that stacked up in his palm. He had no idea what order they came in. He could only pray it was something deadly as his hand limply bounced off the coiled armour's chest plate, trying and trying and failing again and again to find a way in.

An enormous, dizzy wave flowed through his head as Vorric's visage merged with that of a woman's, one with yellow eyes filled with a burning hatred before it snapped into a sharp focus. Her fingers were around his neck, pressed like knives as he thrashed again. But this time he was strong! His right hand gave a mighty punch to sweep her aside, revealing a boundless blue sky.

Spiric was standing before he knew it, the city of Andias surrounding him, a dozen red-robed guards closing in on the emaciated woman.

'Hold back!' Spiric roared. 'She's mine!'

He felt the sword at his hip, the smooth, well-oiled, and silent glide of it emerging from its sheath. The glinting sun caught it as he readied the tip at the woman's throat. He'd never yet drawn blood, he'd never been old enough, yet it was today that fifteen years had passed from his birth. Today was the day he proved the rage that was his birthright. But then a voice cried out. His voice.

'No!'

Spiric felt his head turn, his heart suddenly a motor in his chest, not from the attack, not from the fury that burned in his lungs, but something otherworldly as he looked to his prince. Into very his own face.

'We have laws!'

Spiric couldn't find the words to respond. His eyes felt so wide they were about to pop out of his own skull. His entire body rumbled with his pulse as it raced faster and faster and suddenly the prince's expression matched his.

'She...' Spiric stammered, frowning. He'd never stammered. He never ever stammered! Arallak had taught him to speak perfectly in the presence of his duty, to the point they'd practiced long into the night to be the seeds of perfect royal wardens. He blinked, meeting the face that was his own once again as he composed himself. 'She leaves us no choice, Prince Ozim.'

His vision blurred and warped again, Vorric's face dashing across it before the blue skies returned, his royal guards surrounding him as he stood in the square of the city he wanted no part in, while a beaten and destitute woman glowered up at the wielder of the sword pressed to her throat.

At his friend.

His lost brother.

At Spiric.

Being knocked to the ground had ruffled Spiric's usually sleek and cropped black hair, his face twisted into a rage that Ozim had dreaded seeing each time he was forced to walk among the city that rightfully despised what his family and The Hytharo Empire had subjugated them to. But now he could feel that rage awakened, burning in his heart, that murderous intent that terrified him to the core.

'I've never seen you kill,' he growled at Spiric. 'I don't want that to start now.'

The memory twisted again, the sword now in his hand as he withdrew it. Hateful tones tumbled clumsily from his mouth.

'Then don't come to her trial. But there will come a day. You cannot live a lifetime without death.'

He turned away from himself, from Ozim, from whoever the hell he was now, and found Arallak among the guards. He'd expected to see pride. Instead he was met with horror. The rest of the crowd matched his expression and Spiric decided to capitalise on it. He thrust his sword skyward with his right, burning rune after rune in his left before he clapped that to the hilt, charging the blade with blinding lightning.

His vision faded as screams reached his ears, the crowd scattering in fear until their panicked shouts trickled from earshot, one by one, until a single, long howl of pain remained ringing in Spiric's ears.

Vorric was on top of him again, howling, thrashing, and screaming, his hands off Spiric's neck, Spiric's own arms entangled in Vorric's armour as pulse after pulse of lightning swept across the metal in crackling waves. With a shocked gasp, Spiric let go, clutching his battered throat with both blood-soaked hands as he coughed and hacked, the sound of his own pathetic struggle to breathe still drowned out by Vorric's cries of pain.

The lightning was gone, but it had attracted something far, far worse. The echoes surrounded him, reaching out with ethereal hands that formed into flesh for only the moment they touched him, each contact producing a dark flash that left absolutely nothing in its wake. The coiled armour fell away in pieces as Vorric rose and began to flee, the crowd of echoes following, their touch now stripping away cloth and flesh.

Vorric took off with a blast of air that engulfed Spiric, and he clambered to his feet, doing his best not to trip over as his head swam. Breathing didn't make him any less dizzy, the only remedy would be to unsee what he'd just remembered, but as he looked to the cavernous ceiling, up at the retreating shape of Vorric through the steel canopy, he resolved to block it out. For just one more moment he could hold off the truth of who he was meant to be.

He still needed to be Spiric.

As Vorric disappeared behind Memory, Spiric strode to the edge of the pit, the echoes following him at ten paces as he drew Byreth's hand cannon with his right hand, readying one last axiom in his left.

'Come on. Come on,' Spiric muttered under his breath. 'Come get me!'

## CHAPTER THIRTY-FIVE

# TO DUST

L IGHTNING CRACKLED IN HIS palm. His lightning. His power. In his right, Byreth's cannon felt featherlight, the rusted metal grip practically welded into his skin. Spiric ignored the gathering echoes as they drew closer and closer. Close enough he'd feel their breath if they exhaled.

But they didn't.

Neither did he.

Vorric's form emerged from the other side of Memory, pulsing gusts of wind already preceding him that washed across Spiric as staggering waves, but he didn't budge as the bastard closed in. Instead, he raised his left hand, arcs and coils of energy dancing along the length of his arm as he let the axiom burn.

A whipping tendril of lightning lashed out, spanning the void to Vorric in the blink of an eye, seeking him out like a bird of prey diving on its target. A flash of pure light filled the cavern, blinding Spiric for just a moment, just long enough to miss the strange way that Vorric's entire body shimmered in mid-air, a single second of skipping in and out of sight as the energy searched for a mark before extinguishing itself.

Spiric caught the briefest glimpse of Vorric's flapping navy robes before he tackled him, a punishing impact that lifted Spiric clean off his feet. It took him another second to gather his wits and realise he still hadn't hit the ground. The undercity swirled and dipped far below, Vorric's blood drenched arms clutched around Spiric's chest as he was carried away from the steel forest.

Vorric's trajectory began to plummet as the void surrounding Memory rushed up ahead. Spiric thrashed but he was unable to get his pinned left hand close enough to Vorric to plug one last axiom into him as they fell.

They were low now, so close to the dunes that Spiric could almost kick the tops of them. With only seconds until they were over the pit, Spiric swung his right arm around, jamming the muzzle of Byreth's hand cannon into Vorric's guts and hammering the trigger.

The gunshot rang out, and suddenly Spiric was falling. He spun in utter silence for barely a second before he hit the sand with a dull crunch, still sliding down the dune as he scrabbled hopelessly for purchase. Somehow he'd landed on his back, and he couldn't tell if the shimmering lights above were coming from his ringing, aching head or simply another quirk of the undercity.

He looked down at himself, almost mistaking his blood-soaked clothes for the red robes he always wore in those horrific memories. Gingerly, he ran his hands down his body, but found nothing but deep scrapes and bruises waiting to rise to the surface.

A low and mournful groan reached him from the other side of the sand dune. Spiric shambled over the top of it, almost slipping at its crest, a mistake that would've sent him sliding down into the void only a few metres beyond. It was a fate Vorric had almost found himself.

He was slumped on his side, his feet dangling out over the edge and his head resting further up the foot of the dune. His body crumpled with each rasping breath. Both of his hands were clutched over a gory wound in his stomach, but he was unable to staunch the oozing flow. Blood spilled onto the sand, unable to drench it before being absorbed, adding to the pool of crimson mud growing under him.

'Is that how Grethard went?' Spiric spat. 'Did you let him die slowly, like this?'

He staggered over to Vorric, half sitting and half collapsing down into the sand next to him, savouring the pained grimace the man regarded him with. Blood coated his teeth.

'No,' Vorric wheezed. 'I did to him... what he did to them... It was only fair.'

'So then what do I do to you? For what you did to Basarod, Kurkress, and who knows where else?'

Vorric groaned and tried to shift onto his back, a pathetic lurch that barely moved him. Spiric didn't feel inclined to help. Not even with a swift kick. Vorric tried again, revealing his entire left side to be caked with a sandy slurry of blood and muck.

'He got a better death than this. Reythurists... are meant to die under the sky.'

Spiric glanced up at the cavern's ceiling, dark spare for the refractions of the skyscrapers that pierced it.

'I guess it wasn't meant to be.'

'You weren't meant to be, Spiric!' Vorric spat.

'You're right. I wasn't,' he replied slowly. 'Spiric is not my name.'

'You... what?'

'Ozim,' Spiric continued. 'My name was Ozim. This whole time I thought I was a murderer. A warrior. An executioner. But I wasn't. I was a prince of The Hytharo Empire. I abhorred the violence that we wrought, and I wanted nothing more than to end the cycle it perpetuated. The one which Onassis guaranteed. I couldn't face it again. I wanted to forget it all, but when I got here, I had forgotten myself. I remembered only what terrified me. It was enough to turn me into exactly that. I suppose that's why you wanted to kill me, wasn't it?'

'It was,' Vorric hissed back. 'But I was trying to save you just then.' He held up his left arm, using his right hand to wipe the blood away from its underside to reveal it blank. 'Last axiom. Last chance to get to the surface. Last chance to show the world that I was right.'

'So they wouldn't remember you as a butcher.'

'Exactly...'

'And that's what you're afraid of?'

Vorric nodded weakly.

'It wouldn't have mattered. Even if you'd won, it's what you always were. It's what Onassis turned you into.'

'It's what was meant to be!' Vorric roared.

His words reverberated around the cavern and Spiric watched the sound travel, catching sight of the shadowy figures that perked up across the way as they seemed to hear it.

'Because of what Onassis told you? He's gone now. What makes you so sure he's right?'

'Because... Because...' Vorric stuttered.

His eyes were unfocused, his brow twitching into a frown as he stared up, confusion lurching across his face. His hands were trembling, weakening their hold on the wound.

'Because he's a helixic,' Spiric said. He was on his feet, his fists balled at his sides, and he only wished he had Byreth's hand cannon tight in his grip, but he'd lost it in the fall. 'But so am I! He and I share a memory that I've now changed, that all this is now permanently a part of, but now nobody knows what happens next! There's no record! There's nothing that's meant to be! I've spent weeks believing that I was someone I am not, knowing it to my core despite seeing things I should've realised proved me so damn wrong. Who's to say that anything we believe is "meant" to be?'

'Onassis!' Vorric grunted with a gurgle of blood. 'He is the anchor that—'

'But he's gone!' Spiric cried out. He spun around theatrically, pretending to search the cavern for the shadow dancer but only catching sight of more approaching echoes. 'He said it himself that he'd never done this before, that anything could happen, so why doesn't it?'

'Because it hasn't.'

'But it already has!'

An empty pause lingered after Spiric's words before Vorric mustered his last words.

'So why shouldn't it?'

Spiric finally looked down at Vorric. His hands began to still and his breathing weakened. Blood had finally stopped flowing from the wound. If anything, it seemed to be retreating. More shadows were gathering, only a few paces away, staring at the both of them with a hungering curiosity. Spiric met Vorric's eyes again. They were bloodshot, bruised, and—

Spiric thought it was a trick of the light. The blue gaze had flickered to black. It happened again, longer this time, then rage and betrayal suddenly carved Vorric's face into a primal scream as every muscle in his dying body spasmed, lurching him to his feet as he grabbed Spiric by his collar.

He thrashed against Vorric's grip, but before he could break free, a colossal blast of air launched them both hurtling at the cavern ceiling. The echoes below formed into a black morass, surging after them as one great wave, on the cusp of consuming them whole, hands of living flesh nipping at their feet as the sand above was rent open, blinding them with sunlight and driving back the darkness below.

Spiric and Vorric only remained airborne long enough for the ground to snap shut under their feet. Their flight halted abruptly and Spiric was dropped unceremoniously on to the fresh dune. He screamed as he fell the last foot or two, landing on his back with a dull thud.

He backpedalled, kicking up hot sand as he went, but Vorric didn't follow. His feet still hadn't touched the ground. His blue and blood-soaked robes were gone. Sleek, black, embroidered garments had taken their place, the pattern a perfect match to the monolith of Memory that stood beyond him. His face was clean of the scars and welts that had shaped it, and when he turned to Spiric, it was with a gaze of bottomless black eyes.

Spiric rose as Vorric's feet touched the ground. He approached slowly, paying more mind to his own form than the boy that had once been his quarry.

'What happened to me?'

'The thing you most feared,' Spiric replied. 'Same as happened to me.'

Vorric fixed him with a confused look.

'When I was Ozim, I feared the violence. The hatred and the rage. I wanted to run from it. Hide from it. But it only hunted me harder and harder as I did.'

The sands suddenly shifted beneath his vision, flattening and warping into carpet as the skyscrapers above crashed into each other, the debris landing to form the interior of the two clashing structures. Vorric was gone. Memory was gone. He was underground again. All that remained was the dim orange light that filtered in through the glass which held back the desert sands.

It was silent.

A silence that stretched for eons as Ozim waited. Waited for the frantic footsteps coming from the stairs on the other side of the room. He could've gone further, hid deeper, but the exiled prince's body ached.

He was alone.

Alone and afraid.

The source of the clambering footsteps hurtled into view,

looking much the same. The man's pace slowed as he scanned the room, each of his cautious steps pounding in Ozim's heart. He looked down to his wrist. There were seven runes left.

A wild shout came from across the room, heavy pounding footfalls following as Ozim finally, for the first time, levelled his arm and took aim. The first power rune burned, crackling painfully in his palm as he looked away, clenching his eyes shut as the piercing snap of lightning lanced out.

The man wailed in pain and collapsed, tumbling the last few feet before he lay twitching at Ozim's feet. He could only look up at him, terror across his face, silently pleading as Ozim readied the next rune.

But this time when it burned white, when the blue arcs of energy danced between his fingers, it didn't hurt. It was glorious. It was a rush of power he'd never imagined as the man's entire body seemed to warp again, replaced now with that of a woman with wild yellow eyes that glowered up at him with a lifetime of rage as she lay twitching on the cobblestone plaza of Andias.

Spiric let out a victorious roar as the second power rune burst forth, stopping her heart once and for all. As the smell of burnt flesh filled his lungs, he looked up to the cheering crowd, but this time he fixed his eyes on Prince Ozim, flanked and safe among all his guards.

Spiric held up a hand, two fingers stretched towards the sky as he stared at him. Two axioms. It always took two axioms. When he lowered his arm, Ozim was gone. As was everyone else. Sand lay at his feet again, skyscrapers stretching up at his sides and Memory framed in the distance between them.

'I've remembered myself as the one who would deal out the violence. Because when I was Ozim, I believed that I was destined to rule over it.' Spiric said to Vorric. 'That I was meant for it. That's what The Hytharo Empire was. That's why it should not be forgotten.'

'Then you must think the same of the Scythes.'

'I do.'

Vorric cast his face down, unable to meet Spiric's eyes. 'Then prove that we were wrong. That I was wrong. That you were meant to be. That I'm sorry, even if there's nothing I can do to make up for it.'

It was little more than a muttered apology. One that would never make up for the waking nightmares he'd inflicted upon the land. For the lives he'd taken away. But even if Spiric couldn't dignify it with a response, he knew Vorric meant it. That he understood him.

It was strange watching Vorric as he struggled to stand there. There were moments where he'd fade, or his feet would sink just a bit too far into the sand. Spiric could recall Arallak telling him that existing in this world was a struggle. Not that Arallak ever would again. His sacrifice, his offer for everything until the end of time to delay Onassis' return, was a fate beyond death. Instead it would be Vorric that took his place, an eternity stretched out before him to dwell on his mistakes.

'What will you do now?' Spiric asked.

Vorric shrugged, a gesture unnaturally casual for the new shadow dancer.

'For the first time, I'm not sure. I am nothing. No one. Nobody. To the rest of the world, no more. Onassis had given me meaning. Purpose. But he's gone. I think I'll have to wait for him to get back. When he returns, I shan't be on his side.'

'So you'd be on mine?'

Vorric chuckled. 'I wouldn't deserve it. But what of you?'

'I think the same.'

Another quizzical look crossed Vorric's face.

'I wasn't the only Hytharo that was thrown through time,' Spiric explained. 'I was just the first to get here.'

'Then when do the others come?'

Spiric shook his head. 'No idea. But if I could remember myself as Spiric, instead of who I was as Ozim, perhaps I can remember them, too. I just worry they won't be as peaceful as the prince I once was.'

'Or if they'd still be loyal to Prince Ozim of Andias.'

Vorric smirked, but Spiric failed to see the humour in it. He still didn't understand what a helixic was, but if it ran in a bloodline as he suspected, then he had two more royal siblings to contend with, along with two more survivors of The Hytharo Empire whose nature he could not fathom. If he was meant to stop the Hytharo Empire from existing in the next life, and

Onassis along with it, he wouldn't be able to do it alone.

'It's a bridge I'll burn when I come to it. But first I have to wait for my friend.'

'The one who came with you? Who failed to shoot me with the cannon you ended up killing me with?'

Spiric nodded. 'She's stuck at the top of one of these skyscrapers, saving her brother from a place where time stands still. I don't have a chance of making it back to civilisation without her, so I'll have to follow her in.'

'Show me.'

It was strange travelling through the ruins with Vorric at his side. Half the time he wasn't even there, simply flitting in and out of sight, either far ahead or further behind as Spiric slowly scaled the tower. His aching muscles, bruised and battered from the fight, made it slow going and he wondered if enough time had already passed that Byreth would be free of the fracture when he reached the top.

Yet when he finally got there, she was exactly where he'd left her, still only two steps in. Vorric watched on from the catwalk as Spiric hobbled to his side.

'Ephemeral,' he said quietly. 'People used to think it was a paralict, but I just thought it the source of this phenomena instead. A fracture disguised as a dangerously tempting trap.'

'What would've happened if they got to the ball in the centre?'

Vorric placed a hand on Spiric's shoulder, causing him to

flinch.

'I once found an Academy record of an expedition to get one of these things. They'd set off almost sixty years ago. There was no summary of return. When I found the site, I found why.' He squeezed Spiric's shoulder tighter. 'Let's hope she doesn't.'

High above, the sun accelerated, plummeting towards the horizon before shooting up the opposite side, its entire journey repeating every five seconds, then four, then so quick that day and night was a blinding blue and black blur.

Byreth's pace picked up, Vehli only just managing a yelp of shock as she crashed into him. A mighty roar rang out from somewhere inside the tussle, and suddenly she was bodily carrying her brother up the other side of the metal surface. Each clang of her boot slowed the sun's cycle above until she was out the other side, dumping him on the catwalk before straightening up, the now-setting sun making her face radiant.

The grip disappeared from Spiric's shoulder as she looked over and a look of confused exasperation twisted on a face he never thought he'd see again.

'Spiric?' Byreth said, stomping over to him. 'Is that you?'

'Yeah. It's me,' he said weakly, the second half of the words knocked from his lungs as she tackled him into one more excruciating bear hug. 'It's me.'

# A NOTE FROM THE AUTHOR

Thank you so much for reading THE HYTHARO REDUX! Writing this novel and discovering Spiric's story was an amazing journey that I've undertaken over the almost nine years before I could finally publish it and I'm now so glad to share it with the world.

If you enjoyed your read, please consider leaving a review on Amazon or Goodreads. Your endorsement is the most vital thing in getting the book in front of other readers and is greatly appreciated.

# Pronunciation Guide & Glossary

A NOTE FROM THE author: The course of this novel will explain all concepts as you come across them, so referring to this glossary is not necessitated, and it has been included as an extra.

(If a term or pronunciation is not included here, then it has either been omitted to avoid spoilers, is minor enough to not be worth mentioning, or would be pronounced exactly as read. Bolded parts of pronunciations indicate emphasis on that particular syllable.)

## Major Characters (roughly in order of appearance):

- Spiric: *Spir-ic*

- Grethard: *Greth-ard*

- Byreth: *By-reth*

- Vehli: *Veh-li*

- Leerukhart: *Lheer-rue-cart*

- Vorric: *Vorr-ic*

- Tetran: *Tet-tran*

- Arallak: *Ar-a-llak*

- Greely: *Gree-ly*

- Voss-Ela: *Voss-El-a*

- Braiyth: *Bray-ith*

## Runic Peoples:

- Kretatic: ***Kre**-ta-tic*

  - Born with green eyes, these peoples use their magic to magnetically bind scrap metal into arcanites.

- Reythurist: *Rey-thur-**ist***

  - With blue eyes, they have a keen sense of the air around them, their magic giving them the ability to manipulate it in unexpected and often deadly ways.

- Curiktic: *Cu-rik-**tic***

  - Drawing the roots of their magic from the ever-burning sun, yellow-eyed Curiktics can summon blinding light or blazing fire, the latter of which either causing or cauterising wounds.

- Hytharo: ***Hy-thar***-o *(The "Hy" sounds like "high", and "thar" almost sounds a bit like "their", but with more of an "a" sound.)*

  - Extinct for eons, the Hytharo people were the ones responsible for bringing rain to the Droughtlands. Their blood-red eyes and matching runes meant either this, or bolts of deadly lightning were coming. Their disappearance is a mystery, almost completely forgotten aside from myth and legend.

## Objects:

- Arcanite: *Ar-can-ite*

  - An arcanite can refer to any piece of magically bound metal created by a Kretatic's axioms. A Kretatic can use these for many purposes, be it as weapons, beasts of burden or other ingenious uses. While under their control, a Kretatic must commit a portion of their mind to the metal to control it. In return, they can sense things through the metal as if it was their own flesh. The larger and more complex the arcanite is, the greater the stress that is placed on a Kretatic's mind.

- Paralict: *Par-a-lict*

  - A paralict is an unnatural object often found in the ruins of those-of-glass. They carry bizarre and incomprehensible magics with them and are as dangerous and forbidden as they are valuable.

- Respark: *Re-spark*

  - A paralict often found in areas cursed by lightning. Taking the form of small orange discs of ceramic appearance, they spin perpetually. Attempts to stop this motion have disastrous and explosive consequences.

- Molten Flux:

  - Molten flux was a self-replicating liquid metal that was injected into fresh corpses to create autominds. It was highly volatile and would quickly swell to fill whatever container it existed in, to the limits of surface tension. Contact with skin was lethal. Despite these dangers and the punishment for being found in possession of a single drop, it was the subject of a roaring trade until it was destroyed at the end of a time known as The Flux Catastrophe.

- Automind:

  - An automind is a fresh corpse that has been reanimated by molten flux. Entirely docile, autominds are used by some Kretatics to control arcanites far larger and more complex that they are normally able to.

## **Magic:**

- Ink:

    - Concocted from impossibly rare liquid water and a number of other ingredients, ink is used to draw runes onto the skin of one who wants to use magic. Each vial is specially brewed depending on which type of magic they were born to use.

- Runes:

    - Each piece of magic, or axiom, is made up of a number of runes. A single rune will mean a word, or a number of words, which are often determined by the intention of who is using it at the time.

- Axioms:

    - An axiom is the resulting magic itself, a statement of words summoned into the world to change it. It can also refer to a sequence of runes that are ready on someone's skin.

- Those-of-Glass:

    - The name that the people of the Droughtlands
      to those who built the various forbidden ruins
      that are scattered across the dunes. Little else is
      understood about them, other than their magic
      being impossibly different from what is known.

- Fracture:

    - The name given to areas of anomalous
      phenomena usually contained within the ruins of
      those-of-glass.

## Places:

- The Droughtlands:

  - The name given to the stretches of desert wasteland which is known to those who live upon it.

- Breggesa: **Bre**-*gges-a*

  - The largest city in the Droughtlands, an enormous trade hub at the crossroads of several regions and home of the Academy of Breggesa.

- The Lightning Cage:

  - An area of ruins left by those-of-glass, one of the largest in the region. Extremely difficult to enter, due to the seemingly impenetrable fence of ancient lightning from which the place gets its name.

- Kurkress: *Kur-kress*

  - A mining town nestled in the mountains to the west of The Lightning Cage, which draws great mineral wealth by extracting the excavated remnants from a dormant ruin left by those-of-glass.

- Revance: **Reh**-*vance*

  - Revance is the gargantuan walking fortress that wanders across the Droughtlands, both as a cargo hauler and a mercenary outfit. Despite being one gigantic arcanite, its creator and controller are still unknown.

- Basarod: *Bas-a-rod*

  - An ancient citadel which serves as one of the primary trade hubs in the region of the southern sands, standing largely independent from Breggesa.

- Kyrea: *Kye-re-a*

  - Factory town infamous for its factories and the murky underworld of autominds and traders of molten flux that supply them.

- Iroka: *I-**row**-ka*

  - Mining town that serves as a trade hub at the end of Revance's journey across the Droughtlands, the beginning of which lies just outside of Breggesa.

# Also By

The Flux Catastrophe Series:
Rising Flux: The Prequel Novella to Molten Flux
Molten Flux

The First Hytharo Series:
The Hytharo Redux

# About the Author

Jonathan Weiss is an Australian Fantasy & Science Fiction author of THE FLUX CATASTROPHE and THE FIRST HYTHARO series. Ever since being a small boy, he hunted for the best way to tell stories, dabbling in film and stop motion before eventually finding a passion for novel writing as a teenager. More than a decade later he'd gathered a bachelor's degree of Journalism from the University of Wollongong and a career in commercial cloud sales, yet they were never as satisfying as the time spent writing.

With the support of his artist wife and the cacophonic trio of their pet budgies, he's now dedicated himself to a full-time career as an author. When not writing, Jonathan can be found reading halfway through books and being so satisfied he forgets to finish them and painting his way through a never-ending pile of Warhammer 40,000 models.

Milton Keynes UK
Ingram Content Group UK Ltd.
UKHW011819130923
428619UK00004B/117